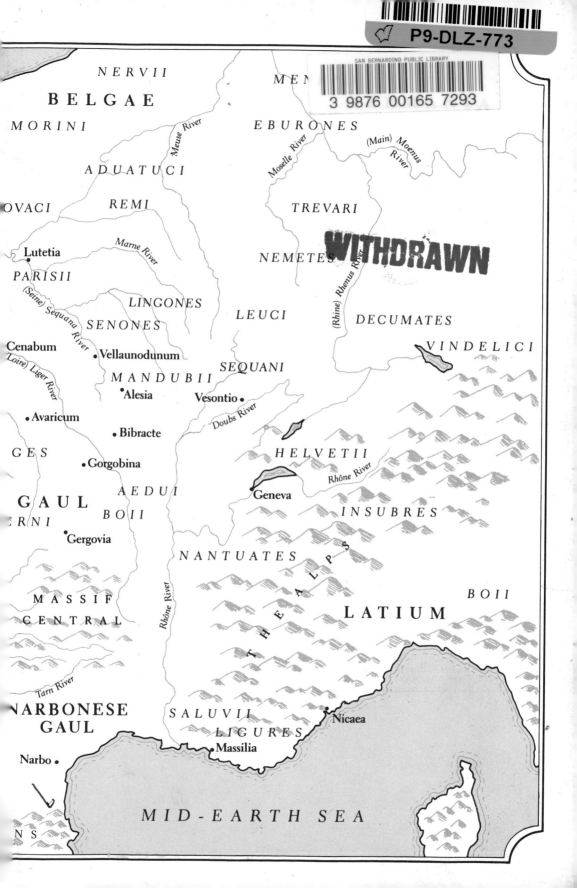

NERVII

BELGAE

MORINI

M E N

EBURONES

Meuse River

(Main) Moenus River

ADUATUCI

Moselle River

OVACI

REMI

TREVARI

WITHDRAWN

Lutetia

Marne River

NEMETES

PARISII

(Rhine) Rhenus River

LINGONES

DECUMATES

(Seine) Sequana River

SENONES

LEUCI

VINDELICI

Cenabum

SEQUANI

(Loire) Liger River

Vellaunodunum

MANDUBII

Vesontio

Alesia

Doubs River

Avaricum

Bibracte

HELVETII

Rhône River

G E S

Gorgobina

Geneva

GAUL

AEDUI

INSUBRES

RNI

BOII

Gergovia

NANTUATES

BOII

MASSIF

LATIUM

CENTRAL

T H E   A L P S

Tarn River

NARBONESE
GAUL

SALUVII

Nicaea

LIGURES

Narbo

Massilia

MID-EARTH SEA

N S

DRUIDS

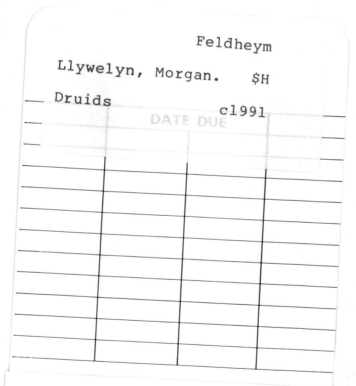

20√ 5/97

By Morgan Llywelyn

The Wind from Hastings
Lion of Ireland
The Horse Goddess
Bard
Grania
Red Branch
Druids

DRUIDS

Morgan Llywelyn

WILLIAM MORROW AND COMPANY, INC.
New York

4/24/91
Feld

Recognizing the importance of preserving what has been written, it is the policy of William Morrow and Company, Inc., and its imprints and affiliates to have the books it publishes printed on acid-free paper, and we exert our best efforts to that end.

Library of Congress Cataloging-in-Publication Data

Llywelyn, Morgan.
    Druids / by Morgan Llywelyn.
      p. cm.
    ISBN 0-688-08819-8
    1. Gaul—History—58 B.C. to 511 A.D.—Fiction.   2. Druids and Druidism—History—Fiction.   I. Title.
PS3562.L94D7   1991
813'.54—dc20
                             90-44292
                                CIP

Printed in the United States of America

First Edition

1 2 3 4 5 6 7 8 9 10

BOOK DESIGN BY PAUL CHEVANNES

MAPS BY GDS JEFFREY L. WARD

For the druids.
You know who you are.

They [druids] desire to inculcate as their leading tenet, that souls do not become extinct, but pass after death from these present to those beyond.—Gaius Julius Caesar

The druids, men of loftier intellect, and united to the intimate fraternity of the followers of Pythagoras, were absorbed by investigations into matters secret and sublime, and, unmindful of human affairs, declared souls to be immortal.—Ammianus Marcellinus

The druids joined to the study of nature that of moral philosophy, asserting that the human soul is indestructible.—Strabo

Prologue

He had been dead a long time.

With a profound sense of shock he realized he was no longer dead.

Beyond an increasingly vivid sense of self he was still aware of the tender network from which he was being separated. From its fabric those who were dear to him reached out, calling to him, seeking one more communion.

Do not abandon me! he cried to them. Follow me, find me!

Tightening around him, existence throbbed with the pulsing of a giant heart. He was expelled into lightlessness, he was tumbled into the unknown.

Down and down he spun.

Gradually he began recalling long-forgotten concepts such as direction and distance and time. Concentrating on them, he found himself spiraling amid stars. Constellations bloomed around him like flowery meadows.

He reached out, hungry for the suddenly remembered sensation of touch . . . and slipped and slid and came to rest in a warm chamber lit by a dim red glow.

There he lay dreaming. Sheltered and content, he was suspended between worlds, floating on tides regulated by the rhythms of a universe. In this building-time he sorted among his memories, deciding which to keep. So few could be retained and it was hard to anticipate which he might most need. Yet a voiceless command urged him to remember, remember. . . .

He drifted and dreamed until the pounding began. Shocked, he tried to fight back, but he was seized and squeezed and ultimately ejected into a place of hard surfaces. A burning flood poured into his nostrils and open mouth.

The infant used that first breath to scream his outrage.

CHAPTER ONE

I AWOKE to terror because I heard them singing.

Yet we were a people who sang. We were of the Celtic race, that tall people famed for their fierce blue eyes and fiercer passions. Most of my clan, my blood kin, had fair hair, but in my youth mine was the color of dark bronze.

I have always been different.

Nine moons after my birth our druids gave me the name of Ainvar. I was born of the tribe of the Carnutes in Celtic Gaul; free Gaul. My father was not considered a prince, as he had no swords sworn to him personally, but he was of the warrior aristocracy and entitled to wear the gold arm ring, as my old grandmother frequently reminded me. My parents and brothers were dead before I was old enough to remember them, so she raised me alone in their lodge in the Fort of the Grove. I remember when I believed the fort with its timber palisade was the entire world.

The air always rang with song. We sang for the sun and the rain, for death and birth, for work and war. Yet when I was startled awake by the druids singing in the grove, I was badly frightened. What if they had discovered me?

I should not have slept. I had meant to stay alert in some hiding place until dawn, watching until the druids came to the grove. But I was raw with youth; the events of the night had exhausted me. When I finally found a refuge, I must have tumbled into sleep between one breath and the next. I knew nothing more until I heard the druids singing and realized they were already in the sacred grove. They must have passed very near me.

Spying on them was strictly forbidden, subject to the direst punishments, unnamed but whispered.

My mouth went dry, my skin prickled. I had not expected to be caught. I just wanted to see great magic done.

With agonizing slowness I got to my feet. Every dead leaf rustled my betrayal. But the druids continued without interruption until I began to think they were unaware of me.

Perhaps I could creep close enough to watch them after all, I told myself. My fear was not as great as my curiosity.

It never has been.

My refuge had been a depression between the roots of a huge old tree, a hollow filled with dead leaves. As I eased out of it, a winterkilled twig snapped beneath my foot and I froze. If the druids had not heard the twig, surely they could hear my heart pounding. But their singing went on. And so, in time, did I. Very cautiously.

Everyone in the fort had known our druids were going to try to force the wheel of the seasons to turn. The traditional ceremonies for encouraging the return of the sun had failed, and the druids had devised a new and secret ritual said to be of great power. Only initiates were to be allowed to see the attempt, born of desperation.

We were suffering a winter without end, a season of blowing granular ice and icy granular wind. Gaul was cloaked in clouds. Livestock was emaciated, supplies exhausted, people frightened.

Naturally we looked to our druids to help us.

When I was only a knee-child my grandmother had caught me staring, finger in mouth, at several figures swathed in robes of undyed wool. The robes had hoods like dark caverns from which eyes glowed mysteriously.

"They are members of the Order of the Wise," Rosmerta had said to me as she took my hand and led me away, though I continued to look back over my shoulder. "Never stare at them, Ainvar; never even look at them when their hoods are raised. And always show them the greatest respect."

"Why?" I was always asking why.

Knees creaking, my grandmother had crouched down until her face was level with mine. Her faded blue eyes beamed love at me from amid their network of wrinkles. "Because the druids are essential for our survival," she explained. "Without them, we would be helpless against all the things we cannot see."

So began my lifelong fascination with druidry. I wanted to know everything about them. I asked a thousand questions.

In time I learned that the Order of the Wise had three branches. Bards were the historians of the tribe. Vates were its diviners. Though all members of the Order were usually called druids for the sake of simplicity, in truth that title belonged to the third division, who studied for as long as twenty winters to earn it. Druids were the thinkers, teachers, interpreters of law, healers of the sick. Keepers of the mysteries.

No subject was beyond the mental scrutiny of druids. They measured the Earth and the sky, they calculated the best times for planting and harvesting. Among the practices attributed to them, in avid whispers, were such rituals as sex magic and death-teaching.

The learned Hellenes from the south called the druids "natural philosophers."

The principal obligation of the druids was to keep Man and Earth and Otherworld in harmony. The three were inextricably interwoven and must be in a state of balance or catastrophe would follow. As the repositories of a thousand years of tribal wisdom, the druids knew how to maintain that balance.

Beyond our forts and farms lurked the darkness of the unknown. Druid wisdom held that darkness at bay.

How I envied the knowledge stored in those hooded heads! My young mind was as hungry for answers as my belly was for food. What force pushed tender blades of grass through solid earth? Why did my skinned knees ooze blood one time, but clear fluid another? Who was taking bites out of the moon?

Druids knew.

I wanted to know, too.

Druids instructed the children of the warrior class, who comprised Celtic nobility, in such skills as counting and telling direction by the stars. We met in the groves and sat at our teachers' feet in dappled shade. Sometimes there were girls in the group. Celtic women who wished to learn were allowed the privilege. But our teachers never shared any real secrets with us; they were only for the initiated.

I wanted to know.

So of course I found a secret ritual of sufficient power to change the seasons irresistible.

The diviners had declared the fifth dawn after the pregnant moon to be the most auspicious time. The ritual would be conducted in the most sacred place in Gaul, the great oak grove on the ridge north of our fort. The fort itself had been built to garrison warriors like my father who guarded the approaches to the grove, which must never be profaned by foreigners.

Other fortified villages and towns in Gaul were the strongholds of princes, but not ours. Ours was the Fort of the Grove and the chief druid of the Carnutes was its supreme authority.

On the night before the secret ritual was to take place I had lain in a froth of impatience, waiting for my grandmother to fall asleep. I had always lived with Rosmerta, who tended to my needs and scolded me as she saw fit. She would never allow me to go out on an icy night to spy on the druids.

Of course, I had no intention of asking her permission.

On this night of all nights, unfortunately, she seemed wide awake, though usually she was nodding by sundown. "Aren't you tired?" I kept asking her.

She smiled her toothless smile at me. Her collapsed mouth was as soft as a baby's. "I am not, lad. But you sleep, that's a good boy."

She hobbled around our lodge, doing little woman things. I lay tensely on my straw pallet, burrowed amid woolen blankets and fur robes, letting my eyes wander from Rosmerta to the faded shields hanging on the log walls. They had been untouched since my father and brothers were killed in battle shortly before I was born. My mother, who was really too old for childbearing, had given birth to me and promptly followed her men into the Otherworld.

The shields were a constant reminder of my warrior heritage, but their dimming glories did not excite me.

I wanted to see the druids work great magic.

My supper lay in my belly like a stone. Rosmerta glanced in my direction occasionally, but she seemed preoccupied. At last she pulled her three-legged stool close to the central firepit and sat down, gazing into the flames.

I waited. I feigned a yawn, which she did not echo. I closed my eyes and made snoring noises. Old woman, go to bed! I thought, peeping at her through slitted eyelids.

When I thought I could stand it no longer, she finally got up, joint by joint, in the manner of the very old. She took a small stone bottle I had never seen before from the carved wooden chest that held her personal belongings, and drank its contents in one long swallow. Her wattled throat trembled. Then, with one hasty glance at me to be sure I was asleep, she took her heavy cloak from its peg and left the lodge. An icy blast of air eddied through the briefly opened door.

I assumed she had gone outside to relieve herself. The bowels of old people are unreliable. Seizing my chance, I bunched my bedding to resemble a sleeping figure, then grabbed my own cloak and hurried from the lodge.

The fort was asleep. The only living creature I saw was a cat hunting rats near a storage shed. The moon was shrouded in cloud, but the wintry night had an icy luminosity that allowed me to see well enough to make my way to a section of the palisade concealed by the sheds of the craftsmen. The lone sentry at the main gate was dozing at his post in the watchtower.

With a run and a leap I scrambled up the vertical timbers of the wall, a forbidden feat that every boy in the fort, and not a few of the girls, had mastered by the time they had all their meat-eating teeth.

We were a people who dared.

The palisade was built atop a bank of earth and rubble with a considerable drop on the far side. Though I landed with bent knees, the shock of impact took my breath away. As soon as I recovered I set off for the grove.

Carnutian tribeland included much of the broad plain traversed by the sandy-bedded river Liger and its tributaries. Beside one of these, the Autura, a great forested ridge thrust upward from level land, dominating the landscape, visible for a day's march. This ridge, which was considered the heart of Gaul, was crowned with the sacred grove of oaks that was the center of the druid network.

Sacred sites are not chosen by Man, but revealed to him. The earliest settlers here had felt the power of this place. Anyone who approached the oaks was gripped with awe. They were the oldest and largest in Gaul, and Man was nothing to them. Through their roots they fed on the supreme goddess, Earth herself, while their uplifted arms supported the sky.

The clamor of human habitation must not be allowed to disturb the atmosphere of so sacred a place, so the Fort of the Grove had been built at some distance from the ridge, but close to the river which was our water supply. Upon leaving the fort I fixed my eyes on the dark mass of the ridge against the slightly paler sky and settled into a ground-covering trot.

I had gone over halfway when I heard the first wolf howl.

In my excitement I had forgotten about the wolves.

The terrible winter had deprived them as it had us, making game scrawny and scarce. The wolves were hunting closer than ever to the settlements of men, seeking meat.

I was meat.

I began to run.

Only an idiot, my head tardily informed me, would have left the fort in the middle of the night with no weapon and no body-guard. But youngsters hold only one thought at a time. Years of study are required before one can think, as druids do, of seven or nine things at a time.

I might have no years left me.

I did not run; I flew.

If I could only reach the grove I thought, in my panic, that I would be safe. The grove was sacred, everyone knew that. Even the animals of the forest were said to revere it; surely the wolves would not kill me there.

Surely.

At fifteen, one believes any amount of nonsense.

I had run until I thought my lungs would burst. Frozen grass crunched under my feet. Another howl sounded, closer than the first. My heart was pounding so hard I thought it would leap into my throat and choke me. Could a person die that way? I did not know, but I could imagine. I was always imagining.

The ground lifted, the ridge rose before me, black against black. Miraculously my feet found the way without stumbling over a stone and pitching me headlong. The trees swallowed me. But even then

I was not safe, I had to get to the grove of the oaks, the sacred grove. I pushed through a tangle of undergrowth, holding an up-flung arm in front of my face to protect it. My harsh breathing was so loud the wolves could have tracked me by the sound alone.

A stitch of pain tore through my side like a bolt of lightning. Perhaps it was lightning. Perhaps I had been struck dead and would not have to run anymore. Then the pain ebbed and I struggled on, tripping over roots, sobbing for breath, trying to hear if the wolves were behind me.

The undergrowth thinned; I was on the last steep rise leading to the grove of ancient oak trees. I gave a gasp of relief. Next moment I stumbled and fell forward into a hollow filled with dead leaves.

The leaves closed over me.

I lay panting, listening for the patter of feet. Nothing. Only the thunder of my blood in my ears. I dared to hope the wolves had not been after me at all, but on the trail of some smaller, easier game.

When it seemed I might be safe, I settled deeper into the bed of dry leaves. It was as good a place as any, and warmer than most. I could wait in relative comfort until the dawn, knowing I was well concealed at the very edge of the grove. The druids would come with the dawn. . . .

Then I heard singing and the night was over.

They must have come right past me on their way to the grove.

Cautiously I crept forward, trying to get closer to the clearing in the center of the grove where the most powerful of druid rituals took place. An immense holly bush barred my way. It stood at the very edge of the glade; if I could get inside it I could see without being seen. Or so I thought.

I flopped down on my belly and wriggled forward, propelled by knees and elbows, smelling cold earth and leaf mold, until I was beneath the lowest outstretched arms of the holly. Meanwhile, the druid song for the oaks gave way to a rhythmic chant that hid any sound I was making.

When I reached the holly trunk, I wormed my way to my feet between the branches, only to discover my view into the glade was still blocked by its evergreen leaves. Impatiently I started to push a branch out of the way . . . just as the central figure in the glade turned in my direction.

Brandishing the carved ash stick that was the symbol of his authority, Menua, chief druid of the Carnutes and Keeper of the Grove, seemed to be looking straight at me. I froze. Cold sweat ran down my bare legs below my tunic.

If I were already counted as an adult, which I should have been after surviving fifteen winters, I would have been entitled to wear the tight-fitting woolen leggings grown men wore. But I had not been initiated into adulthood. My legs had not officially reached their final length. My manmaking was to take place in the spring, and spring would not come.

The full weight of the danger struck me. I could be classed as a criminal for breaking a druid prohibition. Criminals were, at the option of the druid judges, fodder for sacrifice.

I stared in horror toward Menua, convinced that he with all his powers could see me through the most solid leaves.

But to my enormous relief, he did not. The chief druid continued the slow turning of his body. Murmuring in counterpoint to the chanting, he began weaving designs in the air with his hands, letting the ash stick fall.

There was a sudden tingling on my skin such as one feels before a storm breaks. The hair stirred on my forearms and lifted on the nape of my neck, moved by the inrush of unseen forces. The murky morning dimmed and the air grew colder, denser, thick with tension.

In the glade the druids began circling sunwise around a central hub. Between their moving bodies I glimpsed something white lying on the raised stone slab used for sacrifices.

I thought I understood. A gift of life would be offered in exchange for a gift from the Otherworld.

The adult members of the tribe were privileged to attend all the sacrifices except those which involved some secret ritual, like this one. Children, however, were forbidden. But we boys sometimes re-created the sacrifices for ourselves, using some hapless lizard or rodent.

For the son of a warrior, I was strangely squeamish about seeing blood shed. It troubled my belly. I always let someone else take the role of the sacrificer, and I dropped my eyes at the crucial moment when the others were watching the knife. I was great at chanting and exhorting, however.

Now the real chanters and exhorters were at work. Their voices filled the grove, calling on the sacred names of sun and wind and water while their feet wove a complex pattern on the earth. Chanting rose to thunder amid the oaks.

Then Menua lifted his arms. Like the bare twigs of the trees, his fingers clawed space. By his gesture, sound was torn from the grove, hurled into the air, gone. The other druids halted in mid-step, freezing the pattern.

The air crackled with gathering magic.

Menua flung back his hood. In the style of the Order, his head was shaved across the front from ear to ear, leaving a bald dome of forehead surrounded by a flaring mane of white hair. In sharp contrast were the black eyebrows that almost met above his nose. Menua was only of average height for a Gaulish man, but he was wide and solid, and the voice booming from his chest was the voice of the oaks.

"Hear us!" he cried to That Which Watched. "See us! Inhale our breath and know us for a part of you!"

I shrank inside my tunic. My crawling flesh informed me of a Presence, larger than human, occupying visibly empty space, aware of Menua and the druids. And of me. A terrible, awesome power, gathering itself in the grove.

"The seasons are entangled," Menua was saying. "Spring cannot free itself from winter. Hear us, heed our cries! Your sun does not heat the earth and soften her womb so she will accept seed and grow grain. The animals will not mate. Soon we will have no cows for milk and leather, no sheep for meat and wool.

"The pattern of the weather is damaged. Our bards tell us that we came to Gaul many generations ago because the patterns of existence had been damaged in our homeland to the east. We had too many births and not enough food. We fled here to save ourselves, and in this land learned to live in harmony with the earth.

"Now that harmony has somehow been disturbed and must be put right. The confusion of the seasons threatens not only the Carnutes, but our neighbors the Senones, the Parisii, the Bituriges. Even such powerful tribes as the Arverni and the Aedui are suffering. All Gaul is suffering."

Menua paused to draw breath. When he spoke again, his voice was thick with pleading. "We implore the help of the Otherworld. Aid us in healing the pattern. Inspire us, guide us. In exchange we shall offer the most precious gift we have to give, not the spirit of a criminal or an enemy, but the spirit of our oldest and wisest, a person revered by all the tribe.

"We send you the spirit of one who bore the deaths of her children with courage and never failed to give good counsel in the circle of elders. Her spark comes to join yours, life moving to life. Accept our offering. Help us in our need."

Gesturing to Aberth the sacrificer, Menua lowered his arms. Aberth stepped forward, throwing back his hood to reveal himself to That Which Watched. He had a foxy face and fox-colored hair behind his tonsure, and a curly red beard that never grew below his jaw. On his arm a circlet of wolf fur denoted his talent for killing.

Strapped to his waist was the sacrificial knife with its gold hilt.

The chanting began again, low but insistent. "Turn the wheel, turn the wheel, change the seasons." The druids were circling again. "Turn the wheel, change the seasons, join with us, accept our gift, now. Now!" The voices rang with desperate urgency.

Aberth paused beside the shrouded figure on the altar stone. He pulled away the cloth, baring the body for his knife. In the moment before I meant to drop my eyes, I had a clear look at his intended victim.

My grandmother lay with her gentle face turned toward the sunless sky.

Chapter Two

"**N**o!"

At first I could not imagine who screamed. Who would dare interrupt a druid ceremony?

Then I realized I was screaming. Like some madman, I had burst from concealment and was running recklessly into the glade, waving my arms and yelling for the druids to stop.

I expected lightning to strike me and shrivel me into a cinder at Menua's command.

Instead, he and the others merely stared at me. Aberth's upraised arm hung in the air, holding the knife above Rosmerta. Only the chief druid seemed able to move; he tried to catch me as I flung myself protectively across my grandmother's body. I beat him off with clubbed fists, then took the old woman in my arms. I was surprised to discover how thin she was. It was like holding a bag of sticks.

We lay together on the stone of sacrifice with the knife poised above us. I did not look up. I pressed my lips against Rosmerta's cheek, feeling the dry old skin, inhaling her scent, her individual odor of woodsmoke and desiccation.

Her flesh was cold to my lips.

Menua's hand clamped on my shoulder. "Step aside, lad," he said, more kindly than I expected.

I intended to obey him; we always obeyed our druids. But instead my arms tightened around Rosmerta. "I won't let you kill her," I said in a muffled voice, my face against hers.

"We aren't going to kill her. She's already dead." Menua waited for his words to sink in. Aberth took a step backward, perhaps in response to some signal from the chief druid.

I lifted my head so I could look down at Rosmerta. Her eyes were closed, sunken into pits lost amid the wrinkles. When I raised myself higher I could see her scrawny neck, where no pulse beat. Her chest did not rise and fall.

"You see?" Menua asked in the same gentle tone. "The knife is only a formality to conform to the ritual of sacrifice. Rosmerta chose, with nobility and fortitude, to die for the common good. When she thought you were asleep last night, she drank a potion we had given her. Winter-in-a-bottle, we call it. She took winter into herself, she became winter, the season of death. Then she came to my lodge and we brought her here before dawn. Her spirit left her body just before sunrise, which is the time spirits prefer for migrations.

"This is the new ritual, Ainvar. Rosmerta shows winter how to die so spring may be born. In such ways, with such symbols, we encourage the healing of the pattern."

He was only speaking words, they meant nothing to me. All that mattered was my grandmother, who could not be dead. As clearly as if I still saw it, I remembered the look on her face the night before as she gave me my meal—a thin gruel and a lump of badger meat. She had claimed she was not hungry.

Now I held her with arms nourished by the food she had denied herself. I would never surrender her.

Above my head Menua said to the others, "This may be the help we sought. The Source of All Being has sent this lad to us. Think on this symbol. What better way to show the seasons how to change than by tearing a boy in the spring of his life away from the corpse of winter?"

He seized my shoulders and tugged. I sobbed in grief and defiance. Later they told me I had actually twisted around and bared my teeth at the chief druid.

"She isn't dead. I won't let her be dead."

"You have no choice. Come now, Ainvar." He pulled harder. There was an edge to his voice; the time for handling me gently had passed.

I shouted again, "I won't let her be dead! Rosmerta? Live, Rosmerta!"

Then it happened.

The corpse opened its eyes.

The knife fell from Aberth's fingers. One of the other druids muffled a cry by cramming her knuckles into her mouth. They fell back, leaving us alone.

Rosmerta's body shuddered. Air hissed into her mouth.

"Grandmother! I knew you couldn't be dead, I knew it. . . ." I shook her bony shoulders, I rained kisses on her defenseless face.

Her voice was the papery whisper of dry leaves. "I should be dead. I'm so tired. So tired. Let me go, Ainvar. I need to go."

Tears choked me. "I cannot. What would I do without you?"

She fought to draw another breath. "Live," she whispered.

Menua urged, "Listen to her, Ainvar. The law says we must respect the requests of the old. Rosmerta's body is worn out. Would you have her remain in a collapsing dwelling?"

I could not think, I did not know what to feel. I was all knots inside. I looked from Rosmerta to Menua and back.

When my grandmother breathed she made a dreadful rasping noise, a sound of agony. The next breath she drew was worse.

Menua was wrong. I did have a choice, but making it was the most difficult thing I had ever done. Something seemed to tear loose inside me as I gave Rosmerta one last, urgent hug, and pressed my lips to her ear. "If you truly want to go," I murmured, "go. I salute you as a free person," I added, the words one Celt customarily said to another when parting.

She sank in upon herself. A rattle sounded in her throat. A strange, bitter odor came from her gaping mouth.

Something as insubstantial as a sigh sped past me into the morning.

For a few heartbeats no one moved. Then Menua gently pulled me away. There was no resistance left in me. He bent over the old woman's body. His examination of her was thorough. Later, when I had more wisdom, I would recall that, among other things, he had pressed his fingers very firmly against Rosmerta's windpipe and held them there for a time.

He straightened up and looked around the glade, seeking the eyes of the other druids. "Winter is dead," he announced. "Gone beyond recall." He flicked a glance at me.

The ritual resumed, swirling around me like a mist. I paid no attention, I could not make sense of it. I was numbed by a sense of being alone which I had never imagined before. I would not starve, my blood kin occupied the Fort of the Grove and no clan allowed any of its members to be abandoned. But the warmth of affection Rosmerta had blanketed me with would not, could not, be replaced.

I felt cold and naked.

The druids chanted and circled. A hole was dug among the roots of the oaks. Rosmerta would sleep forever as I had slept the night before, embraced by the trees. Her shrouded body, wrapped in a cloth painted with eyes and spirals, was reverently returned to Earth's womb together with a small selection of grave goods to show her status in life.

My eyes saw. My spirit was somewhere else.

When the ceremony was concluded we left Rosmerta in her very special grave. She was honored; usually only druids were given to the oaks. We started back toward the fort, a group of druids singing one of the songs of praise to the Source, and me among them, small. Alone. Cold.

Except I was not cold.

Gradually I realized I was growing warm.

Sunlight was pouring over me like melted butter.

Looking at the others, I saw golden light on their faces. The druids had thrown back their hoods and were walking bareheaded, and the sunlight struck sparks from hair of russet and gold. It cast a sheen on the graying locks of Grannus and haloed Menua with silver.

Sunlight.

We slowed, we stopped, we stared at each other.

The chief of the vates, Keryth the seer, broke into a grin. A generously proportioned woman with half-grown children of her own, she seized the usually diffident Grannus by the hands and swung him around in a wild dance. "Sunshine!" she exulted, laughing. Grannus laughed with her.

Giddiness overcame us all. I felt a cloud lift from me, leaving in its place the glow of life.

We walked on. The druids began singing a jubilant song of thanksgiving, and though I did not yet feel like joining in, something inside of me sang with them . . . until I saw the palisade of the fort ahead of us and realized I would be returning to an empty lodge. No Rosmerta to keep the fire going, to cook the food, to mend my clothes . . . to rumple my hair with a fond and loving hand. Most important of all, that.

My steps faltered.

As if he heard my thoughts, Menua put his hand on my arm. "You are coming home with me," he said.

I almost wriggled with gratitude, like a puppy given a bone. But my relief was short-lived. When I smiled thankfully at Menua, he did not smile back. His face seemed carved of stone.

A horrid thought occurred to me. What if he was taking me to his lodge, not to save me from loneliness but to punish me for my behavior?

No matter how I screamed, no one would dare enter the chief druid's lodge without permission to rescue me. My blood kin, my clan, would leave me to whatever fate he chose for me. Cousins and aunts and uncles would go about their affairs; Rosmerta was the only person who had been truly my own, who might have defended me.

The darkest whispers I had heard about the druids flooded into my mind.

You have been a fool, my head informed me now that it was too late.

There was nothing for it, I thought miserably, but to act like a man now at least, even if it was my last act. Particularly if it was my last act. We Carnutes were Celts. I clenched my fists, took a deep if shaky breath, and followed Menua with my chin up.

The captain of the guard was standing sentry at the main gate, as he did once every moon. When he saw us he reversed his spear, turning it point downward. Then his eyes widened in surprise, recognizing me among the druids.

Ogmios, whose name meant "The Strong," was a mighty-thewed

man with a drooping moustache in the style favored by warriors. As guard captain he possessed a two-handed sword with coral set in its hilt, and his oval shield was elaborately ornamented in swirling Celtic patterns. Wearing a plaid tunic of red and brown and crimson leggings that encased his muscular legs like sausage skins, he was an impressive figure.

Privately, I thought he was as stupid as a barrel of hair. Perhaps I was prejudiced because of his treatment of Crom Daral, his son and my cousin.

Crom was small and dark-visaged, born of a woman with crooked shoulders who had been stolen from the Remi tribe. Ogmios made it plain he was disappointed in the boy, who was a replica of his mother. Though boys were not allowed to speak to their warrior sires in public, Ogmios also avoided the lad in private, showing such distaste for him that Crom became a morose and bitter child.

When I felt sorry for him and offered him my friendship, Crom attached himself to me like moss to a stone. We got into all sorts of mischief together—usually at my instigation.

Then my fascination with the druids had begun to take over my life to such an extent that I began neglecting Crom. When I sought his company out of guilt, he was sarcastic. "I'm surprised you bothered to look for me," he said. "Is there no druid in the fort for you to tag behind?"

Our relationship grew strained. Yet I continued to think of him as my friend, someone I would get back to, someone who would always be there. When I had time.

I was very young.

As I entered the fort with the druids, I looked around for Crom, but I could not find his somber little face among those of people hurrying to greet us, praising the druids for their success.

Menua accepted their thanks impassively, with a grave and dignified nod. Later I too would learn the value of an opaque expression for guarding one's thoughts.

People were emerging from every lodge, throwing off their cloaks to bathe in the sun. The men wore tunics and leggings, the women were dressed in heavy woolen skirts and round-necked bodices dyed red and yellow and blue. They resembled flowers as they turned their faces eagerly to the light.

Several of the druids were married. Their partners hurried to congratulate them, but the chief druid, who had no wife, stalked on alone. I trotted miserably after him like a bullock to the sacrifice.

He did not bother to look back. He knew I must follow.

The lodge reserved for the Keeper of the Grove was the largest in the fort, as fine as the home of a tribal chieftain, a king. It stood at a slight remove from the other buildings, an island in a sea of footbeaten brown mud. A sturdy oval building of well-chinked logs, Menua's home was thickly thatched—grass-headed, as we used to say. An oak door hung on iron hinges that had been rubbed with fat until they gleamed. Above the doorway was a perch for a tame raven such as many druids kept.

The raven watched as Menua swung open his door and beckoned to me.

The lintel was low enough to make me bow my head, but the single room inside was high and spacious . . . and nothing like I had imagined.

No matter what the tribe, houses in Celtic Gaul followed one general pattern. They were constructed of logs or wattle-and-daub, and every one was crammed with the paraphernalia of living. A lodge invariably had shields hanging on the walls and spears stacked by the single doorway, a loom monopolizing floor space, carved wooden chests for personal property, clothing drying on ropes strung from the rafters, pallets of wool stuffed with straw lying on the floor or in wooden bedboxes set against the walls, cages of woven willow fastened high on the walls so hens would not lose their eggs to small children and roving hounds, a clutter of tools and benches and baskets and pots and Greek amphorae and Roman pitchers and, perhaps, an imported bronze brazier, a luxury much prized this past winter.

By contrast the lodge of the chief druid of the Carnutes was starkly bare.

In the center was his stone hearth, graced by a splendid set of iron firedogs in the Celtic style of swinging, swelling curves. An age-blackened bedbox held his bedding. There was one carved bench, one carved chest, a net of borage suspended from the rafters, and a single shelf holding bottles and jars and some red-glazed pots. His wardrobe hung from three pegs. All else within the walls was space and air. Even the flagstones of the floor were swept clean.

"You live here?" I asked incredulously.

"I live here," Menua corrected me, tapping his forehead.

My eyes swung round the lodge again, looking for the instrument of torture with which he would punish me. Something terrible. There was nothing. Then I realized he needed nothing tangible; with one magical gesture the chief druid could probably turn me into a toad.

Yet he did nothing more threatening than to stretch, yawn, and hoist his woolen robe to his belly so he could scratch the skin beneath.

Then he turned to me. I had backed up against a wall. In a voice every bit as stern as I had been expecting, Menua said, "You and I must talk. A very serious talk indeed."

He took two ominous steps toward me. My shoulder blades pressed against the rough logs behind me, feeling a thread of cold air blowing through where some of the chinking had dried and shrunk. I willed myself to melt into the timbers, but instead my belly growled ferociously.

Menua's eyes began to twinkle. "I suppose you would like to eat something first, eh? I had forgotten that boys are always hungry."

I was as astonished at his suddenly solicitous voice as by the smile that accompanied it.

I would soon learn that a disconcerting change of mood was one of Menua's tools. It threw people off guard.

"I only had gruel to eat last night, and nothing since," I blurted out as my stomach knotted and gurgled. "I'm awfully hungry."

He nodded. "Seeing death makes the living want to eat and to mate. So life asserts itself, Ainvar," he added in a new tone of voice, stressing each word carefully as if he were instructing me.

Which he was, of course. That was the beginning.

My second lesson came hard on its heels. "Go to Teyrnon's lodge; it is his turn to provide for the needs of the chief druid. Tell his wife that you require a meal. Explain you are with me now." When I hesitated, he added, "Didn't you know that every family provides for the druids in turn? Our gifts belong to all. Run along now." He aimed a slap at my buttocks.

I ran.

Teyrnon the smith and his wife, Damona, were sitting on a bench beside the door of their lodge, watching their children play and soaking up sunshine like sponges from the Mid-Earth Sea. They were sturdy people who looked as if they missed few meals, even when times were lean. The armorer of warriors was not allowed to grow weak with hunger; his clients saw to that.

I repeated Menua's words to Damona, a sallow woman with an ugly, good-humored face. She exchanged a long look with her husband, then disappeared into the lodge. Teyrnon leaned back against the wall of his house and eyed me speculatively, picking his teeth with a goose quill. I offered no conversation. I did not know what to say.

Damona returned with a wheel of coarse dark bread with a hole in the center, and a copper bowl of boiled roots drenched in melted fat. I mumbled my thanks and started back to Menua. Behind me I heard Teyrnon saying, "You might as well begin making a new tunic for the lad, too. He needs it. His legs are long and growing longer."

By the time I entered Menua's lodge I was embarrassed to find that the smell of the food was making my mouth water. In spite of the chief druid's words, it seemed disrespectful to gobble food on the day my grandmother died. But the fragrance of the melted fat was irresistible. Fat had become a rare delicacy during the endless winter.

Fat, my head surprisingly observed, had also recently greased the chief druid's door hinges.

When I offered the food to Menua first, he waved it aside. "Not for me but for you," he insisted. He sat on his bench and watched me without expression as I ate right- and left-handed, swallowing as fast as I could. For all I knew, at the end of the meal I might be slain, and if so I wanted to die with a full belly.

The endless winter had done that to many of us.

When I picked the last crumb off my tunic and wiped my mouth on my forearm, Menua's smile returned like the sun. "Was it good?"

"The best food I ever ate!"

"I doubt that. But your gift for appreciation does you credit. You have a lot to learn, however." The smile vanished, his voice darkened. A fire leaped into his eyes. In spite of myself I flinched before the power of the druid's gaze.

"First," he said, in a voice so cold I thought I must have imagined the earlier smile, "you will tell me how you recalled the dead to life."

He sprang forward in one motion. I would not have thought a square-built man could move so fast. His fingers clamped on my wrist and he shook me as a hound shakes a hare.

The attack was so unexpected I nearly vomited my meal into his face. "I didn't . . . I don't know . . . I don't know what happened, what I did! Was she dead? I can't bring the dead back to life!"

The chief druid shook me back and forth, his compelling eyes fixed on mine. "Of course she was dead, Ainvar!" he roared at me. "Are you implying that a druid death potion might have failed? Never!" His face was no longer impassive. The skin was mottled with red and his eyes bulged from their sockets.

Any fear I had felt before was nothing compared to this.

He shook me and shook me and I babbled and babbled. I was incapable of measuring my words, I could only blurt out what I knew. And I knew I could not possibly have restored Rosmerta's life if the druids had killed her. I was young, I was ignorant, I was . . .

"You are gifted!" Menua shouted at me. "Didn't you know? At your birth, our seer saw portents of talent in you that would be of great benefit to the tribe and would involve a long journey. So you were named Ainvar, meaning 'he who travels far.' We thought at the time you would be a great warrior who would attack some distant tribe and bring back its wealth to the Carnutes.

"We were wrong though, weren't we? You journey in a very different way. This morning you traveled to the Otherworld and brought back your grandmother."

The idea was so incredible I stopped breathing for a moment. But he was the chief druid. He knew more than all the kings. If he thought such a thing was possible, perhaps it was.

Suddenly the strength went out of my legs.

Menua caught me before I fell to the floor. He guided me over to sit on his bench by the fire, and stood watching me narrowly until I summoned enough spit into my mouth to speak. "Do you think that I . . . ?"

"What I think isn't the issue. Do you think you did it?" He was relentless, the chief druid.

Be careful, my bruised brain warned me. If you brought Rosmerta back to life you acted in defiance of the druids, who meant her to die.

Menua must want me to admit it, thus confirming that his potion had killed Rosmerta in the first place. But such an admission would condemn me.

I could think of no defense, so fell back on honesty. "If I did what you suggest it was accidental," I told him. "Truly." My ears were ringing; my bones felt hollow.

Menua continued to fix me with an unblinking stare. "Ainvar," he said as if bemused. "Young Ainvar, who is to travel.

"We harbored too small an ambition for you, I think." Sighing, he rubbed the high bald dome of his forehead with his fingertips. "You shall need to be properly trained, of course . . . ," he said as if to himself.

He was not going to kill me? Or turn me into a toad?

"Even with training you may have nothing to contribute," he went on. "Still, the omens are undeniable. The sun is back."

"You did that," I said quickly.

His gaze softened. "Ah yes. I did that. We did that, we druids working together.

"You just might be worth some effort, young Ainvar. But listen to me. Right now people are busy celebrating, they won't think deeply. But when they crawl into their beds tonight some may recall that you were with us when we returned from the grove, and wonder what part you played."

The dark shelf of his eyebrows met in a frown over Menua's nose. "Druids answer only the questions they choose to answer," he told me. "Remember that. If you are asked about what happened today, look through your questioner's eyes to the back of his skull and say nothing. Do you understand?"

"I understand." He is including you with the druids, my head told me. My heart leaped.

"You will live with me for a time and we will learn together what talents you may possess, Ainvar. Whatever they may be, it appears your gifts are of the head, not of the arm."

"Gifts of the head?"

"Powers of the mind. Those who have them may, if they submit to the necessary years of study and discipline, aspire to entering the Order of the Wise. They may have an aptitude for reading omens or memorizing the poems that contain our histories. Or they may be sacrificers, or healers, or teachers like myself. Each of us has an invisible ability, you understand, unlike obvious gifts of the arm such as swordwielding or craftsmanship."

Cautiously I raised my hand and fingered my head; the head that Celts held sacred.

"Am I to be a druid?" I dared to whisper.

Menua assumed a dubious expression. "There is the remotest possibility. Very remote, mind you. Druids must be obedient to the law and you showed a shocking disregard for the law today. If that is the way you intend to proceed we should have Dian Cet as chief judge declare you a criminal now and be done with it."

Knowing the use to which druids could put criminals, I shook my head violently. "I'll never again break the smallest prohibition, not as long as I live."

Menua's eyelids crinkled at the edges. "Ah, I think you are going to cause me seven kinds of trouble, no matter what you say. But you may just be worth it if we can tolerate each other long enough to find out. Now go collect your bedding from Rosmerta's lodge. I have no provisions for guests."

That night I slept in the home of the chief druid. Our old lodge would be assigned to the first couple to marry and conceive a child after Beltaine, the festival of spring and fertility.

In the darkness I lay wondering.

Was it possible I had somehow worked the greatest magic of all, the magic reserved for the Source of All Being? In ignorance and passion, had I struck the spark of life?

CHAPTER THREE

SOMETIMES I caught Menua watching me narrow-eyed, stroking his lower lip, and knew he was wondering, too.

My formal instruction began with criticism of every aspect of my being. Nothing I was or did, it seemed, was right. For example, I was unforgivably awkward, an insult to Menua's eyes.

"Look to nature," he advised me. "Every creature that emerges from the Cauldron of Creation is as graceful as it can be according to its physical abilities. Thus do willow tree and water rat alike honor the life within themselves. Life is sacred, a spark from the Source of All Being.

"But you blunder about as if your joints were untied, Ainvar. You bump into this and stumble over that, you spill your precious food and tear clothing it took someone much effort to make. As you come from a line of warriors, I assume you began learning how to handle weapons in your ninth summer. Tell me: Are you as inept with a spear as you are clumsy in my lodge?"

My ears burned hot. "I'm good with a spear. And a sling. And last summer I became tall enough for a sword."

"Aha!" Menua pounced. "So we must assume you have some control over your muscles if you choose. Then why isn't every gesture you make, in public or private, a way of thanking the Source for an able body?"

Pointing his forefinger at me, Menua roared in a voice like thunder, "Celebrate yourself!"

My bones obeyed. My spine, slumped in the customary curve of growing boys, straightened itself. My hand, which had been grabbing for a lump of Damona's bread, stopped itself, then reached out slowly and with restraint. My eyes observed for the first time how cleverly hand and wrist could work together to create a harmonious line.

Menua nodded approval. "Now you no longer resemble a pig rooting through a midden heap. That is appropriate for pigs but not for people. From now on, you will take pleasure in human grace."

The chief druid never made an awkward gesture, even when he scratched himself. Every movement was fluid, celebrating the ability to move.

I was so impressed I even believed he farted musically.

Nantorus, king of the Carnutes—we always called the tribal chieftains kings—came north from his stronghold at Cenabum to congratulate the druids on the success of the new ritual. I had seen him before, for he was a frequent visitor to the sacred grove. To maintain his position a king needed the support of the Otherworld. He was not born to kingship but elected to it by the elders and the druids, and needed all the support he could get.

Though he did not impress me as Menua did, Nantorus was splendid and fierce-looking in a crested bronze helmet and coat of leather incised with lozenge shapes picked out in red. Tall and broad, with a flowing brown moustache, he was the symbol of Carnute manhood. Also he moved with a kingly grace, my head observed.

Menua entertained him in our lodge. I hovered in the shadows beyond the hearth, trying to keep my mouth closed and my ears open.

Nantorus asked about me. "What plans have you for this tall lad, Menua? Shouldn't he be out training to replace his father on the battlefield?"

Menua chuckled. "Perhaps I'm saving him to eat when our supplies run low again."

Nantorus laughed too, then sobered. "I hope you don't say things like that when the Roman traders are around. They don't understand druid humor; they might carry back tales of Carnutian maneaters."

"Romans." Menua twisted his mouth with distaste. "The Greeks were better. I remember those we used to see in my youth, longheaded men with a nice appreciation for irony and sarcasm. I would no more joke with a Roman than I would with a bear. Who could understand me better," he added.

"I see you still dislike the Romans."

"I merely meant I would be careful what I said around them, as you yourself just advised," Menua replied. My ears had grown sensitive to his tone; I detected the faintest stiffness, a guarded quality that had not been there before.

Nantorus turned toward me. "Your father was a good man with a shortsword. Are you?"

"Ainvar may have other gifts," Menua interjected smoothly. "He is apprenticed to me, for now."

"You intend to make a druid out of a potential warrior?" Nantorus did not sound pleased.

"We have a number of warriors. But every generation there are fewer druids."

Nantorus fixed me with his eyes. "I revere the druids as must we all, Ainvar, but surely you are aware that honors and status within the tribe are won in battle. You might aspire to be a prince someday with men of your own at your command."

"The value of a druid is the equal of a prince, because of his worth to the tribe," I replied.

Menua's face remained impassive, but there was a smile in his voice when he said, "The lad knows the law. I've beaten it into his head."

"Have you? And is there anything else in that head? Or is it, as I begin to suspect, solid rock? If it is rock I want him for a warrior, Menua; hardheaded men are worth their weight in salt when someone tries to bash in their skulls." Suddenly Nantorus reached out and caught me by the ears. He pulled me toward him until he could look deep into my eyes.

I made myself meet his scrutiny without flinching.

"Those eyes!" He released me and passed a hand across his face as if to wipe out the sight of me. "Those eyes!" he repeated. "They are like doorways opening onto endless vistas, Menua. . . ."

"Extraordinary eyes," the chief druid agreed. "I think whatever is in him is worth exploring before it is lost to a spear thrust or a sword slash. Don't you agree?"

The king nodded slowly. He still seemed shaken. "Perhaps. Still . . . he will be a big man, and he comes from the blood of fighters . . . Tell me, Ainvar: Is there nothing about being a warrior that interests you?"

"There is one question I would like to ask."

"Yes?" said Nantorus eagerly. "What is it?"

"You are a champion with both sword and sling," I reminded Nantorus. Young as I was, I knew that kings never object to flattery.

"I am." He stroked his moustache.

"Then you are the person to tell me. Why is a stone thrown from a leather sling so much more deadly than one thrown by hand? I've always wondered."

"*Why?*" Nantorus opened his eyes very wide. Once or twice he started to say something, then stopped. He shook his head, a rueful smile forming beneath the brown moustache. "This one is all yours, chief druid," he said. "I should never have questioned your decision to keep him."

But he did not answer my sincerely meant question. He was just a warrior. He did not *know*.

The two men shared cups far into the night, discussing tribal matters and the concerns of men. As I had not passed my man-making, I was not invited to join them.

I resented being excluded. There was hair in my groin, my voice had deepened, my penis could stiffen like a stallion's. What more, I wondered, was necessary for manhood?

As my studies continued, spring blossomed with a radiance all the more welcome after such a bitter winter. Our sunseason songs were blended from the rustle of new leaves, the liquid outpourings of the nightingale, the drumming of the woodpecker. Beyond the gate of the fort we began building a tower of timber to feed the great bone-fire that would herald Beltaine. Beltaine, Festival of the Fire of Creation.

From Menua I learned that the Source of All Being is the single and singular force of creation, yet has many faces. Mountain and forest and river, bird and bear and boar, each reveals a different mood of the Creator, a different aspect. Each is therefore a symbol of the one Source, but we reverence these nature gods separately with individual rites, showing that we understand and respect the diversity of creation.

Every entity must be free to be itself.

The sun is called the Fire of Creation and is the most powerful of symbols, because without light there is no life. Life is both Creator and creation, Menua explained; the closing of the sacred circle.

For this reason we Celts made our temples the living groves.

As the days grew longer, we carried the last gnawed bones of winter out of the fort to pile on the bone-fire, which would be a sacrificing of the old, a cleansing and a preparation for the new. It was an exciting time. Some mornings when I awoke I thought I would burst from my skin for sheer exuberance. Then I thought of Rosmerta, who would not see this spring. . . .

I said nothing of this to Menua, but druids do not need words. One evening, when the twilight shadows were long and blue and my throat closed up with melancholy, he took the net of dried borage down from the rafters. From the herb he prepared a drink sweetened with the last of the stored honey.

"Drink this, Ainvar. Borage eases a sorrowful spirit. Your long face is not appropriate for the season, and soon we shall go out to the bone-fire and begin the singing."

I recalled Beltaines of other years, and Rosmerta's cracked but enthusiastic voice, and her arm around my shoulders. In one long gulp I drained the cup.

The beverage was musty tasting, but it cleared my head. By this simple magic my sadness was eased, and I was grateful.

Some of the kindest magics are small ones.

We went out together to sing at the bone-fire.

Beltaine was, among other things, the season of generation, of marriages and of manmaking. At Samhain, which was the opposite festival on the wheel of seasons, druid judges settled disputes and punished crimes. Debts were paid if they must be, broken partnerships dissolved, broken pots returned to the earth from which they were formed. Samhain, season of endings.

Beltaine was the season of beginnings.

For the first time in bardic memory, spring came to the territory of the Carnutes that year while other tribes, even the Arverni in the south, were still being pelted with sleet. This did not go unremarked. Word traveled fast in Gaul, shouted from village to village in relays. Soon the achievement of our druids was common knowledge.

As a result, a prince of the Arverni, a man called Celtillus, sent his oldest son to us, requesting that the powerful druids of the Carnutes conduct the youngster's manmaking themselves. He would share in the ritual with the lads of our tribe.

Menua tried not to let me see how flattered he was.

In due course one of the boy's uncles, a man called Gobannitio, brought his nephew to the Fort of the Grove in a four-wheeled, shield-hung wagon drawn by two wintershaggy horses. We had heard they were coming long before their arrival, and the fort was thrown into a frenzy of preparation. Even uninitiated boys, myself among them, were given weapons and sent to stand among the men at the gateway to impress the Arverni with our numbers.

The wagon came rumbling up the rutted trackway from the south, accompanied by an escort of Arvernian warriors with weapons at the ready. In tribeland not their own, they shot suspicious glances at every rock and bush.

Gobannitio was easily recognized. He stood in the front of the cart, wearing a massive torc of twisted gold around his neck to protect his nape and announce his status. His arms and fingers gleamed with rings of gold and bronze. Earrings of imported enamelware dangled from his ears. Luxury goods from the Mid-Earth Sea were very popular among Gaulish princes.

In spite of his splendor, my eyes were drawn to the person who rode beside him, a youth of my own age and height. This must be the lad come for his manmaking.

I could not help staring.

From the first glimpse I sensed in the boy a surging urgency, as if he might explode at any moment. Though he was affecting a glaze of princely boredom for our benefit, he seemed more alive than anyone I had ever seen.

He felt my eyes on him and turned toward me. Our gazes met and locked. For one heartbeat his eyes were cold, measuring me. Then his aloof expression dissolved into a grin that went all the way to his ears.

"My nephew Vercingetorix," Gobannitio was announcing to Menua and the waiting druids. "The name was given him at birth by our seer. It means 'King of the World.'"

Vercingetorix. I knew from that first moment that we were as different as ice and fire. We were not going to like each other.

Instead of stepping from the wagon, he put one hand on the side panel and vaulted out. Gobannitio followed in the more customary way, and Menua, together with Dian Cet and Grannus, escorted the pair into the chief druid's lodge.

I was left outside.

After a little stylized posturing, the Arvernian escort relaxed and mingled with our own warriors. Fighting men have a common language beyond tribal dialects. Soon they were sharing cups. I was left to slink around outside the lodge on my own, wondering if Vercingetorix was drinking wine with the adults.

The life of the fort went on around me. Metal clanged; the craftsmen, who were honored next to warriors, were getting the tools ready for planting season. Meanwhile, women swept and scrubbed and baked and sang the songs of work and weariness. Knee-children scrabbled in the dirt, whooping and shrieking.

Eventually Vercingetorix emerged from Menua's lodge and glanced around. "Where is the lad with the bronze-colored hair? Ah, there you are. Help me with my things, I'm going to be sleeping here."

"*I* am the only other person allowed to sleep in the chief druid's lodge," I retorted, prickling with indignation.

He flashed me another of his engaging grins. His sandy-gold hair entitled him to a face full of freckles. He had a sharply chiseled nose with little indentation below the brow, like a Hellene's. His eyes sloped downward at the outer corners, giving him a deceptively lazy expression as he drawled, "But Menua just told me I am to share his lodge. So you are wrong. Wrong often, are you?" he added insultingly.

Menua might accuse me of being wrong, and often did, but no stranger from another tribe could saunter into my birthplace and insult me. I hit him, of course. I am a Celt.

He hit me back, of course. He was a Celt.

At once we were rolling in the dirt, grunting and swearing and pummeling each other. He sank a fist under my ribs that knocked the breath out of me, but not before I managed to strike him

squarely in one of those sleepy, hooded eyes. It would be rainbowed before the sun set.

Rough hands pulled us apart. I looked up to see Menua glaring
at me, and beyond him an amused circle of onlookers. "You disgrace
me, Ainvar," said the chief druid.

Vercingetorix and I scrambled to our feet. He had the nerve to
try to help me brush myself off, but I shoved him away.

Menua regarded me sourly. "Having an Arvernian prince en-
trusted to us for manmaking is a singular honor, Ainvar, yet you
have welcomed the boy with your fists. This is a very bad beginning,
and the first step shapes the journey. No sooner do the Arvernians
acknowledge us as the preeminent druids in Gaul than you em-
barrass our entire tribe with your behavior."

"All the blame isn't his," Vercingetorix spoke up. "Nor all the
credit yours. I was sent to you because our chief druid is very
old and the long winter has enfeebled him. In my opinion, you
were simply the next best thing. And this fellow and I fought
because I baited him deliberately. I wanted to know what sort of
man he is."

I wanted to throttle Vercingetorix. How dare he defend me—
and insult Menua! I waited for the chief druid to wither him where
he stood.

But Menua never batted an eyelash. In a tone that implied he
gave no weight to the opinions of children, he said, "Like you,
young Vercingetorix, until Ainvar undergoes his manmaking he is
no sort of man at all."

The Arvernian turned his hooded gaze toward me. "Oh, I think
he is," he said softly. "I think this Ainvar is a man." Then he simply
walked away.

I looked at Menua in bafflement to find him laughing with the
others. "Two wolf cubs in one sack," said Grannus. Gobannitio
added, "In a moon's time I'll collect whichever one of them sur-
vives."

Everyone seemed to think this was very funny. I was not laughing, however. I was watching the tall lad with the golden hair who
was wandering around the walls of our fort as if assessing the
strength of the palisade.

So it was that I met the audacious warrior, irresistible and relentless, whose star we would one day follow where none of us
ever thought to go. Vercingetorix.

Just then Menua's raven cried from the roof, an omen I had already learned to interpret. The raven's voice above the bed meant a guest was welcome; I could not argue.

"If the raven calls 'Bach, Bach!' a visitor is a druid from another tribe," Menua had taught me. "If the cry is 'Gradh!' it is one of our own druids. To warn of warriors approaching, the raven says 'Grog!' If it calls from the northeast, robbers are near; if from the door, we can expect strangers. If it chirps with a small voice, saying, 'Err, err,' we can expect sickness in the lodge."

For Vercingetorix the raven called from just above the smoke-hole, and that same night the Arvernian lad spread his bedding so close to the fire that he blocked all the heat from me.

CHAPTER FOUR

Vercingetorix and I were able to take instruction for our man-making together. The eligible youths were divided into groups of three, a powerful number. Each group would be tested as a unit to strengthen the sense of tribal brotherhood. The Arvernian was not of our tribe but was arbitrarily linked with me by Menua—as was Crom Daral, who would be our third.

The choice of Crom surprised me. Memories of our friendship came welling back, and I was glad when Menua said I could tell him about the arrangement. I found him throwing spears at a straw target by himself. But in spite of what I thought of as good news, he was cool to me, even though I gave him a fond blow on the shoulder. His face remained closed and sullen. "Did you ask that I be your third?" he wanted to know.

Before my head recognized the hope hidden in his voice, my mouth blurted out the truth. "No, it was Menua's decision. He wants us with the Arvernian."

"Ah." Crom half-turned away from me. I observed that his mother's legacy of uneven shoulders had grown more pronounced, now

amounting almost to a deformity, one was so much higher than the
other. Poor Crom. If Vercingetorix was gold and I was bronze,
between us Crom Daral would be like some dark and baser metal,
introduced for what purpose?

Only the druids knew.

"Do you like the Arvernian?" he asked abruptly.

"I don't know yet. I don't think so."

"Do you like him better than you used to like me?"

I had forgotten how exasperating Crom could be. "I still like
you!" I snapped.

"No you don't." He thrust out his underlip sulkily.

"Have it your own way, then. But you don't know everything."

"Neither do you. Nor your precious druids!" he retorted.

In a bad humor I returned to the lodge in time to meet Vercingetorix coming out of it. As wary as two hounds meeting in a narrow
doorway, bristling and sniffing the air, we circled each other. Then
he went his way and I went mine.

That night in my bed I thought about Crom Daral. With the
self-centered callousness of children, I had been unaware of the
depth of his hurt at my perceived defection. But he obviously was
hurt, and I knew him well enough to know he would nurse his
grievance interminably.

I had lost a friend.

Too late, I realized I had lost more than I could spare. Rosmerta's
death had already robbed me of the cushion of love that had supported me through my childhood. I had not appreciated it until it
was gone. Menua saw that I had what I needed, but he was no
substitute for a grandmother.

Or a friend.

I lay curled into a tight knot in the darkness and fought the fangs
of self-pity.

For three days, Crom, Vercingetorix, and I met daily with various members of the Order of the Wise, as did the other candidates
for manmaking. The omens were read, our teeth and bodies examined for weakness, our minds tested with riddles.

On the evening of the third day, Grannus told us to prepare
ourselves for purification.

The candidates for this particular manmaking came from the fort
and the region surrounding it for one day's walk. More distant
youths would attend rituals held by their local druids. We com-

prised a large crowd, and members of the Order took turns supervising as we were bathed, purged, bathed again, given spring water to drink, made to sweat in the sweat lodge, then rubbed with oil of anise and crushed bay leaves and switched with willow twigs.

Throughout the day Vercingetorix was in a high good humor. He ignored Crom Daral's dour silence and treated my cousin as if the two were good friends. He was equally amiable toward me, and I discovered that when he chose, the Arvernian could exert an overwhelming charm. But when I burst into laughter at one of his jokes, I saw a look of hurt and anger on Crom Daral's face. I clapped my hand over my mouth, then thought better of it and went on laughing.

I was beginning to resent Crom Daral.

When we were clean inside and out, we were ordered to stand a night's vigil, naked, under the stars.

We took up positions around the wall. Each of us was determined to stand heroically, wide awake and impervious to the lingering chill in the night air. I was stationed between Crom and Vercingetorix. The latter endured, with little footshifting from sunset to sunrise. Whenever I looked in his direction, he flashed a grin at me, his teeth gleaming white in the gloom.

Crom, however, had difficulties. He shivered uncontrollably. He sneezed, he yawned. Once or twice he swayed and I feared he would fall, but he managed to jerk himself awake at the last moment. The rising sun found him red-eyed and miserable.

Vercingetorix, however, contrived to look as fresh as if he had spent the night in a bed, though I noticed that even he had gooseflesh. "Today is our day," he said cheerfully. "We become men." He narrowed his eyes. "Ainvar, did you ever wonder what womanmaking is like?"

I shrugged, pretending I was not interested in such things. "Different, that's all I know. Each girl's ritual happens individually, when she has her first bleeding."

Someday I will know all about it, I promised myself silently. Druids know.

The druids circled the fort to collect us. We were still naked; chilled, yawning youths trying to look manly. In the cold, Vercingetorix's shriveled genitals were no larger than mine. In spite of, or perhaps to compensate for, his crooked shoulder, Crom Daral was more impressively equipped than either of us. As we accompanied the druids to the forest, however, I could smell fear on him.

Fear smells like the green rot that eats away bronze.

We climbed the ridge toward the grove as the sun climbed into the sky. We were not taken to the grove itself; manmaking took place in a glade on the other side of the ridge. The trees watched us approach. Their arboreal darkness reached out for us; the wet weight of their shade lay heavily upon us.

Hooded druids and shivering boys came to a halt. Grannus called us each by name, then introduced us each, formally, to Menua, who would conduct the ceremony.

He called us forward in groups of three. When our turn came, Vercingetorix and I stepped toward him without hesitation, our strides matching perfectly. Crom Daral was half a step behind us.

The chief druid held out his hand, and Grannus placed a thin, sharp dart of polished bone on his open palm.

"Men must know they can endure pain," Menua intoned.

I had expected something of the sort, but not at the start of the ritual. Though it was worse than I anticipated, I gritted my teeth and endured. When the bone needle entered Crom's chest skin behind the nipple and came out again, I heard him gasp. Menua had pinched up the skin to avoid having the dart pierce the chest cavity, but the procedure was acutely painful in such a sensitive area.

Vercingetorix never flinched. A smile lifted the edges of his lips where the warrior's moustache was already sprouting. "Perhaps they'll have us demonstrate our prowess with a woman next," he said out of the side of his mouth to me.

He was mistaken. Next we were each given a stone and told to place a bare foot on it while water was poured over our outstretched arms. "Stone does not yield," said Menua. "There are times when a man must be like stone. Take the spirit of the stone into yourself.

"Water does not resist. There are other times when a man must be like water. Take the spirit of the water into yourselves."

I closed my eyes obediently and tried to feel like stone; like water. Somewhere between the two I encountered a shifting line that made me queasy. Startled, I opened my eyes.

"What about women?" Vercingetorix muttered.

Menua heard him.

The chief druid whirled on the Arvernian. Thrusting his face

into the boy's, he roared, "You have a confused idea of manhood!
Tell me, child with a presumptuous name—if your people were
attacked, would you defend them by climbing onto a woman?"

Several of the watching youths sniggered.

Vercingetorix took a step backward; Menua was almost on top
of him. "Of course not. I'd take up a shield and attack the attackers
with sword and spear."

"Would you?" In the blink of an eye, Menua's demeanor changed
completely. He went from furious to courteous, he became a benign
fellow calmly seeking information. "Would you really? And would
that impress them?"

Vercingetorix was off balance. Having experienced the chief
druid's disconcerting changes of pace myself, I could almost feel
sorry for him. He tried to sound as calm as Menua, but there was
a faint stammer in his voice as he replied, "I'm wonderful with
sword and spear."

"Are you? Isn't that nice for you." Menua lifted his bushy eyebrows. Expecting it, I saw him change again. With sudden with-
ering sarcasm, he snarled, "And if you had no weapons, *King of
the World,* how then would you impress your enemies? With empty
hands and a mouth full of wind, how could you frighten anybody?"

He turned away, as if Vercingetorix was no longer worthy of
interest. The Arvernian burned red beneath his freckles. I doubted
if anyone had spoken to the son of Celtillus in such a way in his
life. I wondered if Menua had made an enemy.

The manmaking resumed as if there had been no interruption.

We were tested throughout a wearyingly long day. I tried to
keep my sleepy head alert and not scratch my skin where the blood
dried in itchy crusts.

When the sun was low in the sky, we faced the final challenge.
Beyond the trees a wide pit had been dug, and in it Aberth the
sacrificer built a fire of blackthorn, the wood-of-testing. Each group
of three was told to select its heaviest member. Ours was obviously
Vercingetorix. Carrying the heaviest between them, the other two
were to leap across the pit where the flames were highest.

"A man must know he can exceed his own limits," Menua told
us. "And a man must honor his promises. Each of you will promise
the other two not to fail them."

The pit was dauntingly wide. If the two jumpers did not make a mighty effort, or if the one balanced on their locked arms moved at the wrong moment, all three would fall and be burned, perhaps fatally.

Crom Daral's nerve broke. He shrank against me. "I can't do it, Ainvar," he whispered.

Vercingetorix spared him only a glance, then said to me as if issuing a command, "Ask for someone else to be our third."

Part of me was grateful for that instant, confident leadership. I almost surrendered to it. But Crom was blood kin and had long been my friend. I would not deny him his manmaking to please Vercingetorix. The Arverni were of Celtic blood like us, but they were not us. We Carnutes had gone to war against them in the past and would again; that was what tribes did.

My head would decide the matter.

"We three are going to jump together," I announced firmly.

Crom protested in a faltering voice. "But I'm too tired."

My temper frayed. "We're all tired! We're supposed to be, this isn't meant to be easy for us. Neither is it impossible or they would not ask it. The tribe needs new men."

Crom's lower lip jutted forward. His eyes were blank, reflecting the flames. "I can't."

"Leave him," said the Arvernian.

A voice murmured in my mind. I clutched the idea before it could fly away. "I know what we can do, Vercingetorix. Help me. Collect an armload of rocks, hurry!"

He stared at me. He was not accustomed to taking orders from someone his own age. Feeling the powerful tug of wills between us, I became very aware of the awesome strength of his.

Summon the spirit of the stone, said the voice in my head.

I obeyed. I concentrated; I became stone.

A heartbeat passed. Another. Then Vercingetorix grinned and I knew I had won.

We loaded Crom's arms with rocks until he was heavier than either of us. Then he sat on our locked arms and Vercingetorix and I leaped the blazing pit.

We left the ground in stride like a team of trained chariot horses. Up, up! Beneath us the fire snarled and crackled. A thrill ran through me, but it had nothing to do with the danger.

We soared!

Linked together we became more than two, Vercingetorix and I. For that brief flight we were one creature with the combined abilities of both, and something more. Something glorious.

When we landed on the far side of the pit and set Crom down, Vercingetorix looked at me and I knew he had felt it too, that numinous moment when together we could have leaped a pit twice as wide, over flames twice as high. We exchanged a glance of exultation.

Crom intercepted that glance. He sagged and sat down cross-legged on the earth, staring dully at the pit.

Five sets of boys fell. Two were badly burned.

The manmaking concluded, Dian Cet laid hands on each of our heads in turn. I hardly felt the touch of the druid judge, or heard his voice as he said, "Tonight you are a man, Ainvar of the Carnutes."

My senses were still flooded with the feeling of Vercingetorix's hands clamped on my arms, and the memory of transcendence as we soared above the fire.

When we returned to the fort, Vercingetorix and I walked side by side. We did not speak, but I was increasingly aware of the tidal pull of his personality, drawing me to him. Whatever was in him had been intensified by his manmaking.

Of course, my head affirmed. That is the purpose.

A small feast was served to the newly initiated men. I sat beside Vercingetorix, and we shared a few oatcakes and a lot of wine. At some point in the festivities I found myself calling him Rix.

We had a succession of sun-soaked days together before Gobannitio returned to take Rix home. During that time I told him of my family and he told me of his, particularly of his ambitious father, Celtillus, who was warring against the Aedui in the south. Celtillus dreamed of making the Arverni the supreme tribe in Gaul, Rix confided, although the king of the tribe had smaller goals and was content with things as they were.

"My uncle Gobannitio agrees with the king," Rix said. "He says we would lose more men than we can afford to lose if we tried to subjugate all the tribes of Gaul."

"What do you think?"

Rix smiled. "I like a bold dream."

"You'll never defeat the Carnutes," I assured him, but I laughed as I said it and there was no hostility between us. We had become friends. We fished in the river and rolled our eyes at the women and the time we had together was too short.

"Perhaps you have found a soul friend," Menua suggested to me in private.

"What is a soul friend?"

"A person you have known . . . before. And almost remember. A person with whom you have a special link. When one of such a pair is a druid, the druid is obliged to serve as guide and counselor for his soul friend."

"Does Vercingetorix know about soul friends?"

"I doubt it."

"Should I tell him?"

"He might laugh at you; he might not understand," Menua replied with a perceptiveness I would only appreciate later.

My head knew Menua was right; the Arvernian and I were soul friends. I recognized the spirit that looked out at me from Rix's long-lidded eyes.

I began taking my obligation seriously, giving him much gratuitous advice. To my surprise, he accepted it, or at least listened.

Rix had a habit common to those who live with others. He announced what he was going to do before he did it, often in unnecessary detail. "I'm going to bed now, I'm sleepy and I want to be fresh for hunting tomorrow," he would say. Or, "I'm going outside for a piss, my belly is too full of wine."

As Menua had advised me, I advised Rix. "Don't announce your intentions so freely. The less others know, the better."

"Secrecy is for druids," he replied.

"Secrecy could be good strategy for warriors, too," I suggested.

Rix studied me through narrowed eyes. "You are clever, Ainvar."

His compliment embarrassed me. "I use my head," I said diffidently.

"If you find anything else in that head of yours that might be of use to me, share it. I'm trying to assemble an armory."

"The King of the World will need one." I could not resist teasing.

He hit me. I hit him. We rolled in the dirt, punching and pounding, until laughter broke us apart.

When Gobannitio came for Rix our leavetaking was awkward. We had almost been enemies; we had become more than friends. We were not bards and so did not have the agility of tongue to express our feelings.

In near silence, I helped Rix collect his things in the lodge. When he lifted his rolled bedding onto his shoulder, he said, "Beware of the man with the crooked shoulder, Ainvar. He failed himself at the manmaking and you were a witness. He won't forgive you for having seen his weakness."

"You don't understand, Rix. Crom was my friend."

"Just remember what I said. You have a clever head, but I am a pretty good judge of men."

"I'll remember," I promised.

At the doorway he turned back toward me. Had we belonged to the same tribe we would have hugged fiercely, grabbed one another by the beard, and kissed both cheekbones. But he was Arvernian and I was Carnutian. A chasm yawned between us.

Rix grinned. "We jumped the pit together, Ainvar," he said unexpectedly.

We threw our arms around each other then and hugged hard enough to crack bones.

His parting words to me were, "I salute you as a free person!"

"And I, you!" I shouted as he strode away.

I did not follow him to the gate. I did not want to stand with the others, waving as Gobannitio and his nephew drove away. I knew Vercingetorix would never look back.

I was alone, and I was a man.

I would be a druid.

CHAPTER FIVE

MY INSTRUCTION resumed; my classrooms were the glades of the forest. Menua wanted me to absorb the wisdom of the trees. Druid, as he explained to me, meant "having the knowledge of the oak."

He said, "When men were as vapor, trees were vapor. The forests are older than memory and time is stored in their roots and branches. It is the nature of trees to be generous, so open yourself and be still. Receive what they impart."

I learned to listen to the trees.

Of my generation, I was the only person within a day's walk being trained in druidry. Menua spoke wistfully of bygone years when many gifted youngsters had presented themselves for training and the forest had rung with voices reciting in chorus. He could not explain the shortage of hopefuls for the Order, and it weighed heavily on him.

"But things are as they are," he told me with a sigh. "Until the pattern presents us with more talented people, I have only you to instruct in the natural sciences."

We were sitting in a small glade, he on a fallen tree and I cross-legged at his feet. The current topic for study was the Greek language, and we had been discussing the term "natural science," by which the Greeks meant the druidical arts. Menua admired the Greeks; he knew their writing and their customs. Menua knew everything, almost.

"The Greeks understand us better than the Romans," he told me. "The Romans call us 'priests,' which is a mistake. The Hellenes who used to trade with the Carnutes in my youth referred to druids as 'philosophers.' When I learned to understand their language, I realized the term was appropriate.

"Once the various Greek tribes traveled more or less freely throughout Gaul, before their subjugation by the Romans. I miss them, Ainvar. They were interesting people with subtle minds. I once had a discussion with a Greek who called himself a 'geographer,' and appeared to grasp the concept of the pattern as readily as a Celt."

"I'm not certain I understand about the pattern myself," I admitted. "You speak of it so often. But just what is it?"

Menua pointed toward the interplay of light and shadow among the branches above us. "There is the pattern. From star to tree to insect, each fragment of creation is part of one design, the pattern of being, that extends unbroken from the Otherworld to this world. The pattern is constantly in motion, connecting us in life and in death to the Source of All Being."

"But how do you recognize the pattern?" I asked, staring at the branches that were only limbs and leaves to me.

Menua nodded slowly. "Now you give voice to one of the greatest of questions. When you know the answer, you will know yourself to be a druid. You will have learned from experience to feel the pattern in your bones and your blood."

Having hoped for a more specific answer, I must have looked dubious, for his expression softened. "I cannot transfer my own experience to you, each must find his own. But I can tell you about the pattern.

"People who pray for luck are really seeking to grasp the pattern, Ainvar. There is no such thing as luck, that is only a word for being able to control events. The few who intuitively follow the pattern as it applies to themselves appear to have luck, for they are, without knowing it, drawing on the forces of creation. When they deviate from the pattern they lose contact with those forces, and thus with the power that influences events. Then we say they have become unlucky. When things work out well for you, you will know you are following your pattern as you should."

My mind had snagged on one of his words like a strand of wool snagged on a bramble. "What does 'intuitively' mean?"

A fine webbing of wrinkles fanned outward from the corners of Menua's eyes when he smiled. "Intuition is the voice of the spirit within you."

"I've heard it already!" I cried, remembering the night something had told me to pile Crom Daral's arms with rocks. "At least, I think I have. Once."

"You must hear it more often than that, Ainvar. You must listen to it every day."

"Can I learn how?"

"Of course, that is one of the things I am to teach you. You will begin by listening to the songs of the earth. The natural world and the world of spirits are connected through the pattern, remember? But most people do not bother to listen to nature's voices, just as they do not look for the pattern."

I glanced at the treetops again and he chuckled. "Not with your outer eye, Ainvar. Use your inner eye."

"My inner eye?"

"One of the senses of your spirit."

I considered this. "I don't think I have any."

"Of course you do, everyone does. We are all born with them, they come with the spirit that animates the flesh. Little children use them every day. Think back to your early childhood, Ainvar. Were you not aware of many things adults did not hear and see? Remember. Remember."

His voice reached inside me, summoning.

Memory flooded through me.

When I was only a knee-child, my head not yet reaching Rosmerta's hip, I had known there were other presences in our lodge. Since I was aware of them I assumed everyone else was. Every shadow was intangibly occupied. The night beyond the door was peopled with potential. I knew without question and without doubt.

I was not afraid of the dark; I had so recently emerged from the darkness of being unborn. An elusive memory lingered like a prom-

ise at the edge of my awareness, calling to me. Even then. Luring
me out into the darkness, making me curious.

How could I have forgotten the many times I ran eagerly into
the night, trying to recapture a lost magic, while Rosmerta scuttled
after me, clucking and scolding like an old hen.

"I remember," I said softly.

"Good. Then we can train you." Menua pushed up the sleeves
of his robe, revealing still-muscular forearms covered with wiry
silver hair. Bees were humming in the glade. Soil smelled hot,
leaves smelled green.

"First you must learn to be still," the chief druid told me. "Be
truly still, so your body is like an empty sack, gaping open.

"Whether you know it or not, your spirit is only held in your
flesh by an act of will. You must relax your will and allow spirit to
move as freely as mist among the trees. Otherwise your spirit,
which is the essential and immortal You, might someday find itself
trapped in a decaying body it must accompany into the tomb."

The image of my spirit being imprisoned in my dead body was
so horrific I determined to learn to free it no matter how hard I
must work. I practiced being still, which was difficult, and letting
my soul float, which seemed impossible. I felt as if I were sealed
in a stoppered jar.

"Don't squirm when you're supposed to be concentrating,"
Menua scolded me. "You are listening too much to the demands
of your joints and muscles. Your body is not in charge, Ainvar.
You are."

I redoubled my efforts. The summer we had courted and won
came to us sweetly and lingered long, and in time I learned to stop
thinking of my body as myself. It was merely an outpost of me, a
companion, a home in which I lived for a time. I grew easy in my
skin.

Then one morning I heard a lark sing; *really* heard a lark sing.
As I listened spellbound, the piercingly pure cataract of musical
sounds became echoes of a greater glory I experienced with a sense
beyond hearing, a sense belonging to my untrammeled soul.

I ran to tell Menua. Words shaped for only five senses were
inadequate, but he understood.

"Now it begins for you, Ainvar. You can find the pattern anywhere. Hear it, see it, feel it. Where would you like to begin?"

I knew at once. "Can I have a man with a spear?" I asked.

Menua nodded. He did not even ask me to explain.

Taking a warrior called Tarvos with me to watch for the wolves I still remembered with a shudder, I left the fort to spend the night in the forest. Among the trees, without the barriers of walls and roof.

I went to seek the magic in the night with my newly awakened senses of the spirit.

I found a snug place for myself in the lee of a hillock and sent my bodyguard to stand a distance away, where he could hear me if I needed him but would not distract me. His expression told me he thought I was mad, but I was the chief druid's apprentice. It was not given to warriors to question my actions.

After singing the song for the setting sun, I wrapped myself in my cloak and lay down to wait.

I had a long wait. Nothing happened. By sunrise I was stiff and hungry, yet determined to persevere.

Every night for eight nights I slept in the forest, with barrel-chested, bandy-legged Tarvos poking his spear into every clump of shrubbery and muttering to himself. During the days I continued my studies with Menua, who was currently teaching me the motions of the stars.

On my ninth attempt I heard the music of the night.

Sometime after the moon disappeared a wind arose. The trees became its instruments. It played them with undulating volume, with sweeping susurrations of sound, with a great plumy movement billowing through, sighing away. Each tree had a voice. Oaks creaked, beeches moaned, pines hummed, alders whispered, poplars chattered.

I lay absolutely still, drowning in sound.

Then everything came together.

I was caught up in the rhythm of a dance, ecstatic and sublime, that had been going on long before there was any such being as Ainvar. I was dissolving into wind and moss and leaves, into a rabbit huddled in its burrow, into an owl swimming through the night on silent wings.

Disturbed by the rushing wind, cattle lowed in a distant meadow. Every cow had a distinctive voice their herder would have recognized among hundreds; each voice filled a particular space belonging to it alone in the larger pattern of sound, a pattern that included my own breathing and the scattering of insects in the leafmold and the pattern of raindrops striking the leaves.

Water rolled down my cheeks. Perhaps rain. Perhaps tears summoned by beauty.

The night sang. The earth smelled of rotting wood and tender shoots unfolding in darkness, feeding on decomposition, death and birth together in the pattern, one springing from the other.

Both in me. Both of me. I of them. I was the earth and the night and the rain, suspended at the apex of being. There was no time, no sound, no sight, no need of them.

I *was*.

Rapture.

"Ainvar? Ainvar!"

I opened my eyes to find Tarvos crouched over me. His face was twisted with worry. His hair held the shape of the wind. "Ainvar, are you all right? If anything has happened to you the chief druid will hang me in a cage!"

Dawnlight filtered through the leaves above us. The air seemed gray and grainy. I sat up, surprised to find myself dizzy. My clothes were sodden. "I'm not dead," I assured the warrior. "I've had the most wonderful experience. . . ."

"Mad," said Tarvos with conviction. "All you druids are mad." He extended a hand to help pull me to my feet.

I liked Tarvos. His jaw was too broad and there were gaps between his teeth—and he had called me a druid. I tried to smile at him, but my legs were shaking under me. My wet clothes clung like ice and I began shivering.

"You look terrible," Tarvos informed me. "Like an owl in an ivy bush, all staring eyes surrounded by leaves." He briskly brushed the leaves off my clothing, but I kept on shivering uncontrollably.

"We'd better get you moving," Tarvos said, giving me a shove. He might think of me as a druid, but he did not let that intimidate him. I liked him all the more for it.

As we walked back to the fort, I heard a sound in my ears like the sound a glass bottle makes if you strike it with metal. Tarvos somehow eased himself into my armpit and took part of my weight on himself. "Crazy druids," he muttered.

"I'm not a druid yet," I felt constrained to remind him.

"I'm a warrior because I was born a warrior," he replied. "You're a druid for the same reason."

Menua was not in our lodge. I yearned for my bed. Since I had given Tarvos no instructions, he followed me inside.

"Grog!" screamed the raven on the roof.

"Druids don't live very well," commented Tarvos, looking around. "I thought you'd have a lot of gold in here."

"It's in here," I told him, tapping my forehead.

He looked dubious. "If you say so." He shrugged his burly shoulders as if shrugging off a cloak; a characteristic gesture, I was to learn. "Do you want me to build a fire to dry your clothes?"

My head reminded me I should not have brought anyone into the chief druid's lodge without Menua's invitation. And a druid's fire was sacred; no flame could be kindled on the summerdead hearth without an elaborate ritual.

I was chilled, my teeth were beginning to chatter. I had lain for a long time in the rain, I suppose. I started to say, "I can take care of myself, you can go now . . ." but the ringing in my ears grew louder and I wandered off into a grayness.

From a distance came the raven's voice, chirping like a wren.

I awoke to a sense of urgency. My skull was filled with cobwebs. Sorting among them, I could not find the thought I wanted. Menua was bending over me and I wanted to tell him about the night and the music, but my tongue refused to obey me. Tarvos is more obedient than my body, I thought angrily.

I became aware of a fire blazing. Raising my head dizzily, I saw Tarvos feeding sticks to the flames. . . .

The next time I emerged from the grayness, Sulis the healer was rubbing a foul-smelling paste on my chest. "You should not have let him stay out all night in a storm," she said over her shoulder to Menua.

"He's a strong young man, and it was important to him. He must be given every opportunity to discover his abilities; our numbers are too small as it is. This is not the safest of times."

Sulis bowed her head. "It is not. I don't question your judgment," she added submissively. Menua was the chief druid.

And Tarvos had dared to build a fire on his hearth! I struggled to sit up. Sulis pushed me back onto my bed with one firm hand in the center of my chest. As she bent over me I saw the valley between her breasts in the deep neck of her gown.

"Where is Tarvos?" I demanded to know. "Did you put him in a cage? It wasn't his fault!"

Menua's face swam into my wavering sight. "Of course I didn't put him in a cage. He took care of you, we are grateful."

"I want to see him now," I demanded feverishly. To my surprise, for I was not used to commanding the chief druid, Menua nodded and beckoned to someone. Tarvos stepped forward, unharmed.

"I'm here, Ainvar. You didn't dismiss me, so I stayed."

I lay back bemused, imagining Tarvos stubbornly holding his place when the chief druid returned to the lodge.

Sulis rubbed a fragrant liquid onto my upper lip. As the fumes drifted into my nostrils, I fell into an easy sleep, from which I eventually awoke, clearheaded but weak.

Tarvos was sitting on the floor near me, sharpening a knife on a whetstone. The bulky shape of his shoulders was reassuring. He wore the only tunic and leggings I had ever seen him in, garments unacquainted with washing, and the hair flowing down his back was the indeterminate color of old thatch. He was neither polished nor prepossessing, but he had refused to leave me when I was ill.

Tarvos the Bull, he was called.

I was young, my strength returned quickly. Later in the day Sulis came to check on my progress. Tarvos followed her with his eyes. "She has a nice haunch on her," he commented when she had gone.

"She's our healer!"

"She's a woman," he said with a shrug.

Menua allowed him to stay, though I never knew why.

Tarvos spread his bed outside the door to our lodge, but during the day he was inside with me, feeding me, bringing me water, encouraging me to get up when I was ready. He also provided me with an unexpected opportunity to enrich my head. Only a few winters older than I, the Bull had served as a warrior in several tribal battles and experienced many things I had not.

"Tell me what it's like to be a warrior," I said.

He looked blank. "It's something to do."

Tarvos was not a wordy man, but I persisted. "Druids need to know all they can about everything, including battle, Tarvos. If you share your feelings with me I can experience war through you."

He considered this, then stared into space for a time, obediently seeking words for things not usually discussed outside the brotherhood of battle. While he pondered I poured him a cup of wine from Menua's personal store, thankful that the chief druid was away, supervising the castrating of the bull calves.

I held out the cup and Tarvos accepted it eagerly. When he had taken a long drink, I urged, "Now. Tell me what it means to be a warrior."

"Being a warrior is about getting killed," he replied simply. "Warriors are born to be killed."

"Are you afraid of dying, Tarvos?" It was a druid sort of question.

He took another drink. "You druids teach that death is merely an incident in the middle of a long life, don't you? So why fear it? It's no more lasting than fucking or farting." He drained the cup. "What warriors fear," he went on, "is losing. Most of us are more afraid of losing than we are eager to win. The losers are usually badly injured, perhaps crippled for life. I don't fear death but I don't like pain. The wounds you get in battle may not hurt at the time, there's too much going on, but they are a misery after. Some say they don't mind. I do mind."

"So you fight to avoid losing?"

He nodded his shaggy head. "Most of us. Or to avoid being called coward. And for a share of the loot, if there is any. Of course, a few men are different: the champions. The warriors with the greatest style fight for their own reasons."

"What do you mean by the greatest style?"

He held out his empty cup and waited. I filled it. Tarvos nodded again, solemnly. "Style is what sets a champion apart, Ainvar. They are crazy-brave, they do things that would get any other man killed but they walk away laughing. When you see the style of a champion, you recognize it, it's like a glowing inside him."

Vercingetorix has style, my head informed me. He is one of those rare beings who achieve because they never deviate from the pattern that applies to themselves.

Yet how does he know? Do champions, like druids, receive some special guidance from the Otherworld? Or is it accidental, so they are subject to failure at any time?

Tarvos was watching me over the rim of his cup. "Do you want to be a champion, Tarvos?" I asked him.

He looked startled. "Not me! I'm content to carry my spears and try to kill the other man before he kills me. All that fancy style just makes me tired. I think it's as unnecessary as teats on a boar."

He finished his second cup and rubbed his belly, spreading the warm glow. "Can I ask you a question, Ainvar?"

"You may."

"Why did you choose me that day? To be your bodyguard, I mean."

I thought back. "I was actually looking for Ogmios, to ask him—"

"You were looking for Ogmios yet you chose me?" Tarvos interrupted.

I was learning to listen: I recognized the concealed pleasure in the Bull's voice. I bit off the words I had meant to say about Ogmios and his son, Crom Daral, and said instead, "When I saw you, Tarvos, I found the man I needed."

My reward was the expression of satisfaction on his blunt face and the flash of his teeth in his beard when he smiled.

He left the lodge to get some food for me from Damona, and I lay back on my bed, thinking. I had spoken the truth, I now realized. I had chosen the right man, though on that day I was looking for someone very different.

I had gone in search of Crom Daral to ask him to be my bodyguard, hoping that would somehow be a start toward mending the breach between us. But he was hard to find, even in our small fort. He had been deliberately avoiding me since the manmaking.

I had thought Ogmios, as captain of the guard, would surely know where his son was. I went in search of him among the company of warriors who could usually be found near the main gate of the fort, boasting and wrestling to pass the time. But before I saw Ogmios I discovered his son embedded in the group, listening with unsmiling face to the rough banter. I shouted "Crom!" and raised an arm in greeting.

He turned at the sound of my voice and met my eyes. Then he deliberately turned his back on me.

I halted in midstride. My head echoed Vercingetorix's words: "He failed himself and you were a witness. He won't forgive you."

My eyes chanced to meet those of a burly young man with hair the color of dirty thatch, lounging at the edge of the cluster of warriors. Impulsively I shouted to him, loud enough for Crom to hear, "You there! You're the very one I want! Bring your spear and come with me, on command of the chief druid."

Tarvos had been with me since, proving to be the ideal ally. Solid and steady, he conformed to my need, fitting exactly into my pattern although I had taken him on impulse.

What, then, is impulse?

Such questions roil the brains of druids.

In any event, I could not hold Tarvos to my side much longer. My strength rapidly returned; soon I did not even need to lean on him when I went to relieve myself at the squatting trench.

Before I could dismiss him formally, he was taken from me by his primary obligation.

A great shout came thundering across the land. The warning was cried from plowman to herdsman to woodcutter until it reached our fort, and it would be shouted on from there by a network of the common class all the way to Cenabum, which was two nights from us by foot but only a short distance by voice. "Invasion and attack!" came the cry.

Details followed. A large war party of the neighboring Senones had moved into Carnute territory east of the fort and was plundering the more prosperous farmsteads there. Our fort and its warriors were sufficient to defend the grove and to shelter nearby farmers, but for this sort of problem we needed Nantorus and a larger army. The shouts soon brought him from Cenabum with a full complement of fighting men. Our warriors ran to join them, yelling and clashing their weapons to make a frightful racket.

We all crowded the gateway to see them leave for war. In the crush a small red-haired boy who was jammed against my knee tugged impatiently at my tunic. "What do you see?" he kept asking.

I started to lift him up so he could see for himself, then realized he was blind. I knew the boy; he belonged to a clan of smallholders who planted barley just beyond the fort. He was always wandering away from his distracted mother. His pale gray eyes were covered with a milky film that Sulis the healer had never been able to clear. Sundered from the sun, his was an endless night.

I picked him up and held him so my lips were close to his ear. He was very young, he hardly weighed anything. But he vibrated with life. "I see the king," I told him. "Nantorus rides with his charioteer in a wicker-sided war chariot. He wears a tunic of iron links taken from the Bituriges in battle; they have iron mines in their territory," I added, unable to resist teaching. "His horses are matched brown stallions seized from the Turones, and his long hair flows below a bronze helmet crested with a boar's head, a trophy of war taken from the Parisii."

"Ooohhh!" breathed the child, clapping tiny hands. "Are there many chariots? How do they fight in them?"

"They don't, not anymore. Once they did, but a chariot is an unstable platform for battle, and now the tribes only use them for the initial display before the real fighting begins. In their chariots the two war leaders will charge at each other, hurling spears and insults, while their cavalry and foot soldiers try to intimidate each other with more threats and insults. Each side wants to look larger and more ferocious than the other."

"What are cavalry?"

"Warriors mounted on horses. My father was horse rank," I added with sudden pride. "My grandmother had me taught to ride by our warriors when I was not so much older than you."

"Will I learn to ride a horse and be part of the cavalry?" the child asked eagerly.

I had a painful vision of the limitations of his world. "No, because your clan belongs to the common class," I said as gently as I could, unwilling to remind him of his blindness. "Only warriors of horse rank can be cavalry. But most warriors, although belonging to the noble class and entitled to wear the gold arm ring, are foot soldiers."

As I spoke, I caught a glimpse of Tarvos running forward with the other foot soldiers, yelling with excitement and beating his spear against his shield.

"Tell me about the battle," the boy urged.

"One of the ways our kings have earned their kingship is through proving themselves as fighting champions," I explained, "so the opposing kings have their chariots driven in huge circles, trying to make their horses look as if they are wild and out of control. Then when they feel they have impressed each other sufficiently, they dismount and fight on foot, with swords. Their warriors watch and cheer their style, then join in the general battle. Some throw off their tunics and fight naked to intimidate their opponents with the size and rigidity of their manhoods. Each side hurls itself against the other in wave after wave, until one side is overcome."

"I would like to be a champion with a chariot," the little boy confided, snuggling against me. His coppery hair smelled of the sun. One of his clan came elbowing through the crowd to us.

"There he is! We've been looking everywhere. . . ."

He was taken from my arms with reluctance on both sides.

"The boy often wanders," his kinsman said apologetically. "He's quite fearless, blind as he is and small as he is."

"He's safe anywhere near the fort," I assured the man. "We're all tribesmen. Even the current enemy wouldn't hurt him, you know. Children, like druids, are sacrosanct."

I watched the bright head being carried away through the crowd. There was a tap on my shoulder. "You can help me," said Menua.

He was frowning. Taking me by the elbow, he steered me away from the crowd. "Did you observe how thin the warriors are, Ainvar? Planting went well but we haven't yet harvested, and the effects of the bad winter can be seen on gaunt faces. Our men have not rebuilt their full strength. They are running with excitement now, but by the time they reach the Senones they will be dragging their feet. They need the aid of the druids. Particularly yours," he added.

His eyes twinkled mysteriously.

We went to the lodge together. There he rummaged in his carved wooden chest, then removed a mirror of polished metal. Its back was inlaid with bronze and silver wires in a curvilinear design that represented nothing but suggested everything.

"Here," said the chief druid, handing me the mirror. "Use this to part your hair into four equal sections. Here are strips of cloth to bind each section, blue for water, brown for earth, yellow for sun, red for blood. Be certain the partings are straight, and tie the strands securely so no strength can run out of them."

I must have given him a quizzical look, because Menua almost, but not quite, smiled. "Strength must be hoarded until it is needed. There is strength in your hair, it being the part of you nearest your brain. The brain, in the sacred head, is the source of all strength, all vigor and vitality.

"We are going to use your strength, amplified by the power of the grove, to send our warriors the vitality they need to win in the coming battle. So you must prepare yourself precisely as I instruct, young Ainvar.

"Today you will learn about sex magic."

CHAPTER SIX

I HAD never seen myself in a mirror made by one of our skilled craftsmen. Rosmerta had not kept one; long before she died her face had ceased to be her friend.

During my childhood, ponds and puddles had given me glimpses of unformed features to be grimaced at and splashed away. For the first time I was seeing those features firmed into maturity and reflected in polished metal. If I did not know who he was, I would not have recognized the young man staring back at me.

He had an elegant narrow head with a long skull suitable for storing knowledge. The eye sockets were deeply carved, the cheekbones high, the nose prominent and thrusting. It was a strong clear timeless face full of contradictions, brooding yet mischievous, reserved yet involved. Fathomless eyes and curving lips spoke of intense passions carefully suppressed, concentrated in stillness.

Those somber, smoldering features startled me so badly I almost dropped the mirror. "I look like *that*?"

"You do now. We cannot know what you really look like until

64

your spirit has had many years to carve your face into a representation of itself. Perhaps it will be much like the face you wear now, perhaps not. Now stop staring at yourself and get to work, prepare your hair as I instructed. You must do sex magic soon."

Menua handed me a bronze comb, but for some reason I could not carve straight partings in my hair. Nervous fingers make mistakes.

Sex magic, I kept thinking.

As we left the fort and set out for the forest on the ridge, we were joined by several other members of the Order of the Wise. Though their hoods were raised, I recognized Sulis the healer, Grannus, the judge Dian Cet, Keryth the seer, and Narlos the exhorter. I was thankful that Aberth was not among them. The sacrificer's gifts were essential for the welfare of the tribe, but his presence made me uncomfortable.

Sulis also made me uncomfortable, though in a different way. She was good to look at, with a fine strong face and, as Tarvos had observed, a tempting curve to her hips.

As he walked beside me, Menua saw me glance toward her. "She pleases you?" he inquired pleasantly.

One could never be certain what hidden meanings lurked in his words. I nodded but made no reply other than a random noise in my throat that Menua could interpret as he chose.

"She is our youngest initiate," he remarked. "She comes of a talented family. Her brother, whom we call the Goban Saor, shows remarkable gifts of craftsmanship. He can make anything with his hands, from jewelry to a stone wall. Sulis's hands are also gifted; her touch relieves pain. She is a fine healer. A fine woman in many ways," he added thoughtfully.

He turned toward me. "Have you had much experience of women, Ainvar? Aside from the games children play, I mean?"

The memory of some of those games came vividly back to me. I must have reddened, for the chief druid chuckled. "Good, good, we want boys and girls to explore each other's bodies, it's the best way to learn. Then you can be comfortable together later on, when you are old enough to mate.

"Sex takes practice, Ainvar. And appreciation. It is like the channel of a river, directing the life force that flows from the Source of All Being. Think of it. A man and woman join their bodies together, life flows through them, and a child is born. What greater magic?"

There was a sense of awe in his voice, awe that had not faded with the passing of the years.

"Our winterweary warriors are going to need a strength they do not have, something the Greeks call 'energy.' The energy of bulls fighting, of rams rutting, of young men hot with passion. Energy is the life force and it flows through everything created by the Source, even through stone. The trees, always our teachers, sink their roots into the soil and draw out energy. Life. Take off your boots as we walk and feel the earth with your bare feet. Feel, as you have learned to hear."

I did as he commanded, drawing off the soft leather boots that covered my feet and were tied around my shins with thongs. When I stepped barefoot onto the ground at first, I felt only pebbles and hard-packed dirt. Then there was . . . a flicker like a whisper running through the earth.

Only a flicker, but it startled me into awareness and I stopped walking.

Menua stopped with me. "You felt it?"

"I think so. It was like putting my fingers to my throat and feeling the blood hum inside."

"Very good, Ainvar. Some druids have such a feeling for the life force as it courses through the earth that they can follow it like a pathway. Its paths intersect in certain, special places, where the life force gathers so strongly that—"

"The grove!" I interrupted with a flash of intuition.

"The grove." Menua's voice rumbled deep in his chest. "Yes. There, more than any other place in Gaul, the paths of power meet. The great grove of the Carnutes is sacred not only to Man, but to the earth. You sense it; all who go there sense it.

"There are other places with similar properties. Some are forceful and invigorating, others are peaceful and contemplative. Men are drawn to them; they become holy sites. Some places excrete noxious forces from the earth as your bowels excrete waste, and they are to be avoided. If you listen, your spirit will warn you of them.

"As for this grove, we druids discovered long ago that the life force here is so intense it heightens our own abilities many times over. Therefore we hold our most powerful rituals in the grove . . . like the sex magic in which you will take part tonight, Ainvar."

We were walking again. My forgotten boots dangled from my

fingers. My eyes were fixed on the ridge rising before us with its crown of trees dark against the sky.

Menua said, "In the grove we will add your young male energy to the power of the sacred place and hurl the combined force after our warriors like a spear. When it reaches them they will have strength they did not know they possessed. They will win their battle against the Senones and come back to us free persons."

We were climbing toward the grove. My feet found their way along the path of brown earth, studded with occasional sharp-edged stones of mottled reddish-brown. My lips moved of their own volition, silently imploring That Which Watched to make me capable of the task before me.

The druids had brought torches; the one Sulis carried was lighted. From this the other torches were now set ablaze and then positioned at intervals around the glade in the heart of the grove. Beyond the forest the setting sun still shone, but among the trees was twilight.

Menua had me stand in the center of the clearing. Narlos led a chant and the druids circled me, sunwise. A wind rose and sang with them, movement and movement and flowing.

I saw Sulis looking at me from beneath her hood.

The chanting stopped. Menua stepped forward and took a handful of leather thongs from a pouch tied to his waist. He motioned me to hold out my hands, and he bound each wrist separately with a leather strip tied so tightly my fingers grew cold at once. Then he repeated the procedure with my ankles.

Sulis stepped out of the circle and took off her robe. Beneath it she was naked.

Her skin gave off a scent like warm bread. I had seen naked girls before, but Sulis was a woman.

"Lie down," she said to me.

I did, feeling awkward. The druids and the trees watched, expecting me to participate in something I did not understand.

There are many kinds of fear.

Sulis knelt beside me and arranged my body, head to the north, arms extended east and west. She began stroking me, slipping her warm hands under my tunic. This time hers was not a healing touch. Wherever she touched me, I burned.

The chanting began again.

Sulis smoothed her palms along my rib cage. She pulled up my tunic, working it off my body, and I squirmed to help her. My skin was unbearably hot, I longed for the cool air.

When I lay back down, she gently pressed the balls of her thumbs into the base of my throat. My pulse beat against the pressure. Her thumbs moved along my body, pressing at various points. All my awareness of self followed her thumbs. I could hardly breathe, I could only feel.

Feel feel feel.

Feel the pounding excitement building in me like floodwater behind a log jam, desperate for release, trapped by the thongs strangling my wrists and ankles.

Sulis's hands stroked down the centerline of my body, her fingers trailing fire. I felt as if ants were swarming over me. When her hands reached my belly, my penis stirred and rose like a creature with a will of its own, so achingly sensitive I was afraid I would scream if she touched it.

She separated my legs and knelt between them. Using her thumbs again, she caressed the insides of my thighs. My fingers flexed and my toes curled in spite of the tight thongs. Leaning forward, Sulis breathed on me. Her warm breath stirred the hair of my groin. I shuddered.

Sulis began to sing.

Her song had no words. It was pure melody, a skein of sound spun round us, becoming part of the chanting as I became part of the chanting, and my penis became part of the chanting, all creation expressed in vibrant sound, heard in my soul as I had heard the music of the night.

The energy Menua had described pulsed through me, and Sulis sang, and touched me, until pleasure became excess became agony.

I would die without release of the force building in me. I would burst like an overripe fruit.

But there was no release. There was only Sulis caressing me and singing to me, using her fingernails and her teeth on my flesh in patterns of torture, dragging her unbound hair over my body until the force in me grew to an intensity beyond bearing. Without my head's permission, my body began to writhe. Instantly four druids seized my hands and feet, holding me in place. Menua had my left hand; when I twisted around to look at him his hood was thrown back and his eyes were closed in the torchlight, but his lips were moving, chanting, part of the power, power, flowing through me now, scalding through me now, thundering with the rhythm of the chant and the gorgeously insistent hands on my body, the power gathering itself . . .

 . . . *the power in the grove, gathering itself* . . .

and exploding out of me in great aching spasms that arched my spine and made me cry out as Sulis gasped and the trees spun around us and the strength sped from me, the magic released like a spear to go singing invisibly through the air to our distant warriors, to strengthen their arms, to add vigor to their bodies, to being them home alive and safe.

And free.

They returned victorious. The Senones had been routed and driven back to their own land, northeast of ours. Our warriors abandoned the pursuit and came home to celebrate.

Tarvos sought me out to tell me about the battle. In spite of victory he had not avoided pain. A spear had thrust through the fleshy part of his upper arm, and a sword had laid one cheek open from eyebrow to jaw. Using the wounds as an excuse, I went to find Sulis to ask her to care for the Bull personally. I watched as she poulticed his arm with herbs, then stripped a sheep's kidney of its membrane, which she dipped in milk and spread very carefully over the gaping wound on the warrior's cheekbone. Recalling the touch of her fingers, I envied Tarvos his injuries.

When she dismissed us I took him back to the lodge with me to give him some wine and plunder his memories.

He sat with his back against the wall, exploring the drying membrane on his cheek with tentative fingers. "It doesn't hurt," he said unbelievingly.

"You were talking about the battle. . . ."

"Ah. Noise. Noise is what I remember most. It's always that way in a war, Ainvar. Yelling, swearing, screaming, grunting, bashing, clanging, one terrible roar that goes on and on until you think it will split the stones. I did what I always do. I ran into the middle of the noise and tried to make a louder noise."

"Why?"

He shrugged the shoulder above the uninjured arm. "We all do it, that's all. It gets you through. As long as you're running and yelling you don't have time to think, and you believe you're going to be all right." He drew a deep breath and winced as some new soreness surfaced. "While the battle is going on noise is the center of it and everything else is off at the edges."

I pondered this after he left the lodge. Later, at the celebration feast, I told Menua what Tarvos had said. Menua did not seem as surprised as I had been. "Noise is sound and sound is structure and structure is pattern," he told me.

"The harmony that holds the stars on their courses and the flesh on our bones resonates through all creation. Every sound contains its echo. Before there was Man, or even forest, there was sound. Sound spread from the Source in great circles like those formed when a stone is dropped into a pool.

"We follow waves of sound from life to life. A dying man's ears still hear long after his eyes are blind. He hears the sound that leads him to his next life as the Source of All Being plucks the harp of creation."

As so often before, I marveled at the scope of the chief druid's knowledge. A thousand years of observation and study and contemplation, stored in one head . . .

Our warriors had taken prisoners. Some thirty of the Senones were brought to our fort with halters around their necks. We greeted them with the contempt they deserved for having let themselves be captured rather than dying heroically in battle.

As prisoners of war they were turned over to the druids. When Nantorus formally delivered them to Menua, he had one request to make. "Before I go on to Cenabum I want to question one of these men. He is said to be a runaway Aeduan who has been fighting as a mercenary for one of the princes of the Senones."

"A runaway from his own tribe?"

"He committed some crime and feared the punishment of the druids, it seems. But that's not why I want to question him. I'm more interested in rumors I've been hearing of the increasingly close relationship between Rome and the Aeduans. There are reports of Roman soldiers serving with Aeduan warriors. If that is true, I want to know, and I am hopeful this disaffected Aeduan can tell us."

"I'll question him with you," Menua said. "I am doubly interested in his story."

No one had invited me to go along, but I had learned that if I looked as if I knew what I was doing, I was rarely challenged. So

I trotted in Menua's shadow as he and the king went to the pens where the prisoners were being held under guard. The man they sought was soon identified by his companions and taken to a low, dark shed for questioning.

The space was small and stank of woolen dyes. The guard pushed the man inside and then stepped back so Nantorus and Menua could enter. I scuttled in behind them. The guard only gave me a bored glance. He knew me well enough.

When the prisoner realized one of us was wearing a hooded robe, the blood drained from his face. "Don't touch me," he hissed in a thickly accented voice.

"I can do anything I want with you," replied Menua in a tone of mild reproof. "You know that. You let yourself be captured. No one escapes the judgment of the druids."

A sly expression flitted over the captive's face. He was a meatless man, all bone and gristle, with lank brown hair and prominent teeth. "I did once," he whispered.

"No, you merely prolonged the inevitable. I understand you fled druidical punishment before, but now you see you cannot avoid that which is meant for you."

"I don't know what you're talking about."

"I think you do. And if you don't want to make things worse for yourself than they already are, you will cooperate by answering a few questions."

Nantorus stepped in by saying, "Tell us what you know of your tribe's relations with the Romans."

The sly look intensified. "The Senones do a little trading with the Romans."

Menua gave such a roar even Nantorus jumped and the guard, who was waiting outside, poked his head around the door and pointed a spear at us all indiscriminately. "Not the Senones!" the chief druid shouted at the prisoner. "Don't try to deceive us, your accent tells your origins. We want to know about the Romans and the Aeduans."

Defiance oozed out of the man like sweat from his pores. He was naked except for a plaid battle kilt; his heaving ribs revealed the pounding heart beneath. "I am Mallus of the Aedui," he admitted reluctantly.

"Then, Mallus, answer every question put to you or we shall return you to the Aeduan druids tomorrow."

Mallus's eyes rolled in his head. "What do you want to know?"

"Are there Romans among the Aeduan warriors?" Nantorus asked.

The prisoner hesitated. "Some, perhaps. It's a complicated situation. There has been a certain, ah, alliance between the Romans and the Aeduans for a long time now, surely you know that. We are not too far from their territory and we do a lot of trading with them. They are a powerful people—"

"They are foreigners and not to be trusted," interrupted Menua.

Nantorus had been watching the captive closely. "I think this is a person of some rank," he remarked.

Mallus inflated his chest and lifted his head. "I was a captain of Aeduan cavalry. Before."

"Before?"

Another hesitation. Menua leaned toward him, and the man spoke up hastily. "Before I killed a Roman ambassador in a quarrel over a woman."

"Ambassadors, even foreigners, are sacrosanct," said Menua in a shocked voice. "No wonder you fled to the Senones to escape the reach of Rome."

"No one is beyond Roman reach any longer," Mallus said sadly.

The king and the chief druid closed on him from either side. "I think you'd better tell us," Menua said with deadly calm.

Words spilled out of the captive then. I could tell how serious the situation was by the expressions on the faces of Menua and Nantorus as they listened.

The land of the Aedui lay southeast of us, adjoining that of their age-old rivals, the Arverni. Aeduan strength and influence had begun to wane in recent generations. They were increasingly reliant upon Roman trade for the materials and luxuries they had begun to think necessary for a way of life based on Roman standards of prosperity.

Not all of the tribe agreed, however, and internal strife had divided the Aedui. Their Arvernian neighbors had decided they might be ripe for attack and plunder, and began assembling war parties in the borderlands. To counter this threat, those Aeduan princes most kindly disposed to the Romans had begun trading grain for Roman warriors in order to build up their own personal armies.

Menua's bushy eyebrows caterpillared across his forehead. "Do you hear, Nantorus? The Aeduans have invited Roman warriors into Gaul! Every Gaulish settlement already has its Roman traders; now there are armed men here as well. If what Mallus says is true, no one is beyond Roman reach."

"I speak the truth," Mallus said indignantly. "I am an honorable man, that's why I was in charge of the escort for the Roman trade delegation."

Ignoring the temptation of that remark about honor, Menua said silkily, "And it was an ambassador of that delegation whom you killed? Some foreign woman-stealer who couldn't keep his hands off Celtic women?"

"Exactly!" agreed Mallus, such easy prey to the druid's manipulations that for a moment Menua looked bored and I almost laughed. The Aeduan said, "Imagine how I felt, being elbowed aside by a short man who was losing his hair. So many men from Latium go bald. They don't have manly manes like ours, and to make themselves more ugly they scrape their jaws as bare as their heads. I don't know what a woman would see in any of them."

"I can't imagine," said Menua dreamily, tenting his fingers. "Go on. Tell us about it."

"There was a woman of our tribe who liked me, but this Roman saw her and the prince I followed sent her to him. I went after her. There was a struggle and I stabbed him. Then I put the woman behind me on my horse and fled.

"But she was ungrateful, the perverse creature. She slid off the horse and ran back to sound the alarm. I had to ride for my life. I knew the druids would condemn me for killing an ambassador. I must have ridden for many days until at last I came across a party of Senones who were willing to let me join them and go north with them.

"But I left that foreigner weltering in his own blood," Mallus added with satisfaction.

When the interrogation was over, Nantorus appeared relieved. "It isn't as bad as it sounded," he told Menua. "Some of the Aeduan princes are enlarging their warrior bands with a few Romans, but what harm? Mercenaries are common enough. It isn't as if we were being invaded by Latium."

"Isn't it? Have you forgotten the history the druids tried to teach you? Wherever Rome sends warriors, she leaves them. They take women, sire children, build homes, and eventually Rome claims the lands they occupy."

"If the Aedui are so foolish as to let Rome gain control of their land that way, they deserve to lose it."

"It isn't just a matter of Aeduan land," Menua insisted. "We're talking about a part of Gaul being taken over by the foreigners. They already have the southern part, the Province; now they move into free Gaul, and we live in free Gaul. The rat that nibbles the Aeduans will nibble us next, Nantorus!"

"You overestimate the Roman threat."

"I don't think so. My own travels have never taken me into Roman territory, but when the druids from throughout Gaul meet each Samhain for the great convocation held in our grove, I talk to many who have. And what I have learned of Roman ways worries me.

"Inevitably, given the nature of human ambition, a little grain exchanged for a few mercenaries will become a lot of grain exchanged for entire armies—in other words, a major military alliance carrying Roman influence into the heart of Gaul.

"And I tell you this, Nantorus: Roman influence frightens me more than Roman warriors."

"Influence!" Nantorus scoffed, dismissing the idea with a wave of his hand. Our king was a man of the sword; amorphous concepts had little reality for him.

The amorphous was Menua's realm, however. He continued to press the point until at last Nantorus agreed to call a meeting of the tribal council at Cenabum and let Menua express himself to it.

By virtue of clinging to Menua's cloak I could go, too. I was wildly excited. This would be my first real journey.

Nantorus rode off in his chariot, leaving a swirl of dust to mark his passage, but it took Menua and me two long days of hard walking to reach the stronghold of the tribe. Menua disdained the use of horses and carts. "Druids need to keep their feet on the earth," he reminded me.

The land we traversed was level, sometimes gently rolling, thickly forested and fertile. On cleared meadowland we saw prosperous farmsteads, each capable of supporting a small clan. Crops thrived in the sandy soil; the clear air carried the smell of cooking fires, and the sound of people singing.

In those days, we were a people who sang.

Since then I have seen larger forts and mightier cities, but my first sight of Cenabum is with me still. Compared to the Fort of the Grove, the stronghold of the Carnutes was immense, a sprawling, irregular oval of timber-reinforced earthen banks studded with watchtowers, the sky above permanently stained with smoke. Cenabum stood on the bank of the river Liger from which it drew its water supply, and a number of small fishing boats thronged the wide river, defying its occasional treacherous currents and pockets of quicksand.

"Five thousand people can be comfortably sheltered within these walls at a time," Menua said with pride, pointing toward the palisade. "I myself was born there."

Everything about Cenabum impressed me. The main gate was a double one, with two watchtowers connected by a bridge. As I passed beneath the bridge, the sentries looked down and one waved. Entering the fortified town, for Cenabum was truly a town, we were immersed in the music of ironworkers at their forges and the lard-fat cackle of geese a day away from the roasting spit. A team of carpenters brushed past us carrying some heavy timbers, then halted in confusion, stammering apologies, when they recognized Menua's hooded robe. Everywhere I looked I saw people at work or in conversation. My nose wrinkled at the mingled smells of excrement and fish and midden heaps.

Just within the gates I noticed a group of square, flat-topped buildings unlike Celtic lodges. As I watched, several dark-haired men in pleated tunics emerged from one of the buildings, chattering away among themselves and waving their hands in the air.

Menua followed my gaze. "Roman traders," he said sourly. "They live here more or less permanently and everyone assumes they are harmless and makes them welcome for the sake of their trade. But I wonder if they are harmless. Would they throw open the gates of Cenabum, do you suppose, for invaders?"

The druids who lived at Cenabum escorted us to a guest house, a well-appointed lodge set aside for the purpose. Menua cast a contemptuous glance at the carved benches and cushioned couches. "Roman softness," he said under his breath to me. "We'll sleep outside tonight, in our cloaks."

We did. That night it rained.

At highsun the next day the council met in the assembly house.

Like all tribal councils, ours consisted of the princes and elders of the tribe. The princes arrived, each with his own band of armed followers, and left their shields and weapons stacked outside the door. The elders came wrapped in cloaks and trailing wisps of time behind them like long gray hair.

Holding aloft the ram's horn that designated him as speaker, the chief druid addressed the council while I stood at the back of the lodge, trying simultaneously to listen to him and read the reactions of his audience.

"In the flight of the birds and the spattering of bullocks' blood I have seen patterns that disturb me," Menua announced. "I have seen armies marching. Now I have learned that the Aedui are making Roman warriors welcome in Gaul."

"Celtic people are famous for their hospitality," commented the prince Tasgetius, a rawboned, loose-jointed man with thickets of sandy-red hair on the backs of his huge hands. "And some of my best friends are Roman," he added, glancing down at the imported arm rings he was wearing.

"Don't judge a people by its traders," Menua warned. "It is in their self-interest to appear affable, but the Romans are nothing like us and you must never think they are.

"Many generations ago they abandoned the reverence of nature and began substituting man-made images in human form to serve as their gods, an idea they stole from the Greeks. The Romans are great thieves," he added contemptuously.

"But while the Hellenes retained a certain sensitivity to the natural world, the Romans have none. I have heard that the only nature gods they acknowledge are sun and moon and sea, and even those have human forms and identities.

"Making gods in their own image has given the Romans an exaggerated idea of Roman importance. They assume that because they make gods they have the authority of gods. They have acquired a lust to control, which they call a desire for order and seek to impose on everyone else.

"The Roman concept of order does not suit Celtic people. Our free-flowing spirits are not comfortable in square boxes and communities where even access to water is regulated. We are accustomed to free water and tribal ownership of the earth upon which we live, we elect our own leaders and celebrate the Source.

"The Romans have chosen the rigidity of their man-made order over the flow of nature's pattern. Such an arrangement cannot endure forever, of course. A paving stone can be laid over grass, but the pattern is never still. Beneath the stone, the roots will continue to grow. They will press against their barrier until someday they break through and lift green arms toward the sun.

"Meanwhile, the Romans have chosen to disregard the inevitability of natural law and have created their own lawmaking body, which they call the senate. The senate designs laws to fit the world the way Romans want it to be, not the way it is."

Some of the council were listening intently, I noticed. A few looked bored. Generally the elders were paying more attention than the princes.

Menua said, "I am told that its citizens believe Rome is the center of the universe. Because the existence of the Otherworld challenges Rome's authority, they ignore matters of the spirit and concentrate on the flesh. Those gods of theirs are only to satisfy fleshly needs and have nothing to do with keeping Man and Earth and Spirit in harmony.

"As interpreters of natural law, we druids have always sought to clarify our vision of nature in order to see beyond the visible to the invisible, the forces that underlie and shape existence. We know that humans are inseparable from the Otherworld because our bodies house immortal spirits. The Romans, however, believe one brief lifetime is all they have, and the belief has made them frantic and greedy.

"I cannot understand the Roman way of thinking but it dismays me. If such people ever gain dominance here we will find ourselves trapped in their rigid world and it will cripple us."

I found the idea as terrible as having my living spirit trapped inside my dead body. But strangely, some of the council were unmoved. Men like Tasgetius refused to see any danger in the Roman presence in Gaul. "We need the Romans here," Tasgetius insisted. "They are our source for wine and spices and our market for furs and surplus produce."

Others agreed there might be some eventual military threat but were swaggeringly confident that Gauls could defeat any soft southerners. As for the idea of something as nebulous as Roman influence being a danger, they scoffed.

A third group, including Nantorus and Menua's own kinsman the prince Cotuatus, was finally convinced but was not able to sway the rest. The factions fell to arguing among themselves with much shouting and fist pounding, resolving nothing.

Menua left in disgust. I trotted after him. We had not gone far when Nantorus hurried up to us, panting. Too many wounds had left him a battered man. "It is unfortunate, Menua," he said. "But you know how they are. . . ."

"They're fools," the chief druid replied shortly. "Fools who have been seduced by traders' trinkets."

"I say this to you, Menua. As king of the Carnutes, I charge you and the Order of the Wise to take whatever precautions you deem necessary to protect our tribe from this threat you foresee. You need no one's support but my own. Protect us, druid, because we are free people and not to be crushed beneath paving stones." With this injunction Nantorus turned aside to the warmth and comfort of his own lodge, leaving us in a darkness that had fallen like a stone upon Cenabum.

Instinctively I understood that the king felt he had fully discharged his duty by putting the responsibility onto the druids. Nantorus would sleep this night with a peaceful mind. Menua, however, shifted his shoulders uncomfortably as we walked on, like a man carrying a heavy burden.

The wind had swung around and came howling out of the north, ending our golden summer. Cold rain lashed us. Menua abandoned his resolve to sleep under the open sky. Together we ran for the shelter of the guest lodge.

The rain followed us only to the eaves. The cold followed us into our beds.

Next morning the chief druid told me we were returning at once to the grove. "We have work to do, Ainvar." *We.* He had said *we.* "We are going to raise a cry for assistance in protecting the tribe, a cry so loud it will ring throughout the Otherworld."

"How do we do that?" I asked eagerly.

His face was somber in the sunless dawn. "We are going to sacrifice the prisoners of war."

CHAPTER SEVEN

ATTENDANCE AT the public sacrifices was a privilege afforded to every adult member of the tribe. Being denied that privilege was considered the most cruel punishment the druids could inflict, for it meant denying an individual the right to participate in direct communion with the Otherworld.

But there were not as many human sacrifices as had once been offered in Gaul. In recent generations the number had dwindled drastically, and since my own manmaking there had been none. Only oxen went to the sacrificial altar.

Seeing the Senones sacrificed would be my first such experience. As Menua's apprentice, I would be expected to assist in the ritual; I, who looked away when the blood bubbled from the throat of a sacrificial animal.

The meat on the roasting spit was sacrificed for your sake, my head reminded me. And you ate it with a good appetite, you even licked the grease from your fingers.

That is different, I argued with myself. My brother-in-creation died that I might live, and its spirit was propitiated before the slaughter. When I eat flesh I always do so in full knowledge of the gift given me.

My head replied, The prisoners will die that you and the tribe may be protected, and their spirits will be propitiated. It would be cowardly not to witness their dying, when they are giving so great a gift.

Cowardly, I agreed. But the thought chilled me just the same.

"For this aspect of your education in druidry, Aberth the sacrificer will be your instructor, of course," Menua informed me.

Of course.

It was whispered that Aberth loved shedding blood for its own sake, that it gave him the sort of pleasure other men found in women.

He came for me at dawn. Standing in Menua's doorway, with his narrow features half concealed by the folds of his hood, Aberth infected the air with a charnel reek. I drew back involuntarily.

His thin lips tightened over his teeth and his eyes glittered. "You do not welcome me, Ainvar?" he asked mockingly.

"I welcome you as a free person." My voice was thin.

Aberth looked past me to Menua. "That isn't a very warm greeting for such an auspicious occasion. Has this man no enthusiasm for sacrifices?"

"He has not yet had his deathteaching, so he isn't fully prepared. In the normal course of events . . . but the pattern has presented us with the sacrifice of the Senones long before Ainvar was ready for deathteaching, so it will be his first experience. Take him, Aberth." The chief druid surrendered me to the sacrificer and turned away.

Aberth's lodge was as crammed with objects as Menua's was free of them. On a shelf stood a long row of stoppered containers. Winter-in-a-bottle, my head surmised. Various types of knives, finely honed, were fitted into slotted containers of yew wood. Following the direction of my eyes, Aberth said, "Yew is the wood of rebirth. A yew's branches grow down and into the earth to form new trunks while the center of the tree rots away with age. No man can tell the age of a yew, since it is dying and being reborn simultaneously. Sacred is the yew, which is why we use a club of yew wood for the blow of mercy to stun a sacrifice before the knife."

He selected a blade from its holder and ran his thumb caressingly along the edge. A thin red line appeared. Tiny drops oozed. Aberth licked them from his thumb with dreamy eyes.

The sacrificer showed me every knife in his extensive collection, explaining how one was specially designed to be driven into the back of a heavily muscled man—"so he will fall forward on his face and our diviner can read his death throes without being distracted by his facial grimaces." Another knife, smaller and finer, was for the tender throat of a baby goat. The curved blade with the gold hilt was reserved for the sacrifice of the Oak's Child, the tumor-shrinking mistletoe.

When I had examined, with an inner revulsion, the entire assortment, Aberth squinted at me and folded his arms. "Now you tell me, Ainvar. Use your intuition. Which of these would be most appropriate for the Senones, the prisoners of war who were not willing to die in battle?"

I had no idea. The voice in my head told me nothing. How does one kill thirty people at once? In my all-too-vivid imagination Aberth stalked among bound and kneeling victims, scything them down until he waded in a sea of blood.

He read the sickened conjecture in my eyes and laughed. "You will not make a sacrificer, Ainvar, no matter what other talents you may possess. But you will assist anyway; in a ritual of this magnitude we need everyone.

"As it happens, I shall not be using any of my beautiful blades. The Senones lost their courage or they would not have allowed themselves to be captured alive. We shall give them an opportunity to correct the balance, a second chance to meet death in heroic style. Theirs will be the glory of returning to the Source on wings of fire!"

Aberth's face was radiant, his voice resonant. He seemed to envy the Senones the death he had planned for them.

I, however, was appalled. "You're going to burn them alive? All of them?"

"You don't understand, do you?" he asked almost pityingly. "Sacrifice is not an act of cruelty, Ainvar. The most gifted sacrificer is the one who can release the spirit from the body with the least pain. When a person, or an animal, dies in agony, its spirit is dazed and confused.

"Remember that the purpose of sacrifice is to return a spirit to its Creator as an act of propitiation, always. And remember, furthermore, that every spirit is a part of that Creator. If we send one of its own parts back to the Source frightened and bewildered, we are insulting the very power we wish to propitiate.

"Therefore the Senones will burn, but they will not suffer. I am the best sacrificer in Gaul. Before the prisoners go to the fire they will be given myrrh in wine to drink to dull their senses and enlarge their courage. Then they will be placed in wicker cages raised high above the ground. Certain powders thrown into the flames will thicken the smoke and suffocate the captives before the fire reaches them. Knowing this will enable them to face death more bravely, so the bards of the Senones can sing of them afterward with pride."

To hold the prisoners, three massive cages were built of osiers lashed together with leather bindings. Fire would cause the wickerwork to disintegrate quickly, so it was doubly important that the captives be unconscious by the time the flames reached them, or they might escape.

As in so many other druidical customs, the practical blended seamlessly with the mystical.

When the cages were ready, Aberth supervised the workmen as they set each one atop a tall pair of wooden pillars. The fire would be kindled around and between these pillars so the smoke would rise upward through the slats of the cages. The entire assembly looked like a pot-bellied giant on sturdy legs, lacking only arms and a head to make the illusion complete.

Keryth the seer declared the most auspicious time for the sacrifice would be the next dark moon day. To my relief, Menua took me with him when he went to prepare the Senones for their ordeal. I was not sorry to leave Aberth.

I stood to one side listening as the chief druid explained what would happen and exhorted the Senones to die nobly so they would be a credit to their tribe. He promised to see that word of their courage was carried to their people.

"We offer you an easy death and a good death," he told them. "Not many men have that assurance. That is, we offer you an easy death provided you do what we ask.

"We request that once your spirits are freed from your bodies and rejoined with the Source of All Being, you use all your powers to implore the protection of the Otherworld for the Carnutes. If any one of you is, in his secret heart, unwilling to do this, I promise you that man will feel the flames!"

Most of the Senones stared tensely at Menua as if devouring his words, though a few appeared almost indifferent and sat or stood propped against the wall of the pen, gazing dully into space. Mallus, the former Aeduan, I noticed crouched in a corner by himself, his eyes darting incessantly like those of a trapped animal.

Another man caught my attention. Tall and strong, with light brown hair and a broad brow, he was looking straight at me with an expression of hopeless longing. It is not you he wants, my head told me, but the life inside you, the future you possess and he does not. I turned away, unable to meet his eyes.

On the morning of the sacrifice the entire fort gathered for the song for the sun. Then the gates were thrown open and the procession set out for the grove. Excitement flickered through the crowd like a grass fire. This would not be the simple sacrifice of a docile animal.

The druids led the way. The prisoners came next, shambling sleepily, their faces flushed as if from drink. A guard led by Ogmios accompanied them, spears at the ready. The inhabitants of the Fort of the Grove followed, their numbers constantly increasing as smallholders and herders from the surrounding area hurried to join us. Many of them had little idea of the reason for the ritual; the prospect of spectacle was enough.

I must behave well, I reminded myself. Menua will be watching me. I was queasy and very nervous.

The earth lifted, the trees rose above us. We passed through the forest to the mighty stand of oaks on the crest of the ridge. Chanting, the druids circled the grove sunwise while the rest of the crowd jostled for position, each person trying to get where he could best see the three cages waiting just beyond the grove itself.

At first sight of them one of the prisoners cried out.

Around the legs of the headless wickerwork giants we had stacked trimmed branches to form crisscrossed layers as high as a man's head. Leaves and green wood had been stuffed into every crevice to create more smoke. Wooden ladders were propped against the cages, just below the open doors.

Ogmios did not give his charges time to panic. "Send them up the ladders quickly," he ordered his warriors. A wall of armed men suddenly surrounded the Senones and pushed them forward. Drugged as they were, some stumbled. Our men helped them, not unkindly. The prisoners were up the ladders and in the cages almost before they realized it. The doors were quickly barred behind them.

Aberth stepped forward, carrying a lighted torch. Suddenly everything was happening very fast.

Looking at the men in the cages, I saw that most were standing with deliberate fortitude, setting their jaws in the heroic image for which they wished to be celebrated. If their eyes were glazed, at least their hearts were stout. I was proud of them. They were not of my tribe, but they were Celts.

Mallus, however, was clutching the bars and whimpering. One or two others appeared on the verge of collapse. The stench of someone's bowels opening filled the air.

The chanting rose in volume as the spectators added their voices to those of the druids.

"Faces of the Source!" cried Aberth. "I appeal to the three gods who accept sacrifice, to Taranis the thunderer, Esus of the water, Teutates, lord of the tribes. Accept our offering!" He put his torch to the wood beneath the first cage.

Flame leaped. He ran to the other cages and set them alight. The men inside stared down, white-eyed. Smoke began to pour from the stacks as the green wood started to smolder. Sulis opened a bag of white doeskin from which she flung handfuls of powder into the fire. A haunting fragrance arose like that of sweet hay. Menua motioned us to step back so we did not breathe the fumes.

Among the stacked branches flames twisted and glittered. The first of them licked at one of the cages, and a high, thin wail rose above the sound of the chanting, a disembodied shriek of despair.

But only one of the victims screamed. The rest were already slumping in the cages as the smoke did its work. Some of the druids had brought rolled oxhides, which they now unfurled, waving them to keep driving the smoke into the cages. Mercifully it soon obscured our vision.

This isn't so bad, I told myself.

A second, more agonized scream tore the air as the fire exploded into an inferno.

The billowing smoke receded long enough to reveal flames devouring the cages. Soon whatever had lived within lived no longer and screamed no more. Above the gleeful gobbling of the fire, those who stood nearest could hear the sizzling of fat and the popping of bones. My belly heaved.

Three headless giants writhed, blazing. The heat pouring from them scorched my face. The druids were frantically flapping their oxhides to keep the fire away from the trees. The rest of us leaped back just in time as the cages collapsed in a shower of sparks.

Sulis told me later that I screamed then. I only recall standing transfixed, staring at the glittering sparks. Some arced out and down like a fountain of burning gold. Others—in memory I would count them as thirty—did not fall but rose on a wave of heat, leaping into the sky above our heads, above the oaks, rising up and up and up and . . .

Gone.

"Gone to the Source!" Menua exulted. "Plead our cause, brave Senones!"

A force as mighty as a thunderstorm boomed through the grove, a colossal drumbeat that seized and shook us. Aberth shouted in triumph, "Taranis the thunderer accepts our sacrifice!"

Awe rose in a flood we could not contain, expanding our spirits until they burst from our bodies in a frenzy. We were all screaming now, lost in the roar of the fire, leaping upward and outward from the grove to storm the vault of the sky, to claim the protection of the Otherworld, not to be ignored, not to be denied, the combined will of the people expressed as one will, one cry, one sacrifice, one moment when there were no barriers between worlds and earthly events could be transcended and reshaped.

I threw out my arms and wheeled and tumbled amid the stars.

The sparks, the living golden sparks on their way outward!

Slowly the passion ebbed. I clung to it for as long as I could. But at last I could not deny the walls of flesh around me, the weight of my body holding me.

I opened my eyes.

The druids had gathered around the pyre. I joined them. I was numb; my eyes looked at but refused to see the twisted, blackened shapes amid the seething coals, the horribly familiar angles of bent knee and elbow. If I closed my eyes I could still see the sparks against my eyelids.

Behind me I heard song swelling from countless throats. The Carnutes were raising their voices in a hymn of praise for the sacrificed Senones, describing their courage in the most extravagant terms.

The druids were singing, too. We were all singing, putting the sound between ourselves and death and fear and horror.

Singing for joy.

Much later, the bones and ashes would be gathered and a ritual performed for them.

When we returned to the fort, I felt drained. I had at least not disgraced myself, I had taken my place and added my voice, sending my effort of will out with the rest.

Out . . . where? Into a void where Something watched. Had we won its favor, its protection?

Who could know?

Druids knew.

As our procession returned homeward, I followed Menua's broad back, grateful for its solidity. I was attempting the impossible feat of thinking and not thinking at the same time. No one seemed in the mood for talking. Some of the faces around me wore the rapt expression of those who have briefly touched the immensities. I wondered what they had felt, amid the chanting and the flames.

I wondered what was on my own face.

The silence of Gaul's russet and gold autumn enfolded us. We heard no whoosh and crash of a tree being felled, no herder singing to his animals, no crack of stonemasons at work. The woodsmen and herders and stonemasons were with us.

Neither did we hear the clatter of spears or the thud of thousands of feet marching to a single rhythm. For though they would soon appear in ever-increasing numbers elsewhere in Gaul, the warriors of Rome would come last to the territory of the Carnutes.

In the meantime I would have replaced Menua as chief druid. And found Briga.

CHAPTER EIGHT

SEX MAGIC was wonderful. My first experience had left me avid for more, which only amused Menua. When I kept suggesting an application of sex magic to solve every problem that came along, he laughed at me. "The ritual must be appropriate to the need, Ainvar, and is never celebrated for the gratification of the celebrant. You're letting your body think for you again."

I could hardly help it. My body was young and virile, I could feel the tension building in me, waiting to burst out again, to explode like a star.

Could stars explode? I must ask Menua.

In the meantime I was preoccupied with Sulis. Menua had turned me over to her during the short, dark days of winter, for instruction in the healing arts, which did not always require that we be outside. Drying herbs and preparing potions could be learned within the warmth of a lodge.

I did not seem to be learning much, however. "You are not paying attention, Ainvar!" Sulis snapped at me. "You are supposed to acquire some knowledge about every aspect of druidry, but that does not include the construction of lodges. Why are you staring into the rafters?"

How could I tell her I was staring at the rafters to avoid staring at the roundness of her breasts?

"What was I just saying to you?" she demanded to know.

I cleared my throat and struggled with my rebel thoughts. "Ah . . . about mistletoe . . . "

"Indeed. And why is the Oak's Child the most sacred of all plants?"

"Because . . . because . . . "

"Because the decoction of its berries is the only thing that can stop the burning growth that eats people from the inside out."

"Ah. Yes."

"And is the simple essence enough?"

I was thinking hard, trying to hear her recent words in my memory. "Ah, no. You add other things. . . ."

"Which are?" She was not quite, but almost, tapping her foot. Her lips were pressed into a thin line.

Just before she completely lost her temper with me, I was able to name the ingredients to be combined with essence of mistletoe. I understood the value of the brew well enough; to die from the burning growth was a prolonged and shrieking agony. I had seen a man who put off coming to Sulis until too late, when the monster had taken hold of him to such an extent even she could not kill it.

I would prefer to be burned in the cage than suffer what he suffered.

Because the druids knew how to use the Oak's Child, very few of us ever succumbed to the burning growth, however. Using her healing magic, Sulis could shrink a tumor away night by night, as the moon shrank in its waning.

Everything about Sulis was wonderful. Her square, capable hands with their spatulate fingertips could touch an aching head and relieve the pain at once. She could stroke broken limbs . . .

. . . she could stroke my limbs. . . .

"Ainvar, you are *not* paying attention!"

"I am! I was thinking about healing. Could sex magic be used to heal people?"

"Perhaps it's time you moved on to study with someone else,

Ainvar. You could be memorizing the law with Dian Cet instead of wasting my time."

"But couldn't you and I together use sex magic to restore strength to the earth?"

"Perhaps. In the spring. If Menua feels it is needed."

"Or even now," I insisted. "With sex magic couldn't we encourage the wool to grow denser on the sheep?"

"They are so heavily fleeced now they pant like dogs," Sulis pointed out. "If you are so eager for a woman, Ainvar, go look for one! Beyond the walls of this fort there are many not of your blood who would smile at you."

"But will there be magic?"

There was something sad in her smile as Sulis replied, "Ah, Ainvar, magic is not so easily found."

I was tall and well grown, and when I took her advice I found there were, indeed, women to smile at me. Women who licked their lips when our eyes met, and women who turned away but glanced back. There were warriors' daughters and women who tended the land; there were girls who were ripe for marriage and widows who were ripe. In due course I tried every one who encouraged me within a half-day's walk of the fort.

But Sulis was right. Magic was not easy to find.

I enjoyed myself anyway and tried my best to give as much pleasure as I took. My best, the women assured me, was very good indeed. Not a few openly expressed their interest in dancing around the symbolic phallus at Beltaine and bearing my children. References were made to sizable marriage portions.

A druid, however, need not concern himself with his wife's property. His tangible needs were provided by the tribe in exchange for his gifts. If I married at all, I could marry a woman because she pleased me, whether her father sent twelve cows with her or she arrived at my lodge with only a needle and loom.

Winter faded into spring, and we repeated the ritual that had begun with Rosmerta's dying to speed the process. We no longer sacrificed a living person, however; the oldster we chose to be winter only pretended to die, yet winter died anyway and a bright, hot spring followed, making the blood run quick in me. I lost myself in women, in touch and taste and scent. One had creamy skin and one had grainy flesh and another was doughy and dimpled, but every one was a new experience. A fresh exploration. Each in her turn was dear to me.

But none had the gift of magic.

Marrying Sulis was out of the question. Her clan of craftsmen was not blood kin to me, so that prohibition did not stand in our way. But when I made the suggestion she bluntly refused. "A woman marries to have children, Ainvar, and I am not going to have children."

"But why not?"

"Try to understand this; I have given it much thought. My body is an instrument of healing. You have watched me sponge my urine on burned flesh and seen the blisters disappear. My other fluids are also useful in healing preparations. If I carried a child in my body, its properties would affect my own. My sweat, my saliva, my very tears would be changed. My gift might be compromised and I will not take the risk. When I take part in sex magic I use certain precautions to prevent conception, but if I married I would have to give my husband children if I could. So what you ask is impossible."

"Other healers have children. You once told me your own grand-mother was a healer."

"She made her choice, I have made mine. I am following my pattern and ask you to respect that, Ainvar."

I was too young to know that emotional climates change, and that the independence Sulis wanted might someday weigh heavily upon her. I accepted her at her word, but with sorrow in my heart.

Occasionally Menua used the two of us for sex magic, which somehow made everything more painful for me. Yet I never refused. I had learned that sex at its most magical is a sacred rite of such power and excitement that anything else left me strangely unsatisfied.

Tarvos the Bull did not seem to require magic from his women, I observed, watching him enviously as he rutted through the fort. He would marry whoever was nearest when he was ready to marry, and she would admire his scars and bear him a litter of warriors, and they would be content.

At night I walked beneath the stars. Among the lodges, with no roof over me, and the darkness for company. Through open doorways I overheard random bits of conversation, no thought completed but only half spoken between people who knew each other well enough to guess the rest. Comments on food and work and weather, personal criticisms, a rumbling laugh, the sharp edge of anger erupting.

People encased in timber shells.

Theirs was the tripping tedium of walls and chores and living crowded together, climbing over each other sometimes, smelling each other's farting, suffering each other's snoring. They were embedded in the ordinary.

I was not. Mine was the vast dark sky and the spaces between the stars that called out to me; mine was the promise of magic.

Perhaps Sulis was right, I thought.

Beneath the stars I walked dreaming, and the families in their houses did not hear me pass by.

The wheel of the seasons turned and turned.

Thirty years was considered a full generation among us, but the passage of time was not so simply measured. I spent long days studying the sheet of bronze upon which was incised our calendar, dividing and delineating the year so the festivals were always observed on their proper days in relation to Earth and sky. The calendar consisted of sixteen columns representing sixty-two lunar cycles subdivided into light and dark halves, with two additional intercalary cycles to make the whole correspond to the solar year. I studied it until I knew it as my tongue knew the roof of my mouth.

And this was but one of many lessons I must master. I could feel my brain stretching inside my skull.

My teachers were legion. I learned from the stems of wheat and the exhalations of cattle, or the arrangement of pebbles on a streambed or the pattern of geese winging overhead. But my chief instructor was always Menua. I studied him until I could assume his mannerisms like a cloak.

The seasons were passing for him, too. Each winter found the chief druid more crusty and irascible. "You will be my last student," he told me. "You are the one who must follow me."

My spirit soared inside me and I began gobbling wisdom, staking my claim to the dominion of the mind. Working in the cold heat of concentrated intellect, I memorized the law contained in the rhyming syllabic verse called *rosc*, a chant of stressed, alliterative lines. The law was beautiful, I discovered.

At the annual Samhain assembly when all judgments were rendered, Dian Cet always concluded by reminding us, "Our decisions are made in accordance with the law of nature, for nature is the inspiration and model of law. No law counter to nature can be upheld."

Menua taught me the language of the Greeks he had learned in his youth, and polished the smattering of Roman I had picked up from traders, though he dismissed the language as harsh and guttural and of no value. He showed me the writing of the Greeks and the Romans, shapes cut into wood or on tablets of wax or painted on parchment or calfskin. "Put no trust in these, however," he cautioned me. "What is written can be burned or melted or changed. What is carved in your mind is permanent."

He also taught me *ogham,* which was not the written language of the druids but merely a way of leaving simple messages for one another by slashing marks on trees or stone. No wisdoms were committed to *ogham,* yet it was useful enough, and the common people were in awe of us for understanding it.

"Always maintain that sense of awe in them!" Menua insisted.

He was putting more and more responsibility on my shoulders. When I needed a runner to carry messages between myself and other druids, Menua had Tarvos seconded to me.

I would have asked for Crom Daral if things had been different between us, I thought sadly.

One morning I came around the lodge and almost collided with Crom. From the other side of the fort came the sound of a hammer beating iron at the forge. "I didn't hear you for the noise," I apologized, though in truth the noise was not that loud. But I had to say something.

Crom shrugged without replying and started to edge past me in the narrow laneway.

I caught his arm. "Crom, what's wrong between us? Can't it be mended?"

"Mended?" He swung around to face me. "How? Are you willing to admit you're no better than me?"

"Of course I'm no better than you. I'm just different."

"You say that, but you don't mean it."

He is right, my head observed. "You don't know me at all," I said aloud, too quickly.

"You don't know yourself," he snarled. "You should see yourself as I see you, walking around here as if your feet were too good to touch the mud." He pulled free of me and hurried away.

I haven't changed, I'm just Ainvar! I wanted to shout after him. But I did not.

After a long time I wandered miserably back into the lodge. "Menua, is it difficult to be both a man and a druid?"

He pondered the question. "Impossible," he said at last.

Would I ever be able to learn all I needed to know? Twenty years of study was considered the minimum necessary for a chief druid. I could be initiated into the Order long before then, because the time of initiation was determined by omen and circumstance. But those twenty years of learning were a feature of the druidical schools from Bibracte in Gaul to the distant and storied island of the Britons.

And everything must be committed to memory.

"Tell me again about Rome and the Province," Menua would command for the thirtieth time, leaning at his ease against the trunk of a tree and chewing on a blade of grass. "And don't change a word of it, mind you."

"The Romans are a tribe from the land of Latium," I began dutifully. "Once they were but one of many tribes, and they occupied a straggle of huts on a cluster of hills and fought with their neighbors. But they were more ambitious than their neighbors. In time they built up an army capable of exterminating the Etruscans on their north and taking over the rich valley of the Po River.

"Next they destroyed their commercial rivals, Corinth and Carthage, so they could take over their trade routes. While defeating Carthage they also undertook the conquest of Iberia. The Romans ground into dust anyone who opposed them and established a virtual monopoly of trade, sending a constant stream of wealth flowing back to their stronghold, the city of their tribe."

Menua nodded. I observed that the whites of his eyes were turning yellow with age, and there were freckles on the backs of his wrinkled hands. "Now tell me what the Province is, Ainvar."

"The southernmost part of Gaul. Once the Celtic tribes there were as free as the rest of us. But that was before Rome overran the region, before I was born. They renamed it Narbonese Gaul, after the capital city of Narbo which they built there. Usually, however, it is simply referred to as the Province, for it is Rome's chief province outside Latium."

Menua sighed. "The Romans overran it. Brought in warriors and left them there, to marry, sire children, claim the land as their

own. Romanized." He shook his head. "And to whom was the city
of Narbo dedicated, Ainvar?"

"To Martius, a Roman deity."

The chief druid blew his nose in the air in an expression of
contempt. "Martius. Spirit of war. Not the spirit of some living
thing, a tree or a river, but of *war*." His disgust was palpable.
"They have no instinct for naming."

"No," I agreed. "Naming is of principal importance. Everything
has its own, innate name, which must be discovered."

The chief druid almost smiled. My answer had pleased him.

"What do we know of the lives lived by Celts within the Province?"

"The southern Gaulish tribes," I recited, "cannot do any business
without the authority and partnership of a Roman citizen. No coin
changes hands or debt is contracted without being written on the
scrolls of the Romans."

"Written," Menua echoed in disgust. "A man's debts written
down to survive his death and torment his descendants."

He stood up and began to pace, back and forth, with his arms
folded behind him. "I know too much and not enough, Ainvar. We
hear things, I catch a scent of something on the wind. . . . I cannot
sleep for thinking of the power of Rome. I feel it growing like a
living thing, a vine to strangle the oak.

"But I am not sure of the danger, neither its degree nor its
source. If it were possible I would go into Roman territory myself
and observe what is happening there. Some claim the Gauls live
better than we do here; others say they are wretched and enslaved.
I need to know the truth, but I am the chief druid and these are
dangerous times, I dare not leave the grove for long enough to
visit the Province."

Suddenly he turned and fixed his eyes on me. "But you are
young and strong. You could make the journey for me. You could
be my eyes and ears in the Province and report back to me on all
that you find."

My heart leaped in me. The thrilling promise of adventure was
like a drink of strong wine.

Menua sat down again and leaned against the tree. His eyes
gazed up at me but I do not think he was seeing me.

"Ainvar," he mused. "One who travels far."

I held my breath.

He said nothing more.

I waited.

The chief druid retreated into his head, leaving me to study the clouds in the sky and the pinkish-yellow stones emerging from the soft brown soil. Our little river, the Autura, sang to herself below the ridge of the grove.

"You are still young." Menua's voice startled me out of some reverie involving Sulis. "You need more training. Before you can be initiated into the Order you must have studied in the groves of other tribes. I myself spent much time at Bibracte, where my head was greatly enriched by the druids of the Aedui.

"We could send you southward to visit the druids between here and the Province . . . then you could cross the mountains that separate us from Roman territory and continue your learning on the other side. A different sort of learning, eh?"

"As your eyes and ears?"

"As my eyes and ears. Are you willing?"

I tried to reply with decorum, but eagerness betrayed me. "Yes!" I shouted.

Menua's eyes twinkled. "You needn't think it will be easy. The way is long and travel is always hazardous."

"I don't mind! I'm very strong and I can take care of myself!"

"Mmmm. To be sure. But we'll give you an escort anyway, someone a little more seasoned than yourself to guard your back." Menua stretched, scratched himself in both armpits, and got to his feet. He moved with unfailing grace in spite of his bulk, but I heard his bones creak the song of their years.

Together we performed the sunset ritual that thanked the sun for having given us the day. Then we returned to the fort, our faces suitably sober. But once Menua was asleep, I slipped out of the lodge and out of the fort, to stand alone and free under the night sky and give a mighty yell of sheer exuberance.

Menua informed the other druids of his plan. His choice of me for such an undertaking stressed, more than actual words, his faith in me; his desire that I be his successor someday. When that day came the chief druid would be elected by the Order, of course, but Menua's preference would carry great weight. They knew it and I knew it.

Keeper of the Grove.

Shortly after the announcement, Sulis sought me out. "Perhaps we should work some sex magic together to assure you of a safe journey?" she suggested.

Her hair was soft against my lips and the magic came strong and sure.

The route Menua chose for me would take me through the lands of the Bituriges, the Boii, the Arverni, and the Gabali. "Learn something of value in each tribe's sacred grove," Menua told me, "but remember that your ultimate goal is the Province. Once you get there, don't call attention to yourself. I have heard that the Romans regard druids with suspicion. Be a simple traveler, perhaps someone in search of new trading connections. Trade is the language the Romans like best."

I would take with me one bodyguard and a porter. At my request, Tarvos would be my bodyguard. To identify myself as one entitled to instruction in the groves, Menua had the Goban Saor make a gold druidic amulet, called a *triskele*, for me to wear. It was in the form of a large wheel with three curved spokes dividing the circle into the trinity of Earth and Man and Otherworld.

"Before you go," said Menua, "there is one final thing we must do for you. If you aspire to the Order of the Wise, you must be prepared to show the world a fearless face. So you will meet with us in the grove three dawns from now.

"For your deathteaching."

Chapter Nine

THEY WERE hidden in their hoods. Even Menua was concealed; I recognized him by his shape. In the same way, and with a stab of pleasure, I recognized Sulis.

And beyond her, Aberth the sacrificer.

Deathteaching. He had to be present, as opener of the gate into the Otherworld.

We were one moon past Imbolc, festival of the lactation of the sheep. The days were growing longer, anticipating Beltaine two moons hence. Above our heads that sunrise, larks were spilling song into a clear sky.

I had come to the grove to learn about death.

The druids surrounded me in a large circle, with a measured space separating me from them. Whatever happened, I would in the most essential sense be alone.

Menua spoke. "Death," he intoned from his position sunwise of me, "is the reverse of birth. It is the same process happening backward. If we escape death by injury or illness, we grow old, feeble, helpless, infantile. We become as the unborn in preparation for returning to the unborn state.

"Think, Ainvar. Does the idea of being unborn, not-yet-born, frighten you? Look back beyond your earliest memory."

I concentrated. "No," I said at last. "It does not frighten me."

"Good. Then you must have no fear of death, for it is the same state. Death is a way of washing your memory clean of burdens too painful to carry. Death rests and refreshes you, so you are ready to begin a new life in a new body spun from the strands of creation."

Menua raised his pointing finger on his heart hand and rotated it in the air. At once, a number of druids stepped out of the circle and laid firm hands on me. There were more than enough of them to hold me even if I struggled. Deathteaching drew every member of the Order within a day's walk.

Before dawn the chief druid had weighted me down with the wealth that had once ornamented my father and brothers. Finger rings of massy gold, arm and leg rings of copper and bronze, brooches set with amber and coral and chunks of crystal. None of these were of Mediterranean workmanship; they were of the old, true Celtic style, massive but beautifully crafted with so much intricate detail you could study one piece for half a day without seeing all of it.

Now at the chief druid's command the others began stripping the jewelry from me. As each piece was removed, Menua said, "Life is loss."

Strangely, I found myself feeling progressively lighter and more free. The riches that had been the pride of my warrior kin were taken from my sight, but I did not yearn after them; they had been a weight and a discomfort, I realized. I had grown too accustomed to the druid habit of being unencumbered.

When I stood in only my tunic and the skin that held my bones in a package, Menua told me, "What you have lost was an accretion. What you have left is your self. And when you lose even the flesh you wear, you will still have your self."

The chanting began, softly, under his voice.

Sulis came forward to tie a bandage across my eyes. It was fragrant with clove-scented gillyflower and other, more subtle scents, one a sour tang that made me wrinkle my nose. Without sight my other senses intensified. My ears detected the first faint crackling of a fire being built some distance away. Then my nose reported the smell of burning cinnamon, an imported spice so costly it was used only for the most important of rituals, or in the meat cooked for a king.

"We cannot know what will come to you," I heard Menua say. "The pattern dictates differently for each of us. Be open; accept."

The druids suddenly spun me around like a wheel until I did not know if I faced night or morning. Fingers pried open my mouth and a noxious paste was forced onto the back of my tongue. I gagged violently, but they held me so I could not clear the stuff from my mouth. They did not release me until I inadvertently swallowed some.

The vomiting was explosive. I thought my guts were being torn loose. Staggering, I clutched blindly at the air as the supporting hands abandoned me. My fingers closed on empty space. The druids had gone back to the circle, leaving me alone. I cradled my heaving belly and doubled over, fighting for breath in a body gone out of control. Life was gushing out of me on waves of bile. My knees gave way. The last clear thought in my head was a question: Why had the druids poisoned me?

I lay in a knot on the ground with my knees drawn up to my chin. I was no longer even retching, everything in me had been vomited out. The chanting had never stopped. Gradually I realized it seemed to be coming from the earth beneath me also, from the soil and the stones, flowing into me, reverberating with a rhythm that matched the tides of my blood. I was desperately tired. I only wanted to sink into the chanting earth and be part of its song, thought-less, pain-less. . . .

I was drifting free with the familiar sensation that comes in the last moments before sleep. A thudding of the earth near my head told me that feet were treading around me, and a deeper instinct born of both bodily and spiritual senses informed me that the druids were dancing a pattern around me, spiraling in toward me and then out again, leading. . . .

I was gliding away from my body, lured by a beckoning dream beyond the rim of awareness. Warm light. Voices calling. I thought I reached out. I thought I cried a glad reply. . . .

There was a sound in my ear like the dry slithering of a snake across a stone. Aberth whispered, "Death is but a breath away."

The edge of his knife drew a ribbon of flame across my throat.

Shocked back from the dream, I fought mindlessly, flinging myself as far as I could from the sacrificer, clawing at the bandage over my eyes, kicking out, trying to scramble to my feet so I could face whatever threatened me like a man. But I was terribly dizzy. It seemed to take me forever to stand up and tear off my blindfold. . . .

To find myself in a place of lurid red light, teetering on a narrow knife-edge between two abysses. Deep in one was a misty meadowland, dimly seen, peopled by vague forms that seemed to be gesturing toward me.

When I looked into the other I saw Aberth below me, grinning up at me, holding his knife.

The strip on which I stood was shrinking with every beat of my heart.

Inevitably I must fall. But which way? That seemed the only decision left to make.

Which way?

Think.

Was the dreamlike meadow the Otherworld, reachable only through death?

Were Aberth and his bloodthirsty blade still in the land of the living?

Or was it the other way around?

I cried for help but only in my head; I had lost the use of tongue and jaw. I want to live! I protested silently. I have so much yet to learn, to experience. Which way? *Which way to life?*

Out of the red mist a figure approached. At first I thought I had an ally and I redoubled my efforts to keep my balance until help reached me. Then I saw the thing clearly. Saw a massive disembodied head, like some monstrous version of the trophies our warriors used to take from their enemies in battle.

This head, however, had two faces, one on either side.

The faces were not identical. Nor was either human; they were stylized distortions of humanity. One, noble of feature and serene, with a pointed chin and long-lidded eyes, resembled a man entranced. The second was coarse, brutal, with glaring and rapacious eyes. Yet this face was vividly alive. The other's aloofness might have been the distancing of death.

"Do you look toward life?" I cried to the savage face.

The soundless answer thundered in my head: *I do.* But before I could seize upon this as a sign, the voice continued, *I also look toward death.*

And I, murmured the enraptured other, *look toward death. And life.*

"Is there nothing to choose between you, then?" I cried despairingly.

Nothing, they answered in unison.

I stopped struggling and let myself fall. Fall into one of the abysses, not caring which, spinning down, endlessly down. And in my falling I was not alone. The void was filled with presences that cushioned my falling, turning me gently this way and that, guiding me without hands, murmuring to me without words. And among them was Rosmerta; I was certain, though I could not see her. But I knew her as in the long nights when she had bent over my bed to tuck my blankets around me or soothe me after a bad dream.

A voice said, *Whichever way you fell she would have been there; she and the others.*

"What others?" I tried to ask, but I was falling again, falling away, tumbling down and down until . . .

. . . until gradually I began recalling concepts of direction and distance and time. Concentrating on them, I found myself spiraling amid stars. Constellations bloomed around me like flowery meadows and I reached out. . . .

Hands touched me. Someone smoothed my hair back from my forehead. Someone else caught me under the arms and helped me sit up. I was an emptied husk. When I touched my neck with my fingers, I felt the stickiness of blood.

Sulis bent over me to spread a salve on my wound. Beyond her I heard Aberth say, "There is no harm done, I know my art. I merely parted the outermost layer of skin, so stop fussing over him."

My voice creaked as I asked, "Am I dead?"

"What do you think?" said Menua somewhere above me.

I fumbled for the truth I had glimpsed. "I think . . . life and death are . . . two aspects of one condition."

He crouched down and gazed earnestly into my eyes. "Good. Good! It went well for you.

"Death is not the last thing, Ainvar, but the least thing. Remember that. Death is a cobweb we brush through. It has lost its power to frighten you."

I recalled one of the many sayings he had taught me. "The dark moon is but a passing phase of the bright moon."

The chief druid nodded and started to stand up, but I caught hold of his arm. "Why is deathteaching limited to the Order?"

He bent toward me again and something flickered at the backs of his eyes. "Different people are born with different abilities. The gifts that dispose one toward druidry include a certain strength of mind and spirit that allow the person to survive deathteaching intact. A warrior or a craftsman or a plowman has other gifts; the experience would destroy him. But because we can walk into death and out again, it is our responsibility to make that journey on behalf of the tribe and assure others there is nothing to fear."

A dozen eager hands helped me rise to my feet. Druids crowded around to congratulate me. I was hugged repeatedly.

I felt as if I were filled with bubbles.

Then I realized that one of the druids hugging me was Aberth. Before I could stop myself I pulled away. He smiled at me without rancor. "Did you recall living before?" he asked pleasantly. "Some of us do, you know."

"Don't question him," Menua ordered. "Deathteaching is private. If there is anything Ainvar wants us to know of his, he will tell us himself."

That night the members of the Order held a private feast in celebration. Looking around at the others, I wondered how many of them remembered living before. If they did, then death did not always wash away memories. The recollection of sorrow could travel through time with us.

Or the recollection of joy. Two faces.

What waited in the future for me, I wondered, beyond my dying? It was like wondering what lay outside in the night.

A tingle of anticipation prickled down my spine.

When I had drunk enough wine to make my tongue dance, I leaned over and whispered to Menua, "I know another reason why druids reserve deathteaching for themselves."

"Oh?"

"Professional jealousy," I explained with drunken assurance. "If anyone could do it, who would need us?"

Menua laughed. "You are definitely growing wiser, Ainvar."

Still later, after a lot more wine, I had something else to tell him. But I saved it until we were alone in the lodge. Then I described the figure I had seen as I teetered between two worlds.

Menua's reaction was jubilant. "You saw him! You actually saw the Two-Faced One! Such a vision has not been granted to a druid within living memory, though I have heard of it, of course. Ah, Ainvar, you fulfill my expectations for you!"

"You know of him?" I was astonished.

He nodded. "My predecessors described him as the eternal observer, looking ahead to the next world and simultaneously back toward this one. A representative of the duality of existence," he added.

"Is he . . . it . . . a god, then?"

"If you will. An aspect of the one Source. I always longed for such a vision but it was never given to me. And now you . . . such a powerful symbol. I envy you," he said wistfully, heaving an old man's sigh.

I was not prepared to think of Menua as being old, in spite of the fact that the white hair beyond his domed forehead had grown very thin, and he had become increasingly peevish and demanding. To me Menua had seemed eternal. He had so often stressed the immanence of the Creator in creation that I had come to equate him with both.

How could he be old? Yet when I looked closely, I saw how loosely the flesh sagged from his bones.

"But perhaps I should not be surprised that he came to you in the deathteaching," Menua was saying. "You were no stranger to him. Had he not once before helped you to cross the gulf between worlds?"

I stared at him. Suddenly I knew where this was leading. "What do you mean?" I asked, however, playing for time.

"You know what I mean! Don't think you can misdirect me. Why do you suppose I've lavished so much time and effort on you? The tribe is approaching an era of trials, according to the omens and portents, and the chief druid who succeeds me must be the strongest and most gifted ever born to the Carnutes. Who should that be, Ainvar, but a man capable of bringing the dead back to life?"

My first reaction was a sense of wrenching disappointment. There had been no love, he had not cared for me as a father cares for a son. His only interest in me was because he thought I could restore a spirit to its body.

I was as furious as if he had willfully deceived me, and I was suddenly, totally, sober. I opened my mouth to lash out at him and smash his erroneous belief into splinters.

But he had taught me to hear.

The ears of my spirit heard the hope underlying his words. His desperate hope. He had survived more than sixty winters and he was tired. The responsibility of the tribe was weighing heavily upon him. He needed to believe he would pass that responsibility into capable hands and was staking everything on me because of a gift he hoped I possessed.

I bit my lip and said nothing.

Into the silence his voice came with an old man's querulousness. "You can do it, Ainvar. Can't you?"

I drew a deep breath. "If it should ever become necessary, I remember what I did for Rosmerta," I said very carefully.

Which was not a lie. I remembered exactly what I had done for Rosmerta: nothing. But I intended him to draw a far different, and reassuring, inference.

"Ah," he said. "Ah. Good."

What else could I have done? No matter how he felt toward me, I loved the old man.

Soon I heard him begin to snore, but sleep did not come so easily to me.

The next morning I went to find the Goban Saor.

True to his name, which meant "the smith-builder," Sulis's brother could make anything with his hands. He had begun as Teyrnon's apprentice but far surpassed his master, and now had a shed of his own, where he crafted everything from jewelry to weapons.

He was applying a bellows to the forge fire as I approached. I saw a muscular man stripped except for a leather apron. Sweat oiled his body, his hair lay in wet strings along his broad shoulders. When he saw me he straightened up and wiped his forehead. "Ho, Ainvar."

"I need a figure made," I told him.

"Of what?"

"Of something you've never seen. But I can describe it to you. It's to be a gift," I added.

Menua presented me with the gold amulet to identify me. Aberth killed an animal from the herd we bred solely for sacrifice, white cattle with black muzzles and thin, upright manes on their

necks. Wrapped in the hide, Keryth the seer lay nightlong beside
the Autura, and returned with the prophecy of a successful undertaking.

Then when all was in readiness, we had word of invasion. The
warning shouts rang from the hills. A band of Sequani had detached
itself from the vast main tribe beyond the eastern mountains, had
crossed through the fringes of Parisii territory, and was attempting
to settle on Carnutian soil not far from us.

The shouters passed the word along and Nantorus soon arrived
from Cenabum with an army of followers, and those of his sworn
princes, at his back.

After the battle Nantorus was carried to our fort on his shield,
severely wounded. He had won, but at a cost. He was taken to
our healing house, where Sulis and her helpers hovered over him.
Men worried, women wailed.

"Will I have to postpone my journey?" I asked Menua, secretly
resenting anything that might keep me from the adventure.

"I think not. Even if Nantorus is permanently incapacitated,
which I doubt, we would not elect a king to replace him without
a lot of discussion. The election could take place without you, but
without your journey and the knowledge you bring back to me we
will not have sufficient information about current Roman affairs to
guide whatever king we have wisely. So you shall go. But there is
just one more thing I would like you to do first, as I have little
time for it right now."

"Gladly."

"Our warriors have driven the Sequani away, but they took their
best breeding-age women in reparation for Nantorus's injury. The
women should be examined by one of the Order—or at least a well-
trained apprentice—to be certain they are of sufficient quality to
mate with our men. When I was much younger I encountered a
similar situation and let Ogmios take a woman with a serious blem-
ish, and I've regretted it ever since. Don't make the same mistake."

"I can take care of it," I assured him.

"I'm certain you can." Menua's eyes twinkled in their network
of wrinkles in spite of himself.

The old fox, I thought. He is fond of me after all.

The Sequani women were being quartered in our assembly
house, a rectangular building with two firepits, one at either end,
and benches around the sides. The captured women were crowded

onto the benches and had overflowed onto the floor, where they had made beds for themselves out of straw and blankets our own women provided.

As I entered, they gathered into a herd to face me. There was much giggling behind hands and nudging with elbows.

"Who speaks for you?" I demanded to know.

A woman cleared her throat—but it did not help. Her voice was naturally both soft and hoarse, curiously but pleasantly roughened like the purring of a cat. "I am called Briga," she announced, stepping to the fore of the group. "I am a prince's daughter."

I was amused. "Everyone claims to be of noble rank when far from home."

She flushed but stood her ground. Wide blue eyes challenged me. "And who are you to speak to me at all, you great gawky pine tree of a man?"

I stiffened. "Ainvar of the Carnutes," I replied with the hauteur of a man born to horse rank. "I am your captor."

She sniffed. "Not mine. I never saw you before." She was glaring at me as if I were a bondservant offering her a platter of rotten fish. There was nothing remarkable about her; she could not make beauty's claim to pride. Her eyes were fine, but her body was short and sturdy, her hair a commonplace dark flaxen color. There were longer-limbed women in her group with more vivid coloring; some of them were as beautiful as the women of the Parisii. Yet for some reason the one called Briga held my eyes.

"Be advised that I have authority over you," I warned, "and show respect."

"Why should I?"

Perhaps I made a mistake by smiling at her in the beginning, I thought. I scowled instead. It made no difference. Her look remained one of frozen disdain.

"I'm here to examine you," I explained, "so if you will—"

"Oh no you're not!" She doubled her fists and came toward me as if she meant to hit me in the face. "We've been through enough already, get out of here and leave us alone."

"But—"

"Out of here, I said!" She opened her fists and made shooing motions at me with her hands, as if I were a flock of hens. "You don't frighten me," she told me. "You're so lean a gust of wind would blow you away." She took another step toward me, rose onto her tiptoes, tilted her head back, puffed out her cheeks, and blew in my face.

Her companions shrieked with laughter. Even the guard at the door guffawed.

Defeated, I fled.

Laughter followed me.

This, I thought darkly, is what comes of the king being incapacitated. No one respects us. May Sulis heal him soon!

What should I have done to demonstrate my authority over Briga—hit her?

My spirit was incapable of such a deed. I hunched my shoulders around me and trudged on, feeling sorry for myself.

When I saw Menua he was so busy, fortunately, that he forgot to ask me about examining the women, and I was careful not to remind him. If I was able to set out on my journey before he remembered, so much the better for me. Someone else could do it.

Yet the Sequani woman lingered in my head. I found myself imagining a score of different and more satisfying endings for my confrontation with her. Though she had publicly belittled me, I did not like the idea of someone else examining her; some other man's hands on her body.

The end of the day found me retracing my steps to the assembly hall. Only a ribbon of rose light edged with gold lingered in the western sky, bringing that moment of reasonless melancholy that is like a toothache in the soul. As I went back toward the captive women, I told myself I must not let the day die without fulfilling my responsibility. This time I would not be deterred. . . .

I heard her before I saw her. A sound of sobbing came from the path that led to the trench where we relieved ourselves. Following the sound, I almost stumbled over a huddled shape in the twilight. The Sequani woman was sitting beside the path in a ball of misery, hugging her knees. She tried to muffle the sound of her crying, but I had a druid's ears.

She was alone, not surprisingly. The guard would have let her go relieve herself on her word of honor to return. She was a Celt.

I crouched beside her. "Are you hurt?" When she did not respond I touched her shoulder. "Are you hurt?" I repeated.

She shrank in on herself. "No." Her voice was strangled by the effort to choke back tears.

"Are you ill, then? Do you need a healer?"

"No. Leave me alone." She covered her face with her hands.

How could I walk away and leave her alone? I had planned to be very stern, remorseless even, when I saw her again, but that would have to wait. I could be remorseless some other time. "Let me help you," I said as gently as I could.

Her small body convulsed with grief. Before I knew it I had gathered her into my arms. She did not resist; to my astonishment she pressed herself against me and buried her face in my chest. She was mumbling something I could not make out.

"What? What are you saying?"

"They burned Bran," sobbed the hoarse voice somewhere below my chin, "but they wouldn't take me."

"What are you talking about?"

"They wouldn't take me!" Briga's voice rose to an ear-tearing wail of purest agony.

I clamped my arms around her, afraid someone would hear and think I was torturing her. "There, there," I murmured inanely. "It's all right, ssshhh. It's all right. Just tell me what you're talking about. Who was Bran? And who burned him?"

"The *druids!*" The words exploded out of her, propelled by unmistakable hatred. "The druids burned Bran because he was the best of us!" She spoke as if the druids were monsters who had acted out of deliberate cruelty, which was unthinkable.

"You must have misunderstood," I tried to tell her.

"No, they said they had to have Bran, no one else would do."

She was giving me bits and pieces that explained nothing. "Tell me all of it straight out, so I can help you," I urged.

"You can't help me. No one can." The anger faded from her voice, leaving it disconsolate. "It began with Ariovistus," she said at last. Then she hiccuped.

"Ariovistus? The king of the Suebi?"

"The same. They are a Germanic tribe, you know, and he kept leading them across the Rhine to attack the Sequani. My father was a prince of the Sequani but he had grown weary of war. He persuaded some of his followers to go in search of new lands. Let the Suebi have the old one, he said. We only want peace. So we set out, but an evil spirit overtook us and burned and blistered and killed many of our people. We tried prayer and we tried sacrifice but nothing prevailed against the spirit of the illness. The Otherworld was deaf to our pleas and would not recall the malign thing that was killing us. Eventually my own . . . my own beloved . . ." She could not speak.

Feeling helpless, I stroked her hair. "Go on."

"My own dear parents died of the plague. Then some of the others began saying my father's cowardice in abandoning our land to the Germans had caused the Source to send the evil spirit of the illness upon us. A bad thing calls a bad thing, they said, and cowardice and plague are both bad things." She hiccuped again.

"But my father was no coward! He was wise and kind and only wanted a better life for us. They blackened his name with accusations only after he was dead and could not defend himself. It was so unfair!"

"Was Bran one of those who blamed your father?"

"No. Bran was my brother." She began to weep again, very softly and without hope. "They burned him. But they wouldn't take me."

Then I understood; I saw the druidic symmetry. The Sequanian druids, those who had fled with Briga's father and his followers, had sacrificed the prince's son so he could plead for mercy from the Source. But they had also, shrewdly, done it to placate those who blamed the dead prince for their misfortune.

"They wouldn't take me," Briga was murmuring almost mindlessly, losing herself in the repetition.

"Why should they take you?"

"I was his favorite sister. We were as close as two fingers on one hand. Wherever he went I always followed, and he wasn't like other brothers, he wanted me along. But the druids wouldn't let me go to the fire with him."

"Did Bran want you to be sacrificed with him?"

She hesitated. "No. But he couldn't have stopped me. The druids stopped me. Two of them held me, but I saw him go with them willingly, bravely, with his head up. He said he was honored to offer himself for the good of his people. Bran was so noble! But he went to the fire . . . he went to the fire." Her voice was sinking into that rhythmic, mindless murmuring again.

"Then what?" I shook her gently, drawing her back.

"Ah? After?" She said it as if nothing that happened after could be of any consequence. "When the people woke up next morning, the boils had faded from their flesh. The fever had passed. While the smoke of Bran's burning still hung in the trees."

Yes, I thought. Yes.

Her voice was dead as she went on. "When we could, we gathered our things and continued looking for a place to settle. But then your warriors attacked us. And here I am. Without Bran. The druids took him from me. I shall hate them until I die."

The vehemence in those flat, uninflected words was somehow more terrible than her spasm of hatred had been.

I ached for her.

Briga lay in my arms as if the life had been crushed out of her. I could not leave her there, so I lifted her and carried her to the assembly house. The guard at the door gaped at us when we emerged from the darkness.

She turned her face into my chest again, and I realized she did not want to have anyone else see that the prince's daughter had been crying.

Her women crowded around us, staring at me accusingly. "I found her outside," I said lamely. "She was . . . distressed." I tried to lower her onto one of the couches, but she clung to my neck.

"You won't leave me, too?" she whispered. Then she hiccuped again.

Ignoring the other women, I sat down on the couch and held her in my lap. "There, there," I said. "There now." And other meaningless things. But they seemed to comfort her. I rocked back and forth and murmured; she nestled against me and tucked her face into the curve of my neck like a weary child. A small sigh escaped her. Her grip on me eased, but did not let go.

I cannot say how long I sat there holding her. The women watched. No one tried to take her from me. Indeed, I would not have let them. Nothing had ever fitted me as perfectly, even my own skin, as Briga of the Sequani fitted against my body.

When her breathing deepened into sleep, I gently disengaged her grip and laid her down, motioning to one of the women to put a blanket over her. Briga stirred but did not waken.

For the second time I left the house of the captives without examining the women for blemishes.

That night I lay awake for a long time, not thinking about the journey to come, but wondering if anyone had mentioned to Briga at any time that I was a druid's apprentice.

With Menua's permission, before dawn I made my way to the grove alone to sing the song for the sun.

As I climbed the ridge, the stars were fading from the coming of the light, yet still they kept their vigil, watching for their brother beyond the edge of the world. I saluted them, the skywatchers. Sparks from the Source, keeping me company in the great silent ringing of the dawn.

Orange slivers tore open a bank of low-lying cloud to the east. I had almost reached the grove when the sky burst into flame and the sun slid upward like a burning coin. I fell to my knees and extended my arms in welcome as the song for the sun poured from my throat.

We were a people who sang.

When the song was complete I went on to the grove.

Later I would discover that the Romans claimed we worshiped trees, but Romans only see surfaces. Druids do not worship trees. We worship among trees, and with trees. All of us together worshiping the Source.

From the radiance of sunrise I stepped into a darkling woodland of eerie vistas and glimmering greenness. Perception altered with every step. Each breath of wind formed new patterns of leaf and twig. Sound was curiously muted by the living columns of the great temple of the Carnutes.

I had come alone but I was not alone; one is never alone among trees. From the corner of my eye I glimpsed the swaying shapes of the gods of the forest pacing in antlered splendor along the borders of reality. I saw goddesses formed of moss and greenery moving out of, melting into, the trees. As long as I did not try to turn my head and look directly at them, they did not hide themselves but kept amicable pace with me, their Otherworld overlapping mine.

Soon, in the Roman province, I would meet creatures more alien to me than the spirits of stag and sycamore.

Beside the stone of sacrifice I made the summoning sign, splaying my fingers and then drawing them together one at a time: pointing finger, pressing finger, tooth-search finger, heartbeat finger. Then the thumbs linked as I silently implored That Which Watched, Help me. Give me an agile mind and a guarded tongue. I must see everything and reveal nothing, for I will be among strangers. Help me.

Then I returned to the fort to collect Tarvos and our porter, and begin my adventure.

Chapter Ten

Menua came as far as the gate with me, and many of my clan followed along to see us off, but I did not see Briga's face anywhere. I had not expected to; I had only hoped.

She probably does not even know who I am, I reminded myself. She may not even care.

Still . . .

"Who are you looking for?" Menua asked.

My head warned me not to remind him of the Sequani women, who were still unexamined. "Crom Daral," I replied quickly. It was not a lie. I should have liked to see him—though not as much as I should have liked to see Briga. Neither appeared.

"Come back to us a free person, Ainvar," Menua saluted me. Something suspiciously like moisture sparkled in his eyes. My own were stinging. I hate farewells.

Nature offers a better model. Animals greet one another with the rituals appropriate to their species, but they part without ceremony. No painful moments. They just go. That is what I wanted to do then: just go.

I was young, that long-ago day on the plain of the Carnutes. I did not know how to cherish the moment. I did not realize how irrevocably the gates were closing behind me. I thought everything would be waiting for me when I returned, just as I remembered it.

The sun flashed on Tarvos's spear and we were on our way.

For a time the journeying was easy. I was accustomed to walking long distances with Menua. However, I made the mistake of letting Tarvos set our pace, and Tarvos was not a strolling, contemplative druid but a trained warrior. At first I could keep up with him, but when the long muscles in my legs began to ache, I started gritting my teeth and pushing myself to avoid falling behind.

We would not delay our journey with a visit to Cenabum, but hurried on toward the land of the Bituriges. From sunrise to sunset Tarvos swung his legs from the hip in an earth-skimming, ground-eating stride that forced me to new respect for him. My own legs became columns of pain. My back ached, my buttocks ached, my heels were bruised, and it felt as if the tendons were tearing loose in the arches of my feet.

How could the simple act of walking become such agony?

It was painful to walk and painful to stop walking. Most excruciating of all was attempting to move again after a night's rest. Then my joints were locked and my muscles like rigid timber. My richly furnished head was merely a weight to carry, conversation was beyond me. All the concentration I could muster was needed to lift one foot after the other.

I could have mounted the mule and ridden, perched ludicrously atop the baggage, but I would rather have died in the ruts of the trackway. So I stumbled on grimly, my mind a blank of all but pain.

From time to time Tarvos cast an amused glance in my direction but said nothing. Even Baroc the porter and the mule he led knew I was hurting. No one offered to help.

I would not have accepted it anyway.

Blisters formed and broke and reformed. We traveled on. When we came to herders' camps and farming villages, we were given hospitality; there was singing around the fires. Day followed night followed day. One night I realized I had joined in the singing and forgotten the pain. The next day it was gone.

Our way took us to Avaricum, stronghold of the Bituriges, a

fortified town like Cenabum. Avaricum was protected by marsh and river and embraced with a wall of huge beams laid crosswise, the spaces between filled with rubble, the whole faced with boulders. Buried in earth and stone, the beams were impervious to fire and could not be shaken by a battering ram. The Bituriges claimed Avaricum was the finest town in Gaul.

Their chief druid, Nantua, made me welcome and promised me instruction in their grove, but the most important thing I learned from him had nothing to do with the Order. He happened to mention, quite casually, that war had broken out among the Arvernians.

"War within the tribe?" I asked in surprise.

"A new leader has taken control and a prince who hoped to be king himself, a man called Celtillus, has been slain."

I almost choked on the wine I was drinking. Celtillus was father to Vercingetorix.

Though I pressed Nantua for more information, he knew little. He had received the message in the usual way, through shouts borne on the wind. No details. Abandoning any further druidic instruction, I told Nantua I must go south at once.

He chose to be insulted. "You won't learn as much from the Arvernians as you could here."

"I am certain you're right," I said tactfully, "but I have an Arvernian friend who may need me."

"A friend? In another tribe?" Nantua lifted his eyebrows at such an unlikely situation.

"He's my soul friend."

"Ah." Nantua nodded, mollified. "Does this Arvernian know you are soul friends?"

"I doubt it," I admitted. Intuition told me Rix had little interest in the tenets of druidry. He was a warrior; his mother had baked him with a hard crust.

We set off again and this time I pushed the pace. Baroc complained that the mule had not had time to rest. Baroc was a bondservant working off a debt to my clan. He was a yellow-haired man with a small mind but a large capacity for complaining. Since the mule was not complaining, I paid him little mind.

Central Gaul was seething with birthing and planting, but already anticipating the sunseason langor that would precede harvest. When the wind blew green and heavy with bee-hum, men

would sing or sleep or drink or contest; women would meet to
exchange ways of plaiting hair, or to gossip by wells and springs.
A free people, we loved our leisure and worked hard to earn it.

But something was wrong. As the newly planted einkorn and
emer sprouted, the fields showed shadings I did not like. Birds
flew in strange, broken patterns. We saw a flock of small-horned
ewes, usually the most placid of creatures, flee in panic from a
configuration of clouds that swept over them.

Something was wrong. I lengthened my stride and increased
our pace.

Following the river Allier, we reached the highland plateau
which signaled that Arvernian territory lay just ahead of us. By
now the air tingled with trouble. To my surprise, Tarvos, whom I
had thought the least sensitive of men, began carrying his shortsword openly in his hand. I pulled the druidic amulet out of the
neck of my tunic and displayed it prominently on my chest, and
told Baroc to keep a tight hold on the mule.

The Arvernians we met along the traders' trackway were close-
mouthed and wary. No one wanted to talk about the death of
Celtillus. If I asked too many questions, people turned surly or
hurried away from us. Not until the walls of the great fortress of
Gergovia rose in the distance did we happen to meet a bard who
was willing to talk.

That was his name: Hanesa the Talker. Florid and stocky, with
a pattern of broken veins across his nose, the bard had a rich, full
mane of hair and a rich, full voice as well. Even in casual conversation he spoke with rhetorical flourishes.

When I told him we were going to Gergovia, Hanesa grew lyrical
about the size and strength of the principal stronghold of the Arverni, claiming it made both Avaricum and Cenabum shabby by
comparison. When I asked if he knew of Vercingetorix, his gran-
diloquence knew no bounds. "That young man is the most ferocious
fighter ever born in Gaul!" he cried, waving his arms. "I have
watched him at play and in training, and I tell you no man is his
physical equal. He has the strength of ten and his character is of
the noblest. He is much admired . . ."

"As was his father?" I asked innocently.

"Ah. Mmm." Hanesa's spate of words dried away. He eyed me
speculatively, pleating his lower lip between his fingers. "What
does a Carnutian know of Celtillus?"

"I heard he was killed recently. And I am concerned; his son Vercingetorix is a friend of mine."

"Why didn't you say so?" The sun came back; Hanesa beamed. "I am a friend of his myself and am just now on my way to find him. He is my destiny."

This statement was so pompous, and uttered with such seriousness, I had to fight to keep from smiling and insulting the man. "Oh, really?"

"Indeed he is! I mean to be the most celebrated bard in Gaul, which requires I have stories to tell that none other can equal. I shall acquire those stories at the elbow of a mighty hero, a man fated to do great things. Since his birth, such an existence has been prophesied for Vercingetorix. Since recent events have driven him from Gergovia, I have, ah, been settling some affairs of my own, and just now am free to join him. If you are a friend of his you are welcome to come with me."

"Why did he have to leave Gergovia?" As I asked this, I conspicuously fingered my gold amulet, so Hanesa, who as a bard was also a member of the Order of the Wise, would know I was someone to be trusted.

Asking a bard a question is like tipping a brimming jug. Soon we were all off the road and sitting in the shade of a tree, and Baroc, at my command, was portioning out bread and cheese while Hanesa described the recent upheaval in his tribe.

As he talked, he ate right- and left-handed. Every bard I have ever known has had a voracious appetite. As the food vanished into Hanesa's maw, I imagined how Baroc would complain about having his share given to a stranger. Princes and druids have to be hospitable. Bondservants do not.

Between mouthfuls, Hanesa told us, "The trouble goes back for generations. As I'm sure you know, the Arverni once were supreme among all Gaulish tribes." He paused for effect, watching to see if I contradicted him.

Since I wanted him to go on talking, I kept quiet, though any number of tribes make the same claim and it is no more true of the Arverni than of any other. Dominance among the tribes has always been a shifting business.

"The noble prince Celtillus became obsessed with a dream of returning our tribe to their former eminence," Hanesa went on. "To that end he sought the kingship when our old king outlived his strength. But the title was contested and another man won the election. Celtillus took it hard. He would not accept his defeat . . . though he was famed both for his wisdom and his magnanimous spirit!" Hanesa could not resist declaiming. His eyes sparkled, his throat vibrated, his speech abounded with chortles and exclamations. Listening to him was a feast.

"To defend his position against the continuing threat of Celtillus and his followers, the new king sought help. He did not, you will appreciate, feel secure in his kingship, and he mentioned this to the Roman traders in Gergovia, with whom he was doing a sizable business."

At the mention of Romans I felt myself stiffen as if Menua had nudged me. Hanesa finished his meal and continued his recital.

"The traders relayed this information to their principals, and in time help was offered. By someone. Arrangements were made, no one will say what or by whom. But within the last moon the body of Celtillus was found hacked to death in a ditch, and when his oldest son, who discovered it, went wild with grief, the new king, Potomarus, had him driven from Gergovia under threat of death."

My heart ached for Rix, the oldest son. "Who actually killed Celtillus, bard?"

"No one admits knowing the answer. But history is my profession; I know how to ask questions so I can pass on the truth of events to future generations. Through sources I must protect I learned that the traders told Celtillus he could make a special deal for weaponry and additional warriors that would enable him to take the kingship by force. Someone—no names given—would meet him in secret and take him to yet another secret location where the deal could be struck.

"But only Celtillus was struck. Those who saw his body afterward say the wounds in his flesh were of the shape Roman swords make." Hanesa dropped his voice to a sinister whisper.

"Why would Roman traders or their principals involve themselves in a struggle for control of the tribe?"

Hanesa shook his head. "Who can say? To protect their established trading partner, Potomarus, I suppose. But Celtillus died and with him died his dream of gathering all the tribes of Gaul under Arvernian leadership. A foolish dream, really," he added with another rueful shake of his head. "But glorious."

The dream was indeed foolish, my head observed; just the sort of dream Celts adored. Free Gaul comprised over sixty tribes, both large and small, who agreed on nothing but the pleasure of fighting one another to demonstrate their manhood. The idea of forcing them to accept a single leadership was preposterous.

"What of Vercingetorix now?" I wanted to know.

Light leaped in Hanesa's eyes. "Ah, they should have killed that one when they killed his father. He has been shaken by what happened, but when he recovers he will take a spectacular revenge, that's his style. I'm on my way to offer myself as his personal bard because I want to be on hand to see it happen."

Of course, I thought. Revenge spawns epics.

"Let us go to him at once, Hanesa," I urged. "I'm anxious to know he's all right."

"As am I. But be careful of anyone we might meet along the way. Tempers are still running high on both sides."

"No one would harm a druid," I said.

Tarvos spoke up unexpectedly. "Which you aren't, Ainvar. Not yet, anyway."

I shot him an annoyed glance that bounced off him like a spear off oxhide. I could not intimidate Tarvos.

Rix had taken refuge below Gergovia, on the west bank of the Allier. To reach him we had to make our way through a stand of second-growth woodland clogged with underbrush. I understood trees; while they clawed at Hanesa I slipped through easily.

"You northern tribes are as forest-wise as Germans," the bard said bitterly the third time his face was scratched.

I bristled. Being classed with the Germans was an insult to any Gaul.

Like ourselves, the people who lived across the Rhine were divided into a number of tribes. We called these tribes by the common title of Germani, or Germans, though some of them claimed Celtic blood and had legends similar to ours. There was no friendship between Gaul and German, however. They were hostile and aggressive nomads; we occupied prosperous, settled territories with fortified strongholds. The Germans had no druids. They lived in dense forests, which they never bothered to clear, and many of them reputedly went naked both summer and winter or dressed in the raw skins of bears. We considered the Germanic tribes to be brutes of low cunning and disgusting habits.

There was no denying they were awesome in battle, however.

They retained a ferocity celebrated in our own bardic legends, but now rarely practiced by the Gaulish Celts. The Germans were a constant threat on our borderlands, where they slaughtered and plundered. The Aedui in particular had lost territory to them.

Tribal pride had led Hanesa to insult me; of course I could not accept it. Making my voice as cold as iron on a winter's night, I said to him, "No matter what your Celtillus believed, the Arvernians are in no way superior to the Carnutes. Quite the reverse, in fact. If anyone should lead the Gauls it should be my tribe.

"May I remind you that the greatest of all sacred groves, the true heart of Gaul, is in our territory?"

That stopped him. For almost sixty paces Hanesa the Talker said nothing at all.

Gnats hummed, thickening the air. I swatted at them to keep them from my ears and nostrils. We were close to the river now; I could smell her water. Rivers are female. Goddesses, each with her own name and properties, though each is an aspect of the Source. The Sequana, for example, which ran through the land of the Parisii, was famous for both healing and . . .

My musing was interrupted by a sudden thud. I whirled to find myself facing a bearded giant who had leaped from the branch of a tree almost directly over my head. A bearded giant who had a naked sword in his hand.

And murder in his eyes.

CHAPTER ELEVEN

TARVOS YELLED and plunged forward, spear aimed for the thrust. The attacker's eyes locked with mine.

I flung myself not at him, but at Tarvos, twisting his spear away from him before he could drive it into the man's heart.

Tarvos vented a howl of outrage and almost turned on me instead. He recovered himself with difficulty and looked from one to the other of us as Hanesa and Baroc came hurrying up. The man who had almost killed me slowly lowered his sword, which was a massive jewel-hilted weapon that any man but himself would have had to wield with two hands. He held it easily in one.

"So I find the King of the World hiding in a thicket," I drawled.

An ivory grin shone through his drooping golden moustache. "Ainvar? Can it be you?"

"Probably. It was when I awoke this morning. That was a long time ago, however, and people do change."

"Your voice hasn't changed, nor your eyes. Lucky for you, or there would be two of you right now, for my sword would have split you down the middle from skull to crotch."

"There is no such thing as luck," I replied.

His eyes fell on my amulet. "Druid?"

"Menua's apprentice."

"A waste of good reflexes," commented Vercingetorix.

Though he was scratched and gaunt and filthy, in the morning of his manhood the Arvernian prince was a song of strength. From his leonine head to his muscular legs, line flowed into line in perfect harmony. He was even taller than I, and massively boned in maturity. But his lazy-lidded gaze was the same, and his irresistible grin had not changed.

We threw our arms around each other and hugged and pounded. Over Rix's shoulder I saw Hanesa staring. "We were manmade together," I tried to explain.

"I almost didn't recognize you, though," said Rix. "When you came crashing through the trees I mistook you for one of the king's warriors come to take my head."

"Is it as bad as that?"

He smiled with one side of his mouth. "It could be better. But it's temporary. I mean to change everything, and soon."

"How long have you been here? I know about your father, of course."

"Ah. I took refuge here two nights later, Ainvar. I have friends who bring me food when they dare, and there are men who will follow me when I'm ready to make my move. Any of them would let me hide out in his lodge but I don't want to put anyone else in danger."

Hanesa pressed forward eagerly. "What move will you make? Will you attack Gergovia?"

Rix responded with a bitter laugh. "Me . . . and a handful of supporters . . . against the mighty walls of Gergovia? Even I am not that reckless, bard. No, I intend to do to Potomarus what he did to my father, lure him into an ambush and kill him."

"That won't bring your father back, and it would leave your tribe headless."

Something glittered in Rix's eyes. For a moment I saw his soul.

Opening up the senses of my spirit, I listened to the weight of the water in the river and smelled the pattern of the geese flying above us. I recalled the shadings of the sprouting grain in the fields, and the panic of the sheep.

"Now is not the time for you to aspire to the kingship, Rix," I heard myself say.

His eyes widened. "Who said I wanted it?"

"Just be warned. The atmosphere is disturbed. The omens are bad for whoever leads the Arverni now."

"Druid talk," Rix scoffed.

"I would listen to this man," Hanesa told him. The Order supports its own.

Tarvos added, "Ainvar has a good head, you know." It was the first compliment I ever received from the Bull.

Rix raked his eyes over the other warrior, measuring him. Then he turned back to me. "You do have a good head, I'll admit that. But you don't understand. Potomarus doesn't deserve to be king. He and his Roman traders . . . "

"Hanesa told me, at least what is suspected. Have you more than mere suspicion?"

The skin tightened around Rix's eyes. "If I had any proof I would take it to the judges. But anyone who might know anything is afraid to speak up. The king and the traders are safe from everything but my sword," he added with a growl.

"The kingship is an elected office, Rix. Take it by the sword and someone will feel free to take it from you by the sword.

"Listen to me. Everything is shifting, the very atmosphere here is as unstable as the quicksands in the Liger. If you act rashly you will find yourself as dead as your father, with nothing accomplished.

"I have a suggestion. Let memories fade and tempers cool, your own included. Come with me. Menua is sending me as far south as the Province to study with the druids along the way and, more important, to observe the Romans in Narbonese Gaul and report back to him on their actions and plans."

The skin was still taut around Rix's eyes; in their expression I read refusal, so I tossed him a quick, and inspired, lure: "On our travels we will meet other traders who might know the truth of what happened to your father. You know how it is, Rix, the members of one class talk to each other. Traders surely gossip to traders. We can question people, we can learn. If the pattern wills it, you could even get the proof you need to present to the chief judge of the Arverni."

"Do you think so?" he asked with touching eagerness.

I had to be honest. "I don't know, but it's worth a try. You cannot accomplish anything here, hiding in trees. Give the situation time. I tell you, the omens are so bad your new king will undoubtedly fail the tribe in some way, and then you could find yourself with a lot of new allies.

"Besides," I added, hoping it was the final temptation, "I want your company."

I could see him teetering. "Know this, Ainvar. If I go with you I mean to come back to Gergovia. This isn't over."

"I know that."

"It was my father's dream to have the Arverni lead the tribes of Gaul." Rix stared into some inner space of his own to which I did not have access. "His dream was like a spark in dry grass. That spark is not extinguished. Someday I mean to finish what he began."

In that moment I was both certain he would, and frightened for him. All the danger I had intuitively felt since entering this land now swirled unmistakably around the form of my friend. "When the time is right I will help you," I said rashly. I would have said anything at that moment. "But come away with me now. I have to return to the great grove by Samhain; Menua wants me to tell the annual convocation of druids what I have learned then."

Pulling Rix with me took all the strength I had, but somehow it was done. We set off together southward, accompanied now by Hanesa the Talker as well as by Tarvos and my porter. The bard had not asked permission, just fallen into step with us. I hid a smile; I had done the same thing myself often enough.

If Vercingetorix were recognized it might prove unsafe, so I convinced him to disguise his very recognizable self as much as possible. At a crossroads fair I had Tarvos bargain for a filthy woolen cape that looked as if some herder had lived in it for years, summer and winter. The cape was cowled, and the cowl could be pulled up over Rix's bright hair almost like a druid's hood. We tucked his father's jewel-hilted sword into the mule's pack, and Rix thereafter carried only a spear, as if he were part of my bodyguard.

He accepted these decisions with a relief he tried to conceal, which told me how terrible the past days had been for him, alone and tormented. He obediently took his place and awaited marching orders from Tarvos.

This caused the Bull difficulties.

"I can't give orders to him, Ainvar," he hissed to me me out of the side of his mouth. "He's chariot rank!"

"You must. I can't have him be in charge of the bodyguard, that would make him too conspicuous."

Overhearing this, Hanesa said with a flourish, "People will always notice Vercingetorix, bright sun of the Arverni!"

"And you be quiet," I ordered irritably. "At least until we are in some other tribe's territory, or you could get your bright sun killed."

With Vercingetorix figuratively tucked under my arm like a valuable package, I made my way southward, visiting various druid groves along the way but lingering in none. The real goal of the journey was the Province, and I was in a hurry to get there, to see a place that must surely be exotic and strange.

Until we left the land of the Arverni, tension was palpable in the air and clung to my skin like a sheen of sweat. The names of Celtillus and Potomarus were whispered on the wind; some said a war within the tribe might yet erupt.

Yet there was no unified effort, merely talk. Some shouting and fist waving, some wine-born boasting. Without a leader it would come to nothing and be forgotten. We were not people to smolder; we burst into flame at once or else the flame died.

The flame walked beside me, hiding his thoughts behind his eyelids.

The increasingly warm weather provoked stirrings in us; we were all young men. Sometimes as we walked we spoke of women. They were a favorite topic of Rix's, who had had a wide experience of them already. Hanesa joined in with his own reminiscences, florid and surely exaggerated. Baroc chewed his lip; a bondservant's access to women was limited until his obligation was discharged. Tarvos was quiet, as usual.

I thought of Sulis, and of Briga. I spoke of Sulis aloud because everyone but Hanesa knew who she was and I was young enough to enjoy boasting.

I never spoke of Briga. But when I lay wrapped in my cloak at night, I saw her behind my closed eyelids.

It would be a long time until Samhain. And surely some man would have claimed her by then. . . .

I tried to keep from thinking about it. Unsuccessfully.

Occasionally on our journey, just because we were young, sheer high spirits overtook us and we romped and yelled and pushed one another while the mule looked on with an expression of aggrieved maturity.

Late one day, when a silence had fallen that I was quite enjoying, Rix fell into step beside me. He did that sometimes when there was no one to see such familiarity. He began the conversation abruptly, as though it had been in his mind for a long time.

"I quarreled with my father shortly before he was killed, Ainvar. We used to quarrel a lot. He hit me on the ear with his fist."

"All families quarrel," I assured him.

"Not like we did. He and I were cross-grained with each other from the very beginning, yet we were much alike. But whatever I said he disagreed with, and following his example, I did the same with him."

"Sounds harmless. I should think that often happens with fathers and sons. Testing each other like two bulls."

It was easy for me to be objective, I had never known my father.

"You don't understand. The last words we exchanged were violent and angry, and the next time I saw him, he was dead. I wanted to tell him he was right; now I don't even remember what we argued about. But I never got to tell him and I just go on and on talking to him in my head, trying to finish the conversation we can never finish."

"You can finish it in the Otherworld when your spirits meet there."

He whirled on me. "Do you seriously believe that nonsense?"

I was so astonished that I stumbled and nearly fell. "Of course! Don't you?"

"I held Celtillus in my arms after he was dead, Ainvar. Nothing remained of him. No life. He was cold and his blood was stiff on his clothes. He was just so much dead meat. I cried out to him, but there was no answer, he was gone. As if he had never been. Destroyed. Not watching me benevolently from the Otherworld, or he would have found some way to tell me so. He could do anything, my father. He was *destroyed*, do you hear what I'm saying? Made nothing! When you die there *is* nothing, I learned that that day. No Otherworld, no continuing. You live and you die and it's over."

The depth of his bitterness appalled me, though I now understood why he was so determined to take up his father's dream.

I was reminded of Briga, weeping for her sacrificed brother who had died in a very different cause. Confronted with such pain I felt inadequate. I had been taught that the living and the dead are part of one ongoing community, that death ends nothing, but I did not know how to hand on my faith like a cup of wine.

I must hurry back to the grove so Menua could complete my education and give me the wisdom to comfort Briga and Rix.

But first I had an assignment to fulfill and other education to acquire.

Our last visit before reaching the Province was with the Gabali tribe in their mountain wilderness. With obvious embarrassment the old chief druid escorted me to their grove, a sad little stand of gnarled oaks from which many trees were missing, like broken teeth ruining a smile.

"What happened here?" I wanted to know, staring at the hacked stumps.

"My people cut down the trees. For firewood." He would not meet my eyes.

"They wouldn't dare!"

"Not many worship here anymore, Ainvar. Some are even setting up clay gods in the Roman style in niches in their walls." The poor little man hunched his shoulders around himself protectively. "They make puddings out of the blood of sacrificial animals, which should be given to the earth instead. I argue, but the young ones don't listen."

He was simultaneously pathetic and frightening, like a tragic, prophetic dream. A skinny old man with little power left, he was being nibbled away.

"How could this happen?" I asked him.

"A day at a time," he said sadly. "It began when the Roman authorities in Narbonese Gaul declared the Order persona non grata there. It means no druids are welcome in the Province anymore. It was an insult, and they made many derogatory claims about us to justify it. People across the mountains began believing them. Then my own people—the ones who have some dealings with Provincials in the borderlands—began losing faith in us, too.

"We are too close to the Romans. Their influence . . ." He extended his hands and shook his gray head.

Ah, Menua, I thought. Great is your wisdom, Keeper of the Grove!

There was nothing more the Gabali could teach me, but the one lesson was valuable enough. The Romans must be afraid of the Order if they were going to such lengths to discredit us.

And if they were afraid of us, it meant we had a power they tacitly acknowledged.

I led my little band through the mountain passes, and into Narbonese Gaul.

We seemed to have crossed into a different world.

The Province prospered beneath a hotter, more reliable sun than we knew in the north. When we came down from the mountains, the land spread out before us like a green lap; we saw well-maintained farmsteads and fat livestock everywhere we looked. Wild flowers bloomed in every unused pocket of soil. The air smelled of butter and cheese.

As we advanced deeper into the Province, I stopped again and again to kneel and crumble the earth between my fingers. Each time its color and texture changed I paused to touch and taste and smell, to familiarize myself with this new place. I noted each change in leaf and shrub, each different birdsong. I walked marveling.

Mindful of the warning of the chief druid of the Gabali, I tucked my amulet beneath my clothes and instructed Hanesa not to identify himself as a bard if anyone asked.

I began noticing that a wild grape similar to one that flourished in the valley of the Liger had been tamed in the Province, and was standing in orderly rows. "Look, Rix! There is the source of the wine we import at such cost. You can see the same thing growing wild at home."

Wild at home. Tame here. Under Roman control, the vine was submissive.

The alien stamp was everywhere. Though we saw grass-headed lodges, the farther south we advanced the less Gaulish and more Roman they became. The natives of the Province, the Celtic Allobroges, the Nantuates, the Volcae, the clever Saluvii, and the strong Ligures, still lived here, but after a few generations of Roman domination they had become Latinized. We saw it in their buildings and heard it in their speech.

We soon learned we could no longer ask for hospitality wherever the night found us. All doors except those of commercial inns were barred to strangers, and the innkeepers demanded to see money first.

I had brought the Celtic coins we used with traders. Among ourselves we preferred barter, but we had learned from the Greeks that southerners preferred cold metal. And the Romans would consider nothing else. So we made coins.

At the first inn we visited, the innkeeper looked at my coins and sniffed. He had eyes like nuts and the face of a hot red baby. "Don't you have any real money?"

"This is real."

"Look what's stamped on them. Who is this savage with wild hair, and what is this figure, a horse or a hound? Give me Roman coin with Roman heads."

"We have none."

His eyes gleamed. "I thought not. You barbarians never do when you first arrive. I have a generous nature, though, I'll change your money for you. For a percentage, of course. You'll have to do it, currency from Hairy Gaul won't buy you anything here."

That was the first time I heard free Gaul referred to by that insulting name.

"You'll need to buy yourselves some decent clothes, too," he went on. "You can't walk around in those gaudy colors; people will know you for savages at once. You're doubly fortunate in that I have a brother in the next town, a shopkeeper who'll outfit you properly. For a price, of course." He laughed—unpleasantly.

A huge stack of Roman coins purchased a meal for us that would have starved a mouse. Everything was drenched in rancid oil. The meat was older than I was. In accordance with our rank I requested the best sleeping accommodation for Hanesa and myself, and space for our bodyguards and porter close by. The bard and I were shown to an airless cubicle we had to reach by climbing a rickety ladder from the main room of the inn. There we spent a miserable night on louse-infected straw listening to the snoring and farting of four other travelers.

Dawn found us grainy-eyed and furiously scratching. By contrast, our warriors and porter seemed refreshed. "They put us in the shed with the cow," Rix confided. "While it was still dark a young woman as round and firm as a loaf of bread came along with her milk pail, and I interrupted her duties for a time." He laughed. "She didn't seem to mind."

"Probably merely part of her job," Hanesa said.

Rix was offended. "What do you mean? She wanted me."

"She wanted to please her master, who probably orders her to entertain the guests."

"Her master?"

"She's a slave, of course. Didn't you know? All the servants here are slaves. I've talked to several of them."

"But she is of Celtic stock like ourselves! Born a free person!"

"Not in the Province," Hanesa informed him.

The expression on Rix's face said he found this information almost impossible to believe. But it was true. I asked a few questions myself. Slaves were the muscle underlying the fat of the Province, and most of those slaves were of Celtic stock. People who, by heritage, should have been free persons.

We left the inn as soon as we could, with me privately deciding we would sleep under the stars thereafter unless the weather was savage.

Instead of the rutted trackways of free Gaul, the Province boasted wide, well-traveled roadways frequently surfaced with slabs of stone already grooved by Roman wheels. One of these roads led us to the nearest town, a cluster of stone houses separated by narrow alleyways incongruously brightened by pots and tubs of cultivated flowers. Everything was scrubbed and tended. Slave labor, I thought sourly. We made a minimal number of clothing purchases in a tiny shop owned by the brother of our former host—who proved to be as big a thief as the innkeeper.

The weight of coins in my bag was decreasing alarmingly. We would definitely sleep outside from now on, and we would make our new clothes last. "I look ridiculous," Baroc complained of his. "This thing is like a woman's gown cut off at the shin. And it's loose, loose all over."

"We could never fight in anything like this," Rix agreed glumly, glaring at his own collarless coat or smock.

Back on the road we encountered travelers of every description and color, from milk white to ebony. Several times I had to reprove Baroc for staring with his mouth open. Most of the travelers were afoot, but there were also carts, wagons, several types of chariot, both two- and four-wheeled, and a variety of ridden animals, including horses, mules, asses, and shaggy ponies with feathered feet. To my dazzled eyes it appeared as if all the world traveled the roads of Narbonese Gaul.

I tried to strike up conversations with some of these people.

Few responded to any variant of the Celtic tongue, though obviously many understood me. When I attempted the Latin Menua had taught me, I had difficulty understanding the replies.

To my delight, Hanesa had more success. His gift was his tongue and he could make almost anyone respond to him. He also had an ear for language, which he proved by quickly learning the various Provincial dialects we encountered.

The pattern had brought me the man when I most needed him.

That night I did not waste time looking for an inn, but Rix and I together selected a campsite out of sight of the road, close to a stream of sweet running water and screened from casual eyes by a stand of alders.

With the warm earth beneath me and the familiar stars above me, the Province did not seem so alien.

The next morning as we set out again, Rix asked me, "What are we looking for?"

"Anything and everything," I told him. The words were hardly out of my mouth when we had to leap unceremoniously into a ditch beside the road to avoid being trampled. A company of cavalry galloped past, eyes ahead as if no one else existed. Only their leader gave us one imperious glance from beneath his bronze helmet as he pounded by. He swore at us briefly and impersonally, then was gone.

"What did he say?" I asked Hanesa as we clambered out of the ditch, wiping muck from ourselves. "Was that even Latin?"

"I suspect army Latin is different from that of traders," the bard replied in a shaky voice. His eyes were wide with fright.

Rix stepped into the roadway and stared after the vanishing horsemen. Over his shoulder he said to me in an awed voice, "Those horses were matched stride for stride, Ainvar, did you notice? Long legs, small muzzles—what sort of horses are they, do you suppose? And the equipment was matched, too, every man just like every other. Shortsword in a scabbard, long oval shield on his arm, leather body armor, bronze helmet."

"Gaulish face," I could not resist adding.

"What?"

"Celtic stock again. All those horsemen were shaven like Romans, but unless I'm mistaken every one was born to some Gaulish tribe. Except their captain, I'd guess him for a Roman."

"Gauls in slavery, working in the inns, Gauls in the cavalry, following a Roman captain . . . what sort of place is this, Ainvar?"

"That," I said, "is what we've come to find out."

Our brush with the cavalry had left Hanesa pale and jumpy. Bards are not accustomed to sudden danger, he told me.

"You'd better get used to it if you intend to follow Vercingetorix," I told him.

"I shall . . . if only I had a cup of wine to stop my hands from shaking. . . ."

"I see an inn ahead," I said, taking pity on him. "We can get you a drink. If it isn't too dear." This constantly having to consider money was new to me, and decidedly unpleasant.

A wall sheltered the stables and courtyard of the inn from view by the road, so we were almost at the doorway before I noticed that the cavalry company had dismounted there and were rubbing their horses' legs. Their captain was standing to one side as if waiting for something. When he saw us arrive his expression did not change by the flicker of an eyelash; he was not waiting for us.

"Shall we go on?" Hanesa asked nervously.

"I think not. I promised you that wine."

"You go on in and get it," said Rix. "I'll wander around out here, perhaps talk to some of these fellows. I'd like to know more about their horses."

Just then the blare of a trumpet, followed by a clatter of hooves, announced other travelers approaching. The Roman captain leaped to attention. Turning, I saw a mounted escort of six galloping up the road toward the inn, followed by a four-wheeled chariot paneled in leather and a second wagon piled high with baggage.

The innkeeper came running out to greet the new arrivals, almost knocking me over in his haste. He had sunken eyes and yellow teeth and was groveling like a bitch in heat by the time the chariot wheeled into the courtyard.

The leader of the escort swung his leg over his horse's neck and slid down, exchanging salutes with the cavalry captain. The Romans, I observed, saluted by beating their breasts with clenched fists.

The driver stepped out of the paneled chariot and turned to offer a hand to his lone passenger. This second man waved aside the proferred assistance and leaped to the earth as lightly as a cat.

Suddenly I experienced such an intense clarity of vision that every detail of him was burned into my brain.

The man was short by Gaulish standards; his head would not have reached my shoulder. His body was lean and youthful. A brief summerweight tunic revealed ropy sinews in strong bare arms and legs. Flung back from his shoulders was a mantle of vivid scarlet held in place by massive gold brooches.

When he turned in my direction I realized he was not young after all. Unmistakably Roman, his was a face that had never been young. He had a broad forehead and sunken cheeks beneath sharp cheekbones. His eyes were sunken, too, and as dark as his receding hair. From a thin, high-bridged nose deep grooves ran to the corners of a mobile and sensitive mouth.

He looked as if he might have a charming smile in the right circumstances. But he was not smiling now.

His eyes flicked over me, dismissed me, moved on. Restless eyes. Then they stopped. He stiffened. I swung around to see what had caught his attention.

Rix, distracted on his way to look at the cavalry horses by the arrival of the newcomers, was walking back toward me. His cowl had slipped so that his ruddy gold hair caught the summer sun. In that dusty courtyard, Vercingetorix blazed.

He towered above the Roman like a giant from some superior race. Yet when their gazes met and locked, I, standing off to one side, felt the jolt of equal personalities colliding.

Rix jutted his jaw beneath his golden beard. The Roman sniffed the air with his aquiline nose like an animal scenting an enemy.

I had seen two stallions face each other that way before a fight to the death.

While my senses screamed a warning, the dangerous moment held and lengthened. I stepped forward, cutting off their mutual line of vision. Simultaneously I turned my back to the Roman and gestured to Rix to accompany me to the far side of the courtyard. Puzzled, he obeyed.

As we walked, I could feel the Roman's eyes on us every step of the way.

A man, apparently a steward, was just emerging from an outbuilding with a cask balanced on his shoulder. I caught his other arm. "Who is that?" I asked slowly so he could understand.

He knew at once who I meant. "The new governor of the Province, of course. We were warned he was coming, he's on a tour of inspection."

"And his name?"

The steward was anxious to get past me, but Rix and I together were so intimidating he stood long enough to answer. "Guy-us Yoo-lee-us Kye-sar," he enunciated carefully. "Proconsul of Rome."

Gaius Julius Caesar. The name meant nothing to me—then.

But I knew I did not want Rix anywhere near him. Something had passed between them when they first saw each other that gave me a cold feeling in the pit of my belly.

Chapter Twelve

As Caesar entered the inn, with the innkeeper walking backward before him and mouthing welcomes, I quickly collected my little party. "We're leaving now," I told them.

Hanesa objected. "What about the wine?"

"We'll get some elsewhere. Hurry now, to the road. And you, Rix, pull up your cowl and keep your face averted, don't draw any more attention to yourself."

My warning was too late, of course. Caesar had already marked and measured him. But we hurried from the place while the Roman officers shouted orders and stableboys scurried and harness creaked and the air smelled of dust and sweat and horse dung.

That night when we made our camp, I collected an assortment of pebbles of roughly one size, and placed them in a heap next to the spot where my head would lie. At dawn, while the others still slept, I lifted the pebbles and dropped them all at one time onto my cloak, which still bore the shape of my sleeping.

The pebbles spilled from my fingers onto the crumpled cloth and rolled among its hills and valleys, each finding its appointed place. From their design I read the map we would follow. The Otherworld would guide us away from Caesar.

As it happened, I could not have chosen a better time to assess Roman intentions than with the arrival of a new governor in Narbonese Gaul. The Province rumbled like a belly with rumor and speculation. I made the most of Hanesa's gift for conversation, having him talk to strangers at every crossroads and inn. The inns proved expensive, for when people talked to you there, they expected you to buy them a drink. But that same drink oiled their tongues. Hanesa talked, seemingly casually; I listened and learned. Rix devoted himself to studying the military with professional interest.

There were soldiers stationed everywhere, even in the sleepiest villages. Many were Gaulish recruits who played with the children and joked with the women, but others were Roman legionaries, hard-faced men who laughed and joked with no one. They all reeked of garlic and were drilled, as Rix commented with grudging admiration, to perfection. Every man's marching pace was the same measured length. They were as impressive in their discipline as a horde of Germanic warriors in their ferocity.

For civilians as well as soldiers, *tavernae* were drinking places, meetinghouses, dens of thieves, and hubs of information. One evening found us entering a low-roofed *taverna* of stone and plaster on the road to Nemausus. Over the doorway a weather-beaten sign depicted a man with his hand around the neck of a red rooster larger than himself. The smell of sour wine, cheap ale, and unwashed bodies flooded out to meet us.

The windowless interior contained a number of wooden tables so close together you had to climb over one to reach another. The tables were obviously never washed; only the forearms of patrons removed the splinters.

We found seats, and I sent Tarvos to get our drinks. We had changed since our arrival in the Province. Now our faces were burned brown by the sun, and we wore the coarse belted smocks favored by native Provincials. Since none of us was willing to scrape off his beard, this was not much of a disguise, but at least we did not look so obviously alien.

"Don't forget to order an extra measure of ale to take back to camp or Baroc will grumble all night about being neglected," I called to Tarvos.

A big-bellied man sitting nearby turned at the sound of my accent. "Gauls, are you? From beyond the Province?"

I nodded.

His eyes swept over us. "You don't look like Hairy Gauls. Where are your plaid trousers? Barbarians all wear plaid trousers." He spoke with drunken conviction.

Hanesa beamed at him. "Who needs trousers in a climate as sunny and welcoming as yours? We wear no leggings here."

The man blinked owlishly at him. "You like this climate, do you? You wouldn't think it was so wonderful if you had to live here. The business climate is terrible."

"Ah? And why is that?" Hanesa leaned forward with an expression of such earnest sympathy that the other responded with a flood of words. People usually did. Hanesa had a gift.

"I'm in trade," the man confided. "I do a nice little business in small pottery figures; idols, mostly, of the more popular gods and goddesses. For the home trade. I sell as far north as the Gabali, in Hairy Gaul. But it's getting harder and harder to turn a profit.

"My principal investor is a Roman citizen with a villa in Massalia overlooking the harbor; he doesn't have to worry. But I must pay bribes and hand-backs almost daily just to stay in business. Fraudulent contractors take my money and disappear with it. Craftsmen fail to meet deadlines and then offer me shoddy merchandise that even the barbarians won't buy. And worst of all, I live in absolute fear of having my personal property confiscated if I can't pay my taxes, and the taxes go up every time the rooster crows. I tell you, barbarian, a little sunshine doesn't make up for all that." He took a massive gulp of his wine.

"You are abused indeed," said Hanesa.

"Fate," replied the other gloomily. "I did not have the right parents, you see. And I wasn't born in the right place. I'm not a Roman citizen. Just a poor man struggling to make a living . . ." His body heaved and let out a mighty belch.

My intuition told me he had reached that state of drunkenness when a man still knows what he is saying but no longer cares. I signaled Hanesa with my eyes. The bard leaned even closer to our new acquaintance and, through skillful questioning, uncovered a treasure trove of information while I listened.

The man's name was Manducios, and he was of mixed blood, claiming Hellenes and Celtiberians among his ancestors. "In the

Province grapes from many vineyards are emptied into one vat," he explained.

He said that the already ruinous local taxes had recently been raised again to support the expanding military force. A new cavalry was being drafted from among the Narbonese Gauls, and additional soldiers—with insatiable appetites, according to Manducios—were being quartered on local people.

"Why so many soldiers in a land at peace?" Hanesa inquired.

Manducios ran a finger up one nostril, probed, withdrew the finger, examined it, then wiped it on his chest. "We're at peace now but no one expects it to last. Peace isn't profitable, and Caesar needs money."

At the mention of Caesar, I saw from the corner of my eye that Rix, who usually sat quiet through such conversations, suddenly straightened and fixed his hooded gaze on Manducios. "I thought the man called Caesar was a proconsul of Rome. Surely such officials are not impoverished."

The trader barked a cynical laugh. "Let me tell you about Gaius Caesar. My principal knows his family well. They were of equestrian rank and Caesar was born to the patrician class, the aristocracy of Rome. But from the beginning of his career he made a point of associating himself with the commoners, the plebeians. There are more of them, of course, and thus he was able to build a large base of popular support.

"With his military background he also had the support of the fighting class, and was able to get himself appointed to Iberia at the time of the last Celtiberian uprising there. He was no indoor bureaucrat; he was personally responsible for leading Rome's armies to a great victory in Iberia that forced the rebels to submit once and for all after years of resistance.

"Caesar went back to Rome in triumph, enriched with the spoils of the Iberian campaign. With money to spend in the right places he was able to form Rome's current ruling coalition with another general, Pompey, and an extremely wealthy merchant, a man called Crassus, who owns part of every warehouse and whorehouse in Rome. Their official title is the First Triumvirate."

I had to ask, "How could three men rule together? If any tribe in free Gaul had three kings they would pull it apart in three separate directions."

Manducios rolled his eyes toward me and took another drink.

"You're right, barbarian, it's a difficult situation. The three of them constantly struggle for power among themselves. In order to hold his own, Caesar originally spent lavishly, using the Iberian profits to create an air of personal magnificence, and showering the plebeians with gifts to keep their favor. Like my own paying of bribes, really, but on a higher level. Everyone does it. Everyone must," the trader said gloomily.

He went on. "According to rumor, Caesar was on the brink of impoverishment when he persuaded the Senate to award him a ripe plum, the governorship of the Province. He needs money and he means to get it in Gaul."

"But how? through continually raising the taxes? He will strangle the very horse he rides," I said.

"Not taxes; war! The surest way for Caesar to acquire another fortune is to mobilize the armies that the Senate has put under his command. Win or lose, armies in the field take plunder, and the cream of the plunder rises to the top. To the generals. Caesar is a superb general. Some claim he's better than Pompey."

"So he will start a war?"

Manducios pursed his lips and eyed his empty cup. I quickly signaled to Tarvos to have it refilled. "He can't just go off and start a war because he wants one," the trader explained. "He is answerable to the Senate in Rome, and the Senate won't sanction a war without some sort of justification. War must appear to be necessary for the welfare of Rome, not just to enrich an individual."

Recalling the history Menua had taught me, I nodded. I could not resist showing off my knowledge to this Provincial who kept calling us "barbarians"—which as I knew and he apparently did not was no more than a Greek word for people who did not speak Greek. Which I could, if necessary. By this time, I had drunk quite a lot of wine myself. "The Roman legions," I said, "were sent to Iberia originally when Hannibal of Carthage was at war with Rome. Hannibal had bases in Iberia and the legions were sent to destroy them, then stayed to establish colonies. Rome subsequently annexed the Province because Narbonese Gaul is the land link between Latium and her Iberian colonies. Justification!"

Manducios squinted suspiciously. "How do you know so much?"

Close your mouth, my head warned me. Druids are not welcome in the Province now, the official religion of Rome condemns them.

Hanesa rescued me. "We learn from listening to traders," he said quickly. "Traders know everything."

Manducios was drunk enough to be easily mollified. He looked around blearily; I signaled Tarvos to get him a fresh drink. When he had downed half of it, I murmured, "You were saying? About Caesar? As you can tell, I am always anxious to learn."

"Eh? Oh. Him. The new governor. I can tell you this: If he could lead a victorious army in this part of the world like the one he led in Iberia, he could go back to Rome with enough loot to put even Crassus in the shade. He might even be able to get the Senate to name him sole consul."

Rix spoke up. "To have a war you must have an enemy. Who—"

At this moment a party of Roman officers entered the *taverna*. Talk stopped. Men huddled over their cups and kept their eyes lowered until the Romans had demanded and received the best wine the establishment had to offer. Then the officers arrogantly annexed for themselves the table nearest the door.

Talk resumed, but there was a guarded quality that had not been there before. Rightly deducing we would get little more from Manducios, I ordered enough additional wine for him to cloud his memories of us, and we left.

The eyes of the Romans followed Rix as we passed their table. Even in common garb he had a warrior's style that they recognized and admired instinctively.

Vercingetorix always seemed to have a fire smoldering in him.

We traveled farther, we listened and learned more. Rix was an excellent companion, but was proving to be something of a handicap. When he was not scrutinizing the military, he was scrutinizing the local women, and they him. He might be a barbarian, but obviously they found him gorgeous. More often than I liked, Tarvos and I had to reclaim him from beds in situations that might have proved embarrassing or even dangerous.

As we made our way southward, one of Rix's women was the wife of a prosperous olive oil merchant. Considerable ingenuity was involved in having Tarvos and Hanesa sneak a reluctant Rix out the back of the merchant's large house while I, at the front, persuaded the merchant I had come all the way from Hairy Gaul just to purchase some of his wares.

He was both flattered and suspicious. "I find it difficult to believe that my oil, fine as it is, is known as far north as the land of the . . . what did you say your tribe was?"

"The Carnutes."

"Yes, the Carnutes. I do considerable trade with the Aedui, of course, but . . . how much did you say you were interested in contracting for?"

"I didn't say, not yet." He was looking at me intently; I concentrated on imagining myself a trader, my spirit a trader's spirit, and felt my flesh re-forming in that particular combination of affability and avarice I had observed among the breed. "It depends on the quality and how soon you could ship it north. Olive oil is perishable and the summer is hot."

We were standing on the long terrace fronting his sprawling white villa. Beyond a riot of flowers I could see a roadway curving behind the house. Out of the corner of my eye I kept watching for Rix and the others to retreat down that road.

"Our oil is bottled in stone and stoppered with the best cork," the oil merchant was saying. "It will stay good indefinitely and I can ship within fourteen days. Or perhaps you would prefer to take it with you?"

"Mmmm." I pretended to be considering. No sign of Rix making his escape. How long could I keep the man distracted? "Did you say you do business with the Aedui?"

"I have a customer among them who has pronounced our oil the finest available. He's been responsible for a lot of business coming my way."

Some intuition nudged me. "Who is this man? Would he vouch for you to our tribe?"

"No Gaul would doubt his word," came the confident reply. "He is Diviciacus, vergobret of the Aedui."

Vergobret was the title the Aeduans gave their chief judge or magistrate, a person of analogous position to our Dian Cet. Such an individual was of course a druid, and his word was beyond question.

My intuition had served me well. The unexpected connection between an Aeduan vergobret and a Provincial oil merchant was intriguing. I probed further, and the merchant, sensing a sale, obliged by being talkative.

He explained that though official policy had made druids persona non grata in Narbonese Gaul, Diviciacus had managed to acquire Roman friends. He had done this by repeatedly urging closer ties between his people and Latium—the opposite of Menua's attitude. Diviciacus liked Roman luxuries.

The vergobret was brother to an Aeduan prince, Dumnorix, with whom he was engaged in an exceptionally bitter brotherly feud. "Dumnorix wants to be king of the tribe," the merchant explained, "and to aid him in this ambition has swelled the ranks of his personal warriors by forming a military alliance with the neighboring Sequani."

The Sequani! Briga's tribe, overrun by Germanic invaders . . .

The merchant was saying, "Diviciacus responded by asking me to arrange for him to appear before the Roman Senate. I was happy to do so, he's a valued customer. I not only got him an audience with the Senate but with the great orator Cicero himself, who was much impressed with him.

"Diviciacus petitioned the Roman Senate to support him against the ambitions of his brother, whom he claimed would be a bad king because he was too much under the Germanic influence permeating the Sequani. But the Senate refused the petition. They said the quarrel between Diviciacus and Dumnorix was an internal and tribal affair and did not involve Rome's interests.

"I suppose they were right," the man added. "What happens in the tribes of Hairy Gaul is really no concern of ours. Those people have always fought one another and always will, they're only savages."

He realized too late that he had overstepped himself. "I don't mean men like yourself, of course!" he said hastily. But from the corner of my eye I had just seen three familiar figures hurrying down the road away from the villa. Drawing myself up into a tower of white-lipped outrage, I said coldly, "If that is how you feel, I can find someone else to provide us savages with oil at a premium price."

I shook my leather purse in his face and left.

Once we were safely back in camp together, well off the main roads, I gave Rix an overdue lecture about his reckless womanizing. His appetite was insatiable. He paid little attention, no doubt dreaming, even while I was talking, about his next conquest.

I was thinking on another level myself. Examining the new
information I had received in the light of Caesar's reputed ambition,
I could almost see the shape of the future.

Leading my band onward, I continued exploring, observing,
learning.

Southern Gaul was rich land. The climate was mild, the soil
welcomed the seed. Roman roads provided a reliable network between farms and towns and ports, so there was a constant movement of goods. For a price you could buy anything; we tasted fruits
and sweetmeats and fishes we had never known existed.

For a price.

Everything in the Province had a price to be paid in the coin
of Rome.

The land was bounteous, yet the farther we traveled the more
I realized the true, unacknowledged poverty of Narbonese Gaul.
Set amid flower-perfumed gardens with sparkling fountains, the
villas of wealthy Romans were scattered across the hillsides of the
Province like jewels flung from a careless hand. But their beauty
was maintained, like the flow of goods along the roads, by the
unremitting toil of people who owned nothing—the native population.

In free Gaul we had three principal classes of society, though
there was a certain overlapping: the druids, the warrior aristocracy,
and the common class, freemen who farmed the land and made
the tools and weapons and built the forts and lodges.

Free men.

Bondservants were not unknown among us, because there will
always be men who find themselves indebted to someone more
prudent and have to serve him for a time in order to clear the debt.
But even our bondservants were not slaves; were never slaves.
Their period of service had an end; they remained, essentially,
free.

In Narbonese Gaul the Romans had suppressed the druids, slain
the nobles, and reduced the entire population to the rank of common class with neither its dignity nor its freedom. Those who were
not outright slaves to be bought and sold like cattle were little
better off, since they were constantly reminded of their inferior
position. They were tolerated only so long as they produced for
Rome.

The labors of the southern Gauls, whose tribeland this had been, were now a sacrifice poured into the voracious maw of their conquerors.

There were lessons to be learned here.

Under Roman tutelage, the people of the Province grew row upon row of grapevines in soil we would have considered useless, thus turning it to a profit. The wines they produced were not as good as the wines of Latium, according to the Romans living in the region, but those same Romans sold Provincial wine to the tribes of free Gaul and represented it as the drink of the gods.

For a long time we had believed them; it had become our principal import.

I wondered if the wild vines that flourished in the valley of the Liger might not produce an even better wine, if properly cultivated.

We began visiting vineyards and vintners. Hanesa elicited information about the techniques of vinegrowing and winemaking; I listened. Under the guise of prospective purchasers, we were welcomed everywhere.

From an old man who had spent his life cultivating the grape I learned more than the art of winemaking. He was delighted when we appeared on his doorstep, claiming we were representing "northern princes" interested in making a new trading connection for their wine supplies. He insisted on personally showing us around his vineyard, an invitation I accepted gladly.

A leathery-skinned, wizened old fellow with hands as gnarled as his vines, he had us examine the stakes, showed us how the vines were pruned, bade us taste both the grape and the soil from which it grew. "The soil must be thin and dry," he explained. "The rain that makes heavy fruit makes sour wine. A bright, hot summer makes small, sweet grapes that taste like honey—here, taste these."

I savored the grapes appreciatively. And wondered, as I put a few grains of the soil to my tongue, if there was a bit of druid in the old man somewhere.

Later we sat in his paved courtyard overlooking the vineyard and haggled over prices I had no intention of paying. Hanesa enlivened the conversation with anecdotes that made the old man laugh. "I haven't enjoyed myself so much in a year," he admitted. "Not since I lost the Arvernian contract, actually. That hurt my business."

"What Arvernian contract?" I asked, feeling a prickle run down my spine.

"A prince of that tribe, a man called Celtillus, had been buying my wine for years, quite a sizable order. Then he was involved in a struggle for power within the tribe and was killed. Rather ironically, it was our own governor, very newly arrived at the time, who is whispered to have been responsible. So I have little to thank Caesar for," he added with some bitterness.

"*Caesar* was responsible?" I repeated tensely.

A flicker of alarm crossed the old man's face, as if afraid he had said too much. I concentrated my entire mind, enveloping him in a cloud of calm until he visibly relaxed. "Not personally," he said. "But Caesar gave the order that resulted in the man's death. It seems Caesar was supporting the other side. He's made all sorts of connections among the barbarians, I can't think why."

"What others, do you know?"

The old man scratched his head. "I think there is an Aeduan druid called . . . Divicus?"

"Diviciacus," I said.

"Yes, that's the one. He was thrown out of Rome for trying to enlist the support of the Senate against his own brother, but Caesar no sooner arrived to take up the governorship than he invited this Diviciacus to his palace at Narbo and made overtures of friendship. I thought at the time, and still think, that it was strange for the governor of the Province to involve himself so intimately in the affairs of barbarians. We have enough trouble here to keep him occupied; he could do something about the taxes, for example. You would not believe what I have to pay!"

Hanesa murmured sympathetically and led the old man into a recital of his troubles, while I sat with a half-smile frozen on my face and watched the pattern take its final shape in my head.

I was thankful we had not brought Tarvos and Rix with us because they would have spoiled our benign image as trade ambassadors. If Rix had heard what I just did, he would have been impossible to control.

So Caesar had been behind the murder of Celtillus! I decided he must have made a study of Gaulish affairs well before arriving in the Province. How cleverly he had established himself as an ally to two of the most powerful men in Gaul, the king of the Arverni and the chief judge of the Aedui.

Thinking further, I saw what Caesar must have foreseen. Given the Gaulish nature, sooner or later one or the other would find his people involved in a war. What could be more natural than to call upon the new and powerful ally, Caesar, for aid?

Then Caesar's armies would march into free Gaul by invitation, looting and plundering, enriching their commander. When the war was over the warriors would stay, because that was the Roman pattern. They would marry local women, build homes, and Rome would announce that Gaul was now Roman territory by right of occupancy.

A chill ran from my head to my belly. Like a spider, Caesar had spun his web to entrap free Gaul while most of us were unaware of his presence.

Chapter Thirteen

At THE time I thought Caesar more calculating than any druid. The genius of his plan, as I had pieced it together, alarmed me.

But the passage of time has taught me not to be so quick to credit any man with infallibility. No matter how shrewd the scheme beforehand, in practice the outcome of almost any venture is determined by a combination of the inevitable and the unexpected. The Otherworld provides the unexpected.

Afterward, when all is resolved and the tangled threads unraveled to their beginning, historians like to attribute success to the brilliant planning of the winner. But the truth is, there is usually less contemplation than inspiration behind any victory.

I know.

I wanted to hurry back to Menua and tell him what I had learned. He alone would know how to combat the schemes of the Roman. The power and support of the Otherworld must be enlisted, of course, and Gaul would need all its strength to withstand the mighty armies at Roman disposal.

All its strength . . .

The dream Rix had inherited from the murdered Celtillus did not seem so foolish after all. Unity was desperately needed in Gaul. How could any one tribe hope to resist an army that conquered and subjugated entire lands?

As soon as Hanesa and I had rejoined the others, I announced, "We're heading for home."

Rix raised one golden eyebrow. "So abruptly? Why?"

"I have to talk to Menua. I'll tell you about it on the way, since it very much concerns you, I think."

To my surprise, I discovered that part of me was reluctant to leave the Province. I had learned what I came for, and more, but the lure of the unknown was still around the bend of every road. New sights, new scents, new sounds . . .

I wanted to lie among the vines and listen to their song.

The place was dangerously seductive. I turned my face resolutely northward and herded my charges toward home.

As we traveled, I told Rix what I had learned, and what I surmised. He was furious at first, then a deadly coldness came over him that would have frightened me all the more were I his enemy.

"Caesar," he said. That was all he said. "Caesar."

He walked beside me like a great gleaming spear, and I knew we had, in him, the weapon to use against the Roman. Men would follow Vercingetorix. Even the kings of other tribes must surely see his splendor, and want to fight beside him. . . .

We stopped in the market square of a Provincial town to have our sandals repaired before we began making our way northward, and amid cages of songbirds imported from the shores of the Mediterranean, my druid hearing heard one woman say to another, "My daughter has been receiving flattering attentions from that Roman officer; you know the one."

"Really?"

"Oh yes!" the first woman boasted. "She might be the wife of a Roman citizen someday."

"Has he asked to marry her?"

"Not yet. But he comes to her almost every day. He's told her that the governor is very concerned about what he calls increasing German incursions into Hairy Gaul. Germans so close to the borders of the Province are a threat to our peace and could hinder trade. My daughter's friend says his legion could be sent into Hairy Gaul at almost any time."

"Your daughter's friend," the other woman observed, "is telling
a tale to enlist her pity so he can sleep with her. I heard that story
myself when I was young. 'I'm off to fight and die,' they say. 'Be
kind to me.' Tell her not to believe him."

But I, overhearing, believed.

The Germans were Caesar's chosen enemy.

Before leaving the marketplace I waited until no one was looking,
then opened the doors of the birdcages. Those trapped little song-
sters had suffered a crime against nature. "Go quickly," I whispered
to them. "You are free persons."

They understood; animals always understand druids. Suddenly
the air was filled with a rainbow of wings and my heart flew with
them.

In the confusion that followed we left the town very quickly.

Back on the road, I told Rix, "I think we can expect Caesar to
enter free Gaul at almost any time."

Walking provides an excellent opportunity to think. I had
learned not to listen to the almost constant monologue from Hanesa
the Talker. I walked cocooned in a druidic silence, communing
with my head.

Diviciacus had strongly objected to the German alliances of his
brother Dumnorix. And Diviciacus had made himself a friend of
Caesar's. And Caesar had chosen the Germans as the enemies he
needed to justify entering Gaul.

So simple, so clear. The only question was, what act would tip
the scale and set the armies to marching? And when?

Celtic people fought small wars, exercises in power between the
tribes. The Romans thought on a larger scale. Carthage. Greece.
Iberia. Gaul.

What spirits spawned such greed? What forces impelled it?

That night I dreamed of the clink of coins in a leather bag.

Our own funds were exhausted; they would not see us home.
Again Hanesa proved invaluable. Taking up position at a crossroads,
he began spinning tales for anyone who came along, while Tarvos,
looking bored and embarrassed, held out a basket.

Soon Hanesa had a crowd gathered to listen, openmouthed, to
the legends of the Celts. The natives of Narbonese Gaul had not
totally forgotten their heritage.

At the end of the day the basket was heavy with coins.

We would buy all needed supplies for the journey in the next town. I was infected with a sense of urgency. Even the seasons were driving me homeward, for the autumn was upon us and the light was changing. We needed to be across the mountains and into free Gaul before the weather turned against us.

I had promised Menua to be back in the great grove by Samhain. I began watching eagerly for a town.

We found one soon enough.

I did not care for Roman towns. In our travels we had gone as far as Nemausus, where we had gazed in astonishment at the Roman construction called an aqueduct that carried water into the town. The aqueduct was a triple-tiered structure composed of arches supporting an artificial riverbed. At one point this man-made river crossed a real river, the Gard. There I felt again the unsettling sensation I had known before, when I tried to imagine being stone and water at the same time.

Roman towns called themselves cities if they were of any size at all. Though they were built of stone and masonry and ornamented with flowers and fountains, they could not disguise their spiritual ugliness. There were beggars in the streets.

Among the Celts no person had to beg. Everyone earned a living through his contribution to the welfare of the tribe or, if totally helpless, was cared for by his clan. But in the Province people begged, and threatened to call down the wrath of the Roman gods upon any who refused them. Unlike Hanesa with his stories, they gave nothing in return for what they got. They were not even honest bondspeople working off debts.

I did not like the towns. But we had to have food and wine and fodder for the mule, and warmer clothes for crossing the mountains, so when we reached the next town I led my little band through a maze of streets and alleyways, looking for the market square.

We arrived just in time to see a slave auction getting under way.

The pavement of the central square was crowded with pens and stalls. At intervals there were wooden pillars swagged with chains, holding men too powerful to be kept any other way. Slavers bawled at their merchandise in a hundred tongues. Around the edges of this noisy, odoriferous mass of people were curtained litters containing the wealthiest buyers. An occupant occasionally twitched a curtain aside to peer out or to bark an order to a litter bearer to move into a patch of shade.

Impelled by curiosity, I began elbowing my way through the crowd. Rix was just behind me.

I kept my amulet well concealed inside my clothing. Not only were druids outlawed in the Province, but all towns swarmed with thieves. As if beggary were not bad enough, many men born with nimble fingers that would have delighted a craftsman turned their gift instead to less prideful purposes. In free Gaul a man wore his wealth proudly. In the Province he must hide it for fear of losing it.

We came to a halt just below the auction platform. The stench was terrible. Slaves waiting to be sold had no place to relieve themselves but around their own feet, and the area swarmed with shiny green flies as large as hummingbirds.

"Ho, barbarians! Have you come to offer yourselves on the block?" a rough voice shouted at us. I had to grab Rix by the arm. "Don't start anything," I muttered under my breath.

One end of the auction platform was shielded from the sun by a red- and yellow-striped awning suspended between two poles. Prospective purchasers milled like cattle as they waited for the next lot to be offered, or visited the adjacent pens to inspect slaves being held for later sale.

The merchandise was of every type and race. Giant Germans, prized for their size and strength, were kept in chains and shackles. A pair of dwarfs of Ethiopian origin, according to their seller, was costumed in silks and plumes and would bring the high price of exotics. Weather-beaten laborers and field workers stood in a sullen group, rubbing their calloused hands nervously against their thighs or staring out at the crowd like mindless animals.

A half-dozen women were brought forward and pushed onto the platform.

Beside me, Rix growled.

Fair women, white-skinned, blue-eyed, flaxen-haired, and freckled. Celtic women with pride still alive in their eyes. In free Gaul each tribe had its own face, and I recognized the look of the southern Boii on these women.

Stripped naked, they stood in the piteous glare of the southern light. The dealers handled them like cattle, pinching their breasts, estimating their breeding potential and more subtle charms that could bring a higher price.

"They were stolen from free Gaul!" Rix exploded. "They are free people, *our* people. Buy them, Ainvar! Let's get them out of here!"

"Be quiet, Rix! Someone will hear you. Besides, we have only enough Roman money to last us until we're back in Gaul. I can't buy all those women."

"You will," he replied in a voice so commanding I almost obeyed him in spite of myself.

"Look around, Rix," I whispered desperately. "These people are here to do business. If we cause a scene they won't thank us for interrupting them."

"You don't have to cause a scene, just buy the women."

"If I made an offer sufficient to pay for them I could not produce the money to cover it, and I suspect we wouldn't live to get out of the square. We're barbarians here, remember?" As I spoke, I was scanning the crowd for some sign of Hanesa and Tarvos to help me, but all I saw were hard-bitten faces and lustful eyes staring past me at the Celtic women.

The auctioneer was speaking more rapidly than Hanesa in full spate. I clung to Rix with both hands, trying to keep him under control until I heard the cry "Sold!"

The buyer's agents stepped onto the platform, wrapped cloaks around the merchandise, and led it away.

Rix turned a bitter gaze on me. "What good is all your druidry if you can't prevent that?" He jerked his head toward the platform.

A lull fell until the next lot was brought up. Rix began arguing with me again and I realized the crowd was turning its attention on us. I tugged at him, trying to lead him away, but he threw off my hands and doubled his fists as if he would hit me. To my dismay I noticed two soldiers in bronze breastplates bearing down upon us, looking grim. The authorities did not like disturbances during an auction, it was not good for business.

The auctioneer began droning away again. Rix was becoming more agitated. The two soldiers were almost upon us. My head presented me with an appalling image of Rix and myself, two strong young barbarians, seized and shackled and auctioned off with the other slaves. Merely part of the day's business . . .

Business!

I waved one arm in the air, trying to catch the auctioneer's attention. The two soldiers hesitated.

I waved even more frantically. With the other hand I held up my leather bag of money.

"Sold to the tall man in the second row!" cried the auctioneer.

The two soldiers halted. They knew better than to interfere with trade. Rix looked from me to the platform and back again, wearing a baffled expression. I took my first look at the slave I had just bought to save ourselves from a similar fate.

Fortunately it was just one slave. She stood alone on the platform, ignoring the jibes of the spectators. "A fine dancing girl, well trained in the seductive arts," the auctioneer assured me as he pushed her toward me.

I saw a woman past her prime. Her eyes and her breasts were tired, she was mottled with bruises, there was a layer of doughy fat around her waist. Olive-skinned, dark-haired, she might have been attractive once, but that was a long time ago. Now she looked a dozen winters older than I.

Aghast, I met her eyes. They pleaded with me.

The soldiers were still watching us. I flashed them what I hoped was a convincing smile and said in a loud voice, in my best Latin, "She's what I've always wanted." Vaulting onto the platform, I led my purchase away.

I did not dare look at Rix.

We descended by steps at the side of the platform. The auctioneer's agent was waiting for me at the bottom with his hand out and quickly relieved me of most of our money. The woman ducked under the platform and reclaimed a few scraps of clothing from the pathetic heap stored there. She was dressing herself as Hanesa and Tarvos finally came pushing through the crowd to join us.

Before they could ask questions, I ordered my band to close ranks and we made our way from the square, taking the woman with us. Rix said nothing until we reached a side street. Then he rounded on me.

"I wanted you to buy the Celtic women, Ainvar, not this, this . . ." He waved his hands, at a loss for words.

I could have wrung his neck quite cheerfully. Thanks to him we were now lumbered with an overage dancing girl and our money was gone. "You're to blame!" I shouted.

"*I* am?"

"You are rash and reckless and a danger to us all."

"But I thought—"

"After this leave the thinking to me, Rix. I'm trained for it!" I spun on my heel and showed him my back.

In return for our money I had been given a parchment scroll. While the others stood waiting, I unrolled it and struggled to read the Latin, which claimed that the possessor of the scroll also possessed one woman called Lakutu, to use for whatever purpose said owner saw fit.

The thing sickened me. I rerolled the parchment and resolved to throw it on the next fire we passed.

The frightened way the woman was cowering against the nearest wall made things worse. "What am I going to do with you?" I asked her as gently as I could.

She essayed a timorous smile, revealing rotten teeth.

When I continued to stare at her she rotated her hips and thrust her belly forward. She was old and her grace was gone; she stank of rotten fish.

Suddenly Rix laughed. "She's all yours, Ainvar!"

I called him a name in Latin that I hoped he did not understand. There are advantages to knowing more than one language.

The woman presented me with sizable problems. There was never any question in my mind about taking her with us; had we left her, she would soon have been on the auction block again. Having seen the look in her eyes, I could not subject her to that fate. But she would make us more conspicuous than ever—and she had cost us practically all of our money.

I bought supplies with what we had left, and that night we made camp beyond the town. The woman attached herself to me with a slavish devotion. When I lay down to sleep she curled herself into a ball at my feet and stayed there all night.

Rix thought it hilariously funny. He began referring to her as my wife.

"Her name is Lakutu," I insisted. "It said so on her document." Which I had burned.

I could not turn around without bumping into her. When I squatted to relieve myself she tried to wipe my backside with moss.

She did not appear to understand Latin or any of the dialects I knew. I had to communicate with her by gesture, and even then

she did not always know what I meant. She seemed unable to
recognize my efforts to push her away. I began to dread the trip
home.

"You're going to have to repeat your storytelling wherever we
can next gather a suitable crowd," I told Hanesa. "We have enough
food to last us a day or so, but we have a long walk ahead of us
yet, and we will need adequate supplies before we go through the
mountain passes."

"Rely on me," promised the bard.

We found a promising place beside a busy roadway and Hanesa
began attracting an audience. Tarvos collected few coins, but someone gave us a chicken and someone else offered fodder for the
mule. I preferred barter anyway; it was our customary method of
payment in free Gaul. Coins were for traders and were considered
as much ornamental as pecuniary.

While Hanesa plied his art the rest of us stood to one side and
listened. When someone laughed and threw several coins not to
Tarvos but at the bard's feet, Lakutu widened her eyes. She ran
forward to stand beside Hanesa, clawing her fingers through her
greasy hair. Then she began fumbling with her threadbare clothing,
tightening it in some places and loosening it in others.

People watched, elbowing each other. Hanesa started to put out
a hand and restrain her, but intuition spoke to me.

"Leave her alone, bard," I said aloud.

Lakutu began to dance.

She was too old and too fat and no luster remained on her skin.
But when she began to move she was transformed. To the accom-
paniment of her own snapping fingers, Lakutu swung her shoulders
and patted her feet against the earth. There were old stains of
carmine dye on her toes. Watching, I noticed for the first time
how small and high-arched her feet were, and how graceful her
hands.

Lakutu swayed from side to side. With a deft flick of her fingers
she bared her belly. The roll of fat she exposed did not bounce, it
rippled, revealing the sinuous play of unguessed muscles. Her flesh
undulated with exquisite control. Her feet moved faster. She closed
her eyes and began to spin, humming to herself, the tiny feet
pattering in rhythm.

I was wrong about her being too old and too fat. In her dance she revealed a lush, ripe opulence, a round richness like sacks of grain bursting with corn.

She twitched away more of her gown. Her sagging breasts had large, wine-colored nipples. As I watched in disbelief she began to rotate her breasts in two opposite directions.

Even a druid could not do that kind of magic.

Rix was leaning forward, the laughter wiped from his face. Tarvos was breathing hard and Hanesa was murmuring appreciatively, with little clucks and exclamations of pleasure. Even Baroc was standing on tiptoe, peering over our shoulders.

The natives were shouting and applauding.

When she had amassed a larger pile of coins than Hanesa's, Lakutu made one final pirouette, bent down and picked up the money, and brought it to me. She held it out in her two hands and offered me a shy smile to go with it.

None of my training had prepared me for this.

As I hesitated, Rix said out of the corner of his mouth, "Take the money."

It seemed an excellent suggestion.

That night when Lakutu curled up at my feet, I could not sleep for awareness of her. At last I sat up and took hold of her arm. She flowed toward me like water, settling down against me with a little sigh.

In the dark she might have been beautiful.

How I wished I could talk with her! But we had only the language of the flesh; our minds could not meet. With hand and hip I studied her, and by dawn I knew her as well as I ever would.

Rix started to tease me that morning, but something he saw in my face stopped him. He treated Lakutu with grave courtesy thereafter, even helping her to mount the mule when it became obvious she could not keep up with our walking pace.

Though I had admitted it to no one, Briga had frequently been in my mind. But only in my mind; Lakutu was now in my bed. I did not have to seek her out and work to win her. She was simply there, like a wife. I discovered that eaten bread is soon forgotten and I paid little attention to her from sunrise until sunset, yet when I lay down to sleep she came into my arms like a gift, and I was glad.

The act of sex did not leave me sleepy and dulled. Even without magic it burnished me. Afterward my thoughts ran clear and strong.

As we neared the pass that would take us from the Province back into free Gaul, a troop of Roman cavalry intercepted us.

"Where are you going with that woman?" the captain demanded.

"She is a slave I purchased," I answered honestly.

"Is she? Or are you trying to steal her? Let's see your documents."

"I, ah, burned them," I admitted, feeling my ears redden.

The Roman sneered—an expression that is twice as ugly on a shaven face. "You burned your proof of ownership? Isn't that a pity. We'll have to confiscate this obviously stolen property, then, and I think you had better come along too, they'll be wanting to talk to you about—"

"I think not," said Vercingetorix.

He spoke in the Arvernian tongue, but his meaning was clear enough. The Roman officer swung round on his horse to look at him.

Vercingetorix grinned.

Swifter than my eye could follow, he thrust a hand into the pack on the mule, behind Lakutu. Then, as nimbly as if dancing a pattern, he darted among the cavalry. Wherever there was an opening he slid through, and I caught the flash of sunlight on the jeweled hilt of his father's sword.

Men screamed and tumbled from their horses.

With an oath, the captain lashed his own horse forward and tried to intercept Rix, only to have one of his legs half-severed above the knee by a terrible downward stroke of the Arvernian's blade. The man fell, spouting blood. His warriors tried valiantly to continue the fight, but Rix was too agile and their efforts were hampered by their own horses; one turned left and another turned right and a third reared, blocking the way.

With a cry of glee, Tarvos sprang forward to join the attack. The mule was braying, Hanesa and Baroc were shouting, and I longed for a weapon to wield myself. But there was no need. Appalled by the unexpected ferocity of the barbarians, the surviving horsemen fled.

There had been twelve of them. Seven were now cooling meat. Rix was scarcely breathing hard. Tarvos was aglow. "Good fight!" he told me.

Rix did not put his sword back in the pack on the mule. With an air of satisfaction he thrust it through his belt and kept it there.

Sometimes action is more productive than thought. And battle can be an art.

We hurried northward, through the mountains, hoping to outdistance pursuit once the remainder of the cavalry raised the alarm. I hardly allowed our band to stop for rest before I had them moving again; I could feel hot Roman breath on the back of my neck. Day and night blurred.

Rix was unconcerned. I think he hoped they would catch up with us.

A cold wind sang through the passes, promising winter in the midst of autumn. Hurry, my head urged my feet. Hurry home.

By the time we reached the edge of free Gaul, bad weather was brewing. We were still in the hills when a savage storm attacked us with lashing rain. We struggled northward through deepening mud. Traversing the mountains had been relatively easy, thanks to the Roman roads, but in free Gaul there was no Roman road. Our pace slowed to a crawl.

Lakutu was terrified of the storm. She cowered atop the mule like a beaten dog, shielding her head with folded arms and moaning to herself. We were picking our way down a steep incline when lightning crackled too close for comfort, singeing the air.

Lakutu gave a shriek of mortal terror. The mule bolted, tearing the lead rope from Baroc's hand. We all joined him in pursuit as the animal careered off down the hillside, bucking and snorting, with Lakutu clinging to the pack straps and screaming every jump of the way.

Taranis the thunder god roared and bellowed in the sky; angriest of all the faces of the Source.

Chapter Fourteen

WE FOLLOWED Lakutu by her screaming, which at least told us she was still alive. We slipped and slid and fell in mud and swore at woman and mule impartially. At last we found ourselves on a grassy plateau where the mule had come to a halt and stood regarding our approach with the cynical expression common to its tribe. Then it lowered its head and began to graze as if nothing had happened.

At once Lakutu gave a final, piercing shriek, released her hold on the pack straps, and fell off.

Though she was quite unhurt, nothing would induce her to remount. For its part the mule would not let her anywhere near it again. There was nothing for it but she must walk with us, sodden and shivering, and we would have to adjust our pace to hers.

"At least she isn't screaming anymore," Hanesa said thankfully.

I would spare no time for visiting in druid groves. As we passed through increasingly familiar countryside, we paused to sample local hospitality, but only briefly; for the most part we hurried on at the best speed we could manage.

Baroc complained, of course. Hanesa kept us entertained with reminiscences of a Province he had obviously seen, but which the rest of us did not remember at all.

Rix needed no urging. As we neared the land of the Arverni, the call of home grew stronger in him, even though he had no idea what sort of welcome he would receive.

Potomarus might still want him dead.

"Don't take a chance on going into Gergovia until you know the situation," I said. "You are welcome to come all the way home with me, for that matter. I know Menua would be glad to see you."

"Gergovia is my home. I've been away too long already."

"I know, but . . . "

Rix set his jaw. "It's time to face whatever awaits me," he said. "I won't run." He held out his big hands and flexed them deliberately, calling my attention to the webs of scar tissue and the asymmetrical muscle development of his sword hand. "I'm a warrior," he said simply.

Now he was stone; there was no use arguing with him. I was disappointed that he would not go on with me. Perhaps I had let myself make too much of our friendship, I thought. I wanted Rix to be attached to me. Something in me longed to tame the hawk.

And that same something would not value any hawk that let itself be tamed.

So we construct the impossibilities that torture us.

"Then let us come into Gergovia with you so you have allies at your side as you arrive," I urged.

Rix grinned. "Tarvos already suggested it. He itches for another battle at my side, I think."

"Tarvos takes a lot on himself."

"Don't be angry with him for that, Ainvar."

I shook my head ruefully. "I'm not. I never can be, really."

Rix gave me one of those penetrating looks that went to the center of a person. "Friendship isn't conditional with you, is it?"

He was more than a warrior, Vercingetorix was an excellent reader of men. "No," I told him.

"Most people give their affection conditionally, except mothers, perhaps. They just don't admit it."

"And you?"

He lifted his chin and stared past me, into his own center. "I don't know," he admitted.

"You're honest, at least."

"Yes," murmured Rix, still musing. "I am that." He made it sound like a failing.

We accompanied him to the gates of Gergovia, where a surprised sentry admitted us after a few moments' hesitation and a brief conference with his superior officer. My companions and I—with the exception of Lakutu—were once more dressed in Celtic clothing, and I had the gold triskele prominently displayed on my breast. We were travelworn and sunburned, however, and Lakutu forming part of our group was enough to attract considerable attention. Those who did not stare at the returning Vercingetorix stared at her.

Rix had set aside his disguise as my bodyguard and entered a few paces ahead of us, proud head held high. I had Tarvos walk at his shoulder, spear at the ready, and though I did not know if I would remember how to use it, I held Tarvos's shortsword in my own hand. If there was an attempt made on Rix, his life would cost dearly.

"Everyone's watching us," I heard Hanesa say under his breath.

"Ignore them. Look as if you belong here."

"I do, I was born here. But . . . the air feels different now."

I knew what he meant. We waded through tension as if through water.

Gergovia was more massive and more impressive than Cenabum, but my recent travels had made me less easy to impress. I noted, with admiration, the walls and banks, the numerous spacious lodges, the planked walkways like bridges over the ubiquitous autumn mud. The smell of adzed timber was familiar, the colorful clothing of the inhabitants warmed my eyes. But fresh from the Province, I could appreciate the difference between Roman style and that of free Gaul. We were stronger, rougher, more vivid.

More alive.

"Barbarians," I whispered to myself with satisfaction.

A brown-bearded man who obviously knew Rix came trotting up to him. "We are glad to welcome the son of Celtillus!" he cried, seizing my friend and hugging him.

Rix held himself aloof. "Do you speak for Potomarus?"

The other man hesitated. "He's not here now, he's skirmishing with the Lemovices."

Rix smiled his half-smile. "So you're my friend, Geron, as long as the king isn't around?"

Geron was indignant. "I am always your friend," he said stoutly.

"I don't recall your speaking up when Celtillus was murdered."

Geron had bright eyes and the face of an earnest water rat. "Ah, Vercingetorix, don't blame me. What can one man do?"

"Yes. What can one man do?" Rix walked past him and the rest of us followed.

Geron fell in behind us. Another man joined him, then another. Soon Vercingetorix was leading a crowd.

He halted before a lodge where a bedraggled banner of yellow and blue sagged on a pole. "This was my father's lodge, Ainvar." He fingered the weather-frayed fabric. "This was his standard."

"No one has lived here since his death," someone said from the crowd.

Rix turned to face them. "How could they? It is mine now."

He swung open the door, ducked his head beneath the lintel, and entered as if he had never been away.

That night the lodge was so packed with people we needed no fire for warmth, but the women of Rix's clan built one anyway and brought us food. Warriors who had admired Celtillus came crowding in to greet his son—and to complain about Potomarus, who was proving to be a weak king.

"He loses more battles than he wins," they claimed. "We've taken no plunder from our neighbors all season. The only reason he's gone to attack the Lemovices is because anyone can defeat them."

"Why aren't you with him?" I wanted to know.

A warrior, who looked as if he had lost an ear to a sword, replied, "We're princes and free men, we follow whom we please."

"I understand, but these are dangerous times to have divisions in the tribe," I said, thinking of the Aedui.

At that moment Rix began speaking as if his words came on the breath I had drawn. He took over from me so smoothly I was hardly aware of the transition myself. "Let me tell you what I learned in the Province," he said, leaning forward on his bench by the firepit and gathering his listeners with his eyes. Then he launched into a thorough and detailed explanation of Caesar's plan as I had told it to him during our journey homeward.

Nothing I had said to him had been lost. It was all carved in his memory and repeated almost word for word. I heard the thoughts of my mind from the lips of Vercingetorix.

He put flesh and fire into my theory; he infected his audience with fear and passion. "We are free men!" he told them. "No Roman can creep into our land by cunning and subterfuge and steal it from us, not if we stand together against him. We must not be deceived by Caesar and his tricks, but know him for the enemy he is."

He gave me no credit but I did not expect it. I was nothing to these men, merely an apprentice druid from another, and sometimes enemy, tribe. But Rix was one of their own, and if he won their respect they would be his from now on.

I caught the eye of Hanesa, who was sitting across the fire from me, and knew what he was thinking. He was as proud of Rix as I was. An angry, grieving boy had left with us, but a man had returned, a persuasive man with natural leadership and the voice of authority. He took what I had painstakingly pieced together as if he had every right to take and use it for his own purposes. And I surrendered it to him gladly, proud to be part of what was being born in Gergovia that night.

The meeting lasted until we heard, beyond the walls of the lodge, the Arvernian druids singing the song for the sun.

I was so embarrassed at missing the sacred moment that I ran from the lodge. In my haste I did not listen to the final words being spoken, but my memory stored them and repeated them to me when the sunrise ritual was over.

Rix had been telling the others, "The Germans are better friends to us than the Romans."

I went back to him, intent on an explanation for those words. The others had gone. Hanesa was snoring in a carved bedbox, and Tarvos and Baroc lay wrapped in their cloaks on the floor, also sleeping.

Rix was still awake. His face was flushed, his eyes gleamed. "They listened to everything I said, Ainvar. They were impressed, could you tell? They told me I had a grasp on the situation that Potomarus did not. They will be back and bring others to hear me, and by the time Potomarus returns I'll have half the tribe won away from him, convinced that he's a dangerous fool and I am wise beyond my years. He won't dare throw me out then. If he's as weak as I think, he'll start courting my favor."

Seeing him aglow in the firelight, with his strength around him like a mantle of gold, I knew the Arvernians would flock to him. He was young and gorgeous and full of confidence; he would draw them as honey draws bears.

"Rix, what did you mean by saying the Germans were your friends?"

He was momentarily caught off stride, but he recovered so swiftly only a druid would have recognized the uncertain shimmer in the air around him. "Just talk, Ainvar. Just talk."

"One would not say such a thing casually. I think you'd better explain it to me."

"It's late and I'm tired." He faked a yawn.

"No one has ever seen you tired, Rix. You're always alert, and never more so than now.

"You had no compunction about using the products of my thinking to impress those men with your shrewdness. You owe me for that. So I demand in payment that you tell me what you meant about the Germans." I sat down on a bench and folded my arms across my chest, showing him I was willing to wait for as long as it might take. "Tell me," I insisted.

Our eyes locked. I felt once again the tug of wills between us. He was stronger than the last time, so strong he took my breath away. Before I could brace myself I felt my resistance slipping and I wanted to give in to him, to let Vercingetorix have his way in whatever he wanted, to surrender to that summoning power and vibrant charm. . . .

Druid! cried my head.

I caught myself and fought back, feeling the sweat spurt on my forehead. I clenched my mind like a fist until I felt Rix waver, then I leaned toward him, silently demanding.

He dropped his eyes. But I had made a discovery. There was a danger in him. Like the man called Caesar, Vercingetorix was inhabited by a spirit of singular determination. I realized he would sacrifice anything or anyone to reach his goal.

His face relaxed into the familiar grin. "I might as well tell you; Hanesa would tell you anyway, if you asked him. The Arverni have employed German mercenaries on various occasions for years now. We use them against the Aedui primarily. I wouldn't have a German in my lodge or let him near my women, but they're ferocious fighters."

I stared at him. "But that's just what Dumnorix has done."

"I suppose so. What matters is winning."

"Your father used Germanic mercenaries?"

"Not enough of them, apparently. And I dare say Potomarus has some, though they don't seem to be doing him much good, either. But that's because he really isn't an able warrior. If it were me, I'd—"

"Rix!" I cried in despair. "Don't you see what you've done? You —all of you—have made it so easy for him!"

"What do you mean?"

"For Caesar, you fool!"

His face was closed. On the one hand I had presented him with new ideas to ponder and a new way of thinking, but on the other I was now challenging a tradition he had always accepted.

"I want your promise," I said urgently, "that you will never have a German following your standard."

"I don't have a standard."

"You'll take up that one out there. We both know it. And when you do, there must not be one member of any German tribe among the warriors you lead."

He gave me a hooded look. "You know I respect your wisdom," he said gravely.

But that night as I lay on the floor of his lodge, my head reminded me that Rix had not actually given me his promise.

I lay awake for a long time, listening to the crackling of the fire and the snoring of the others in the lodge. When at last I fell asleep, with Lakutu curled at my feet, I dreamed again of the Two-Faced One.

As before, the figure came toward me out of a red mist. This time the faces were different, both recognizably human. One was sharp-featured and imperious, with an aquiline nose and sunken, shaven cheeks. The other was square-skulled, fleshy, with heavy features and a broad Germanic jaw.

This time the figure had two arms. They reached out, extended, surrounded me . . . I began to run, but no matter which way I went the image followed me, the mouths opening to swallow me. . . .

I awoke with a gasp to find myself, sweat-soaked, in Lakutu's arms. Clinging to her with all my strength, I fought my way back from the dream. She soothed me wordlessly as a mother soothes a frightened child, pressing my face against her breasts until at last I relaxed and sank back into an uneasy sleep.

Kind Lakutu!

Once I saw a small dog step out of a dugout canoe onto a lily pad, obviously expecting the flat green surface would be solid. At once the lily pad collapsed and the dog sank like a stone. Its head soon popped back to the surface, but the astonished creature had to swim for its life in an alien and unexpected environment.

A similar disaster had befallen Lakutu. She found herself in an alien environment she had never expected, unable to speak a word of the language—indeed, she would not even try. Yet she remained unfailingly kind, helpful, obedient . . . and I never saw her cry.

With vision clarified by time, I realize how extraordinary she was. Only in our afterthoughts do we fully appreciate.

When I awoke at dawn the taste of the dream was still acrid on my tongue. I did not try to forget it; dreams are communications from the Otherworld. And I was eager to hurry to Menua and tell him of this one.

Now it was Rix who was reluctant for us to part. "Surely you could stay for a few more nights, Ainvar. The princes will come to my lodge again, there'll be a lot to talk about. I would like . . . it would be good to have you with me."

I felt the pull, yet I could also feel the grove calling to me, the trees singing to me on the wind. And I felt a growing anxiety to reach Menua that I could not explain, even with all the tangible reasons I had. "One more night only," I told Rix. "Then I have to go."

That day I went to see the chief druid of the Arverni, a man called Secumos. He was dark-haired and thin, with graceful hands that constantly wove patterns in the air as he spoke. He was eager to hear what I had learned in my travels about the Roman gods. He invited me to his lodge and gave me wine and sweetmeats— imported ones, I noticed. "A gift from Potomarus," he explained.

When I was comfortable he began questioning me. "Is it true that the Roman gods grant their followers a prosperity exceeding anything known in free Gaul?"

I wondered from whom he had heard that—the traders? Probably. "Perhaps Roman citizens are prosperous," I told him, "but those of Celtic ancestry in the Province must work desperately hard just to stay out of slavery. Roman gods are not kind to them."

"What are these gods like?"

"Like men," I said contemptuously. "I'll tell you about them, Secumos. I visited several Roman temples along the way and had the bard Hanesa strike up numerous conversations with Roman priests in order to learn what I could of their beliefs, and I was shocked at what I learned.

"In the bustle of cities, which rats and Romans appear to love, the clamor of construction and the rumble of wheels on paving stones drowns out the voices of water and wind and tree. Without the music of the nature gods to guide them, the Romans have lost a vital link with the Source. They no longer listen to the song of creation. They hear only their own voices, so they make gods in their own images. Or rather, the images of themselves perfected, as they would like to be. Men and women of surpassing beauty, but carved from cold stone, with empty eyes and no spirit in them.

"There is a god or goddess for every human requirement: war, love, the hearth, the harvest, wine, commerce, smithcraft, the hunt . . . the list is endless. They worship each of these separately and even claim that the various gods fight among themselves as humans do.

"And perhaps they are right, for these man-made gods appear to possess all the pettiness and spitefulness of human beings. They are jealous, vicious, greedy creatures who must be continually bribed. Except the priests keep the bribes, since statues have no way of spending gold. The only true prosperity is the priesthood," I added cynically.

Secumos was wringing his slender fingers together in an excess of sympathy. "Those poor people. I had no idea they were so misguided, so lost."

"They call us misguided—and worse. Druids are despised by the official religion of Rome, which prevails in the Province now. The entire time I was there I had to keep my triskele hidden under my clothing. The Romans claim that druids worship a thousand brutal gods, each more hideous than the next—which is ironic, coming from them. They who worship so many separate deities seem unaware that we worship only the diverse faces of the one Source."

"Do they not know of the Source, then?"

Sadly I told him, "I have stood in man-made temples throughout the Province, Secumos, opening the senses of my spirit. Yet I found no presence in any of them but that of Man."

The druid's eyes glittered with tears.

"The Roman religion does not recognize the immortality of our spirits," I went on. "The priests say only their invented gods are immortal, and that when men die they cease to be. This terrible belief is, I think, what makes them so frantic and greedy. They believe they have only one life and are desperate to get as much as they can out of it."

Poor Secumos was quite overcome by my revelations. I did not have the heart to tell him any more of my sad discoveries, such as the fact that Roman priests—a name they apply only to sacrificers—have no knowledge of the healing arts. They cannot draw on the forces in Earth and sky to restore a body to harmony, nor can they find hidden springs of sweet water, or recite their tribes' histories and genealogies, or predict the future, or even open up the minds of young people to anything other than their own narrow religion.

Religion, they call it. Priests, they call themselves.

I left Secumos contemplating my words in misery and went back to attend that night's meeting in the lodge of Vercingetorix.

A larger crowd than before made its way to the lodge. There was no room for women, or even for Baroc and Tarvos, and poor Hanesa was so squeezed he turned quite red in the face as he elbowed for position between two powerfully built warriors. Stacked shields were piled high outside the door, and jar after jar of wine was emptied. Wine whose fragrance brought back to me the heady, ripe-apples-and-grapes smell of the Province in winemaking season, when even the air is intoxicating.

I sat quietly beside Rix on his bench, at his invitation, and from time to time I nudged him surreptitiously with my elbow. He would cock his head toward me while I whispered into his ear under the pretext of passing him a wine cup. When he spoke to the crowd, my words fell from his lips, and the gathered warriors listened.

I also was listening—to them.

Among them this time were four princes, men who had led their followers into battles in many parts of Gaul. They had much to tell of the situation among the tribes, and one story in particular was very disturbing.

As I listened, I could tell that Dumnorix's policy of seeking Germanic support to help him win the kingship of the Aedui had had far-reaching consequences. He had made, through the Sequani, an alliance with Ariovistus and his Suebi, the same tribe from whom Briga's father had fled. To win the support of Ariovistus, Dumnorix had apparently led the Germans to believe they would be given Celtic land.

Ariovistus had interpreted this to mean he could occupy the lands of the Helvetii, a Celtic tribe, and had begun moving people onto them.

Naturally the Helvetii resented this invasion. But for them it served a useful purpose. They had long been complaining that their territory, which was limited by the natural boundaries of the Rhine River and the Jura Mountains, was too small for their burgeoning population. Using the German incursion as a pretext, their tribal council of two winters ago had decided that the entire tribe would migrate to broader fields and more fertile lands elsewhere.

"Ask where they will go," I whispered to Rix.

"Where will the Helvetii go?" he asked aloud. "Surely no other tribe will share land with them willingly."

The prince who had told us of the situation replied, "It is believed they mean to head for the land of the Aquitani, north of the Pyrenees. There are two routes by which such a large tribe can go: a difficult way through Sequani territory, or a somewhat easier journey across the northern part of the Province."

I did not have to think for Rix now; the problem was obvious. "The Helvetii can't take their entire tribe through the Province! The Romans would never allow it, they would attack them before they ever got there."

With a sense of inevitability, I realized this was just the sort of problem the druid Diviciacus had foreseen when he had petitioned the Roman Senate for aid against the ambitions of Dumnorix.

Now Diviciacus had Caesar for an ally.

Free Gaul would be crushed between the closing jaws of the Germans and the Romans.

I whispered this to Rix, but when he spoke it aloud, the prince Lepontos, a deep-chested man with hair the color of dried blood, did not agree. "The matter doesn't affect us, unless the Helvetii try to enter our land. Which they won't. Their route will take them farther south. We merely thought you would find it interesting.

"Of course, with the right leadership we might march an army down and intercept the Helvetii. There will be plunder from such a vast body of people on the move; they will be in no position to defend themselves adequately."

I murmured to Rix, "No. They are Celts."

He glared at Lepontos. "The Helvetii are of our blood. We are not vultures to pick their bones, we shall not prey on them in their time of difficulty. Someday we might want them to stand with us."

Lepontos looked baffled. "To stand with us? Helvetians?"

"We might need them as allies against the Roman, Caesar—provided he does not destroy them first."

"Why should we fight Caesar?" asked an older man with more puckered scars than smooth flesh. "You're making too much of this perceived Roman threat, Vercingetorix. We have a long and amicable history of trade with the Romans. If worse comes to worse I'm sure we can always offer this Caesar enough grain for his army and he will leave us alone, no matter what else he may—"

"Fools!" Rix leaped to his feet and hurled his wine cup across the lodge, narrowly missing the last speaker. The wine splashed like blood on the man's tunic. "I am ashamed of you!" Rix cried. "I am ashamed of any man who would attempt to appease an aggressor! We were not born to cringe and crawl!"

Before our eyes he expanded until his presence filled the lodge. The others shrank back from him; something wild and forever free was staring out at them from his eyes.

"I will fight to the death," said Vercingetorix, "but I will never plead."

He was magnificent. I was glad I had stayed.

"If you're brave enough to fight the Romans we'll fight with you!" someone at the back shouted.

"We'll follow your standard," another called out. "Lead us."

The others took up the cry. It rang through the lodge and out into the sprawling fortress of Gergovia.

"Lead us, Vercingetorix!"

CHAPTER FIFTEEN

LONG AFTER the warriors had gone, Rix sat gazing into the flames. I sat with him, saying nothing, understanding that there are times when a man needs to be alone inside his head.

At last he turned to me. "You heard them."

"I did."

"Part of the responsibility for this is yours."

I knew that well enough. More of the responsibility was mine than Rix realized.

"They want me to lead them. They demand it," he said.

"It's what you've always wanted, isn't it?"

He gave me a strange look, one so hooded I could not read the spirit within. "As much as you've wanted to be chief druid of the Carnutes, Ainvar."

His words caught me in the pit of my stomach. For me to be chief druid, Menua would have to be dead. But that was far in the future, of course, I thought; kingship could come to Rix much sooner.

Then something like a cold chill passed over me. My head repeated Rix's words. And in them I heard the sound of prophecy.

"I have to leave at dawn," I said abruptly.

"You can't." Stated flatly, allowing for no argument. "I need you here with me now. Surely you see that."

"My first obligation is to my tribe and Menua is expecting me."

"What if I won't let you go?" Rix said it playfully, smiling, but his eyes were not smiling.

I was torn. Part of me did want to stay with him, to be his companion and adviser in the exciting days surely just ahead. The pattern had brought us together; I was his soul friend. And like Hanesa, I wanted to take part in his glory.

I was also, almost, a druid.

"If you want to keep me here now, you'll have to kill me to do it," I said.

To my great relief he laughed; light, easy laughter. "I would kill anyone who tried to harm you, Ainvar, so how can you suggest I would hurt you myself? Go then, if you must. I know you gave your word to return to Menua. But . . . will you give your word to me, too?"

I looked into his eyes. "If I can. What do you ask?"

"When I have need of you—and I shall—if I send word, will you promise to come to me and help me? I won't call upon you unless it's absolutely necessary. My head is not totally empty, you know. But . . ."

I nodded. Soul friend. "If you send for me, I'll come," I promised.

When my diminished party left Gergovia, there was a sense of anticipation in the atmosphere of the big fortress. People were gathering in knots, talking, and I heard the name of Vercingetorix. I envied Hanesa, who would stay with him.

The air was cold; Samhain was approaching. When we set out upon the trackway northward, I took an extra cloak from my pack and wrapped it around Lakutu, who was shivering. As my hands touched her, my thoughts leaped ahead to Briga.

Briga.

We had not been on the road for half a day when we heard shouting ahead of us. From all over free Gaul, the members of the Order of the Wise were being summoned to the great grove of the Carnutes.

But it was just a little too soon for the summoning to the Samhain convocation.

From the settled spaces and the private places of Gaul, the druids emerged in rivulets to form a river, heading for the grove. As we passed through the land of the Bituriges, a number of them joined us, including the chief druid Nantua from the grove near Avaricum.

There were not as many druids as there should have been, not as many as in former years. My head observed; my heart grieved. Our numbers were indeed diminishing with each generation. Was the clamor of growing Roman might so loud that our gifted young people could not hear the subtle voices of the Otherworld calling them to its service?

None of us discussed why we were being summoned early. There could be only one reason, and no one wanted to voice it aloud.

By the time we reached Carnutian territory, I was running. Tarvos and I left Baroc and Lakutu behind to catch up as best they could.

I did not mean to stop at Cenabum, but as the fort of the Carnutes appeared on the horizon, we began encountering travelers who told us many of the druids were there. "Because of the election of the king, they had to vote," we were told.

"The election of the king?" My head could not take in this latest development. "What king?"

"Tasgetius, new king of the Carnutes. That is why the Carnutian druids were in Cenabum when the chief druid died."

I stopped in the road as if I had run into a wall.

Only the death of the Keeper of the Grove, the sacred heart of Gaul, would have been sufficient to summon members of the Order from throughout the land. My spirit had known though my head refused to consider it. And now we had a new king as well. . . .

I hurried to the stronghold. The gates of Cenabum were guarded by men I did not recognize. "Who are they, do you know?" I asked Tarvos.

"Followers of Tasgetius, I think."

When I showed the sentries my gold amulet, they opened the gates for us. "The chief judge will want to see you," I was told. "You'll find him with the king."

But I did not. Word of my arrival was of course shouted through Cenabum, and Dian Cet came out to meet me long before I could reach the king's lodge. There were new lines in his face and his shoulders were stooped with worry, but he put on a smile and held out his hands to me. "I welcome you as a free person, Ainvar."

"What happened?"

He took me by the elbow. "Come with me where no one can hear us talk." He led me to a lodge used by the druids of Cenabum, and bade Tarvos stand at the door and see that no one disturbed us.

"While you were gone," Dian Cet told me, "Nantorus finally bowed to his accumulated wounds and admitted he no longer had the health to lead the tribe. A new king must be named, and the prince Tasgetius fought hard for the title.

"Menua opposed him most vigorously, claiming Tasgetius was too thick with the traders and might choose their interests over those of his tribe. The two almost came to blows, though even Tasgetius did not actually dare to strike the chief druid.

"The Order and the elders met here at Cenabum to test the candidates. Only Tasgetius succeeded in answering every question put to him, and his demonstration of prowess with arms was impressive. When the votes were cast, he was elected.

"Menua was furious, though to his credit he conducted the king-making ceremonies with punctilious dignity. Afterward, however, he went on criticizing Tasgetius, publicly and often."

Menua would, I thought. He would not take defeat lightly. Having a king elected over the opposition of the chief druid was an unheard-of event, a bad omen.

In a voice I could not keep steady, I had to ask, "How did Menua die?"

"Of a stomach complaint. He ate too many sweetmeats at one of the feasts following the kingmaking; we celebrated for a whole moon, of course."

"Menua ate too many sweetmeats?" I echoed stupidly. "But to my certain knowledge he never overate anything!"

"You forget, we were celebrating a new king. Menua had to partake, it would have been an insult if he did not."

"Yet he did not hesitate to criticize Tasgetius publicly?"

Dian Cet frowned, as if he had never seen the imbalance. "I suppose . . . of course, feasting is different, people are happy and excited . . . Tasgetius served an astonishing variety of imported—"

"Imported! The traders supplied the food?"

"As a token of respect for the new king."

A cold fire ignited in my belly. "Where is Menua's body now, Dian Cet?"

"In the lodge of his kinsman, the prince Cotuatus. Sulis is there now, preparing it. Tomorrow we shall carry it to grove."

"Take me to him."

"But Sulis must not be disturbed while—"

"Take me to him!" I roared with a force that would have done credit to Menua.

Dian Cet hesitated, then nodded. "I suppose you have the right. He left the hooded robe for you, you know. He meant to have you initiated upon your return."

A fist formed in my throat, choking me.

Menua lay in the lodge of Cotuatus. The prince himself stood guard at the door, but stepped aside when Dian Cet told him I could be considered a druid and thus was entitled to enter. Bent over the body where it lay on a table, Sulis glanced around, then straightened in surprise. "Ainvar! The Source has brought you in time!"

I had difficulty speaking. "What killed him, Sulis?"

"A pain in his belly. By the time I got to him he was doubled over and very pale. He died almost at once. Some of the other healers felt it was perhaps a twisted gut, but I've never known that to kill a man so quickly.

"Come here, Ainvar. Bend over. Use your nose."

I did as she bade me, bending above the empty shell that had once housed Menua. I could not see him clearly for the tears in my eyes. I scrubbed them away with my fist, grateful that Dian Cet had remained outside, talking in low tones with Cotuatus.

In preparation for the journey to the grove, Sulis had wrapped the body in layers of cloth painted with druidic symbols. Only the face was still uncovered. I leaned closer.

There was a strange curl to the dead druid's lips.

When I put my face almost to his, I could smell death, but beyond that my trained nose detected the faintest, fading odor of bitter fruit.

I straightened abruptly. "Poison, Sulis?"

She answered in a whisper. "I can't prove it. I can't say who might have been involved. But it took more than a griping belly to kill him, and there are many poisons compounded from plants I have never seen . . ."

". . . in places far from here," I finished for her. "Do the others know? Or Cotuatus?"

"I haven't said anything to anyone. Who would dare murder a chief druid?" she asked in a voice chilled with horror.

I did not answer, but my head knew. Tasgetius must have wanted the kingship very much, and been unable to accept opposition. A king cannot afford to have the chief druid inveighing against him.

The terrible fact lay between us like a snake on the floor. It could not be considered, discussed, acted upon—yet. For the time being, nothing existed but the body of Menua. My shocked head could think of nothing beyond that.

When I left the lodge, Dian Cet was waiting for me. Aberth was with him. Over his arms, the sacrificer held a hooded robe.

"When we reach the grove, we'll initiate you into the Order first," Aberth said. "That way you can attend Menua's funeral ritual with the other druids. It's what he would have wanted." His voice was uncharacteristically kind.

I looked dully at the robe, but it had no meaning for me. It was just empty cloth. Empty, as I felt empty. I was circling the thin edge of a howling void where none of the verities I had depended upon still existed. Loss enfolded me.

Menua was dead.

No chief druid to listen to my discoveries, to give me advice and criticism.

To welcome me home.

No Menua.

No.

No.

I must have swayed on my feet; Dian Cet caught my upper arm in a firm grip. "You're exhausted, Ainvar. You've come a long way, you must eat and rest if you're going with us tomorrow." He led me somewhere, to some lodge. . . .

Sulis came to me, I remember that. She gave me a drink that tasted of sloes, and I slept. When I awoke in a grainy gray dawn, Tarvos was bending over me. "They want you," he said.

The druids carried Menua's body from Cenabum in silence. An equally silent crowd gathered to watch us go. The new king was among them, looking suitably sober.

I turned my face away from him.

The chief druid was borne on a bier of yew wood, which the druids hoisted onto their own shoulders. Uninitiated, I was not allowed to help carry the bier, but I followed close behind it. We traveled without stopping for food or sleep, and when the load grew too heavy for the carriers, a new set took its turn. Northward, northward, to the grove at the heart of Gaul.

A chill wind accompanied us. The days had grown very brief, and very dark.

We reached the Fort of the Grove late in the evening. Menua's body would rest the night in his own lodge, and I was permitted to keep the vigil beside it.

I did not sleep. I did not think. There was nothing in my head but gray fog and red mist, and from time to time I turned to look at the quiet body lying on the yew-wood bier.

At dawn the Carnutian druids came for me first. Menua's ritual would take place with the dying of the sun; the ritual of initiation was for the morning.

Led by Dian Cet, we made our way to the grove. It was crowded not only with our own druids, but with those from the Bituriges, the Arverni, the Boii, and many others, all those who had known and revered the Keeper of the Grove.

The trees watched. How I had longed to see them again, those mighty and timeless oaks. Now I did not even glance at them. My eyes saw nothing. I felt nothing. I did not want to feel. This was so much worse than Rosmerta's death had been.

Deathteaching had freed me from fear of my own dying, but had not prepared me to have the center fall out of my world.

"Are you applying to join the Order of the Wise?" a voice inquired.

"I am," I replied to Dian Cet, but only because that was the correct form of response. The words held no meaning for me. I clung to my numbness as a warrior clings to his shield.

Among the trees the druids formed into two parallel lines, creating a passageway down which the chief judge led me. As we passed the first pair, they began to chant. The chant was taken up by each opposing pair in turn so that it moved forward with us in waves until we reached the end of the passage, where more druids waited in a circle. They were hooded, officially invisible to the eyes of the world of men.

Dian Cet ordered me to remove my soft leather boots. As I stood barefoot on the earth, it began to resound with the rising volume of the chanting.

I tried to feel nothing.

The chanting came up into my bones like the voice of creation, refusing to be denied. At last I began to ring with it too, my bones becoming a sounding board while loss and pain and grief ran through me like music. I tried to cling to my thin edge, to the safe, numb place where nothing hurt. But it was too late. I could not escape the sound.

My naked feet felt the living earth.

Tears scalded my cheeks. I am a Celt. As I surrendered to the chanting, I heard periodic exclamations of gratitude for the wisdom passed from Menua to me, and now stored in my head.

"Druids do not belong to themselves, but to the tribe," said a familiar voice somewhere nearby.

Startled, I opened my eyes . . . and found myself staring at a huge cobweb suspended between the bare branches of the oaks. It was a network of silver spun out of season, for such webs are a summer creation. Yet this one remained intact and shimmering, no higher than my head.

Of their own volition my feet stepped forward. The circle of druids parted to let me pass.

When I reached the great web, I walked through it. The delicate strands brushed my face. Menua's voice, strong and vital and living, reminded me, "Death is a cobweb we brush through; not the last thing, but the least thing."

My throat constricted with joy. I looked eagerly around for him but saw only the trees and the druids. Yet he was there! The senses of my spirit recognized him. Menua permeated the grove so totally I *knew*, beyond words, beyond faith, that he continued to exist. The essential Menua was a permanent part of the immortal Source, creator of stars and spider webs.

As are we all.

CHAPTER SIXTEEN

OF THE ritual that followed I cannot speak, for the initiation of a druid is known only to druids. Many familiar faces were present. With my numbness swept away, I recognized them and was grateful for their company. I managed a special smile for Secumos of the Arverni, who must have come by horse to have arrived so quickly.

They had all come as quickly as they could, and some from farther away than Secumos. They had not come for me, of course, but to honor Menua.

Menua who was watching us with the senses of his spirit.

When we left the grove, intuition prompted me to look back. The great silver web still hung among the trees as it had when I walked through it.

It hung unbroken.

Singing of life, we returned to the Fort of the Grove.

At sunset we made the trip once again with Menua's body. This time I wore the hooded robe, made of tightly woven fabric fresh from the loom, sunbleached but undyed. As the events of my life unfolded, symbols representing them would be embroidered upon the robe by the women of my clan. Now it was blank, waiting.

Led by Narlos the exhorter, Menua's burial rites were solemn but not sorrowful. We who did not believe in death were celebrating life. At the end we gave the chief druid to the trees.

No constructed tomb would have been appropriate for him. Instead we dug a grave among the roots of the oaks. There his discarded flesh would decay as a fallen tree decays, sinking back into the earth that is mother to all flesh. Roots would be nourished by the substance of Menua; living things would grow containing part of him.

I liked to think of Menua becoming part of the oaks.

We buried him wrapped in his robe and accompanied by the grave goods of aristocracy, for he was of noble blood. Each of us in turn placed a stone on the cairn we erected above him to keep the wolves from him. We did not weep; there was no reason to weep. Nothing is ever lost, merely changed.

The druids from other tribes would remain at the fort until the Samhain convocation, which was only four nights in the future. Our women were kept busy tending to the needs of these honored guests.

Amid the bustle, the arrival of Lakutu with Baroc did not go unnoticed. When I heard the sentry shout, I headed for the gate, only to be intercepted by Sulis. Waving an arm at the scurrying women carrying piles of bedding and baskets of food to the guests, she said, "See what I have escaped, Ainvar. The burdens of women."

"The pleasure of children," I retorted, looking toward the gateway, where torches wavered in the night.

She followed my eyes. "Who is that?"

"My porter. He's just catching up with me."

"No, not him. Who is that strange-looking woman?"

"She's my . . ." I stopped. There was no word for what Lakutu was to me. I really did not know what Lakutu was to me.

Sulis was regarding me suspiciously. "She's your what?"

"His slave," volunteered Tarvos, coming up behind us. "Ainvar bought her in the Province."

I could have killed him.

Sulis stepped back from me as she would have from a snake. "You *bought* a woman?"

"A slave," Tarvos explained helpfully.

"Go away, Tarvos," I said.

"Stay here, Tarvos," Sulis said. Then to me, "For what possible use did you buy a woman?"

"It wasn't like that, you don't understand. She was on the auction block and Rix and I were . . . "

"You and Rix bought her to use together?" Sulis took another step back from me.

"No!" I was reaching out in desperation to take hold of the healer's arm and make her listen to the full explanation, but at that very moment Lakutu caught sight of me and ran to me, throwing herself at my feet with an inarticulate cry.

With her eyes Sulis withered me where I stood, then stalked away.

I took Lakutu by the hand and led her to the lodge I had once shared with Menua. Tarvos trotted behind us as if oblivious to the problem he had helped aggravate. People stared.

I kept my face impassive, but it was not easy.

By sunrise, everyone in the fort knew I had bought a slave. No Celt bought slaves. We kept women captured in war, of course, and most princes had bondservants, but outright slavery, the idea of being owned by someone else, was anathema to a people who cherished freedom above life. Even women taken in war—invariably Celtic women, in Gaul—had the rights and status of the freeborn. But a slave had none. A slave was a tragedy.

I had bought one. Everyone knew.

No one dared question me now that I wore the hooded robe, but when Damona brought me food in the morning after the song for the sun, I read the unspoken question in her eyes. She looked from me to Lakutu and back again.

Lakutu had made herself busy sweeping the floor.

"Is that one to do my work now?" Damona asked in a restrained tone of voice.

"If she likes. She is my . . . guest; she can do as she pleases." In truth, I had no way of stopping Lakutu from sweeping the floor or anything else. Although apparently devoted to me, she would make no effort to learn my language. Some part of her mind had closed.

Damona served the food and was about to leave when I asked

her, "Do you remember the Sequani women who were captured just before I left?"

"I do."

"What happened to them?"

"They were all claimed."

"All of them? Even the one who said she was a prince's daughter?"

Damona gave me a look I could not decipher. "She was the last one to accept a man. Briga, the short one, is that who you mean?"

I nodded.

There was a definite gleam in the eye of the smith's wife as she told me, "The other Sequani women seemed happy to accept whatever warrior asked for them and settle down to home and family. But that Briga, she was difficult. She kept insisting she would wait for the tall man with the bronze hair."

I stared at Damona. Her lips twitched with a smile she could not hide. "In time Menua lost patience with her and told her if she did not accept someone else, she would be turned out of the fort and left to survive as best she could. Still she held out for . . . the tall man with the bronze hair. Until someone told her he was Menua's own apprentice.

"The next day she told Menua she would go with whoever asked for her."

My mouth was dry. "Who claimed her?"

"Someone who had shown no interest in the women until he heard that Briga wanted you, and after that he asked for her almost daily. Crom Daral."

"Briga is married to Crom Daral?" I asked incredulously.

"Not married. By the time she accepted him it was after Beltaine, so they will not dance around the tree together until next Beltaine. But she lives in his lodge and for all I know she has begun carrying his children."

Damona left me with my thoughts; doubtless she was hurrying back to her own lodge to speculate with the other women about why I might have purchased a woman when I had a prince's daughter waiting for me.

I sat on my bench letting my food grow cold.

Lakutu bustled about the lodge, neatening and tidying. I had not expected her to possess the domestic arts. She examined the accouterments of the house with intense curiosity, squatting on her haunches in the ashes to run her fingers over the swelling curves of Menua's iron firedogs. She had shown no interest in the other lodges we had visited along our way, all of which had been more richly furnished than this and must have seemed very exotic to her.

Or perhaps I had not noticed.

I was not really looking at her now. My eyes followed her, but they were seeing Briga. With Crom Daral.

My head tried to reason with me, reminding me I was a druid now, that I had more important concerns than who slept in whose lodge, that I already had a perfectly good woman in Lakutu, that . . .

The head is not always able to reason with the emotions. I sat for a long time on my bench, lost in myself, shaken by an unexpectedly deep sense of loss having nothing to do with death.

Death is a small loss. Some are larger.

Briga lived with Crom Daral in the fort, so I would see her; it was inevitable. I dreaded going out the door.

Yet I must. Fortunately, for a while I saw neither one of them. I busied myself in preparations for the Samhain convocation instead.

On Samhain eve the judges of the tribe adjudicated the criminal and civil disputes brought before them, a tiresome process that began at sunrise and lasted throughout the day. Then the great fire was lighted, the chanting began, the feasts were served to the spirits of the dead, inviting them to join with the spirits of the living as one year ended and a new cycle of seasons began.

In case the spirits of the dead were malign—a very real possibility since many living people had malign spirits—special gifts of propitiation were offered to them, and protective amulets were worn by the weak and by children. Samhain, on the cusp of the seasons, was a time of power, and power is neither good nor evil but both together, like life and death.

No one slept on Samhain eve. We were aware that the dead walked among us in the peopled night. Some were frightened, but I thought of Menua, and of Rosmerta, and smiled.

The next day, first of the new year and birth day of winter, the druids of Gaul met for their annual convocation.

I climbed the ridge with Narlos the exhorter. Sulis was avoiding me, and I never deliberately sought the company of Aberth. We, and the other druids of the Carnutes, led the procession to the sacred grove; the other druids followed by rank, according to the size of the tribes they served.

When I looked back, my heart sank to see what a small procession we made.

The need to select a new chief druid was uppermost in everyone's mind. Though I knew Menua had wanted me to succeed him someday, I was still too young, of course, and having just been initiated, I would not even be considered. I understood and accepted. But like the others, I wondered just who could follow Menua; where would we find his equal?

The discussions began. Before long Secumos asked me to rise and speak, to tell the other druids what Menua had sent me to discover in the Province. "So we shall acquire the last gifts of Menua's wisdom," Secumos said.

I reported to the convocation what I had learned and what I surmised of Caesar's plans. I also repeated what I had said to Secumos about the nature of Roman gods and the duties of their priests.

"According to the Roman way," I explained, "priests are the only people who can deal directly with the Otherworld. This in spite of the fact, as we know, that the Otherworld is all around us. In their ignorance the Romans refer to druids as priests also. The Greeks in their wisdom understood us better."

"Wisdom did not help them," remarked a voice from the crowd. "Rome subjugated the Hellenes."

"Indeed—as they intend to subjugate us. Menua foresaw it."

Aberth stepped forward. Without looking at me, he addressed the assemblage. "Ainvar has reminded us how wise Menua was; I shall give you another example. The Keeper of the Grove trained the ideal replacement for himself, a strong young man with large gifts and a good head.

"Now Menua has gone to the trees, but he has left us Ainvar. Of us all, Ainvar is the best equipped and most knowledgeable to deal with the threat that preoccupied Menua in the last seasons of his life."

My ears burned red. I gazed resolutely at my feet.

"Although it is unprecedented," Aberth continued, "I believe the pattern is clear. If, after having heard Ainvar's report you agree with me that Menua was correct in his concern, I ask you to vote with me to make our newest druid the new Keeper of the Grove."

I was stunned. The blankness of the faces turned toward Aberth told me the other druids were equally astonished. Then one by one those faces turned and looked at me. I felt the judgmental weight of their eyes. Enhanced by the power of the grove, trained senses of the spirit probed me, examining and measuring, assessing my weaknesses. I stood naked before the Order of the Wise.

"Leave us, Ainvar," said Dian Cet. "We must discuss this."

But I am not ready! I wanted to protest. Things are happening too fast, this is not what I expected, you do not understand how ill-prepared I am. . . .

Suddenly I had a mental image of Rix at the moment the Arvernians shouted that he should lead them. Was that what he had felt, that terrible sense of being pulled into deep and swirling waters?

My mouth did not open; I said nothing. I let someone escort me beyond the trees, and there I sat down on a rock and gazed at the vault of the sky, trying to be quiet inside myself.

Is this your desire? I asked the Source.

The sky stared back at me, one fierce blue eye, watching.

Occasionally the wind brought me the sound of raised voices. Sometimes there was shouting. The decision was not being made easily.

In my lifetime no Keeper of the Grove had been elected; I did not know what form the day might take. Each tribe's druids elected their own chief, of course, but he who was Keeper of the Sacred Grove of the Carnutes was principal druid of Gaul. I found it hard to believe they would give the responsibility to a man who had not survived at least thirty winters.

I heard more shouting. For one wild moment I imagined sneaking back and spying on the druidic deliberations as I had once spied on the secret ritual for killing winter. No! my head chided me. Such behavior would be unseemly in a man being considered as Keeper of the Grove.

Keeper of the Grove. A sense of unreality swept over me, and I sat weaving my fingers into shapes, uncertain what I should think or feel. Was it like this for you, Menua, I wondered, when it came to you?

Why did I never think to ask you?

A final shout, then silence. A long, long silence.

"We are ready for you," a familiar voice whispered harshly in my ear. I looked up into the face of the sacrificer.

Aberth led me back to the grove. The waiting druids had raised their hoods; their faces were hidden from me. No one spoke, or even acknowledged my presence. Aberth guided me to the stone of sacrifice. There Dian Cet met me and moved to stand behind me, putting his hands on my shoulders.

The druids threw back their hoods. "Hear us!" cried Narlos the exhorter to That Which Watched. "See us! Inhale our breath and know us for a part of you! We have chosen this man to keep your grove and open himself to your secrets. Fill him, strengthen him. He is yours."

The strong, sure hands of Dian Cet turned me around to face the altar. Aberth beckoned me to lie down. I stretched full length on the cold stone and looked up into the pattern made by the leafless branches, reaching for the sky.

"He is yours!" the assembled druids cried with one voice. They made the signs of summoning, they sang the words of power.

I had been empty; I was filled. Filled with strengths and abilities bequeathed by the generations who had lain there before me. Their residue hummed through me. The day was cold, the stone was cold, yet my soul burned with ancient fire.

When I rose I no longer felt young.

That night a feast was served to the Order in the assembly hall and overflowing into the nearby lodges. I have never been more uncomfortable. It seemed that every druid who had ever met me wanted to discuss my gifts and shortcomings publicly, in agonizing detail. Since I was presumptive chief druid, the gifts were exaggerated beyond credence and the shortcomings slighted until I rose to remind the others that everything must be kept in balance.

This elicited another round of praise. "Wise head!" many applauded.

I sat down and stared into my cup. At the conclusion of the feast, we offered the remnants to fire and water and the four winds.

After a sleepless night, I went to my inauguration in the dawn light. No time could be wasted, the Order must not be left headless.

The rite that would make me chief druid of the Carnutes as well as Keeper of the Sacred Grove of Gaul was, as the most important things are, very simple. Using sacred woods of ash and rowan and hazel, Aberth kindled a small fire in the clearing at the heart of the grove. Grannus escorted me to the fire and rolled the sleeves of my robe above my elbows.

"Cross your wrists, Ainvar, and lower your arms to the fire. Slowly," Aberth instructed.

I obeyed. Slowly, slowly, bending my knees for I was tall. And slowly the assembled druids encircling us and standing among the trees began to chant, "You will enter the light but never suffer the flame."

Grannus pressed on my shoulders, pushing me down. I crouched closer to the fire, feeling its heat envelop me. Red-gold tongues of flame licked my arms; I could smell the short hairs on my forearms scorching.

"You will enter the light but never suffer the flame!"

I held my arms in the fire for a measureless time until the chanting rose to a triumphant shriek, then stopped abruptly. I stood up, dizzily. Aberth and Grannus each took one of my arms and lifted them above my head for all to see. I looked up, too.

The flesh was unburned.

A collective gasp of relief sounded through the grove. "The spirits accept you!" cried Dian Cet. The druids clustered around me then, exclaiming over the burned hair and white, undamaged flesh. Someone asked if I had felt any pain.

"No," I answered truthfully. No pain. Nothing but an intense inner quietness like the silence of snow.

"Show the trees," said Aberth.

I raised my arms again and turned in a slow circle, sunwise.

After we had extinguished the fire and smeared ourselves with its ashes, we returned to the fort. The Order of the Wise was complete again. The other druids walked behind me; none with me now.

The Head is alone.

Chapter Seventeen

"I DIDN'T vote for you," Sulis told me.

"That's all right. I probably wouldn't have voted for me, either."

She had come to me with one of the many problems that must be decided by a chief druid: whether one form of dried mushroom could be substituted for another. The fungi were used in making a smoke for alleviating pains in the back of the head. Sulis was healer and herbalist, but formality demanded that any change in ritual must be sanctioned by the chief druid.

Until these endless chores devolved on me, I did not fully appreciate just how demanding the profession was. Menua had made it look easy. I had been chief druid for four nights and gotten hardly any sleep, never mind the luxury of a meal eaten at a leisurely pace.

Everyone had problems. Everyone needed me.

"You can use these," I told Sulis, indicating a selection of dried and blackened fungus.

"Are you certain? I would have preferred the . . ."

If you don't establish your authority with this woman now you never will, my head warned me. "Use these!" I cried in a creditable imitation of Menua's thunder. I turned on my heel and strode away.

A woman cannot argue with you if you do not stand and argue.

I moved about the fort, answering questions, giving opinions, instructing and advising. Whispers followed me, but I pretended to be unaware of them. There was speculation about the propriety of my being chief druid, of course; my very age invited it.

But most of the whispers concerned Lakutu.

I understood Sulis. She prized her independence not so much for the sake of her healing powers as for the sake of her rank. As a druidic healer, she was the equal of anyone; as a wife, she would have been subservient to a man. Sulis could not bear to be subservient. Even forcing from her the obedience due to a chief druid would be hard, I foresaw. I wondered how Menua had dealt with the problem.

But at least I could see into Sulis's spirit. Lakutu's very simplicity rendered her opaque to me. Or perhaps it was the barrier of language. Though she was eager to tend to my needs, she refused to learn my language. She communicated only with her body. If I had invited guests to the lodge, she would not have spoken to them but would have undoubtedly danced for them.

I did not invite guests to the lodge.

A chief druid should be above embarrassment, but I was still growing into my office. Lakutu's presence was a source of acute embarrassment to me. I made no attempt to explain her—as chief druid I did not have to—but I promised myself that as soon as I had the time, I would resolve the problem.

How, I did not know. Menua had trained me to resolve problems for the tribe, not for myself.

The sun had been dead a long time when at last I was able to return to my lodge. Fire and food awaited me; Lakutu had kept the fire alive and had quietly taken over my food preparation from Damona, who raised her eyebrows but did not say anything—at least not to me.

When I entered the lodge, Lakutu was sitting by my bedbox. She turned her dark eyes toward me, smiled shyly, dropped her eyes. No word of greeting.

Perhaps, my head speculated, her refusal to speak is the one way left to her to retain some sovereignty over herself.

I was too tired to eat. I sank gratefully onto a bed made fragrant with freshly gathered pine needles, and I closed my eyes.

The door creaked on its iron hinges. I would have to show Lakutu how to grease them with melted fat.

"Ainvar?"

I sighed. "Come, Tarvos."

He had fallen into the habit of looking in on me every night, to see if I required anything before he took his own rest. It was not customary for a chief druid to have a warrior as an attendant—but neither had a chief druid ever had a female slave in his lodge before.

I could only trust that these breaks with tradition were in accordance with an aspect of the pattern I did not yet understand.

Tarvos sauntered into the lodge, peering into the pot and helping himself to some food before sitting down cross-legged by the fire. "Is there something I can do for you?"

"No. Yes." Images flitted behind my closed eyes. Sulis. Lakutu. Aloud I said, "Tarvos, have you seen Crom Daral's new woman since we've been back?"

He chuckled. "The one who was waiting for you?"

I raised on one elbow to look at him. "You know about that?"

"Everyone knows about it. She made herself a storm center when she found out you were going to be a druid, they say. She yelled, she threw things. Apparently everyone was concerned; she was making us look bad. When one tribe takes a nobly born woman from another and then cannot find a home for her, it reflects badly on the tribe."

"But Crom Daral took her."

"He did. I pity him, a woman who yells." Tarvos devoted his attention to a hunk of stewed meat.

"Have you seen her?"

"I'm not certain, I don't know what she looks like. I've heard him boasting, of course."

I sat up on my bed. "Boasting of what?"

"She turned out to be something of a surprise. During the harvest festival, that little blind boy who is always wandering away from his mother stumbled into Briga and she picked him up. When she realized he could not see, she began to cry. Her tears fell on the boy's upturned face, and the next day he began to see light. Now they say he can recognize faces."

"*Briga?*"

"Briga the Sequanian. Crom Daral's woman. Sulis was so impressed she wanted to take her as an apprentice, but the woman will have nothing to do with druidry. Crom boasts of her, though. Probably the first thing in his life he's ever had to boast about."

Tarvos rose, stretched, helped himself to another piece of meat without waiting for Lakutu to hand it to him. The Bull took a bite, then said, grease running into his beard, "I don't know what she does to this, but meat tastes better the way Lakutu cooks it." He then consumed my untouched bread, a pot of curds, a bowl of honeyed nuts, drank three cups of wine, belched with satisfaction, and said, "If there isn't anything else I'll go now."

"There isn't any more food, if that's what you mean."

"Any messages you want delivered?"

"I don't think so. Perhaps tomorrow . . . no, I'll take care of it myself."

"If you need me . . ." Tarvos said from the door in parting.

When I emerged from the lodge next morning to lead the song for the sun, I walked into a pelting rain. I sang anyway, full-throated, eliciting half-hearted responses from people sheltering in their doorways and peering out into the wintry gloom.

When the song was over, I went to find Sulis. We had druidic matters to discuss. A person with a gift such as that reported of the Sequanian woman could not be allowed to lie fallow. We must talk to her . . . I must talk to her about her gift. For the sake of the tribe, I told myself.

Since she was an unmarried woman, the healer still lived in the lodge of her father. As I approached the lodge from one direction, I saw her brother, the Goban Saor, coming from another.

"Ho, Ainvar!" he shouted and waved. Then he hesitated. When I drew nearer, he said, "I'm sorry, I'm not used to thinking of you as the chief druid." His tone was suddenly deferential.

"Neither am I," I admitted, smiling. "Nothing has changed between us, we're still friends."

He relaxed visibly. "I was afraid you were angry with me."

"Angry with you? Why should I be?"

"For not having already given you that gift you asked me to make for someone."

Memory leaped in me. "The person I wanted to give it to is dead now," I said softly.

"Ah. That's too bad. It turned out very well, really. It just took a long time because I had to find exactly the right stone—you understand about that—and then the carving was more difficult than I anticipated. It was as if the stone came to life and insisted on taking its own form. I would like you to see the result, Ainvar, even if you don't want it anymore. It's complete except for the final polishing."

"Who said I don't want it? Show me."

He led me to his shed. There, crowded among scores of other items of his making, an object as high as a man's thigh sheltered beneath blankets of calfskin. With a proud flourish, the Goban Saor whipped the covering aside.

The Two-Faced One stared at me from blind stone eyes.

They were not the inhuman faces of my first vision, nor the all-too-human ones of my second. A third set of faces was revealed to me: highly stylized, mysterious, yet as recognizably Celtic in form and line as Menua's iron firedogs. No one would ever mistake them for the empty perfection of Rome's statuary deities. Under the hands of the Goban Saor, the stone had come to life.

"Is that what you wanted?" he inquired softly. A large and powerfully built man, stronger than any I knew save for Vercingetorix, the Goban Saor was exceptionally gentle, as if choosing to deny his own strength. Two aspects of one person.

I looked again at his carving. The thing was both compelling and disturbing. For no perceptible reason, a cold snake of fear began to uncoil in my belly.

Attempting to have an Otherworld vision embodied was a mistake. Something had been trapped in the stone, lured perhaps by the energy of the artisan as he worked all unaware. Now whatever it was crouched and waited, its time not yet come.

The Goban Saor was looking at me. "Is something wrong, Ainvar? I know I couldn't capture exactly what you described, but . . . "

"It's fine, it's extraordinary, you have exceeded my expectations," I told him hurriedly. "Cover it up now, will you?"

Puzzled, he did as I asked. "What is to be done with it?"

"I promised you an arm ring of my father's for making it; Tarvos will bring the ring to you before the sun sets. But I want the image left here, covered, just as it is. Don't show it to anyone, don't move it, don't polish it. Don't even touch it again, do you understand?"

He was protective of his creation; I could tell he wanted to argue, but I pulled my authority around me like a mantle and stared him down.

The Goban Saor dropped his eyes. "As you say."

I could not tell him what I had sensed in the image. He had made it of inspiration and innocence; he was not at fault.

I left the master craftsman at his shed and went to talk to Sulis, but part of my mind continued to be aware of the stone figure under its covering, waiting.

Once I could have entered any lodge in the fort without ceremony, but now I was chief druid. The sight of me appearing unexpectedly in her doorway flustered Sulis's old mother badly. She stammered, coughed, glanced wildly around for her daughters to help her, then retreated with many mumbled apologies, asking me to be patient only a few moments until she could prepare some wine and honeycakes.

I was more embarrassed than she.

Sulis rescued me. "I believe the chief druid has come to talk to me, Mother, not to be entertained," she said, reading my eyes.

Gratefully I took her by the elbow and led her from the lodge into the smoke-stained air. The rain had abated—for a little while—and the wind had died. In the lee of the lodge we were comfortable enough, wrapped in our heavy woolen cloaks.

"Tell me what you know of Briga, the Sequanian woman, and some incident involving a blind child while I was away."

Sulis obliged with a recounting that matched the story Tarvos had heard in every particular. She concluded by saying, "It was the talk of the fort for many nights, as you can imagine. But it must have frightened Briga. She retired into Crom Daral's lodge and has hardly put her nose through the doorway since unless she must."

"Is she happy with Crom Daral?" I asked before thinking. Becoming chief druid does not make one all-wise, I was discovering, to my regret.

"What business is that of yours, Ainvar?" Suddenly Sulis's voice had a waspish sting. "Is this another woman you're interested in —though you already have a slave for your bed?"

It had never occurred to me that Sulis could be jealous. She was a druid.

Yet, thinking of Crom and Briga, I was jealous.

"And what business is it of yours if I am interested in a woman or not?" I retorted, taking a spiteful pleasure in watching her try to frame an answer. "As I recall, Sulis, you refused to be my wife a long time ago."

"That was . . ." She clamped her lips.

"Yes? That was before I was made chief druid?"

Sulis turned bright red, an unbecoming color. It made the webbing of lines around her eyes appear white by contrast, accentuating her age.

Perversely this sign of mortality made me feel more tender toward her than I had in a long time, and I regretted my peevishness. "I apologize, I should not have made such an accusation."

She was horrified. "The chief druid never apologizes!"

"I seem to be doing a lot of things chief druids never do." I almost added, "Perhaps I am too young for the office," but I choked back the words. I must not reveal to anyone the vulnerability I was feeling, my head reminded me. It was enough of a mistake to have apologized.

Once I had relished the idea of being alone, being singular, special, beyond the ordinary. Until I was forever thrust beyond the ordinary and realized there was no way back.

"We will speak of the Sequanian woman and her gift," I said in Menua's most stern and formal voice.

We fought silently. I had won the war of wills with Vercingetorix; I would not be defeated by Sulis. As the rain began to fall again, coldly, insistently, she dropped her head. "What do you wish in the matter?" she asked in a voice gone dull.

I was sorry for my small victory, but the pattern is inexorable.

"I shall speak to her myself, Sulis, and try to make her understand about her gift. She has certain resentments against the Order that must be overcome, but with so few new druids developing, we need every one we can get. If I can win her for the Order, we shall have a valuable healer, and I shall want you to take her and train her."

"What of Crom Daral?"

"They are not yet married, not until Beltaine, which is five moons in the future. Until then, she is her own person, she can leave his lodge if she chooses."

"And where would she live?" Sulis's lips were tight as she asked the question.

"With you," I told her. "Are you agreed?"

"As you say." She turned from me and went back into the lodge.

Icy rain was running down the back of my neck. I raised my hood.

Crom Daral's door was tightly closed. I rapped once, twice, with the ash wand of my office. No answer. But smoke was seeping from the hole in the center of the thatch.

I kicked the door.

It swung inward and Briga stood facing me with a flesh-fork in her hand. I had forgotten she was so small, but as soon as I saw her my arms and my lap recalled the exact warmth and weight and measure of her.

Her fair hair was plaited into a sort of ring atop her head. A few strands had pulled loose and clung to her damp, fire-flushed cheeks. Beyond her I could hear roasting meat hissing on the spit over the firepit.

Recognizing me, her eyes widened. I thought she might close the door in my face, so I stepped quickly forward. She became very still, like a deer surprised in the forest. "You," she said.

She made it sound like an accusation.

"I can hardly deny it," I agreed. Her eyes were on my hood. I threw it back, but her eyes followed it and would not meet mine.

"Chief druid," she said.

"I am that, too."

Now she looked into my face. "And I thought you were kind," she said with a faint, distant regret, as if speaking of some incident in the far past. She started to turn from me, but I caught her by the shoulders and held her.

"I'm not a monster, Briga. We are not monsters, we druids. We protect the tribe, don't you understand that? You must have known it once. How could you let your brother's death so blind you?"

Before she could answer I realized someone had entered the lodge behind me, and turned in time to meet Crom Daral's blazing eyes. "What are you doing here!" His fists were doubled.

I held my voice very steady—but I kept one hand on Briga's shoulder, and on some level was aware that she had not pulled away from my touch. "I am here as chief druid," I replied. "This woman may have a gift of the spirit. If so, we need her."

"She's not of our tribe," he shot back. I had not expected Crom to think so fast. "At least, not until I marry her. And I would never allow her to join the Order with you, Ainvar."

"No matter what tribe she belongs to she can be allowed to study in the groves of the Carnutes with the permission of the chief druid," I told him. "We might find she really has no gift. But until we know, we want her to have a chance."

"Why don't you ask her what she wants?" Crom was looking not at me, but at Briga. "And take your hand off her while you're asking," he added. "Now you tell him, Briga. Tell him what you want to do." He kept his eyes on her, as if he would burn holes in her.

Suddenly I wondered if he would hurt her. Was he holding her out of fear?

"Leave us alone, Crom Daral," I commanded in the chief druid's voice, with a confidence I did not totally feel. "If she tells me in private that she wants to stay with you, I'll believe her, but I don't want you standing there trying to intimidate her."

"Hah." His laugh was without humor. "I'm not trying to intimidate her. She's not scared of me, she's scared of you. Of you and all your kind. You've made a mistake coming here, Ainvar, so you might as well leave."

"You leave," I repeated.

His lips skinned back from his teeth. "As you say. But I think you're in for a disappointment." He swung round and sauntered from the lodge, whistling to himself with maddening arrogance.

I pushed the door closed behind him, shutting out the dark man and the dark day. "Now, Briga. You tell me. Are you willing to take instruction from Sulis, our healer, just to see if you really have a gift? Remember that healers don't sacrifice, they help people, they save lives, they ease pain."

"Crom Daral is in pain," she said to my vast surprise.

"What do you mean?"

"His back. It grows worse each season, more twisted and awkward. Soon they won't let him run with the warriors anymore, and he's frightened of the future. Would you have me leave him, too?"

"Are you going to leave me, too?" she had once said to me, tearing my heart.

That was how he meant to hold her, then. With pity, the most cruel of chains.

But if she had that much sympathy for him, she must have a generous heart; a heart that would take pity on anything in pain and distress. "If your gift is large enough perhaps you could heal him, after you are trained," I suggested.

"Sulis has looked at him. She couldn't help, though she made him walk along the star-paths."

"You may become a more powerful healer than Sulis. Think about it, Briga."

Her round little chin set itself firmly. "I want nothing to do with any of the druids. I swore to hate them forever."

"Forever is a long time," I told her. Then a memory rose in me unbidden, a knowledge I did not know I possessed. "Some emotions can last forever, but hatred is outworn, in one life or several."

She stared at me. "What lasts?" she whispered in that soft, hoarse little voice I had never forgotten.

"The fabric that holds the tender network together," I replied.

Then wondered where the words came from.

CHAPTER EIGHTEEN

BRIGA WOULD not leave the lodge with me; the best I could obtain from her was a promise to think about what I had said. As I hesitated in the doorway, unwilling to leave her, she gave me a look I could feel in my bones.

"Do I *know* you, Ainvar?"

I met her eyes. "I think we know each other," I replied.

The tender network . . .

At that moment I almost remembered . . . then Crom Daral's voice severed my thoughts as a knife severs rope. "Going so soon, Ainvar? Couldn't you persuade her?" His eyes alight with triumph, he brushed past me into the lodge. Standing beside Briga, he put his arm around her possessively. "You see? She prefers to stay with me."

I did not give him the satisfaction of an answer, nor did I dare let my eyes meet Briga's again.

Returning to Sulis, I instructed her to begin intercepting Briga whenever she could, without Crom Daral, and urge her to train as a healer. "Tell her how many people you have helped, Sulis;

stress the joy of your gift. Tell her that with enough training she might even be able to help Crom Daral."

"I don't know if that's possible, Ainvar. I tried; I made him align his spine with the paths of the stars as they stood in the sky on his conception day, but his back refused to assume its proper shape.

"Some people are damaged in the womb or at birth, some are damaged because their bodies respond to the form of the spirit within them. Perhaps Crom Daral has a malign spirit. I cannot promise Briga she could ever help him."

"But she might. She cured the blind boy after you had given up on him, remember?"

Sulis bowed her head.

"Persuade her to leave Crom Daral and join you as your apprentice for the sake of the tribe," I urged one final time. "I command it, Sulis." Silently, in my head, I added: Persuade her to leave him before Beltaine!

Thereafter, when I met Crom around the fort he would give me a secret, smirking look, reminding me without words that he had Briga. Once he murmured as we passed in the narrow space between lodges, "I know the taste of her tongue, Ainvar, and the dimples on her buttocks."

Until then, I had not realized how much he hated me. Having acquired Briga was Crom's one triumph over me, the one time he had ever bested me. I could not imagine what he might do if I succeeded in taking her from him.

Menua, I recalled, never seemed to suffer such problems. He floated on the surface like a waterbird, unentangled with the weeds beneath.

Or did he? In my youth, had I simply been unobservant?

Disquieting rumors were reaching the Fort of the Grove. Our new king, Tasgetius, had increased trade with the Romans. Without Menua to criticize such actions, he had invited more traders to establish residence at Cenabum. Those who recalled the former chief druid's misgivings were troubled by this.

I had two options. I could travel to Cenabum myself—a common enough thing for the chief druid to do—and openly attempt to persuade Tasgetius to reverse his policy. Or I could undertake a more subtle course of action.

Menua had made his objections embarrassingly public and paid the price. I would learn from his experience. At first my planning would take place only in the privacy of my own head, and what I thought I would not discuss with anyone except other members of the Order.

Trusted members. I must not forget Diviciacus, vergobret of the Aedui. Ally of Caesar.

We must have no connections with Caesar, or with Rome.

One of the first policies I initiated in the fort drew howls of protest. We would buy no more wine from the traders, I announced. We would search out wild vines and begin to cultivate our own grapes.

"But what shall we do for wine in the meantime?" my people wailed.

I reminded them. "We haven't always had wine. The Romans introduced it to Gaul; before that we drank barley beer or mead or even water, if we were thirsty. Actually we have a small supply left, which will last us for a while, if we are frugal with it. When it runs out, the memory of wine will remind us to work together to produce our own. I do not want us to be dependent on the foreigners any longer."

"What about other goods?" someone wanted to know.

"Begin with the wine," I said simply. In time I meant to wean us away from the luxuries that were making us weak, such as braziers to heat our lodges and silk to caress our skin. We must return to being self-sufficient.

By talking with druids from other tribes who made frequent pilgrimages to the grove, I was able to follow events occurring in the far reaches of free Gaul. I was also having Sulis make regular reports to me on her progress with Briga.

"She's less resistant to the Order than she was," the healer told me. "She's beginning to see the good she might do as one of us. But every time I think I'm really getting somewhere with her, Crom Daral whines about his loneliness and his pain and she gives in to him. She says she cannot leave him."

What about my loneliness? I thought silently.

The moon waxed, waned. The wheel of the seasons turned.

Oozing goodwill, Tasgetius came to the grove to pay a formal call on the new chief druid. Neither Sulis nor I had yet spoken, even to each other, about the cause of Menua's death. She was waiting for me to do something, I knew. Dealing with the murder of a chief druid must be the responsibility of his successor.

As was entertaining the king. He must not know I suspected him; not yet. I mentally gritted my teeth and invited him in to my lodge.

His eyes gleamed when he saw Lakutu. "I'd heard rumors of your dancing girl," Tasgetius said, fluffing his moustache. "Good for you, Ainvar. Our chief druid is vigorous, eh? Eh?" He nudged me with his elbow. I moved out of reach.

He followed. "Is she any good?"

"She's my guest," I replied evasively.

"You know what I mean. Foreign fruit! And a slave! This sets a fine example for the rest of us, one I may follow myself. Unlike Celtic women, slaves don't dare talk back, do they?" He licked his lips and rolled his eyes at Lakutu, who stared back at him with the expression of a rabbit watching a snake approach.

"I approve of these new customs," Tasgetius went on, seating himself on my bench. "Your predecessor was a small-headed man, clinging to outgrown traditions. I myself am more progressive . . . like you, with your slave."

He beamed at me in friendliness. In a moment, warned my head, he will ask you to share Lakutu with him as a gesture of hospitality.

Hastily I poured a large measure of wine and thrust it into his hand to distract him. He took a deep drink from the cup, then gasped and spewed the wine halfway across the room. "What is this! You dare offer your king watered wine?" Tasgetius leaped to his feet, his large hairy fists doubled, his whole being ready to fight. The cup rolled on the floor.

I kept my voice very calm. "I drink the same wine myself, I assure you. No insult was intended."

He looked baffled. "Why would the chief druid drink watered wine?"

I bent and retrieved the cup, then poured a fresh measure. "To make it last longer," I said truthfully, offering him another drink.

He pushed it away, but he relaxed. "You should have told me your wine stores were running low. As soon as I return to Cenabum I'll send my traders to you with a new stock—as a gift from me. To celebrate our understanding, eh? Eh?"

With an effort, I smiled at him. My head warned me not to refuse his offer openly and put him on his guard against me. Not yet . . . be careful. . . .

"There is still a little unwatered wine, the last of Menua's personal stock," I told him. "I'll get it for you. Come with me and help," I said to Lakutu, leading her away from his reach.

Throughout the rest of the day I plied him with wine, dancing a complicated pattern around him to keep him from Lakutu. I could only hope the wine would last long enough to render him harmless. First it made him sloppy, however, and careless with his tongue. He said one phrase that rang in my head like a bell: "Now that we've cleared the deadwood away, Ainvar . . . *all* the deadwood . . ."

While I pondered his meaning, he drank still more wine, and by nightfall was snoring on my floor.

I carefully retrieved the cup he had been drinking from and tucked it into my robe. Then I took Lakutu to Damona's lodge for safekeeping, and made my way to the lodge of Keryth the seer.

"What do you want, Ainvar?" she asked through the half-open door. Behind her I heard the familiar domestic clatter of husband and children.

"I need you to read this for me, Keryth. Come outside in the quiet." I took out the cup and handed it to her.

To a druid seer, many hidden things are visible. By touching an object they can frequently observe past events involving the last person to use it. We are none of us solid. A minute portion of ourselves penetrates everything we touch, leaving impressions.

Keryth said something over her shoulder to her family, then disappeared from my sight long enough to get her cloak. When she came out into the night with me, we walked a little distance away from the lodges together, under the stars.

Then she stopped. She began turning the cup—a vessel of polished silver, the best the chief druid's household had to offer— over and over in her hands. Her eyes glazed, her face was blank in the starlight. The spirit of Keryth withdrew to some distant place.

I waited, concentrating on Tasgetius.

Keryth's voice, when she spoke, came from very far away. "Deadwood," it said thickly.

"Yes, that's it! Go on."

"Deadwood. Should be cut down. One good throw. When his back is turned. A leader can take a spear in the back in the heat of battle and never know where it came from."

A triumphant laugh followed, not in Keryth's voice. She was somewhere else. The being that spoke, spoke to me from the cup. "One good spear throw!" it crowed. "If that doesn't kill the old fool, it will at least shorten the days of his kingship!"

I knew that voice. If I closed my eyes I could see the large, freckled hand of Tasgetius with its thicket of reddish hair on the back; see it launching a treacherous spear at the unwitting back of Nantorus.

Obviously the wound had not been fatal. But added to all the other wounds Nantorus had collected in years of leading our warriors into battle, it was sufficient to force him to surrender his kingship. Our king must be strong and vigorous; he symbolized the tribe.

Assassination, my head pointed out, was not a Celtic custom. Ours was the way of open challenge, of testing and election.

Assassination came to us with the Romans. Its results were kings like Potomarus and Tasgetius.

I stayed with Keryth until she returned to herself. "Did you learn what you wanted, Ainvar?" she asked, her voice sounding weak and dizzy.

"More than I expected," I told her grimly.

When I returned to my lodge Tasgetius was still sprawled on the floor, snoring. I stepped over him as I would have stepped over pig droppings.

He left the next day when he realized there was no more good wine to be drunk. His eyes were red, his skin was pasty. As he rode out through the gates in his chariot, I concentrated every fiber of my being on sending him a headache he would never forget.

Within half a moon the traders' wagons came rolling up to the fort, laden with casks of wine. Wine from the Province, fragrant and luscious. My throat ached for its caress, but I sent the traders away, and their casks with them. They would report the incident to Tasgetius, of course, but it could not be helped.

We would do without what the Romans offered.

The wheel turned. I was involved in a never-ending cycle of ritual, celebration, instruction, supervision, as I strove to keep my people in balance with the earth that supported us and the Otherworld underlying all. Nothing must be taken from the soil without something being given back. Water must be kept sweet. No animal could be slaughtered for food or in sacrifice unless its spirit was propitiated first. The patterns of our existence must conform to the patterns of wind and water, of sun and rain, of light and dark. Move and flow, avoid sharp edges, sing. . . .

Tasgetius sent more traders with more wine. And a second time I refused them.

Sulis continued her efforts to win Briga as an apprentice healer. Inevitably I encountered Crom Daral or Briga or both around the fort. Wearing Menua's impassive expression, I let them see me only as the chief druid, and I would not be drawn by Crom's taunting.

Sometimes, however, I raised my hood and let my eyes follow Briga when she did not know. She looked tired and drawn; the sweet roundness of her was melting away.

As chief druid I knew to the heartbeat how far away we were from Beltaine and the festivals of marrying.

Meanwhile, Lakutu made herself as handy as a little pot. She anticipated my needs so accurately that I need waste no thought on myself, but could give it all to my profession. The only complaint I could make of her was that she refused to learn my language, but I did not have time to talk to her anyway. At night, when I fell onto my bed too tired to enjoy her body, at least she did not complain. She never complained.

The third time the traders came, I was unfortunately away from the fort. Leading a work party of diviners and laborers, I had gone to prepare a vineyard we were establishing across the Autura River. The diviners would walk the earth barefoot, feeling for the hidden pathways of life. There the bare rootstock would be planted and staked into place, then watered with blood and quickened with a ritual I had spent many nights devising.

I had lain on my bed with a cloth dipped in the dregs of Menua's wine—all that remained now, after Tasgetius's visit—pressed to my face while from its scent I divined the music that would summon the magic of the grape.

I was singing that song to the newly planted vines when the wagons of the Roman traders creaked through the gates of the fort.

By the time we returned, the traders had done a brisk business. The air rang with the clink of coins. The metallic sound was a cry of warning to me.

"Who let them in here?" I demanded of the sentry at the gate, a younger brother of Ogmios.

"The king sent them. Who was I to refuse them entry?"

I ran past him and pushed my way into the throng around the wagons, where my people actually ignored me in their eagerness to trade good furs and well-made bronzework for imported bangles of inferior craftsmanship. "Who is in charge here?" I demanded.

"I am. These are my wagons," replied a swarthy man with a professional smile and hard, mean eyes.

"Galba Plancus," I acknowledged. "I thought I told you the last time you were here not to come back unless I sent for you."

"So you did, Ainvar; indeed you did." He wrung his hands together as if rubbing them free of guilt. "And I would never have disobeyed the chief druid of the Carnutes had not the king himself, our noble Tasgetius, insisted. What is a poor merchant to do when he finds himself caught between two fires?" He smiled appeasingly and shrugged in a style more Gaulish than Roman; Plancus had been a long time in our land.

Tasgetius had insisted. So Tasgetius had finally grown suspicious; I was surprised it had taken him so long to realize that Menua's chosen successor must surely have been imbued with his teachings.

"Tasgetius says you must have a season's supply of the finest wine in your storehouses," Plancus was saying, "and the pick of the trade goods recently brought north from the Province. In honor of your position. In fact, the king feels it is time we established a permanent trading post here for your convenience."

The king feels! I hid the anger I felt at the idea of Romans building houses for themselves in the Fort of the Grove. With pretended regret, I said, "But we have very little room here, Plancus, as you can see. Our walls are crowded with lodges and sheds. This is a small settlement and we are at our full complement now, we just don't have room for you. Nor could I allow you to build outside the palisade," I added hastily, killing the suggestion I saw springing to life in his eyes. "There are wolves, of course . . . and constant raiding on the part of other tribes. You simply would not be safe."

The man's smile—almost—faded. "Raiding? I had not heard. . . ."

"This is Hairy Gaul," I said smoothly. "You know how we are, always at war with each other. We would not want our good friends from the south to be injured, so I think it best you return to Cenabum." My eyes were sweeping the crowd as I spoke; I saw

Tarvos a distance away and brought him to me with the slightest nod of my head.

"Get Ogmios and a body of warriors to escort the traders safely back toward Cenabum," I ordered. "Go with them at least a day, to be sure they finish their journey and don't try to turn around," I added under my breath.

Plancus continued to try to argue, but I was in no mood for listening. I had traveled; I had seen how effectively seductive Roman merchandise was when spread out, glittering, before the dazzled eyes of the Gauls. They only saw the shimmering fabrics and gleaming enamels; they did not see the price that must ultimately be paid for welcoming the Roman way.

The people crowding around the traders' wagons had never stood below an auction block as slaves were being sold.

I breathed a deep sigh of relief as the last of the wagons trundled out the gate. I had only bought us a little time. Tasgetius had sided with the Romans. Soon I would be forced to confront him openly—but by then I hoped to be better prepared.

Unfortunately, I let my personal dislike of the man blind me to the possibility that he might be clever.

I stood at the gates for a long time, watching until the last dust had settled behind the departing traders. Just as I turned away, I felt a tug on my arm.

"Ainvar!" gasped a wide-eyed Damona. "Come to your lodge, hurry!"

"What's wrong?"

"Lakutu's ill. I think she's dying!"

I ran.

Lakutu lay across the foot of my bed, curled into a knot. Her arms were clamped across her belly, her contorted face was livid. When I spoke her name, she moaned, then vomited a thin stream of yellow froth that smelled like bitter fruit.

"What happened, Damona?"

"After you ordered the traders to leave I came in here to help Lakutu; I've been teaching her to sew. One of the traders came to the door with a basket of dried figs he said were for you. When she saw the fruit Lakutu was very excited. She grabbed one and ate it before I could stop her. As soon as I realized it had made her sick, I threw the rest on the fire, but it was too late."

Too late for Lakutu, suddenly faced with a sun-kissed treat she had not seen in seasons, a familiar food from the south. She could be forgiven her greed, for it had cost her dearly. She had eaten poison meant for me.

Tasgetius must have ordered the traders to kill me if I refused them again.

Only this time he had hurt the most helpless among us. For Lakutu, even more than for Menua and Nantorus, I would make him pay. In my own time, in my own way, in a style appropriate to his crime.

Lakutu convulsed. I abandoned thinking and ran for Sulis.

At the door of the family lodge, Sulis's old mother told me, "She isn't here, Ainvar. She went downriver early this morning, one of the farmsteads sent for her. A man was gored by an ox."

I spun on my heel and ran for Crom Daral's lodge. "Briga!" I shouted, pounding on the door. "I need you!"

Crom Daral's hostile voice answered. "Go away, druid."

"Briga!" I cried again. I threw my weight against the door, which he had not thought to bar against me. It gave way, the heavy oak planks making the iron hinges squeal. Briga was on the far side of the lodge, rubbing a copper bowl with damp sand to polish it. She stood up as I entered, her mouth half-open in surprise. I crossed the lodge in one bound. "Come with me, I must have someone who can heal."

Crom Daral hit me a ringing blow on the side of the head. I staggered back. He was on me in an eyeblink, pounding at me. His doubled fist caught me on the side of the jaw and stars exploded behind my eyes. As I fell, I was distantly aware that he was reaching for some sort of weapon . . .

. . . with a massive effort I clung to consciousness.

Crom Daral was facing me in a half-crouch. Firelight glinted on the weapon in his hand.

I launched myself from knuckles and knees and hit him squarely under the chin with the top of my head. He grunted and fell backward. The iron poker clattered onto the stone hearth. Even as he fell, Crom twisted his body, reaching for it again.

I threw myself onto him and pressed my forearm across his throat with all my weight behind it. He bucked, writhed, fought for breath, but I held on grimly until he went limp. Then I sat back on my heels, breathing hard.

Crom was still alive, his ragged breathing filled the lodge. He would recover soon. In the meantime, I turned to Briga. "I mean it, I need you."

"You said you needed someone who can heal. What about Sulis?"

"She's away from the fort, and she's the only healer who lives here. Except for . . . will you come?"

"I don't know what you expect me to do," she said in a small voice. But she took her cloak from the peg and followed me from the lodge.

The day was dying.

CHAPTER NINETEEN

"BRING YOUR husband," I snapped at Damona as we entered my lodge. "Have him stand guard at the doorway and let no one else enter—particularly Crom Daral, do you understand?"

Damona nodded and hurried off. Teyrnon the smith was not a young man, but I felt confident he could repel Crom if necessary. Though on second thought . . .

"Bring the Goban Saor as well!" I shouted after her.

Damona had lighted all the lamps both she and I possessed and placed them around the lodge, filling it with light. Lakutu was lying twisted among my blankets, her face drained of color. Her half-open eyes showed white crescents below the lashes, and occasionally she made a feeble, retching sound. One hand beat ineffectually on the bed.

Briga turned to me. "What am I to do? I don't know how to help her."

Menua had trained me to follow him; to instruct, to inspire. But not to impart the sum total of that training between one heartbeat and the next. "Just listen to the spirit within you," I said desperately. "Open yourself up to it; do what feels right to you."

Lakutu moaned. Without hesitation, Briga knelt beside her and put one hand on either side of the woman's face in an instinctive gesture of sympathy.

Lakutu's body spasmed and she vomited, the stinking fluid spattering Briga. I smelled again the odor of bitter fruit.

Briga wasted no time cleaning herself. Gathering Lakutu into her arms, she cast one final, frantic look at me, then closed her eyes.

Her face assumed a fixed, concentrated expression as if she were listening to faraway music.

As I watched, Briga stretched out on the bed beside Lakutu and pressed her body the length of the other woman's—breast to breast, hip to hip, knee to knee. Lakutu writhed, but Briga held her with unsuspected strength.

I heard Damona return with the men to guard the door, but I did not look up; I kept my eyes fixed on the pair on the bed.

Lakutu writhed a second time. "Do you have some milk, Ainvar?" Briga asked softly.

"Milk? No. . . ."

"Find some. Hurry."

"My daughter is nursing an infant, I'll bring her," offered Damona. She soon returned with a younger woman, who stopped to stare openmouthed at the figures enclasped on the bed.

"Hurry," Briga urged.

Impatiently, I grabbed Damona's daughter and tore open the round neck of her gown. Her breasts were leaking thick, ropy milk.

I found a bowl and gave it to Damona. "Milk her into this."

When the bowl was half full, I took it to Briga. She eased herself away from Lakutu and sat up, still wearing that intent, listening look. Then she spat several times into the milk.

The tension of magic closed around us like a closing fist.

When Briga tried to get Lakutu to drink, the other woman clenched her teeth and made a peculiar grinding noise. Briga summoned me with her eyes. Using thumb and forefinger, I pried open Lakutu's mouth. Her tongue was swollen and black. Briga poured in a little milk, closed her mouth, stroked her throat. Lakutu vomited the milk. Briga tried again. At last a little seemed to go down and stay.

Then Lakutu spasmed so violently she flung Briga into my arms. The Sequanian rested against me for one heartbeat before pulling away, back to the sufferer.

Time, which can sprawl or clench, sprawled that night. By lamplight and firelight, we kept vigil. Damona's daughter had not covered herself, forgetting that her breasts were bare. The fight for life commanded our attention.

Briga lay beside Lakutu, holding her, constantly stroking various parts of her body. I watched her press her face against Lakutu's smeared face, nostril to nostril, exchanging breath. Briga murmured softly, a gentle, repetitive sound without words. After a timeless time, she helped Lakutu sit up so she could vomit again, this time with a great outpouring of stinking liquid. Afterward Lakutu slumped exhausted in Briga's arms, but for just one moment her eyes seemed awake and aware.

There was a commotion at the doorway. Crom Daral shouted, "You can't keep my woman from me!"

I heard both Teyrnon and the Goban Saor arguing with him; then a sound like a thump.

Silence followed.

"Poor Crom," sighed Briga.

The fire in the stone pit crackled and roared and eventually subsided into a lake of shimmering coals. Briga resumed stroking Lakutu's body, leaning over it and murmuring as if she were talking to the organs within. Her fingers repeatedly kneaded the soft belly, then moved up the torso toward the throat with long, sure strokes.

Lakutu went rigid. Her eyes flared with terror. Briga helped her sit up, and she vomited again, another gush of vile liquid that soaked both of them. More stroking, more murmuring. An additional outpouring of less quantity, followed by a final stream of clear fluid with hardly any smell to it.

Lakutu rolled her eyes toward Briga.

"It's all right now," the Sequanian assured her in a voice shredded by exhaustion. "It's all out of you." She stroked the matted black hair tenderly.

Lakutu did not need to understand words; the language of touch and tone was quite clear. The fear went out of her face. Her eyes drifted closed and she sank into a natural sleep.

Briga eased Lakutu into a comfortable position on my bed, then stood up stiffly, massaging the small of her back. "That's all I can do, Ainvar."

"It's enough," I said gratefully. Filthy as she was, I ached to take her into my arms, but I contented myself with standing close, towering over her like the great pine tree to which she had once compared me. "You're exhausted," I told her. "Go rest for your own sake." Into my voice I put all the emotion I could not express with words. The most important things are never said with words.

I went to the doorway and looked outside. Crom Daral was stretched on the earth—with Teyrnon sitting on his chest. The Goban Saor was lounging against the wall beside the door, occasionally rubbing his knuckles.

I went back for a lamp so I could take a closer look at Crom. When the flickering light fell on his swollen face, he opened his eyes and stared up at me. "What are you doing to my woman?"

"I'm not doing anything to her. She is helping me."

"I forbid it!"

"You can't, Crom."

"You're forcing her against her will!"

Just behind me, Briga's hoarse little voice, sounding weary but self-possessed, spoke up. "No one has ever been able to force me to do anything I did not want to do, Crom. You of all people know that by now."

She pushed past me and went to kneel by Crom Daral. "Let him get up," she told Teyrnon.

The smith looked to me. I shrugged.

Waggling his jaw with his fingers, Crom got to his feet. I thought he made a more clumsy business of it than necessary, encouraging Briga to help him. "They tried to kill me," he told her. "Come away with me now. I need you." In the lamplight he stood like a sulky child, with his lower lip thrusting through his drooping moustache.

"The woman inside needs me, Crom."

"What can you do for her?" he asked petulantly.

Before Briga could answer, I interjected, "She just saved her life."

Crom looked to me, then back again to Briga. "You couldn't do that."

I told her quickly, "You did. You know you did."

"You're not a healer," Crom insisted. "How could you know what to do?"

Briga shook her head, a small, helpless gesture. "I cannot say. I just . . . knew."

I marveled that she was able to stand on her feet. Exhaustion was pouring off her in waves I could hear and smell. When she swayed from fatigue, both Crom and I reached out to steady her and our gazes crossed like swords. "She's my woman, Ainvar," he growled, taking hold of one of her arms.

I promptly took the other; it was trembling. "She's a woman with a precious gift," I said, as much to her as to him. Then I dropped my voice and addressed her directly as she stood pinioned between us. "You do admit that now, don't you? You must let Sulis train you."

"But what about me?" moaned Crom.

Briga took a deep breath and squared her tired shoulders. "Poor Crom," she said for a second time, and though I did not want to acknowledge it, I heard an unmistakable affection in her voice.

I had misunderstood whatever was between them, I thought ruefully. My efforts to rescue women seemed invariably misguided. I loosened my hold on her arm. She glanced at me so briefly I could not read her spirit in the light of the lamp I still held in my other hand; then she turned to Crom Daral. He folded her into an embrace, pressing her head against his shoulder with a gentleness I would never have expected of him. "I'll take you home now," he said.

He led her away unresisting, we three men staring after them. The first dawn glow was rising around us, but the sky was textured with lowering clouds; there was not enough light to see clearly. I wanted to believe she cast one glance back at me, but I could not be sure.

The first dawn glow . . .

With a shock, I realized that an entire night had passed. Time, which can clench or sprawl, had lost its meaning. Now my blood quickened with an invisible summons.

After the fetid atmosphere of the lodge, the sharp, cold air was sweet. Filling my lungs with it, I began to sing the song for the sun.

Teyrnon and the Goban Saor joined in. Teyrnon had a pleasant voice; the master craftsman sang with a deep bass thunder. Doors creaked open throughout the fort. One by one at first, then in a lyrical flood, my people added their voices to ours as streams rush to swell a river.

Together we sang the light into being.

Lakutu was asleep when I returned to the lodge. Damona had sent her daughter home and stayed to tend Lakutu by herself, insisting she was not tired though we both knew better.

"Men are no good at nursing the sick, Ainvar. You just sit there on your bench and let me clean her and give her some fresh bedding. She'll rest the better for it."

Obediently, I sat. And observed, as druids do.

Damona was simply a blacksmith's wife, a plain woman with iron-gray hair and a face fissured by living. Her hands were chapped and calloused, but they knew instinctively how to make the sufferer more comfortable. A tug here, a pat there, a quick gesture to smooth the woman's hair back from her forehead; a sip of water offered before Lakutu had to ask.

There I was with a head full of learning, yet I could not have done half so well.

As I watched Damona, I thought of my grandmother and of Lakutu herself, and the little kindnesses they had performed for me, the endless givings of everyday that I had hardly noticed at the time.

They made me feel small, the women. Mine was the ministry of instructing the tribe, but theirs was the ministry of caring. I was beginning to suspect that theirs was more necessary than mine.

Humans can thrive even though they are ignorant. But they will wither if they are not cherished.

When Damona began dropping things, I insisted she go home.

Late in the day Crom Daral came to my door. Standing just outside, he said, "She wants to know how the woman is."

"Still alive, tell her. And thank you, Crom," I made myself add, knowing it had not been easy for him to come.

"Unh." He went away.

To my relief, Sulis returned the next morning. With a distaste she did not try to hide, she examined Lakutu and confirmed my suspicion of poison. "Briga has done all for her that I could, and possibly more," she said. "The woman will live. But she is damaged, her bowels pass blood. Whether or not she will ever regain her strength I cannot say. You must ask Keryth."

"I already did. The portents were ambiguous."

"They often are. That just means the outcome will be determined by choices humans have yet to make."

"You do not need to instruct the chief druid, Sulis," I told her frostily. Sometimes I suspected she still saw me as the lanky boy to whom she had introduced sex magic.

It had been a long time since Sulis and I practiced sex magic together. Yet I knew, from the inviting looks she occasionally gave me, that she wanted to do it with me again, to strengthen her ties to the man who was now chief druid.

I was beginning to recognize ambition in its many guises.

I remained fond of Sulis, however. I was still fond of Crom Daral on some level, though I knew he would cheerfully kill me if he could.

For me, once such links were formed they were impossible to break.

Sulis told me, "Briga has an obvious sympathy with . . . this woman. It would be better for her to continue to care for her than for me to attempt to take over now."

"Will you ask her to do it?"

"I'll do what I can, Ainvar. But she's stubborn."

"I know," I replied ruefully.

I summoned all druids living within a day's walk of the grove and told them of the attempt made to poison me. The horror they felt rippled outward, reaching the trees around us, echoing back in shocked arboreal voices.

Like all living things, trees communicate. Their speech is not audible to human ears, but the trained senses of the druids were aware of a coldness emanating from the oaks, a sullen anger.

Then, with a nod to Sulis and Keryth, I detailed what we had discovered about the incapacitation of Nantorus and the death of Menua.

The air in the grove suddenly crackled with a savage, biting frost. Even Aberth glanced nervously toward the trees, where the shadow of murder hung in the branches.

"Tell us what you want done!" several druids cried out.

Dian Cet cleared his throat. "We shall concur with whatever action the chief druid deems appropriate," he announced formally.

"I have given this much thought," I told them. "There must be a symmetry. What Tasgetius has given, he must receive. But we cannot deprive the tribe of a king until there is a worthy replacement for him, a fact which no one regrets more than I."

Let them know that I too hungered for revenge.

Leaving Lakutu to be nursed by the women, I took the first step in the plan that had been growing in my head. With several of my druids and a select bodyguard of warriors, I set out for Cenabum to return Tasgetius's formal visit.

In my hand was the ash staff signifying the office of chief druid. On my breast was the triskele Menua had given me. The hem of my hooded robe had already been embroidered by Damona with a design representing the mountains I had crossed on my journey to the Province.

Fleetingly I wondered if embroidery was one of the things Damona was teaching Lakutu. Dancing girls are surely not trained to cook and sweep lodges and pound clothing with stones in the river. Yet Lakutu had mastered those skills . . . for me. Soon she might progress to doing fine embroidery.

I tore my thoughts from her and prepared to meet Tasgetius.

The king of the Carnutes was plainly disconcerted by my arriving, in apparent health, at Cenabum. He recovered quickly, however. "We are happy to see you looking so well, Ainvar," he said, holding out his arms and embracing me like a friend.

My face was impassive. "I've never felt better."

"Ah? We heard rumors of a sickness."

"Words shouted on the wind can be misunderstood."

"Quite so. Quite so, eh? Now may we know the reason for your visit?" We bared our teeth at each other in grimaces meant for polite smiles. Wolf-smiles.

"To return the pleasure of yours," I said blandly. "My purpose is, in truth, threefold—I have come to instruct couples planning to marry in the grove at Beltaine as to the preparations they must make ahead of time" (I tried not to think of Briga as I said this) "and I also felt it necessary to explain to you that we really do not have room for a trading outpost in the Fort of the Grove."

A muscle jumped at the edge of the king's eye. "So I've heard," he said drily. Neither of us was giving anything away.

He invited me into his lodge and served me wine. Roman wine. When I took nothing to eat or drink he did not ask why, but I caught the faint flicker in his eyes.

My mind danced with his, testing his mental reflexes. While I kept him occupied, the most appropriate member of my retinue was visiting some of the other lodges in Cenabum.

Following my instruction, Aberth the sacrificer told the kinsmen of Menua and of Nantorus just what had been done to them, and at whose instigation.

Tasgetius, shrewd though he was, was no druid. When he accompanied us to the gates of Cenabum to bid us farewell, he seemed unaware of the roiling, troubled atmosphere within the walls of the fortress.

But I felt it, and rejoiced. The spear was hurled at his unsuspecting back.

On our homeward journey Aberth reported. "There was great anger at what I had to tell, but no real disbelief. Tasgetius has lost what popularity he had. It is common knowledge he accepts secret payments from the traders for letting them do business at Cenabum."

"That custom," I remarked, "is not unheard of in the Province, either."

We were walking across the plains of the Carnutes beneath a warm spring sun. The earth's sweet, soft brown flesh was warm beneath our feet. The land smelled fertile. We had poured sweat and blood into that earth to encourage it to produce.

Walking beside me, Aberth had a red gleam in his eye. "The kin of Menua and Nantorus want vengeance, Ainvar. Blood for blood. The two most outspoken are the princes Cotuatus and Conconnetodumnus, both men with many warriors pledged to them personally."

"I know them; at least I know Cotuatus. He was fond of Menua."

"An intense loyalty develops among people who grow up together in a crowded lodge, as Cotuatus tells me he and Menua did," said Aberth. "He would kill Tasgetius today, but I made him promise to wait until he heard from you that the time was right. Meanwhile, he and the others will watch the king and send word of his actions to you."

I had acquired eyes and ears in Cenabum. Tasgetius would not take me by surprise again. I had no doubt he would make another attempt to kill me if I remained obdurate.

Let him try, I thought with dark joy. My father's warrior blood howled in my veins, wanting to fight.

From the lap of the plains the ridge of the sacred grove rose in the distance like a lifted head. My own heart lifted at the sight of our living temple, inviolate and sacrosanct, standing free against the sky.

No sooner had we entered the fort than Sulis ran up to me, eager to impart good news. "That woman in your lodge is much better, Ainvar. The Sequanian has visited her several times and there's no doubt about it, the woman is improving."

"Her name is Lakutu."

"Ah. Yes. Anyway."

"So is Briga with you now?"

"Not yet. She's still unwilling to leave Crom Daral. But I've talked with her and she admits awareness of her gift. When she speaks of feeling it run through her the night she saved the . . . Lakutu . . . her whole face lights up. Sooner or later, she will stop fighting and come to us."

Sooner or later would be too late. Already the young people were peeling and decorating the tree that would be the hub of the Beltaine dance, the symbol of fertility around which the pattern of new lives would grow.

And word came from the south that Vercingetorix had, over the objections of his uncle Gobannitio, formally challenged Potomarus for the kingship of the Arverni.

CHAPTER TWENTY

"SEX MAGIC," I muttered to myself.

"What?" Tarvos cocked his head. "Were you speaking to me?"

"Thinking aloud," I told him. "About ways of helping Vercingetorix. He will need all the strength and vigor he can summon if he is to win the support of the druids and elders over an established king."

"I never thought the Arvernian lacking in vigor," Tarvos commented. "All those women in the Province . . ."

"You sound envious."

"I had my share. You're the only one who didn't indulge, Ainvar."

This was true, and surprising even to myself. The only woman I had enjoyed in more than a cycle of seasons was Lakutu. I was simply too busy.

Sex magic would be the appropriate ritual to help Rix, but I doubted if it would be effective over such a long distance. I also found myself unwilling to suggest it to Sulis, who would have been the obvious partner.

I had other ways of helping Rix; I was the Keeper of the Grove. At once I sent word through the druid network that I was in complete support of the challenge of the young Arvernian, and that the druids of his tribe were urged to give him the utmost consideration. Then I turned my thoughts to the needs of my own tribe.

I tried not to let myself dwell on the needs of Ainvar.

From throughout the land of the Carnutes, men were bringing women to the sacred grove to celebrate Beltaine. Princes were accommodated in the guesthouse and assembly house of the fort; the rest encamped within the walls, filling every available open space, or stayed with their clanfolk on local farmsteads.

The warm sun of summerbirth rode high in the sky and blood ran hot in the veins.

On the day preceding the marriage rituals, I went to examine the site and conduct the final preparations. The attention of the Source must be drawn to this particular place; fires must be lighted, water poured, a solemn pattern danced on the breast of the earth by the chief druid.

Staked in place with ropes, a peeled treetrunk stood upright in the center of the clearing set aside for the celebrations of Beltaine. The clearing was almost at the base of the ridge, far removed from the holy center where stood the stone of sacrifice. Beltaine festivities could become very rowdy.

The symbol of regeneration was painted throughout the tree's length with the colors of the various Carnutian clans, a riot of crimson and yellow and black, gold and blue and carnelian, purple and green and scarlet. Like a vividly tattooed phallus, the tree pointed nakedly to the sky, awaiting the celebrations of lifemaking, the dances of marriage and fertility.

When I had finished sprinkling the earth around the base of the tree with water from our sweetest, most sacred spring, I stood for a long time just looking at the living monolith. I was barefoot and the earth was warm beneath my feet.

In the silence life spoke to me, making its demands.

Thoughtfully, hidden within my hood, I returned to the fort. I made my way through the crowd already celebrating—and complaining about the shortage of wine. Ainvar's feet carried me to the lodge of Crom Daral; the ash wand of the chief druid beat upon his door.

When it swung inward, Briga peered out at me. I said merely, "Come," and caught her by the wrist.

I did not ask if Crom was there. As it happened, he was on the other side of the fort contesting at stone-throwing with some of the other warriors, but if he had confronted me just then, it would have made no difference. I would have taken her anyway.

When life commands we must obey.

I led Briga through the fort, out the gates, down the slope to the banks of the Autura, to a small, crescent-shaped strip of sand sheltered by willow and alder. A secure and sunwarmed haven, the sort of place a druid discovers when wandering alone with his thoughts.

Briga objected but I could not hear her, my ears were filled with the singing of my blood. She did not try to pull away from me, however.

When at last we stood together on the sand, I realized I was trembling. She looked earnestly up into my face, then back along the way we had come.

"I am the chief druid," I said in a thick voice. "No one will interfere."

"Even if you take a woman against her will?" Lifting her chin, she stared haughtily at me, magically reassembling her flesh and bones so that every line of her reminded me she was a prince's daughter.

"I do not take women against their will," I said.

I released her wrist.

She rubbed the red mark left by my grip, and we stared at each other, both of us breathing harder than our walk required. "I'm dancing the marriage pattern with Crom Daral tomorrow," she said.

I could not reply. I just stood and looked at her.

"He needs me," she said. "You don't understand him. He really does need me. If I left him he would be devastated—particularly if I left him for you. He'd never get over that."

I said nothing.

"He's been very good to me. After you just . . . went away . . . without even telling me you were going to be a druid . . . I felt betrayed. I was so angry with you. You left me after I'd let you see me cry." She dropped her eyes then looked up quickly again, her gaze fierce. "I let no one see me cry. Not ever!"

In a softer voice, she went on. "But Crom Daral cries sometimes, you know. In his sleep. I hear him. His back is getting worse and he knows it. If he can't be a warrior and claim his share of the spoils, his clan will have to support him. That means Ogmios, who has always had nothing but contempt for him. Don't you see, Ainvar? Crom has to have something, I can't leave him with nothing!"

She had taken a step closer to me in her anxiety to make me understand. I opened my arms.

Briga fitted into them like a missing part of myself.

When I began fumbling with her clothes, she mounted a token defense, but it was too late. I forced her down onto the sun-warmed sand.

"I'm Crom Daral's woman," she tried to protest, half-smothered beneath me. She twisted from side to side, trying to fend me off with knees and forearms, but every move she made only increased my desire. My flesh was frantic with need of her.

She stopped fighting me with a startling suddenness. "Why did you wait so long to come for me?" she whispered.

When I entered Briga, she responded with a wild, free joy. I knew then what the Source of All Being must have experienced at the moment of creation: the bursting of a passion too great to be contained.

In that explosion the stars were born—and we are made of stardust.

Later, much later, we began exploring one another, tentatively at first but with increasing confidence. Her soft, round little belly charmed me, and I pressed my lips against its warmth. She rose onto hands and knees to crawl the length of my body from head to foot, pausing along the way to touch, to caress, to look back mischievously over her shoulder and inquire, "Do you like this? And this?"

I grabbed her from behind and buried my face between her buttocks, savoring the juiciness of her. She laughed; I laughed. The two of us together were a festival.

The wildness returned, deeper and richer than before.

This time images formed behind my closed eyes. I saw the naked tree rising in the clearing. I saw sunlight gleaming on spears, and golden sparks flying upward . . . and, at the ultimate moment, I caught the briefest glimpse of one particular, dauntless face.

"Vercingetorix," I whispered into Briga's hair as the cosmos crashed around us.

When we lay quiet once more with her head tucked into the hollow of my shoulder, I stared up at the sky and reflected on the nature of the special climax that can occur with a special woman. The climax that takes place not in the loins, but in the head and the spirit.

Magic was not too strong a term.

We slept and woke and slept. No one disturbed us. At last I thought I had nothing left to give; then Briga took me into her mouth and caressed my thighs and belly until they grew heavy with the need to give again. She swallowed my seed in lavish gulps. "Now your body will nourish mine and become part of me," she whispered, pleased with herself.

I had a sudden vision of Menua becoming part of an oak tree.

A calling bird reminded me that the shadows were lengthening and I had responsibilities; we rose and began to dress. Briga turned her back to me. I would not have it. I caught her shoulder and made her face me. "Don't go away from me, Briga. Not even a step."

"I must, sometime."

"No. I want you with me as long as we live. Promise me." It was an extravagant demand. Even in the Beltaine marriage ritual promises were not made for a lifetime. Life is change, a fact that Celtic law takes into account. Free people pledge to remain partners only as long as both are willing. It would be neither natural nor wise to ask for more. Yet I asked it of Briga. "Promise me!"

She looked at me . . . and into me, going all the way into those depths from which Nantorus had drawn back so long ago. I felt her in a part of myself no one had ever touched. "I shall be yours forever, Ainvar," she said softly. "By sun and moon, by fire and water, by earth and air, I swear it."

Embracing her with joy, I was shaken to discover in Briga a depth of intensity to match my own.

What do we do now? my head demanded to know.

After sex, my thoughts always came clearest, and suddenly I found myself—somewhat after the fact—examining our situation with rueful clarity. If I took Briga into my lodge today as my woman, under the law Crom Daral would have every right to come after me and split my skull. By stealing the woman of a fellow clansman I would have dishonored my office.

I must not dishonor the title of Keeper of the Grove!

So I could not take her for myself. No. Not yet. I could claim her for the Order, however. Yes! Then at some future time, when

Crom had accepted it and found himself a new woman, I could dance with Briga around the Beltaine tree.

The plan seemed perfectly reasonable to me.

I need only explain it to her.

We began our reluctant return to the fort. As we walked, I put my arm around her shoulders. "I'm going to take you to Sulis's lodge, so that . . . "

She dug her heels into the earth and stopped. "I thought you were taking me to your lodge. I can't go back to Crom Daral if I'm yours. You said you wanted me with you."

"I do, I do! But there are many factors to consider, Briga, and I think I have found the best way for us. At least for now. Listen to me." Keeping my arm around her shoulders, I resumed walking, drawing her along with me. She paced with her head down in what I assumed to be a listening attitude.

Until we were almost at the gates of the fort. Then she threw off my arm and whirled on me, eyes blazing. "So this was all a trick to force me into the Order!"

I was dismayed. "Of course not! It's simply the best way for us, don't you see? I meant it when I made you mine."

"Being yours doesn't mean I have to be a druid." She lifted her chin and threw her shoulders back, letting her posture remind me that she was a prince's daughter and could not be forced to do anything.

"Briga, you took part of me to become part of yourself, remember? That means that whatever I am, you are also. And I am a druid."

"Druid logic," she said coldly. "I knew this was a trick. You planned it from the beginning, you trapped me." She took a step backward, away from me, then turned and began running through the twilight toward the fort.

I sped after her, but anger gave her legs strength. She hurtled through the open gates with the chief druid in undignified pursuit. The sentry yelled something at us, but I did not understand what he said.

Nor, for that matter, did I understand Briga.

She raced through the fort, dodging people and hounds and hens, leaping over baskets, swerving to avoid midden heaps. I was within a stride of catching her when a nearby lodge door opened and Sulis emerged.

With one swift glance the healer took in the scene: Briga flushed and furious, me exasperated and desperate.

Sulis stepped deftly between us, shook her head warningly at me, and put her arms around Briga. "You poor thing, is the chief druid upsetting you? We won't have it. Come with me now, we can sort this out in the morning. Your clothes are all sandy and you look tired, would bathing in heated water refresh you? And a good meal? There now, just come with me . . ."

Sulis led Briga into her lodge and shut the door in my face.

I had neglected to raise my hood; now my people crowded around me, eager to talk of tomorrow's Beltaine celebration. I had to answer their questions, I belonged to the tribe. They caught me up and carried me away on the tide of their demands, to supervise the purifications, to consult with Dian Cet about the law, to examine the property being exchanged, to share my wisdom and learning and energy when all I wanted to do was be with Briga. And explain. And make it all right somehow.

Late in the night, I scratched on Sulis's door. The Goban Saor answered. "I'll get her for you," he said, not offering to admit me. In a few moments the door opened wider and Sulis slipped outside to join me.

"Briga is sleeping, Ainvar. What did you do to her?"

"What did she tell you?" I countered.

"Not much, only that you had tricked her."

"She misunderstood."

"That's what I suspected. It didn't sound like you. But she's very angry, Ainvar. She accused you of trying to force her to join the Order before she's ready."

Before she's ready—those few words gave me hope. "Is she willing to stay with you now, Sulis?"

"She is; she says she's left Crom Daral for some reason and has nowhere else to go. It's the opportunity we've been seeking, of course. With the two of us under one roof I know I can win her over. But I should like to know how this came about."

"The pattern," I said succinctly.

Sulis gave me a skeptical look.

After a sleepless night, at the next dawn I sang the song for the Beltaine sun.

Neither Briga nor Crom Daral appeared to take part in the ceremonies that followed, though I watched for them when I could.

Mostly I was too busy to think of either of them. Ainvar the man was submerged in the Keeper of the Grove.

At one point near midday, when Sulis and I happened to be standing next to each other, the healer said to me in a private voice, "Briga wouldn't come, even to celebrate Beltaine. She expected to be dancing around the tree today, you know. She's staying in my lodge and wants to see no one."

"Mmm," I replied.

For the nine days and nights of Beltaine, my people celebrated the generation of new life. Even the harvest festival of Lughnasa could not compare with the joy of Beltaine. First Dian Cet recited the laws applying to marriage, gifts symbolic of the property of the partners were exchanged, then the man and woman danced the marriage pattern together around the base of the Beltaine tree. Drums beat, pipes played, druids chanted; the warm air of spring lay like a beneficent weight on dreaming eyes and sweating limbs. The pattern grew more fevered, more and more couples joined the dance. Then they fell away like petals from a flower, to seek beds on the fecund earth. We were a people of passion and passion was a gift from the Source.

For nine nights and days, my people showed their gratitude.

As chief druid, I presided.

The Head was alone.

When the last exhausted couples made their way homeward, I returned to my own lodge to find Tarvos there, looking after Lakutu. Hiding my surprise, I said, "When did you leave the dancing?"

"Early. The dance is for marrying, and I wasn't marrying. So I thought I'd look in on Lakutu, give Damona a chance to be with her own husband."

"That was kind of you."

The Bull shrugged. "I had nothing else to do. But since you're here now, I'll go. Unless you need something . . . ?"

"No, that's all right." I motioned him away. "Ah, Tarvos!" I called when he was almost through the doorway. "Has any message come from the land of the Arverni?"

He grinned. "They're shouting on the wind. Vercingetorix is the new king. Named on the morning of Beltaine."

Yes, I thought, closing my eyes. The election must have taken place the day before, as I lay with Briga beside the river and whispered his name into her hair.

CHAPTER TWENTY-ONE

OGMIOS CAME to me, somewhat disgruntled. "Crom Daral's left the Fort of the Grove."

"What do you mean?"

"He was embarrassed at being rejected by the Sequanian woman. He's run away, to Cenabum, I think. I always knew he was a coward. But his defection has left us a warrior short, though he wasn't much of a warrior."

"Don't be so quick to condemn him, Ogmios. He's your son."

"By a captured woman. And refused by a captured woman. Not worth much."

"You always underestimated him," I said coldly. "You helped shape him, we all did."

"You're standing up for him after he's run off like a thief in the dark?"

"Crom Daral was my friend. And I am not a judge."

Summoning Tarvos, I asked him to send word to Cenabum that the chief druid of the Carnutes wanted every courtesy extended to Crom Daral. "Let it be known that I would be gratified if some prince took Crom into his retinue. But Crom himself is not to be told of my support," I added firmly.

"You wouldn't want the king to take him on, would you?"

"No, Tarvos. Definitely not the king. But there are others . . . suggest him to Cotuatus, he's a good man."

Events were moving swiftly in the land of the Arverni. In spite of his uncle's opposition, Vercingetorix was consolidating his power. The deposed Potomarus, together with Gobannitio and his other remaining followers, had left Gergovia and gone to the fort of Alesia, in the land of the Mandubii tribe. The wife of Potomarus was a Mandubii.

Perhaps he hoped to build a base of support there to attempt another challenge for the kingship, but I doubted it. From what I knew of Potomarus, there was a limited amount of fight in him.

The Arverni had done wisely in replacing him with Vercingetorix.

During that summer I received frequent news of the quiet but constant influx of foreigners into various parts of free Gaul. Some reports were shouted on the wind; others were brought to me by less ostentatious means, through the druid network. Members of the Order from the farthest corners of the land visited the great grove whenever they could, to renew themselves through communion with the heart of Gaul. Each brought me some snippet of news; each was sent away with my strong injunction to speak to his tribe of the need for unity, and the shining promise exemplified by the new king of the Arverni, the one man I believed capable of facing Caesar when the time came.

I was certain the time would come. Everywhere I looked, I saw signs and omens.

Being a druid sometimes means knowing things one would rather not know.

Meanwhile, under my direction our vineyards were taking shape. At first my people had been dubious, but as the vines began to grow so did the enthusiasm of those who tended them. We sang songs for the vines and created a dance among the rows. Though our first harvest was several summers in the future, men and women began dreaming aloud of the day when work and sacrifice would transmute scraggly vines and dry, thin soil into rubies to fill the cup.

Then news arrived from the perimeters of Gaul that the seeds Dumnorix the Aeduan had planted were bearing bitter fruit.

The Helvetii had taken a long time to prepare for their planned migration, abandoning their homeland to the Germans while they sought richer pastures. They had planted an excess of grain to be certain of supplying themselves, and had built thousands of new wagons to carry their families and possessions. When they judged they were ready, they burned their twelve towns and four hundred villages, as well as the grain they were unable to carry, so there would be nothing left behind for the invading Suebi—and so they themselves would have nothing to return to but be forced to go on. They set off on their great migration with sixty thousand wagons, one for every six members of the tribe.

Their initial route took them through the tribelands of the Raurici, the Tulingi, and the Latovici, whom they persuaded to join them. Even some of the vast Boii tribe were caught up in the migrant fever and joined the search for new horizons. As had been predicted, the chosen route of this ocean of people lay across a part of the Province.

Caesar was in Rome when the Helvetii set out, but as soon as word reached him he sped into free Gaul with a legion at his back and the Roman eagle flying above him. "His standard-bearers wear lion skins," eyewitnesses claimed.

Eagle and lion; the symbology was not lost on me. The predators had come to Gaul.

Late into the night I discussed the situation with Tarvos. Since he called in at my lodge every evening, I had begun relying on him to feed Lakutu. She had survived, thanks to Briga, but was recovering very slowly and had no appetite at all. Neither Damona nor I could get her to eat; only the Bull seemed to have any success. I thought it an odd talent for a warrior, but I was grateful.

So, as he sat beside Lakutu and patiently urged food upon her, I spoke of the worries uppermost on my mind. Talking to Tarvos helped clarify my own thoughts. Sound is structure and structure is pattern. . . .

"The Helvetii sent emissaries to Caesar to assure him they only wanted to pass through the Province and intended no harm, but he did not believe them," I told Tarvos. He had just taken a gobbet of Damona's cooked meat and begun chewing it to a soft paste, which he would then offer to Lakutu on his fingers. I marveled at his patience.

Around his mouthful of meat, Tarvos said, "I wouldn't have believed them, either. He knew they would live off the land to a large extent; so many people would have stripped any region they passed through."

I nodded. "Caesar understood that. He told the envoys he must have time to consider their request, then used that time to bring up reinforcements from the Province. When the Helvetian emissaries returned to Caesar, he told them their request for passage was denied. In great anger, the Helvetii tried to break through the defenses he had thrown up against them but they were repulsed, and many women and children were slain. The only way left open to them was through the land of the Sequani; they never succeeded in getting anywhere near the borders of the Province.

"So I am told they went to Dumnorix the Aeduan and demanded of him, as the original cause of the problem, that he persuade the Sequanians to let them pass. His wife is of the Sequani; that's how this unfortunate situation appears to have begun. When the Suebi overran the Sequani, Dumnorix met with the Suebian leaders and agreed to hire mercenaries from them to placate them so they would do less damage to his wife's people."

Tarvos held out his fingers and Lakutu sucked the chewed meat paste from them. "Appeasement does more damage than less," he remarked. "I've heard you say that, Ainvar."

"Here we see it proven," I told him.

"What did Caesar do after turning back the Helvetii?"

"More swiftly than one would have thought possible, he raised additional legions from Latium and has begun bringing them into free Gaul. Meanwhile, the migrants have reportedly crossed the Sequani tribeland and gone on into the territory of the Aedui, where they have begun serious pillaging.

"Just this morning I learned that Diviciacus, the Aeduan chief judge, has sent an earnest request for aid to Caesar."

The Bull used the sleeve of his tunic to wipe Lakutu's chin. Her large brown eyes never left his face. "That's what you expected, isn't it? Caesar invited ever deeper into Gaul? Does Vercingetorix know?"

"That's how I heard of it. Messengers from him arrived this

morning; he keeps me informed. His territory is nearest that of
the Aedui, of course, and he has allies among the Boii who tell
him everything."

"Ah, yes, I met the messengers arriving just as I was going on
sentry duty. I sent for a horseboy to take their exhausted animals,
in fact." Tarvos offered another bit of food to Lakutu, who obviously
did not want it but took it to please him. She must be lonely during
the days, I thought. I was far too busy to spare any time for her,
or even for myself. What little personal life the chief druid of the
Carnutes possessed consisted of occasional brief glimpses of Briga
as she accompanied Sulis on her rounds.

When we met, Briga would not look at me.

Lughnasa, celebration of the harvest, was upon us almost before
we were ready. Sunseason had been good to us, the crops were
abundant and the new wives had swelling bellies. As we prepared
for the festival to thank the sun and conclude the growing-time, I
avidly followed the news of Caesar's Helvetian campaign through
a constant stream of messengers, visitors, and rumors shouted on
the wind.

Caesar had brought wave upon wave of warriors northward to
defend the Aedui—at least those that were loyal to his ally
Diviciacus—from the plundering migrants. The Helvetii were actually fine warriors themselves; had they chosen to stay in their
homeland and fight, they might well have defeated the Suebi. But
their greed for new lands had betrayed them. Now they were
trapped with no land of their own, and Caesar's armies were everywhere they turned. They fought heroically, but in the end they
were no match for the Romans.

I was not surprised when the shout came up the river: "The
Helvetii are broken! They flee in panic!"

I went to see Sulis. "I need your professional opinion, healer.
If something should happen to Tasgetius, is it possible Nantorus
might resume the kingship? How permanent is his disability?"

She looked doubtful. "Very, I should say. But I can go to him
if you wish and see what can be done."

"Do so. Use every skill at your disposal, and take with you as
many other healers as you can summon."

"There is a shortage of us, as of all druids. . . ."

"I know that!" I snapped. "Just do your best for Nantorus. I don't want the tribe to face what is coming under the chieftaincy of a man like Tasgetius."

"If I'm to take other healers with me, what of Briga?" she asked innocently. I sensed the mocking laughter hidden in her words, however.

"Leave her with me. It's time her training was expanded to other areas than herbs and potions. She must be instructed in every aspect of the Order or she will never fully understand us and be able to overcome her fear."

"And you're the best person to instruct her, of course," Sulis said. This time the hidden sound was sarcasm.

I ignored it. "Of course. I am chief druid."

"She may not find that sufficient reason to sit at your feet, Ainvar."

"Then you must convince her. Remind her she's gone too far to turn back now."

"That," drawled Sulis, "is not an argument that's likely to succeed with a woman. We are more flexible in our heads than men," she added smugly.

"Then tell her you want her to serve as healer here in the fort in your absence! She is capable of caring for the ordinary sort of sickness or injury, isn't she?"

"She is. I've been working with her all summer and I am an excellent teacher."

"Good. Once she has accepted the idea of being our substitute healer, then remind her that will entail working closely with the chief druid."

The corners of Sulis's lips twitched. "Put that way, how can she refuse? She will be too flattered at the idea of serving in my stead; our little Briga is proud, Ainvar."

"I know."

Briga came to me when I finished singing the song for the sun the day after Sulis left for Cenabum, and Nantorus. I had just turned from the singing when I realized she was standing almost in my shadow, with her face closed and her thoughts hidden behind her eyes. "Sulis said I should come to you." She sounded very formal, as if it were our first meeting.

Matching her tone, I replied, "I can teach you things that will make you a better healer."

In that hoarse little voice which I found so curiously endearing, she said simply, "If you must."

We both knew she was trapped. By her own act she had made herself part of the druid network. I could appreciate the irony if she could not.

One could never know what to expect of Briga; I must plan my strategy with her as cleverly as Caesar ever planned any of his campaigns.

He was at that moment regrouping after a decisive battle against the Helvetii near Bibracte, which had left, of all the ocean of migrants, only 130,000 still living. While the blood was still wet on his weapons, he was turning his attention toward Ariovistus the Suebian.

Caesar had no intention of withdrawing from free Gaul after winning only one war. He had not yet even skimmed the cream from the prosperity of the Celtic tribes in their rich and fertile homelands.

Diviciacus encouraged him. According to Rix's Boii spies, the Aeduan vergobret complained to Caesar that soon all free Gauls would be driven from their homelands by the Germanic tribes. He accused Ariovistus of being a cruel, arrogant tyrant, a Greek term he had no doubt learned in his druidical studies. The Aedui were totally divided between those who followed Dumnorix and those who agreed with Diviciacus; a once mighty tribe was thus halved and weakened.

If I allowed my opposition to Tasgetius to become public knowledge, the same thing could happen to the Carnutes. The tribe could be torn apart between king and druid. So I must remain personally silent, trusting my work to go on in the darkness, like roots spreading underground, until Tasgetius was replaced with a king we could trust.

The desperate dangers of division were becoming more evident.

A number of Gaulish kings formed a delegation to visit Caesar personally and congratulate him on his victory over the Helvetii. I was disgusted, but glad to hear that Rix was not one of their number, though I would not have expected it of him.

Tasgetius went, of course.

That autumn I took Briga into the woods and began teaching her, as Menua had once taught me, to see the beauty underlying the apparent harshness of existence.

Sulis had taught her the basic skills. She could make poultices of bran and tar for inflamed joints, she could prepare decoctions of parsley roots and seeds to help expel bladder stones. She knew which illnesses were provoked by the swelling of the moon and which were diminished by its shrinking. With my own eyes I saw her squeeze a sheep's kidney from its membrane so the covering was left intact, then moisten this with cream and saliva and apply it to an old man's suppurating leg ulcer. The ulcer healed, and I was proud of her.

I taught her other things. I remember her sitting cross-legged in the grove, chewing on her fingernails while a stray beam of sunlight found gold in her hair. I had found a seed already locked in sleep, waiting for the distant spring; I held it in the palm of my hand and told her to watch. Then I closed my eyes and concentrated.

When the sweat began running down my forehead, Briga gasped. I opened my eyes. The seed's shell had split open, revealing an infinitesimal pale shoot inside. It uncoiled so slowly we could hardly see movement, but the shell kept opening wider until at last the tiny being lifted into the light.

Briga's eyes were enormous. "How did you do that?" she asked in an awed whisper.

I smiled. As I had anticipated, the magic had broken through her own shell of reserve. "You could do it, too," I told her. "There is life in you and life in the seed. When one calls out strongly enough to the other, there must be a response. Would you like me to show you how?"

She clapped her hands together like a child. "Yes!"

We spent the day there. I wanted to teach her everything at once: how to hear rainbows and see music and smell colors.

I wanted to run my hands through her sunscented hair.

But restraint is expected of a chief druid, so I devoted myself to instruction that was also seduction. My purpose was the seduction of Briga's spirit, and to that end I showed her the lightest and brightest of druid abilities. I made water sing for her and called out-of-season butterflies to dance in her hands.

She laughed. I made her laugh. I recited riddles, secrets hidden within secrets like the whorls of a spiral, and she showed me the pads of her fingertips with the same whorls on them, understanding.

I never touched her. Yet we found ourselves touching on some level of awareness where we conversed wordlessly in a language no one else knew.

I never touched her. The next time she must reach for me. There has to be a balance.

But sometimes it is very hard.

Briga was only mine in the daytime, and even then there were beginning to be other contenders for my attention. Having a young, vigorous chief druid was stimulating new life in the Order. Parents began bringing gifted youngsters to the grove once more, asking me to test and teach them.

"We shall win them back with strong new songs!" I boasted to Tarvos. "We may even be able to rebuild the Order to its former size, as it was when Menua was young."

"How many druids does a tribe need?"

"As many as it takes," I told him mischievously.

The Bull shrugged. "Druid humor," he said. "What do you think caused the decline in numbers in the first place?"

"Perhaps the cause lies with the wheel of the seasons that turns and turns and changes all things, so that ancient ages become new and ancient wisdoms are forgotten only to be rediscovered, the necessary cycle of death and birth."

Tarvos scratched his bushy head. "I don't understand. But then, I'm a simple man."

When I repeated my thoughts to her, however, Briga understood.

Teaching was only a part of my function, of course. In the autumn I must oversee the slaughtering, first propitiating the spirits of the animals. Then there was the storing of grain and the harvesting of the precious mistletoe, part of an endless round that must correspond to natural cycles and be performed according to proven traditions. We took from the earth and we gave back, we worked with sun and rain and the spirit of life. At the hub of all this activity was the chief druid, maintaining the harmony.

I learned to live on very little sleep.

Sometimes I went to the grove alone. There, like an overheated man sinking into a pool of cool water, I immersed myself in the tranquility of the trees until I was refreshed.

I needed all my strength when Sulis returned from Cenabum to tell me there was no hope for Nantorus.

"He can never be elected king again, Ainvar. We did everything that could be done for him, but he is old beyond his seasons. The spear in his back must have damaged his lung; his breathing is ruined. It's surprising he's lived this long, really.

"Now that I'm back, I suppose you want me to resume teaching Briga?"

"Not yet," I replied. "Not yet."

Another task was added to my endless list: I must find a new candidate for king, and do it secretly, without alerting Tasgetius.

While my head was turning over this new problem, word came from the south. Vercingetorix of the Arverni urgently requested my advice and counsel. Could I come to Gergovia?

I went back to Sulis and told her she would resume Briga's instruction after all, and possibly take on some other hopeful healers as well. Grannus, Keryth, and our other druids would divide the rest of the neophytes among them in my absence. "But don't send Briga to Aberth," I cautioned Sulis most particularly. "She isn't ready for him."

When I returned to my lodge to begin preparing for the journey southward, I found Tarvos waiting for me. "I'm glad you're here," I told him briskly as I started rummaging in the chest for traveling gear. "I'll want you to be prepared. We're going to Vercingetorix as soon as my responsibilities allow."

He said something behind my back, which I thought I must have misunderstood. "You what?" I asked him over my shoulder.

"I said I can't wait any longer, Ainvar. So I'm asking you now. Set a price on her and I'll pay it."

Chapter Twenty-two

"LET ME understand this, Tarvos. You want to *buy Lakutu?*" I turned to face him, knowing I sounded as astonished as I must have looked.

His lips tightened until his drooping moustache quivered. "I want her to live in my lodge. But she can't just come to me, she isn't a free person. So I'll buy her."

I sat down abruptly on the carved chest. "Warriors don't keep slaves. Bondservants perhaps; never *slaves.*"

"Neither do druids." The Bull faced me with his head lowered, like his namesake. I would have sworn he flared his nostrils.

My own flash of anger surprised me. "You don't have to worry about her. Surely you know I'll always see that she's cared for."

"You don't have any need of a woman in your house, Ainvar, you're never here anymore. The chief druid before you never kept a woman anyway. If Lakutu was mine I could give her her freedom, and then I could even . . . even marry her," he muttered, his face reddening.

"Marry!" I echoed stupidly.

"She would be willing."

"How do you know?"

"She told me."

I was past astonishment. "How could she tell you?"

"We talk."

"But she can't speak our language."

"I've taught her some words."

My imagination presented me with a vision of the two of them chattering away happily to one another while I was away toiling in the service of my people.

With a pang of jealousy, I realized Tarvos had taught Lakutu what I could not.

"She's still a sick woman," I argued halfheartedly.

"She's getting much better, you just haven't noticed. Sometimes we go for walks. I've taken her as far as the river, she likes that. Please, Ainvar. She's nothing to you. But to me . . . "

I could not bear the light in his eyes. "I'll think about it," I promised. Then I almost ran from the lodge.

I would not be able to go to Rix before Samhain at the earliest. I must conduct the rituals ending and beginning the cycle of seasons, and I must also address Gaul's druids at the annual convocation in the sacred grove. I wanted to remind them of the Roman threat as Menua would have done, and encourage them to think of tribal unity rather than divisiveness. Only if we stood together could we hope to resist Caesar.

"One man leads the entire army intent upon overrunning our lands," I told them. "One man. One head. We too shall need one man, one head, rather than many leaders going in different directions. The Roman pattern is to split up tribes and then roll over the fragments. Remember the history you have learned; think on it."

While my warning still echoed in the grove, I prepared to go to Vercingetorix.

Once more Tarvos met me at the door of my lodge. "Have you decided about Lakutu?" he asked bluntly.

"Are you going to the south with me?" I countered.

"It depends." He stood his ground, feet braced wide.

I, who scorned appeasement, tried to make him laugh. "I'm a druid, not a trader, Tarvos. Must we bargain?"

He just looked at me.

"Take her then," I shouted, breaking before he did. "Take her and be done with it! You don't have to buy her, I give her to you as a present."

"Will you make marks that say she's mine, the way they do in the Province?"

The Bull was aptly named. I had never realized he was so stubborn. "Anything you want," I replied. "Is there any particular language you'd like it written in?"

My attempt at sarcasm was unnoticed. "I don't know about things like that," he said.

So I found a piece of soft calfskin and laboriously scribed on it, with fabric paint, words giving one Lakutu, dancing girl, to one Tarvos, warrior. The language I used was the remnant of Greek I had learned from Menua; I would not use Latin. When I presented Tarvos with the scroll, he made no pretense of reading it, but thrust it into his tunic and grinned like a hound.

Feeling that something more was needed to complete this rather strange ritual, I said to Lakutu—more as a matter of form than an attempt at the communication I had never achieved— "I shall give you some possessions of your own to take to your new lodge. It is the custom of our people."

Her eyes met mine shyly. "Of my people, too. But only among royalty. You make me royalty. I thank you."

I was wordless.

Tarvos filled the silence. "I told you I'd taught her our language."

"I thought you meant . . . a few words only . . . I never dreamed. . . ."

Tarvos looked at Lakutu. "I did," he said.

Until our vines matured, I could not share a cup with them, but I poured the three of us generous quantities of barley beer and we celebrated so thoroughly I almost missed saluting the sunset. When Tarvos left he took her with him.

The lodge was unbelievably empty.

A gift, Menua had once told me, should be something you want for yourself, or it is not worthy to give.

When we left for the land of the Arvernians, Lakutu waved farewell to Tarvos from the door of his lodge, not mine.

As I made my way southward with my retinue, I heard that Caesar was on the move again; against Ariovistus. He had condemned some of the drafted Gauls in the Provincial army as cowards because

they were reluctant to fight the German king. A slaughter was in
the offing. Afterward, who would Caesar turn upon next?

At least we had the seasons for our allies. Winter was upon us;
Caesar might manage one good fight before surrendering to ice
and mud and going into winter camp, and in that time Rix and I
would meet and plan.

When I reached Gergovia, I was welcomed with great ceremony
to the lodge of the king. Bronze trumpets were blown to announce
me. I rather liked it; Tarvos was unimpressed.

Tribal kings live well, but the prosperity of the Arvernian royal
stronghold was exceptional by any Gaulish standard. The king's personal lodge was immense, large enough to house several families,
and possessed two vast stone firepits, one at either end of the oval
structure. There were numerous benches covered with furs, and
carved tables holding bowls and cups of bronze and silver and
copper. The lodge was so large it boasted private sleeping com-
partments separated from the rest of the house by carved wooden
screens. The least important of the king's servitors—and the lodge
swarmed with bondservants—wore rings and brooches of enameled
openwork that would have ransomed a prince's daughter.

The gleam of gold was everywhere. Around his neck Vercingetorix wore a gold torc as thick as an infant's wrist.

But he was, in many ways, the same Rix. His grin was as irresistible, his hooded gaze as compelling. "I'm glad you've come,
Ainvar. I wasn't certain you would—an important man like the
chief druid of the Carnutes." His laughter was gently mocking.

I matched the mood. "When the King of the World summons,
who am I to resist?"

After we had feasted together and shared wine, we became more
serious. Rix sent his servitors out of earshot, to the other end of
the lodge, so he could ask me, "Have you heard the latest news
of Caesar?"

"Rumors on the road. What news have you?"

"He's met with Ariovistus. The German refused to go to him,
so they agreed on a place midway between them. Ariovistus was
blustering and hostile, according to my Boii informants."

"You are as well informed as a chief druid," I told him. "And I
thank you for passing your information on to me."

"I wanted you to know what I know, in case I needed to call
upon your head."

"As you have done."

"Yes. It's this matter of Ariovistus, Ainvar. He insisted that his people had won the land they hold in Gaul in fair battle, and that it is no concern of Caesar's. Caesar countered by demanding that no more Germans be brought across the Rhine. He said that if Ariovistus would agree, there could be friendship between him and Rome, but otherwise Caesar would punish the Suebi for their many outrages against his allies among the Aedui."

I massaged my tired calf muscles with my hands. "I can't imagine Ariovistus was willing to accept any conditions laid down by Caesar."

"Of course not, he was furious. He declared there could only be war between them, and the skirmishing has already begun. Ariovistus has drawn together an army from several allied Germanic tribes with which he means to occupy Vesontio, the principal town of the Sequani. The last I heard, Caesar was on his way to head them off. I'm waiting for more news now."

"Why did you send for me at this time?"

"Because since spring Caesar has broken the Helvetians and, unless I'm much mistaken, will soon have crushed Ariovistus. But there's no sign of his armies returning to the south. I hear he is building heavily fortified winter camps, permanent bases, in every area he has thus far penetrated in Gaul. There can no longer be any doubt that you were right in your assessment of his plans. The next step is, what do we do about it?"

We were sitting together beside the fire, lolling at apparent ease on fur-cushioned benches, with brimming cups in our hands. But there was nothing relaxed about either of us.

I considered. "Send word at once to the kings of the tribes of free Gaul. Request them to attend a council meeting here, Gergovia is central enough. But don't call it a council of war. Just summon them now, before the outcome of Caesar's campaign against Ariovistus is known to all. If you wait until Caesar is celebrating another impressive victory, they may be too intimidated by him."

"Do you think they'll come?" Rix asked, his voice calmly curious, his eyes on the flames.

"Most of them. And some of those who hold back will come galloping along soon enough, once they begin suspecting the others might be plotting behind their backs. We've all grown very suspicious of one another here in Gaul. Make it work for you."

Rix turned to face me. "You'll stay here and sit beside me in the council?"

"Right by your ear," I promised.

Mounted messengers sped from Gergovia at dawn. One does not summon kings by shouting on the wind.

While waiting, I explored Gergovia in the company of Hanesa the Talker, who was delighted to see me. He told everyone we met, "The king and I took Ainvar with us to the Province, you know. Ah yes. And now he's chief druid of the Carnutes, the most gifted Keeper of the Grove ever to be born in Gaul. I always knew he had extraordinary gifts, I think I was aware of them before anyone else actually."

I pretended not to hear. Kings require excess; druids do not.

As we walked through the laneways and across the few open spaces of the sprawling fortress, which held hundreds of lodges and was home to thousands, I watched for some trace of German mercenaries. I found none. Of course, what Rix might be doing in the borderlands was another matter. I did not ask him outright; I did not want to force him to lie to me.

But the danger of having Germans among his followers continued to prey on my mind. They would draw Caesar to attack him more surely than gold or cattle, and I had an uneasy feeling that I had never convinced him of that danger.

When next we met in the king's lodge to eat and drink and talk, I began slipping references to the Germans into the conversation. I did not speak against them, I even praised their valor in battle. Yet I referred obliquely to time-honored hatreds; I recalled old stories whispered around the lodgefires of our youth to frighten children. I summoned, like a stain spreading across the floor, the ancient enmity of Gaul and German.

At the king's invitation, Hanesa had joined us, and he became my ally. I drew him with such devices as saying, "You remember the old story about the two Germanic tribes who . . ." and then Hanesa would take up the tale—perhaps one I had never heard at all—and elaborate upon it until he had constructed a masterpiece of grisly horror.

Rix listened fascinated, in spite of himself.

It was like slipping poison into a fig.

"If Ariovistus is any example of his race," I said with studied casualness, helping myself to more roast mutton, "then he is a man

of giant stature and appetites." I glanced toward Hanesa. "Where
do the German warriors get their strength, do you suppose? Do
they still rape their slain enemies and then eat them?"

Rix stopped chewing. "I never heard that."

"Oh yes!" Hanesa obliged. "It was common knowledge. German
tribes have always been cannibals. Why do you think they need
no supply lines when they go into battle?" The bard bit deeply
into his roasted meat, making the skin crackle and the juices spurt.

Rix pushed his food aside and reached for the wine.

In the Province I had learned many lessons, not the least being
the value of discrediting an enemy. I would get those Germans
out of Rix's army one way or another.

But before the first of the tribal kings arrived in answer to Rix's
summons, a messenger on an exhausted horse staggered through
the gates of Gergovia and demanded to see the king. "Caesar has
Ariovistus trapped," the man gasped. His face was white with
fatigue, his clothes spattered with mud and what might be dried
blood. "Though he has sixteen thousand foot warriors and six thousand on horse, Ariovistus fears the battle will go against him. He
begs the Arverni to ride east and stand with him against Caesar."

Rix turned to me. "What say you, Ainvar?"

The eagerness to give battle was rising off him like waves of heat.

This was a major test. If I gave Rix the wrong answer I would
lose my influence with him. As well as I knew the Source I knew
that my relationship with him was conditional. Everything was
subservient to the driving force within him that attracted us all;
that could make him the best weapon Gaul could forge against the
ambitions of Caesar.

But the Germans were also ambitious for Gaulish land, as they
had demonstrated too many times. I remembered my vision of the
Two-Faced One with Caesar's face on one side, a Germanic visage
on the other, and in the silence of my head I prayed, Guide me.

The words came strong and sure. "Do not use one mad dog to
fight another, Vercingetorix, or they might join forces and turn on
you. Let one destroy the other. Then you need only fight the
survivor."

It was not the answer he hoped for; disappointment and anger
warred on his face. Yet he stood quietly, absorbing my words,
never taking his hooded gaze from mine.

At last he said, "Your advice makes sense."

I dared to consolidate my gains. "Ariovistus apparently thinks he has the right to ask you for help."

Rix did not give me a reply, but he turned to the Suebian messenger and said in a voice loud enough to be certain I heard, "When you have rested and eaten you will return to your king. Tell him that I shall order any of his men currently in my territory to return and fight with him, but I shall not send him any other assistance. Now or ever. And he is not to call upon me again."

The messenger grew even more pale. "But there are six Roman legions against him."

"Then you must return at the gallop," Rix advised coolly. "You will be needed to fight." The matter closed, he turned his back on the unfortunate man.

I was proud of Rix. He had subordinated his passion to attack Caesar now and accepted a more prudent policy. He was meant to be a king. I wished we could have him to lead the Carnutes, but he could do more than that.

He could lead the Gauls.

That night as I lay on my bed, listening to Rix pleasure himself behind a screen with one of his many women, I thought, what if Ariovistus won? Rix would not thank me for denying him a chance to be on the winning side against Caesar. . . .

I need not have worried. As we subsequently learned, the Germans were routed and pursued all the way to the Rhine. Caesar made a habit of following up on his victories. Ariovistus managed to save his life by swimming across the Rhine, but one of his daughters was killed and another taken prisoner. Germanic women frequently went to war with their men and suffered the fate of any warriors.

Almost as an afterthought, the Celtic tribes living nearest the Rhine fell on the last of the Suebi to reach the river and killed most of them. Ariovistus, though safe in his forests, died soon after. It was said he stopped eating and turned his face to the sunset.

Leaving his armies secure in winter quarters, Caesar took himself off to Rome.

The tribal kings of Gaul came to Gergovia.

Curiosity brought some, self-interest brought others. Many, such as Tasgetius, and Cavarinus of the Senones, and Ollovico of the Bituriges, were conspicuous by their absence. They led the great tribes who did not, perhaps, think they needed to listen to anyone else.

Some of the lesser kings thought otherwise. And in the new
young king of the Arverni they found a man as tall as the tallest of
them, as strong as the strongest, a man who was clever and fearless.
Even I, who had prepared him diligently beforehand, was impressed. Rix turned the force of his personality on those swagger-
ing, boastful chieftains like a blinding light, forcing them to listen
and respect him.

He described in detail the Roman threat as he—as we—saw it.
He was very convincing. He told what he had learned about Roman
military techniques through observation in the Province, detailing
the organization of Caesar's armies to the last cook and porter. He
had men twice his age listening openmouthed as he described
intricate battle formations.

"We must be united in our efforts to deny the Romans any further
encroachment in Gaul," Rix said earnestly. "Only by standing together
can we successfully confront such an army as Caesar has organized.
We need to form a confederation against him; he cannot be defeated
by one tribe alone, however large. His armies are too well trained
and he can move them long distances at great speed. He can build
roads and bridges to give them access almost overnight. If we resist
him tribe by tribe he will defeat us tribe by tribe. We have to
stand together. A confederation is the only way to survive."

Every king in that council had fought every other king present
at some time. Asking them to form an alliance was asking the
impossible. Only a man as exciting and inspiring as Vercingetorix
could hope to succeed.

Such a man is not born in ten generations. He was given to us
when we needed him most.

At the conclusion of that first council of free Gaul, the kings of
the Parisii, the Pictones, and the Turones had agreed outright to
accept Rix as their commander in the event of war against Caesar,
following his standard and his orders in a unified defense of the
land. The others were half-convinced, but waited to withhold final
commitment until they saw which way the wind blew. At least no
one had flatly refused.

After they left Gergovia, I told Rix, "You have to win Ollovico
of the Bituriges somehow. His tribe is essential if we are to hold
the center of Gaul."

"And what of the Carnutes north of them? Your own tribe,
Ainvar? Tasgetius ignored my summons."

"Tasgetius is so Romanized he all but wears the toga. But he will not long be king at Cenabum. I promise you that."

"How long do you think we have before Caesar attempts to overrun all of Gaul?"

"I've put that question to our seers. They tell me we have at the most five winters; probably less."

"Druid seers," Rix said with contempt. "What do they know?"

The longer I knew Rix, the more his disbelief worried me. Man and Otherworld must work together. Otherwise . . .

Before saying farewell to Rix, I paid the same courtesy to Hanesa. He responded by spouting an interminable epic concerning the coming of the kings to Gergovia and their immediate, unqualified devotion to the brilliant Vercingetorix.

"That isn't quite what happened," I pointed out.

"I know," replied the bard, "but it sounds better."

"Perhaps so. It just isn't the truth."

He gave me a sly look. "That tale about the Germans being cannibals wasn't exactly the truth, either. But it seemed to be just what you wanted Vercingetorix to hear."

I had to smile. "You're more perceptive than I realized. But after listening to you, I'm beginning to doubt the veracity of any history."

"People want their histories to be colorful, Ainvar. If you tell an audience what they want to hear, the way they want to hear it, then they'll listen and believe. Don't you suppose that's the way Caesar reports his deeds to the Roman Senate?"

Wisdom comes from many sources. Hanesa made me wonder, for the first time, just what sort of stories Caesar was telling about the Gauls to those beyond our borders who would never know us except through his reports.

Later I would realize that he told many lies indeed to justify his attempt to destroy an entire people. He was not satisfied with discrediting the druids. He represented all Celts as wretched and ignorant savages whose one hope lay in subjugating themselves to the more enlightened Romans.

His calumnies were not only believed, they were destined to endure because he wrote them down.

Ah, Menua, there you were mistaken! Our truth should also have been committed to vellum and leather, etched in copper and carved in wood and scribed on wax tablets, so there would be voices to speak for us to future generations, to counter the Roman lies.

Now it is too late . . . unless I whisper on the wind. The wind never forgets. Someday, someone may hear . . . with the senses of the spirit. . . .

Knowing Rix would send for me again, I set out for home.

On the way I stopped at Cenabum, having first sent Tarvos to ascertain if Tasgetius was in the town. When the Bull reported, "He's away with a hunting party," I entered the gates and made my way to the lodge of Cotuatus.

Menua's kinsman had changed since I first met him. I remembered a fleshy man with eyes like bright blue stones set in deep pouches. Now I saw a man who had burned off his surplus fat as a warrior does preparing for war. Even the pouches were diminished, the whole being leaner and tighter. "We're still waiting for word from you, Ainvar," was his greeting to me. "My sword hand itches."

"It must itch a while longer. We can't afford to have anything happen to Tasgetius until there is a replacement for him. This is no time to leave the tribe headless."

The blue eyes flashed defiance. "What if I refuse to wait? Tasgetius murdered Menua, yet still occupies a kingly lodge and laughs and drinks and tumbles women. His pleasure hurts me more than my own pain. Blood cries for blood, druid. You understand."

I did understand. I also knew he must not defy me. As we stood facing each other, I gathered the force of my mind and hurled it at him in one concentrated, white-hot bolt.

Cotuatus staggered. His face spurted sweat. Raising a hand to his temple, he groaned, "Terrible pain . . . I've never had such a headache . . . help me, druid."

I folded my arms across my chest. "Help yourself. Abandon any thought of ever acting against my advice."

Even in his agony he understood. His head bowed in silent acknowledgment.

I relaxed, letting my heart slow its thunder. Such efforts cost my body dearly.

"It's easing now," Cotuatus muttered. Then he breathed a shaky sigh of relief. "It's almost gone."

His eyes, when he lifted them to meet mine, glittered with fear.

Then I knew I was no longer imitating Menua but had become chief druid in every particular, able to draw upon the power of generations of my predecessors. Once I would not have risked hurting Cotuatus; I would have sought to make him like me. Now

I understood it was not important for me to be liked. But I must be respected.

Cotuatus, a powerful prince of the Carnutes, had just acquired a deep respect for me. He might in time be molded into a satisfactory candidate for the kingship. He would need guidance and instruction, but at least he was Celtic to the core.

As I left his lodge, my eye fell upon a cluster of his warrior followers loitering near their prince's lodge. A man with swords sworn to him liked to be able to look out his door and see them nearby.

Among them I caught a glimpse of a dark, sullen face, and one shoulder abnormally higher than the other. I nodded to him, but Crom Daral looked right through me.

As I rejoined my retinue and we left Cenabum, I remarked to Tarvos, "I may have found our next king."

"Who?"

"Cotuatus. He has qualities the tribe will need, I think. He needs to learn more about the entire situation, of course, and expand his thoughts to accept new ideas, but he should be capable. I just . . . "

Tarvos knew me; he heard the doubt in my voice. "You just what?"

"I wish I had thought of him as a potential king sooner. Then I wouldn't have sent Crom Daral to him."

"You did it as a kindness to Crom, even if he doesn't know it."

"Kindness," I echoed. "I wonder if my misguided kindness has sent our next king a black bird of ill omen."

"Shall I go back and see about getting him sent to some other prince?"

"No, that would just make everything worse. I would look indecisive and Crom might well figure out that I was behind his assignment in the first place, which could cause all sorts of complications. Leave it alone, Tarvos."

So we left Crom Daral with Cotuatus, but thoughts of him lingered troublingly at the back of my mind, like a small, nagging splinter in the flesh.

I was more glad than ever to return to the fort, and the grove. When my people came out to greet me, my eyes found one bright face in the crowd before any other, and I released a breath I did not know I had been holding.

Briga did not have to smile at me. It was enough to know she was there.

Meanwhile, Tarvos trotted past me, a wide grin gleaming

through his moustache as he hurried toward the open doorway of his lodge, where Lakutu stood waiting.

As if the scattered sparks from the great fire of creation must obey a cosmological command to rejoin, we are compelled to seek the missing parts of ourselves. We collect friends, we require mates. Each of us separately is a fragment; life is the whole.

That night in my bed I was painfully aware that Lakutu no longer slept curled at my feet.

In the dead of winter the work of the druids continues. While our people shelter in warm lodges, we whisper to the seedlings sleeping in the frozen earth. We light the fires that will guide the reluctant sun back from the realms of frost. We supervise birth and burial, keeping the living and the dead in harmony with the earth and the Otherworld.

And we teach. A druid's words are most clearly heard in the crisp silence of a winter's day.

I resumed instructing the hopeful applicants for the Order, Briga among them. "So many new faces," old Grannus commented. "They are drawn to you, Ainvar. Menua began building your reputation long before you became chief druid, you know. He claimed you could . . ."

His jaws snapped shut. The old often become garrulous, and Grannus obviously had just realized he was saying too much.

"What claims did Menua make for me?"

"Ah. You know. He said you had gifts."

"What gifts?"

Grannus twitched a shoulder. "It's been a long time, you cannot expect me to remember everything he said."

But I knew he had not forgotten, not with his druid's memory. Menua must have told him—and others—that I could restore life to the dead.

The idea appalled me. I did not want people looking to me for a magic beyond my ability. I could do many things that seemed impossible to the uninitiated, but were actually only a matter of manipulating natural forces. Yet even I could not lure an escaped spirit back into a cooling body.

Could I?

Sometimes I still awoke in the night, wondering.

CHAPTER TWENTY-THREE

WHILE THE druids were occupied with winterwork, the Romans were also busy. Though Caesar spent most of the winter in Latium, I learned that the officers he had left behind in Gaul were enlarging and fortifying the winter camps and arranging supplies for his next campaign in the spring.

North of us lay the territory of the Belgae, tribes originally of Germanic origin for the most part, who had occupied northern Gaul for so long that they were as Gaulish as we. The fertile, easily worked land they had captured when they first came across the Rhine had encouraged them to abandon their wild ways and become farmers and herders. We of central Gaul took women from them, traded with them, waged war with them as we did with one another.

Caesar announced that the Belgic tribes were conspiring against Rome.

Vercingetorix sent for me.

"You can't go before Beltaine," Tarvos protested.

"Of course not, but I'll leave immediately after. Why are you so concerned about when we go?"

"I . . . I intend to marry Lakutu at Beltaine. She's not a slave anymore," he went on hurriedly before I could object. "You gave me that scroll saying she was mine, so I made her face the sun and then I said, 'I salute you as a free person.' That was enough, wasn't it? To make her free?"

The Bull was nervous as I had never seen him, and equally, desperately, serious. I swallowed a smile as I replied, "I should say so, yes. You have it on the authority of the chief druid: Lakutu is a free person.

"But are you certain you want to marry her? Do you want her to bear children for you? She isn't one of us, she isn't from any part of Gaul. She's not even a German."

"She's from Egypt," the Bull said with shy pride.

"What?"

"She's from Egypt. She told me. Is Egypt very far away, Ainvar?"

I was finding this difficult to digest. "It's very far away," I managed to say. "Why, does she want to go back?"

"Oh no, she says she's content to spend her life here, even if we do smell."

These revelations about Lakutu, former enigma, were unsettling. "What does she mean, we smell?"

"Because of the food we eat. Remember Rix explaining that the reason the Roman warriors reeked of garlic was because they were fed it to build up their strength? Lakutu says we Gauls stink of blood because we eat so much meat."

I stared at him. I had never known that Lakutu found my odor offensive.

For a second season I conducted the Beltaine ceremonies as Keeper of the Grove. I watched as Tarvos led Lakutu in the ancient steps of pursuit and capture, coupling and thanksgiving. Many couples came to the grove to be married that year; the air rang with song.

We were a people who sang.

The poisoning had left Lakutu very thin, and there were now streaks of gray in her black hair. Yet on the day she married Tarvos she was young. Her eyes were as shiny as two black olives and she giggled behind her hand.

Because she had no clan of her own, the women of the fort

provided her marriage costume. They dressed her in a close-fitting bodice of softest fleece, like a spun cloud against her olive complexion. Her skirt was embroidered with red and blue knotwork, and boots of dyed kidskin covered her feet to the anklebone. Around her waist was my own contribution.

"I want you to make a girdle for her," I told the Goban Saor, "superior in value to what I paid for her on the auction block. Under the law it will remain her property in marriage; it will speak for her worth."

When Lakutu danced the pattern dance with Tarvos around the Beltaine tree, she wore gold and silver at her waist, and the watching women exclaimed enviously at its magnificence.

Perhaps she was Egyptian, as she claimed. I never knew. Watching her in her happiness, I saw no different race. I saw only Lakutu, who was part of us.

Part of the whole.

Tarvos would never know how I envied him that day.

In the cycle of seasons since the last Beltaine when I had taken Briga by the river, somehow there had never been an opportunity for us to be just a man and a woman together, to come to the understanding that precedes a marriage. When we were in the grove, I was chief druid with neophytes to teach; when we were in the fort, my people were likely to come to the door at any time of the day or night, requesting my wisdom or my magic.

The demands of my office left me little time for devoting myself to winning a difficult woman.

And Briga was maddeningly unpredictable. Other women ran until you caught them, then they were yours. Briga, once caught, would not stay caught.

When I finally succeeded in bringing together an uncommitted moment and a private place, she shied away from my arms.

"What's wrong?"

"I can't . . . care for you, Ainvar."

I was baffled. "Why not? I am young, strong, healthy . . . I have high rank in the tribe. . . ."

"You don't understand," she said in a voice so low I could hardly hear her. "There is something worse than grief, you know. There is an anguish so deep it becomes a pit of nothingness. I've been in that pit. I'm never going back there.

"I've thought and thought about it—you're always urging us to think. So I have. I've decided the only way to avoid that pit is never to love anyone, so I can never be hurt by losing them." She set her chin, she stiffened her spine. Prince's daughter.

The irony was, I knew the irrefutable answer. "But no one ever really dies, Briga. You haven't lost those you loved, their spirits are immortal. Death is merely an incident in the middle of a long life."

"I know, I know," she said dismissively. My facile words had not reached the suffering core of her. She refused to be freed of her fear. She wanted some proof that went beyond words, she needed a confirmation of the soul's survival that would permeate her blood and bone.

That gift came with being accepted into the Order by the Otherworld. Its season could not be rushed. Even the Keeper of the Grove could not force it. I must be content with teaching her and preparing her.

So I did not dance with Briga around the Beltaine tree that year. I stood in the shadow of the oaks and watched her broodingly from the darkness of my hood as she laughed and clapped with the other celebrants surrounding the dancing couples. In my pride, I did not go to her when the pattern dance was over and the married pairs stretched themselves upon the earth. Some of our people joined in a general coupling, with which we traditionally supported the newly married. But I stood aloof, wretched in my dignity.

I would have killed anyone else who tried to touch Briga. But no one did. Her erect posture forbade it, and for once I was glad she was a prince's daughter.

The season of celebration ended; Vercingetorix needed me. Tarvos and I set out with a complement of warriors as my bodyguard. It was unwise for anyone to travel unarmed in Gaul anymore, not even a chief druid. The predators had come.

As we were about to leave, Grannus drew me aside. "Are you certain it's wise for you should go off like this to the Arvernian? It's one thing to leave your people during the honey moon, Ainvar. But this is different."

"Are you questioning the wisdom of the Keeper of the Grove?"

"I'm questioning the wisdom of your going so far away from your own people for long periods. I'm an old man," he added in a voice as thin as the skin on boiled milk, "and that is one of the prerogatives of age. I can question anyone and anything."

"I'm doing this for the sake of my tribe, Grannus. The Carnutes
are best served by my supporting Vercingetorix in every way I
can."

Grannus was shaking his head. "You're mad if you think the
Arvernian, or anyone, can unite the tribes. Only a man too young
to know better would dream such a dream."

"Only young men dream, Grannus. When a man stops dreaming,
he knows he is old.

"As for my leaving the grove, I am appointing someone I trust
fully to serve in my absence and protect the grove with his flesh
and his spirit."

"Dian Cet?"

"Aberth."

Grannus peered at me from rheumy eyes. "You continue to
surprise me. Why the sacrificer? I would have thought the chief
judge was the obvious choice."

Thinking of Diviciacus of the Aedui, I replied, "I have become
reluctant to put too much power into the hands of judges. Aberth
is a fanatic, the one person who can never be swerved from his
course.

"The only restriction I have laid upon him is that he is not to
give the neophytes any instruction until I return," I added. I did
not want Briga to learn about sacrifice from Aberth's lips. I had
enough problems.

On the morning we left the fort, the region was bathed in the
sultry golden light that precedes thunder. It was too early in the
year for such a storm, yet one was gathering in the air. The weather
made our horses nervous.

We would be traveling on horseback like a company of cavalry,
riding animals Ogmios had arranged for us. Walking took too long
and events were moving too fast. To deal with constantly changing
situations, I had determined to take my feet from the earth and
let them dangle at the sides of a swift-galloping horse.

I missed the walking, however.

The Gaulish style of riding differed from the Roman. Caesar
mounted his cavalry on animals with African blood in them. They
were thin-skinned, thin-legged animals with nostrils flared for

drinking the desert wind. The horses we bred in Gaul were sturdier, with good strong heads and dense leg bones. We rode them bareback; Roman cavalry sat on felt pads held in place with breast-collar and crupper.

Our horses were allowed to gallop freely so long as they went in the desired direction; Caesar's troops rode in rigid ranks with every animal under tight rein. Yet, surprisingly, most Roman cavalry comprised Celtic auxiliaries drafted in the Province and the outlands. This was because the Romans were more often than not indifferent horsemen, while everyone admitted the Celts were magnificent riders even when conforming to Roman order.

We were riding down a long, narrow valley when a dark ribbon appeared on the skyline to the east. "Look there!" cried Tarvos, reining in. "A Roman scouting party, do you recognize the formation?"

"Unmistakable," I agreed. My every sense was alert, my skin prickled with warning. "They've never come so deep into our territory, Tarvos."

We halted, huddled together, fifteen men on horses staring east while our mounts snorted and pawed, sniffing the wind blowing toward us from the invaders.

Tarvos said tensely, "They've seen us."

The column on the horizon halted in perfect order, every rider maintaining his exact distance from the others. The figure in the lead was the only one who moved, turning toward us and coming a little way down the slope to get a better look.

My warriors reached for their weapons.

"Don't move," I ordered.

They hesitated, turning their eyes toward me.

Tarvos said crisply, "You heard the chief druid. Don't move, any of you."

The Roman officer advanced, drew rein, stared in our direction for a while, then turned and cantered back to his men, his short campaign cloak billowing from his shoulders like a farewell wave to us. The column moved away down the other side of the slope and out of sight.

"Where are they going?" Tarvos wanted to know.

"North, obviously. Not to attack, there aren't enough of them. They're looking for something, and I don't like it. There is nothing for them in the land of the Carnutes . . . at least nothing I'm willing to let them have.

"I want to discuss this with Vercingetorix."

We kicked our horses into a gallop and surged out of the valley, riding southward across the gently undulating plain.

In order to talk with Rix this time, I would not have to go as far as Gergovia. We were to meet in the fortified town of Avaricum, where he was trying to convince Ollovico, king of the Bituriges, to join with us in a confederacy of Gaulish tribes resisting Caesar.

We reached Avaricum shortly after midday. The sun shone with a flat, metallic light, and the sky was dull in spite of a lack of cloud. The air smelled like dust. As we neared the town, I saw a sea of leather tents pitched in a random sprawl outside its walls, with vivid Arvernian standards fluttering from poles around the perimeter of the area. "See that, Tarvos. Vercingetorix has brought an army with him."

"He's a king," the Bull replied sensibly.

We had ridden hard and I was more weary than I would admit. But the sight of the largest tent, with the standard of Rix's own clan fluttering proudly above it, lifted my heart and I urged my horse into a smart trot toward the tent.

The sentry on duty outside shouted. Rix emerged, saw me, and ran forward to meet me. "I greet you as a free person!" he called while I sawed on the reins and tried to make my lathered horse rear on its haunches to impress him. The horse declined, shaking his head and backing up several paces instead. I should have known better; he was not a being who enjoyed having demands unexpectedly thrust upon him.

I managed to halt him and slid gratefully onto the unmoving earth.

"I didn't know you rode," Rix said as he came up to me and we hugged.

"My father was horse rank," I reminded him. "My grandmother made certain I learned to ride, though I haven't done much of it since my childhood."

His eyes twinkled. "So I see. You can't put your knees together, can you?" He laughed; we hugged and pounded each other. But when I drew back to get a good look at him, I saw new lines in his face. "Remind me to show you the black colt I'm training for myself," he said as he led me to his tent. "A superb animal. For experienced riders," he added, laughing again.

An aide poked his head through the tent flap. "Bring hot water," Rix ordered. "And wine, and food for my friends. But hot water first."

I had never been more grateful for the Celtic tradition that says a man must be allowed to bathe his face and feet after a journey before anything is expected of him.

When we were sitting at our ease in Rix's tent, with my own Tarvos standing guard outside the door as well as Rix's Arvernians, I told him of the Roman scouting party we had seen.

Rix scowled. "That's a bad sign. I didn't know they were in your territory."

"Neither did we."

"They probably hoped to stay out of sight, but your plains offer little cover."

"Can you make a guess as to their destination?"

Rix rubbed his jaw thoughtfully; his fingers made his crisp beard crackle. "Looking for a site for another of Caesar's camps, I'd say. There's no doubt he's begun a campaign against the Belgae, so he'll be wanting fortifications to guard his supply lines."

"Not in my land," I growled.

Rix grinned. "You're sounding very belligerent for a druid."

"There's no question of not fighting. It's only a matter of when and how."

"That's why I asked you to join me, Ainvar. I'm going to need your help to convince Ollovico to stand with us. I've done everything I could think of, I even brought an army with me to let him see how ready we are, what splendid fighters he would be joining forces with. But he's decided any form of union would be a threat to his personal sovereignty. He insists he can protect the land of the Bituriges without outside help, and says there is no reason why his tribe should shed blood to defend some other tribe."

"I doubt he's the only king thinking that way. How many others have you succeeded in convincing?"

Rix rose and began pacing the limited confines of the tent. It was too small for him, but any enclosed space was always too small for Vercingetorix. "Not enough," he said. "Not enough at all. I've spent the winter traveling from tribe to tribe, letting Hanesa tell them how wonderful I am, contesting at arms with their best war-

riors, but I'm not making much progress. Perhaps I'm the wrong
man for this, Ainvar."

Self-doubt was so unlike him it worried me more than the Roman
scouting party. "You're the only man capable!" I insisted. "You're
made for it . . . and it was your father's dream."

Rix stopped pacing. "It was my father's dream to make the
Arverni the dominant tribe in Gaul. That's what some of the kings
fear. They suspect I'm using this as a ploy to seize control of their
tribelands. I repeat to them the words you said to me, but they
don't seem to have much effect when you're not with me."

"Perhaps one man cannot use another man's magic," I suggested.

He raised his hooded lids to glare at me. "I'm not talking about
magic, Ainvar! Druid smoke and muttering. I'm talking about the
real world."

"You have a limited vision of reality."

"Ah no! You won't get me involved in one of those convoluted
druidic conversations! Surely you know by now that I don't believe
in the Order and what it stands for; I only believe in my good
sword arm. *That's* real."

It was neither the time nor the place to attempt to restore Rix
to harmony with the Otherworld. But someday soon I must, I
realized, before disharmony made achievement impossible for him.
As it was, he was right to doubt himself. Man cannot succeed by
flesh alone. Earth and Otherworld always interact.

Even Caesar, though he sacrificed to Roman gods, operated on
an instinctive level, obeying the pattern as it applied to him. The
proof was in his accomplishments. If Rix was to be the weapon
Gaul would use against Caesar, he must be as whole and as in
balance as we could make him.

Like Briga, though for a different reason, he would have to be
taught. But would he accept? Menua had once told me, "Men do
not believe what they cannot see, and they will not see what they
do not believe. That is why magic is a mystery to them."

But when would there be time to convince Rix he was galloping
down the wrong path? If only I could take him, alone, to the grove,
I thought . . . if only it were possible to subject him to the rituals
reserved for druids . . .

"Ainvar?" he said sharply.

"I'll go with you to Ollovico," I said aloud, "and you will try
again to persuade him. It must be your voice he hears, Rix, for it

is your leadership he will have to accept. But before we go I'll rehearse your arguments with you. Then you must say your own words, not mine. Say them your way."

By the time we emerged from the tent a savage storm had swept out of the north, driven by a baleful wind. The sky was a sickly greenish color and forked spears of fire flickered on the horizon.

"We'll ride into Avaricum together," Rix told me. "Ollovico is tiring of the sight of my face, but he'll welcome you."

Hanesa appeared out of nowhere, slowing us down, spewing words from his mouth as if they were pebbles too hot to hold. I appreciated his pleasure in seeing me, but was glad when Rix told him he must stay behind this time. There would be only Vercingetorix and myself and thirty of his warriors—and Tarvos, of course.

I always insisted on Tarvos.

The storm was drawing closer. "Lakutu hates this sort of weather," Tarvos said as I stepped into his cupped hands and swung my leg over the back of my horse. I did not have time to reply. The skittish animal bolted forward at the sound of thunder, and I had to fight to bring it under control.

Rix rode up to us on a tall black colt with a fine head. The young stallion was snorting and rolling his eyes, but Rix controlled him deftly between leg and hand, turning him so he could not see the lightning. "Do you like him, Ainvar?" he asked as he patted the glossy, arched neck.

"Very much. But I doubt if I could handle him."

Rix grinned. "I doubt it, too. He accepts no one but me."

"Horsemen always like to claim that," Tarvos muttered to me from behind his hand.

Following Rix's standard-bearer, we entered the gates of Avaricum, watched but unchallenged by the sentries. As servants were taking our horses, the storm broke over our heads; we ran the last few paces to the king's lodge.

"I welcome the chief druid of the Carnutes as a free person," Ollovico told me. "And you also, Vercingetorix. Though we've seen rather too much of you recently."

Rix has indeed pushed too hard, I thought. "The impetuosity of youth," I said, smiling at Ollovico as if we were two mature men together in a conspiracy against the overardent young. As I spoke, I envisioned myself old, gray-skinned, with the tracks of the seasons carved deep in my face. Concentrating, I forced flesh to obey spirit.

The druid whom Ollovico saw seemed of an age with himself.
Wise, experienced, more to be trusted. "You're older than I remembered, Ainvar. Perhaps you can help me talk sense to this
foolish fellow, since I know him for a friend of yours. I've given
thought to the idea of a confederacy among the Gaulish tribes and
decided it is madness."

"Is it?" I asked innocently.

"Indeed. Here, sit . . . do you want water for your face? Or
wine? You sit too, Vercingetorix, of course. . . . As I was saying,
Ainvar, trying to get the tribes to accept each other as allies will
never work. Why, Vercingetorix has been telling me I would have
to serve in the field with the Turones, and we're on the verge of
war with them now over some women of ours they've stolen."

I lifted my eyebrows. "Haven't you ever stolen their women?"

Ollovico shrugged. His was an interesting face. Beneath thin,
pinched nostrils shaped for sniffing disapproval, his mouth was a
wide and amiable curve. He was caught between two poles of
expression, never able to surrender completely to either. His frown
could not frighten or his smile hearten.

"That's different," he was saying. "We need wives to bring fresh
blood into our clans."

"So do the Turones. You could have intermarriage between your
tribes without warfare."

"But there must be war, Ainvar! Victorious warriors get the pick
of the best women, and women respect you more when you fight
for them and win them.

"It's only through tribal warfare that we prove ourselves as men.
Vercingetorix wants us to set aside centuries of tradition and flock
together like sheep. I tell you, the women would laugh at us."

Since the chief druid of the Carnutes had not proven himself an
expert on female behavior, I decided it was time for Rix to take
up the argument. "You will have all the fighting you want if you
join Vercingetorix," I said. "He tells me Caesar is now attacking
the Belgae."

Ollovico turned for the first time to Rix. "How do you know
this?"

"I have sources among many tribes who are cooperating to keep
an eye on the Roman. Working together, we follow his every move
as one tribe alone could not."

Well done, I thought.

"If Caesar does attack the Belgae, what has that to do with me and my people?" Ollovico wanted to know. "You still haven't convinced me that any of this concerns the Bituriges."

Rix leaned forward, fixing Ollovico with a compelling, hooded gaze. "Caesar has trained his legions to move at a speed no other army can equal. In the Province I watched them drilling, day after day after day. Every man is taught to adjust his stride to the length of a short thrusting spear, then to quicken that pace to a speed near running and maintain it for half a day at a time.

"If Caesar has armies in the north and decides to bring them into central Gaul, he can be upon us before any tribe is prepared, as things are now. If his legions are within seven nights of any one of us, they threaten us all, Ollovico."

Rix paused for breath and glanced at me. I nodded encouragement. He continued. "This very day I have learned from Ainvar, here, that Roman patrols have been seen in the land of the Carnutes, no great distance from your Avaricum, Ollovico. No distance at all, to a Roman.

"Think on it. Roman warriors in the heart of Gaul.

"For that reason the chief druid of the Carnutes has come at the gallop to confer with the chief druid of the Bituriges . . . you know how members of the Order like to confer with one another in times of danger."

Ollovico turned to me. "Is this true?"

"I'm very concerned about the safety of the great grove."

His pupils dilated. "Caesar wouldn't dare—"

"Caesar would dare anything," Rix interposed. "He's bringing more and more troops out of Latium and the Province, and they're reportedly building both roads and permanent fortifications. They mean to stay in Gaul, Ollovico, within striking distance of your tribe and mine."

"Not that close, surely . . ."

Rix leaned back and folded his arms across his chest. "From the great grove to Cenabum is not two days' march at the speed of the legions," he said in a matter-of-fact tone. "The same again would bring them to the walls of Avaricum."

Ollovico was wavering. I could see him trying to imagine distances and envisioning men marching. "Is it possible?"

"I assure you it is," Rix told him. "I might be wrong by half a day, but no more than that. You are very vulnerable to Caesar,

Ollovico, we all are. We can very easily be caught in his closing fist. The sooner the tribes of free Gaul can be made to understand this and prepare for their mutual defense, the safer we'll be.

"We need you and your Bituriges, Ollovico, and you need the rest of us. Every tribe can guard its neighbors' borders, and in the event of total war, all our numbers together would be a match for Caesar's legions. It's very simple," Rix concluded with an air of almost negligent disdain. "Stand with us or die alone." Then he winked at me.

Because I was with him, he was sure of himself again. He denied the Otherworld, but when I, a representative of the spirits, was beside him, his balance was restored and his confidence returned.

Confidence is a powerful magic.

Rix moved in relentlessly; Ollovico gave ground rapidly. By the time we left his lodge, Rix had his pledge to join the confederacy, though with a stipulation. "If Caesar attacks the center of Gaul with his armies, and the other tribes agree to follow your standard, Vercingetorix, I shall also. But I demand your word that you will make no attempt to usurp the kingship of the Bituriges."

"I have my own tribe," Rix assured him. "All I want is to keep them free."

Free.

It is a simple word. Yet if the great grove was the heart of Gaul, freedom was Gaul's lifeblood.

Fleetingly, I wondered if the Belgae felt the same way about their freedom. . . .

Chapter Twenty-four

Vercingetorix was elated. His success with Ollovico left him too excited to sleep, so we passed the night in his tent in earnest conversation. Sometime before dawn I hoped to be able to insert a few subtle references to the importance, and the reality, of the Otherworld; to begin tearing down the dangerous walls of resistance he had erected.

But Rix had more tangible matters on his mind. "I'm going back to the kings I visited before, Ainvar. Now that I have the support of Ollovico to use as a lever, I know I can persuade more of them to join with us. I may even go to some of the tribes on the fringes of free Gaul. They'll be the first Caesar gobbles up. I won't need you to go with me, I know how to handle them now."

That night he felt he could do anything.

I was glad; it was a feeling he needed if we were to succeed at all. So I kept my lips sealed on the topic of the Otherworld. Why run the risk of alienating him now? There would be other opportunities, other conversations.

Besides, my concentration was fragmented. The patrol we had seen was very much on my mind. Rix had spoken the truth when he told Ollovico I was concerned for the safety of the grove.

Now Caesar was occupied with the Belgae; but when the time came to turn his attention to free Gaul, his initial attack might be against its druids. I had observed how Rome discredited and ultimately outlawed the druids of Narbonese Gaul in order to eliminate any influence other than Roman upon the people.

If Caesar meant to do the same thing in free Gaul, what better way to begin than by destroying its sacred center? A dreadful intuition warned me that the scouting party we saw might have been seeking the exact location of the great grove.

For Caesar's future reference.

I was relieved that Rix did not feel he needed me to go with him to the other kings. More than anything else I wanted to be riding north again, to assure myself of the safety of the fort, and Briga, and Lakutu. And the trees.

Rix and I had a final conversation in the morning before I left. All around us his warriors were breaking camp, taking down the leather tents, packing supplies, leading horses to water, sorting weapons, laughing and challenging and insulting one another, tripping over tent pegs, urinating noisily onto bare earth, singing and swearing and swirling with the customary confusion of Celtic warriors about to march.

Rix surveyed the chaos. "Ainvar," he said thoughtfully, "in the Roman army camps each man has specific duties that he performs in a certain order. No more, no less, the same way every time. None of this scrambling around and two men arguing over who gets to pack the mule."

I saw the direction his thoughts were taking. "Can you imagine ordering Gaulish warriors to measure every stride they took? It wouldn't suit our style, Rix."

He rubbed his jaw. His eyes brooded below their hooded lids. "Caesar's bringing us a new face of war. The old reasons for fighting—the sort of thing Ollovico was saying yesterday—it's all changed, hasn't it?"

"Yes. I've had that thought myself."

"And there's no going back."

"No." Recalling a favorite saying of Menua's, I recited, "The inexorable rhythm of the seasons brings an end to all, to joy and sorrow alike. Winter to summer, death to birth, the wheel turns, and we must turn with it."

"Druid," Rix said sourly.

"But true."

"You're always beating that drum, aren't you? Oh, you're very subtle, Ainvar, but I know what you're doing. You hate it that I don't believe anymore. But you just said yourself, everything changes. Perhaps mine is the new way. Perhaps we don't need all that chanting and pattern-dancing and sacrificing any longer. Caesar doesn't dance patterns."

"Caesar sacrifices to Roman gods. I've heard their priests say so. No king dares openly defy the deities."

"If gods exist. You say the Roman ones are invented by Man. How can you prove that ours are not? 'Believe,' you tell me, but I don't believe; yet no bolt from the Source has struck me to punish me.

"What I do believe in, Ainvar, is your intelligence and your sound advice when we're dealing with practical matters and you're not off in a mist somewhere."

I bit off the words that leaped to my tongue. I must not indulge in the luxury of arguing with him now; any sort of division between us would be dangerous. "I have to get back to the grove," I said stiffly.

"You're angry with me."

"No."

"You'll come to me again if I need you?"

I met his eyes. "When you need me."

He swallowed but he did not blink, "I'll send word to you," he said.

Before leaving, I had the most cursory of meetings with the druid Nantua, to repeat my warning about danger to the grove in case Ollovico should say anything to him about it. I also used the opportunity to stress that he must keep encouraging Ollovico to support Vercingetorix.

"The arrangements of war are matters for warriors," the chief druid of the Bituriges said reprovingly.

"I'm talking about naked survival, Nantua! And that is the concern of *druids!*"

Galloping northward, I remembered the shock on his face. The

danger was still not real to him. It was not real to any of them yet.
Caesar was a shout in the distance; they could not comprehend
the threat he posed.

Yet every day that threat grew nearer.

As we came pounding across the plain, I saw, with a sense of
indescribable relief, the great grove standing inviolate against
the sky.

I had barely entered the gates of the fort before I was needed
for this and for that, to go here, run there, confer with him, demonstrate to her. I plunged into summerwork, and when I could
spare a thought at all, I thought of Vercingetorix in the south,
riding from tribe to tribe, trying to gather a following.

Children who wanted to become druids followed at my heels as
I went about the fort or walked in the surrounding countryside.
One of them, my most ardent follower, was the boy Briga had
cured of blindness. Remembering myself walking in Menua's
shadow, I saved a special smile for the lad.

"Has he a gift?" I asked his mother, a farmer's wife with creamy
skin and a generous mouth. I recalled her from the first hot seasons
of my manhood.

"None that I know of, except for his fascination with the druids."

"When he's old enough for instruction send him to me, then.
He's already received one gift: He can see, while remembering
the darkness. We'll make something of him."

Harvest brought Lughnasa; autumn brought Samhain with the
winter stretching ahead. At the Samhain convocation that year I
told the assembled druids, "Caesar has spent the summer fighting
the Belgic tribes. After building innumerable fortifications and killing countless women and children, he has finally defeated them,
and then on some pretext attacked the Nervii and their allies, the
Aduatuci. He cuts a swath across the northland from the Rhine to
the Gallic Sea. So far, the protection Menua gained for us with
sacrifice has held, and we have been spared Caesar's attentions.
But who can say how much longer that may last?"

"I have been told that for the purposes of campaigning he has
divided Gaul into three parts. He intends to subdue each part
separately. The Belgae are the first, the Aquitani in the southwest
will be next. The central region will be his final target. Free Gaul.
Including us.

"If Caesar succeeds in turning Gaul into one of the Roman provinces, he will make certain there are no druids left, except men like his misguided ally, Diviciacus of the Aedui. He will destroy the Order of the Wise so no thinkers are left to resist him, and he will sell our people into slavery. I have seen Celtic women on the auction block while the crowd leered at them and their captors fondled them and rubbed against them and laughed at their shame. I have seen this and worse—I have observed children of our race begging in the streets of Roman towns because their clans have been forced to adopt Roman ways and no longer care for their orphans as we do."

I went on spinning a web with my words until the smell of fear rose like a fecal stench from my listeners. I wanted them to be afraid. Not of death, which is the least thing, but of entrapment, of square pens, square houses, paved streets, shackled legs, crushed spirits. . .

"Persuade your tribes to unite under Vercingetorix," I urged, "or tribe by tribe Caesar will conquer us all."

During the long, cold winter, the druid network fanned out across Gaul, speaking in favor of the Gaulish confederacy under Rix's leadership. I could only hope the Order still had enough power in the land to make a difference.

A visiting druid from the north, making his first pilgrimage to the sacred center of Gaul, told me about the aftermath of Caesar's campaign against the Belgae.

He was one of the Remi, neighbors of the Belgae who, fearing for their own safety, had bowed before Caesar and been the loudest in accusing the Belgae of conspiring against Rome. For standing with Caesar they had expected to be left in charge of the region when he withdrew his armies.

"But when the fighting was over, Caesar did not withdraw his troops," lamented the Remian. "Nor did he leave us in charge. Because he wages war on women and children as well as warriors, he had depopulated vast areas, and his own soldiers moved onto them and began building settlements!" The man was quivering with the indignation of the betrayed. "We are left with nothing to show for supporting Caesar."

"I could have warned you," I told him. "If you had come to me sooner, I could have told you about Caesar's pattern."

"It is a long journey for us . . . and there are not so many of us anymore . . . you don't understand. . . ."

"I understand that you've come running to the grove when the trouble grew serious enough. What is it—are the Romans now moving onto your lands also?"

He bowed his head.

The druids of the Remi were not the only ones who had rarely made pilgrimages to the grove since I became Keeper. Diviciacus of the Aedui had never appeared among the oaks.

I wondered if he still considered himself a member of the Order—or was he totally Caesar's man?

He had betrayed the Order, allowing himself to be seduced by the glittering metal and the clattering hooves of Roman might into thinking that Caesar's power was all he needed to protect his tribe. Perhaps he thought he had made the wisest choice for his people.

The weight of responsibility surely sat on Diviciacus as heavily as it did upon me.

Since returning from Avaricum I had questioned every sentry, every warrior, every craftsman and freeman and bondservant at the fort and in the surrounding area, to discover if any of them had seen a Roman patrol near the grove. No one had.

Yet at the base of my spine, I knew. I could smell danger to the grove.

"Ogmios, we need more lookouts at all times," I demanded. "You let too many men sleep when they should be watching every cart track and fold in the land. I want the grove protected, Ogmios, do you understand? Protected!"

"Are you afraid someone will steal the trees?" he asked, making a ponderous attempt at a joke.

"Yes!"

He stared at me with the blank expression of a genuinely stupid man trying to think. "How could they take so many without us knowing?"

I saw that Ogmios must soon surrender to the seasons and be replaced by a more alert and able captain. Knowing it was useless, I sent a message to Tasgetius requesting additional warriors for the fort.

"He'll never give them to you," Tarvos told me. "That man would not willingly put a single weapon in your hands."

"I know it. But I must observe the traditions."

"You still won't break with him openly?"

"Look what's happened because of the open break between

Dumnorix and Diviciacus. The Aedui are split in half, too weak
ever to resist Caesar. No, Tarvos, when the break comes with
Tasgetius it must appear to come from the people, not from a
member of the Order."

"When will that be?"

When. Everyone wanted to know when.

So did I.

Using the need for more guards for the grove as an excuse, I
visited Cenabum repeatedly, ostensibly to persuade Tasgetius but
actually to spend as much time as I could with the prince Cotuatus,
training him to think, to be prudent, to hold his temper, to recognize patterns, to plan ahead. I was preparing him for the very
special sort of king we would need in the near future.

As I had expected, Tasgetius refused to give us any more warriors. "You are mistaken about the Romans being any threat, Ainvar," he told me in the privacy of his lodge, where the antagonism
between us was open and naked now. "I think you are just using
that to try to get more armed men and build up your own power,
but I am too clever for you."

"Druids have never required the power of weapons."

"Times change."

"The very point I'm making. I am Keeper of the Grove, Tasgetius, and times are changing. If there is any threat to the grove
I am obligated to—"

"There isn't," he said harshly. "I don't know why you keep
making the trip to tell me there is. You've let the foolishness of
your predecessor infect you, you see shadows where there are
none."

"I saw a Roman patrol deep in our territory."

"No one reported it to me."

We glared at each other. He did not offer me food or drink,
knowing I would not accept. Knowing I knew. Not caring.

As chief druid, I visited each of the princes resident at Cenabum
before returning to the grove; I was within tradition to do so. I
was careful not to spend appreciably longer with Cotuatus than
with the others, but our conversations were held in desperately
earnest whispers.

He was not perfectly suited to our need, but he would have to
do. We were running out of time.

I invariably saw Crom Daral somewhere near Cotuatus's lodge

every time I visited the prince, the dark face turned toward me, the sullen eyes watching. Once I asked Cotuatus about him.

"Ah, the hunchback? He's all right. Not much good with weapons, but he's fiercely loyal to me. Won't let me out of his sight."

"That is his way," I said, remembering.

"I'm grateful to have someone like that to guard my back, Ainvar. He's like your Tarvos."

"No one is like Tarvos," I replied.

The seasons changed. Caesar had vanquished the Aduatuci on the pretext that they were a Germanic people, descendants of the Teutoni. Their punishment for daring to try to help the Nervii stand against him was for all who survived to be sold into slavery.

Without a qualm Gaius Caesar sent 53,000 people who had been born free to the auction block. He then went back to Latium for a time, leaving one of his strongest legions to attack and subdue the tribes on the western seaboard.

Though the heartland of Gaul was still free, Caesar had the temerity to announce in Rome that he had brought "peace" to the entirety of Gaul.

His peace including blatantly establishing a winter camp in Carnutian territory.

As soon as I learned of this, I almost killed a horse under me riding to Cenabum, Tarvos and my bodyguard pounding along in my dust. The gates of the stronghold were thrown open for us, but when I left my men and went to the king's lodge alone to avoid appearing provocative, the sentry on duty barred my way with his spear. Barred the chief druid!

Spitting in his face, I paralyzed the man with magic. Then I kicked open the heavy oak door; my leg ached for days afterward. I strode inside roaring, "Caesar has a camp on our tribeland! What do you know of it, Tasgetius?"

The king met me standing with his big freckled fists on his hips and belligerence in every line of his body. "Why shouldn't he? He's a friend."

"Caesar is no friend to any free person."

The king surveyed me coldly. Any pretense of normality in our relationship fell away like the shed skin of a snake. "He says my enemies are his enemies, druid."

I ignored the bait. Instead, I said, "Are you aware that one of his legions has overrun the tribe of the Veneti on the northwest coast, killed thousands of them and smashed their boats? With that one blow Caesar has cut off our entire supply of tin from Briton-land. Is that the act of a friend?"

"The Romans will sell us tin."

"I'm sure they will! At five times the price! Tasgetius, you fool, can't you see what's happening?"

I should not have called the king a fool to his face—I, who constantly urged prudence on others. But a Celt can ride his passions for only so long before they run away with him.

Tasgetius turned purple with outrage. "Guards!" he bellowed.

The sentry I had spat upon peered dizzily in through the doorway, still trying to shake off the effects of my magic. "Get help!" the king commanded.

The sentry blinked, swayed, backed out of our sight.

"I'll have you thrown out of Cenabum, Ainvar."

"You dare not publicly exile the chief druid," I told him confidently. "The people would rise against you, terrified that you were courting the wrath of the Otherworld."

"Then I'll kill you here and now and say you died of a fit!" He lifted those big fists and advanced toward me.

I did not take one step backward. I thought of stone; became stone. Cold granite on a winter's night. "Raise one hand to me and before your next breath I call down the lightning on this lodge," I warned. "You and everything in it will be burned to ash." Even as I spoke, thunder boomed.

Tasgetius hesitated. "No chief druid has ever killed a king," he said. He did not sound entirely certain, however.

I drew my lips back from my teeth in a grimace that was not a smile. "Not yet, Tasgetius."

The thunder spoke again. The stiffness went out of the king's spine. "Just leave, Ainvar. Leave this lodge and leave Cenabum. You may not realize it yet, but the time of the druids is over."

"You think it dies with the coming of Caesar? Then you are doubly a fool. We will always be needed. Who else understands the rhythms of the earth and the strength to be drawn from the patterns of the stars? Who else knows what sacrifices are needed to feed and reward the land for its fertility? Who else can placate the spirits of the insects so they don't devastate our crops?

"Without the intervention of the druids, Tasgetius, Man in his ignorance would rape and plunder the earth as surely as Caesar rapes and plunders the tribes. The earth would cease to provide then. There would be disaster."

The king sat down on his bench but did not invite me to sit also. With a sigh, he said, "Let me tell you a little plain truth, druid. There will be disaster if we shake our fists in Caesar's face the way you and your followers are advocating. Those who oppose the Roman suffer more when he overruns them than those who accede to him from the beginning."

He sounded tired, perhaps tired enough to listen to reason. "Don't you see? We don't have to be overrun, or to give in!" I said eagerly. "We can fight and win, Tasgetius. One tribe alone cannot defeat Caesar, that's been proven, but all of us together can—"

He snorted. "I've heard of your Gaulish confederation, heard of it until the very mention turns my belly. I tell you now and forever: I'll never surrender the Carnutes to any other leader."

"If you would just talk to Vercingetorix," I urged, "and get to know him, you would—"

The king gave me a sardonic smile. "When I'm talking to you, I am talking to Vercingetorix—don't you think I know that? My own chief druid supporting another king." He sounded very bitter and I knew I had lost him. No matter how persuasive Rix, or Rix and I together, might be with the other tribes, Tasgetius would resist to the death anything that involved me. Yet how could I be extricated from the pattern?

While I searched inside my head for something to say, the king asked, "What turned you against me, Ainvar? Once I thought we might be friends, colleagues. Then you insulted me by rejecting my traders and the gift of wine I sent you not once but three times. I knew then you were as opposed to my kingship as Menua had been."

The coldness returned to my voice. "My refusal was not meant as an insult to you. I merely wanted to have no trade with the Romans. We are growing our own grapes now; with one more warm summer we will be making Gaulish wine. Think of it, Tasgetius. We don't need the traders; we don't need Rome or anything it might offer. There is nothing that we cannot do for ourselves, in our own style—"

This time I was interrupted by a flurry of activity at the doorway as several armed guards shouldered through together, carrying daggers in their hands. When they realized they were confronting the chief druid, they halted, confused, and looked to the king for instructions.

For perhaps the only time in our lives Tasgetius and I thought the same thought at the same time; I could hear our two voices echoing in my head. There must be no public break between the king and the Keeper of the Grove.

At least there was that much kingship in him.

But he should not have mentioned Menua.

"The chief druid is just leaving," Tasgetius said rather stiffly to the guards. "Will you escort him to the gates?"

One of the guards asked in surprise, "Isn't he accepting the king's hospitality?"

"The king is famous for his hospitality but I have too many demands on my time," I replied smoothly. Then I gave Tasgetius a smile so insincere it made my lips sting, and he returned the gesture with a nod of his head that must have hurt his neck.

I left the lodge. There was no storm outside, of course.

The king's guards walked with me all the way to the main gates of Cenabum, though they did put their daggers, a form of short-sword, back into their scabbards. When Tarvos and my men saw them coming, they put their hands on the hilts of their own weapons and the two groups of warriors eyed one another uneasily.

"It's all right, Tarvos," I said. Then added under my breath, "But I have to see Cotuatus before I leave. Where is he?"

"He isn't in Cenabum, Ainvar. Crom Daral came by while I was arranging to exchange our tired horses for fresh ones. He was looking as sour as always, but I spoke to him for the clan's sake. He complained to me that Cotuatus had gone off and left him because he isn't a good enough horseman to keep up; they planned to travel fast."

"Who planned? To travel where?"

"Cotuatus and the prince Conconnetodumnus have gone to spy on the Roman encampment. Tasgetius doesn't know they've gone, but Crom says the king will bar the gates of Cenabum against them when he learns of it. And you know Crom, he's just resentful enough at being left behind to tell Tasgetius himself."

Indeed I did know Crom.

Once, on the banks of the river, I had watched as fishermen spread their nets in the sun to dry. Some of the network was tangled and I observed them patiently separate and unknot the strands. I was younger then; my fingers itched to take a knife and simply cut out the tangle.

How convenient it would be if human tangles like Crom Daral could be cut out when they threatened the integrity of the fabric. But Crom had a right to exist. He was, for all his flaws, part of us.

Nor would I have called down the lightning on Tasgetius—this was a standard druid threat none, to my knowledge, had ever actually succeeded in doing. I had made the thunder roll—or made Tasgetius think he heard the thunder roll—and that was sufficient.

"Did you say you've already arranged for fresh horses?" I asked Tarvos.

"I did, though I told the horsekeeper we wouldn't need them until tomorrow at the earliest."

"We need them right now. We're leaving."

His shy, eager smile surprised me. "We're going home? I'm going home? To Lakutu?"

Torn between amusement and envy, I replied, "Not yet. First we're going after Cotuatus."

Chapter Twenty-five

WE LEFT Cenabum at the gallop, ostensibly heading north to the Fort of the Grove. Once out of sight of the watchtowers, however, we circled back and rode south toward the Roman camp. If my information was correct, it was located within striking distance of both Cenabum and Avaricum—and not much farther from the stronghold of the Senones, Vellaunodunum.

The sheer arrogance of Caesar was impressive. He behaved like someone who has already conquered and may go wherever he likes. That in itself gave him an advantage; people believe and accept what they see.

My head reminded me that this was the man who had impoverished himself in order to appear sufficiently magnificent to be a proconsul of Rome.

Perhaps Caesar appeared most confident when he was weakest?

If so, what weakness was he protecting by establishing a winter camp at the edge of the land of the Carnutes, whose king was his avowed friend?

I felt as if Caesar and I were in a deadly contest of heads in which I had one small, but perhaps crucial, advantage. I knew of him, but he did not, to the best of my knowledge, know of me.

It was Vercingetorix he had noticed and would remember.

A stain of smoke in the sky ahead warned us that we were approaching the Roman camp. Drawing rein, Tarvos and I left our horses with the other warriors and advanced cautiously on foot, climbing a ridge mantled with tall grass. As we neared its crest, we bent low, then crawled the last few lengths on our bellies until we could peer over the top and down into the valley where the camp stood.

This was my first view of an invading army in free Gaul. A chill swept over me. Here was the embodiment of Menua's horrific vision of rigid order, straight lines and exact edges.

A legion consisted roughly of 5,300 men, divided into nine fighting cohorts and a tenth cohort composed of clerks and nonfighting specialists. The camp before us would have sheltered perhaps three cohorts and attendant personnel. It had been precisely constructed according to an unvarying plan by the engineers the Roman army always carried with it. A protective ditch surrounded the facility, which had been built on a tributary of the Liger to assure a fresh water supply. The walls were of crisply cut turf blocks and timber, reinforced with an outer fence of timber stakes as level across the top as the horizon of the sea. Within the walls the Romans had already stamped the earth smooth and had erected blocks of identical buildings to house the troops, each holding a century, a group of about eighty men plus their equipment. At the end of each block was a larger room for the commanding centurion. There were horse pens, storehouses, and a long row of workshops. The winter camp looked almost like a town, but it was not a town; no one would ever be born there. Life was not its purpose.

In the center of the compound a headquarters building flew the legion's standards. To one side stood a small wooden structure built to imitate stone, complete with columns—obviously the camp's temple. I wondered what lifeless god stood on a pedestal inside.

A rustling in the grass made us whirl around, ready to fight for our lives; it was only Cotuatus coming up the slope behind us. "My men are stationed in that woodland back there," he said, pointing. "You did not approach undetected, Ainvar."

"What about the Romans?"

He grinned. "They didn't see you, they have no guards on this side of the camp right now. They've all wandered to the other side, where some Carnutian women from the nearest farmstead are bathing in the river. Even Roman security is not proof against man's desire to look at naked women."

"A victory for nature over paving stones," I commented. Cotuatus looked baffled. One could wish he had a better head, but at least he was born of a kingly line and was smart enough not to mistake the Romans for friends.

He crouched beside us until I had filled my eyes with the winter camp, then we slithered back down the hill together and my group went to join his in the distant woodland.

I told him of my conversation with Tasgetius, and he told me what he had learned of the Romans. "They threw up this camp in an incredibly short time, even working through the night by torchlight. They have their own ditchers, surveyors, smiths, carpenters—fighting men who are also trained to do all necessary construction work. They can build anything wherever they need it. They're like tortoises who carry everything they need with them, Ainvar. Every legionary has, in addition to his weapons, a saw, an ax, a sickle, a chain, rope, a spade, and a basket. And a straw mattress, though they don't do much sleeping. They're up at first light, drilling. Their drills are like bloodless battles."

Rix, who had made a point of observing Roman drills in the more pacified Province, had told me the same thing. In these drills there was none of the spontaneity of Celtic warfare that encouraged individual acts of bravery and style, there was only regimentation and repetition, wearing deep grooves of behavior into the men of the legions so they would behave the same way every time, in every circumstance.

Therein might lie a weakness. I must remember to suggest this to Rix.

That night we held a cold conference beneath the winter stars. We did not light a fire for fear of alerting the Romans, but we were safe enough among the trees. As we sat, huddled and shivering, while the wind sang, Cotuatus remarked, "I wish I had one of those hardy women who was willing to bathe in the river today to keep me warm tonight." He turned to his cousin with a chuckle. "You have no wife, Conco; why don't we take one of them back with us to Cenabum?"

Conconnetodumnus replied, "They're daughters of a farming clan. I'd rather have a warrior woman, a wife suitable for a prince."

"Any woman who can bathe in an icy cold river in the dead of winter is suitable for a prince," Cotuatus argued. He was beginning to take the matter seriously. I saw that once he fixed onto something he held on. "We could circle the Roman camp and go down to them in the morning, then—"

"You may not be able to go back to Cenabum yourselves," I interjected, "never mind taking a wife with you for Conco."

There was startled silence in the darkness. Then Cotuatus said, "Why shouldn't we go back to Cenabum? The Romans haven't seen us. We've learned what we want to know about them but they know nothing of us."

"I approve the idea of spying on the invaders," I said, "but Tasgetius won't. He's begun calling Caesar 'friend.' If he learns what you've done it's within his authority—and his character—to bar the gates of Cenabum to you."

Conco cleared his throat with a sound like mud gurgling among pebbles. "How could he find out? We left the town very quietly before dawn, bringing only a few men with us, and we told no one what we intended."

"No one but your own men," I contradicted. Reluctantly, I explained about Crom Daral. Where he was involved I felt both responsibility and guilt. Crom Daral always infected me with guilt, that most corrosive and unnatural of emotions. Neither ferns nor foxes know guilt. Crom spun a web of guilt, the stuff that trapped those who most wanted to like him, ultimately making affection impossible.

Cotuatus was angry. "If the man is that small-spirited I should have been warned. Ainvar, why didn't you tell me this would happen?"

"I didn't know; I certainly didn't anticipate this particular situation."

"You should have. You're a druid."

I gathered myself into myself. "Are you questioning me, Cotuatus?"

He hesitated, fumbling among memories of pain. "I . . . ah . . . no."

"Good. Now listen to me. When we return to Cenabum—without a woman for you, Conco, we can't afford to be burdened right now—we'll make camp some distance away and send my Tarvos to the town to find out what's happened. How many supporters have you within the walls?"

In the gloom I saw the two princes turn toward each other. "Between us," Cotuatus spoke, "at least half the population of Cenabum. Perhaps more."

"An uprising against the king must come from the people, from a majority of the people," I stressed, "and not from the Order. If you go to earth outside of Cenabum and send word, have you enough followers to take care of Tasgetius?"

"You think we'll find the gates barred to us, don't you?"

"It might be the ideal opportunity," I said. "An act on the part of Tasgetius that would bring about a natural, and from our point of view desirable, result. Without meaning to, Crom Daral may have given us just what we need. I assume your followers would be very upset at any barring order against you?"

Conco laughed. "I promise you that!"

Before the sun rose, we were on our way back to Cenabum. I waited until we were far from the Roman camp before singing the song for the sun, but then I sang it full-throated and the warriors joined in as we rode.

We made a hidden camp some distance from the stronghold and sent Tarvos in alone. For all his size and strength, the Bull could appear innocuous. He had a gift, as I had observed before, of being able to saunter through any crowd without being noticed simply because he seemed so casual, so uninvolved.

He returned to us with sparkling eyes. "Crom Daral told, all right. Tasgetius was furious. Cenabum is officially forbidden to the princes Cotuatus and Conconnetodumnus."

"How are the people responding?"

Tarvos grinned. "With a buzz, like a disturbed nest of hornets. The traders take the king's side, of course, and accuse Cotuatus and Conco of every sort of villainy. Though Tasgetius has barred them from the town, he has not explained the reason why, so I, ah, did that myself. I visited several people I know and informed them of the Roman camp set up in our own territory, and told them these two brave princes here had gone to spy on the treacherous invaders. The invaders the king had made welcome."

I clapped the Bull on the shoulder. "Tarvos, you're a treasure!"

Embarrassed, he ducked his head and scuffed his toe in the dirt. "That uprising you wanted is under way, Ainvar," he muttered. "I had little to do with it. Tasgetius brought it on himself."

"We all had something to do with it, Tarvos. Even Crom Daral. Most important, Crom Daral." I could not help laughing.

I gave Cotuatus his instructions. "You will remain here for now, and I shall go back to the grove to be as far from events as possible, so no one will accuse the Order of being involved. Send word to your followers that you support an uprising against Tasgetius and are just waiting for them to overcome him and open the gates of Cenabum to you again.

"When that happens, of course, it will mean Tasgetius is no longer king. Shout the word, summon the elders. I shall convene the Order and we will prepare to elect a new king, one who will not give away our land."

We had hidden in a woodland. I walked a little distance away from the others and stood silently for a time, feeling the trees around me. Exulting. My patience had been rewarded. With the unlikely Crom Daral as its hub, the wheel of events had turned until the right set of circumstances occurred. Soon I would be able to inform Rix that the heartland of Gaul was securely behind him.

Before any human agency could inform me, I would know. The wind would carry the message; the earth would tell me when Tasgetius was no longer king. As man shouts from valley to valley, the trees shout silently to one another, even over great distances. In the sacred grove I would hear; I would know when the deed was done.

Druids know.

Leaving Cotuatus and Conco waiting tensely for news from Cenabum, my bodyguard and I rode for the Fort of the Grove.

Along the way a prickling began at the base of my spine. I began urging my horse faster, feeling apprehension building. We did not stop for rest, but destroyed a second set of horses by riding furiously; yet even then we were too late.

As we entered the open gates of the fort, and my people ran forward to greet us, I scanned their faces and saw that too many were missing. Briga, Lakutu, Damona . . . most of the women.

I turned my horse and rode back to the watchtower. "Where are the women?" I shouted up at the sentry.

He scanned the horizon. "They should be back by now. . . ."

"Where are they?"

"They went with Grannus to sing a song to the vines, to protect them from the frost spirit."

"Did they take guards with them?"

He looked down at me with a puzzled frown. "Why should they? They were only going to the vineyard down the river, no great distance."

The vineyard!

We had come to love our vines. Their spraddling, awkward shapes were beautiful to us, because we had trained them to those shapes to enable the sun to reach every cluster of fruit. Stems that were gnarled and twisted but obedient to our design delighted our eyes. Green and new, their leaves were touchingly tender. In their harvest colors of gold and yellow and almost red, they were like jewels.

Our first harvest of the immature vines had taken place following a wet summer, which had caused the soil to be too acid and produced sour fruit and wine that was hardly drinkable. We learned from our mistakes. The druids made all the necessary sacrifices to assure that the next summer would be hot and dry. The grapes we harvested then were as sweet as honey, and the wine was superb.

Breathing the air at grape harvest, with its heavy scent of ripe fruit, was like breathing wine. People paused in their labors to exchange glances, sniff, smile. From sandy and grudging soil they were taking a powerful magic.

The grapes were harvested now. The wine was pressed and waiting. But tending the vines did not cease; they must be given all the love we could bestow to protect them as they slept and prepare them to produce again. And again.

Because they were best at caring, women tended the vines.

You had to boast to Tasgetius about the vines, my head accused me. And he has had enough time to . . .

"Come on!" I yelled at Tarvos. Wheeling my weary horse, I kicked him and galloped out the gate, calling to the sentry as I passed, "Summon every man you can to follow me! And hurry!"

Tarvos never questioned, never hesitated. Even as the startled sentry was shouting orders and the members of my bodyguard, who had begun dismounting, were trying to hold their horses still long enough to allow them to scramble on again, Tarvos was galloping at my side.

Skirting the ridge where the grove stood, we followed the river. A vineyard had been established on the far bank of the Autura, where a sheltered bend trapped and held the sun's warmth. As we approached, the view was obscured by the trees snuggling near the water on our side of the river, but then the Autura made her turning and the scene opened out before us.

Someone—perhaps Tarvos, perhaps I—gave a shout of rage.

The Romans were there.

A century of warriors led by a mounted centurion had invaded our young vines. Theirs was no simple scouting party. Most of them were legionaries, clearly identified by their uniforms. They wore identical bronze helmets with snug leather skullcaps beneath to cushion the head from blows, and upper-body armor of metal plates fastened together with leather straps to give mobility of arm and shoulder. They were armed with thrusting swords, daggers, and two spears each, and carried round, iron-rimmed shields of wood covered with leather.

Accompanying these professional killers were auxiliaries armed with deadly leather slings and bags of stones. The whole mass was sweeping through our vineyard with implacable purpose, driving our women ahead of them and trampling and destroying the young vines.

"Lakutu!" Tarvos screamed, catching sight of her.

The Romans heard him. The centurion reined in his horse, turned toward us, raised his arm in a signal. The auxiliaries, who were in front as was customary, immediately began firing stones from their slings, some toward us and some toward the hapless women in front of them. The missiles hurled at us fell short, falling harmlessly into the water, but I saw several women throw up their hands and fall. One stone hit a girl's head with such force that blood spurted from her nose and ears.

The kicking I had given my horse before was nothing compared to now. He plunged into the river with a frantic bound, sending up a terrific splash. Tarvos was right behind me. The rest of my bodyguard was only a few strides farther away.

We must have looked laughable, a dozen men attacking a Roman century. But we were not just men, we were Celts.

And those were Celtic women trying futilely to find some shelter among the bare rows of vines. When they saw us coming to their aid, they stopped running and crouching and stood tall, yelling their own war cries. They seized stones and dirt and even ripped up grapestakes to hurl at the foreigners. Their spirited assault was as unexpected as our own, and between us we took Caesar's century by surprise.

The auxiliaries, who were neither as trained nor as disciplined as the legionaries, hesitated. The centurion on his horse bellowed an angry command, but the men with slings could not decide whether to continue shooting stones at us and at the women, or to fall back before our advance. As a result, they tightened into a confused knot, causing a perceptible loss of Roman momentum.

I dared glance over my shoulder. Tarvos was still right behind me, galloping through the water which was, because of the season, no deeper than our horses' knees. Behind him a few paces were the other members of my bodyguard, and in the distance I could see a dark moving clot, which must be warriors from the fort hurrying to our rescue. If we could survive until they arrived, we had a chance.

Time was our enemy.

We druids contemplate the nature of time. As part of our training, we develop an intensity of imaginative will that is capable of manipulating any element that conforms to natural law. As I had observed before, time could clench or sprawl, so it must be malleable to some extent.

With an incalculable mental effort I reached out, grasped time, held it. I clamped down with all the strength I possessed, pouring the full power of my will into the attempt. I envisioned the Romans moving slowly, then more slowly still, as if they were in deep, deep water. I imagined time stopping for them.

What my mind was creating and what my eyes were watching began to blend together. The Roman century, frozen in one moment held locked by my mind, ceased moving.

The effort was beyond anything I had ever attempted. I knew I could not sustain it; my body felt as if every fiber were being sundered. I managed to gasp out to Tarvos, "Go get the women. Bring them back across the river."

I never had to tell Tarvos anything twice. He sped past me, up the bank, slid from his faltering horse, and began collecting our people like a hen gathering her chicks. My influence was concentrated on the space occupied by the Romans; the Carnutians were not affected by it, except for two or three who had already been overrun by the warriors and were trapped inside the ranks.

I did not know who was alive, dead, injured. I dare not break my concentration enough to look . . . to look for Briga's face.

My strength was weakest at the rear of the Roman column, and those warriors were still capable of action. They fought their way into the frozen mass of their companions until they too were caught by stilled time. Then they stopped and stood like the others, often with one foot lifted in a step, mouths ajar with yelling, arms raised, weapons brandished.

Waves of nausea swept over me. I was vaguely aware of Tarvos coming back toward me with others around him, splashing through the river. . . .

I faltered. I saw the Romans begin to move again; I clamped down again savagely. But my concentration had been broken finally and irrevocably by the sound of shouting and the whirr of spears in the air above my head, coming from our side of the river.

Warriors had arrived from the Fort of the Grove.

As soon as I let myself hear them, the spell was shattered. The Romans leaped into furious action, hurling a rain of spears in our direction. The Carnutian warriors plunged into the river, meeting the fleeing women midstream. There were glad cries of recognition, and then the women hurried on to safety while the men rushed ahead to attack the Romans.

Dizzily, I slid from my horse and leaned against his heaving flank. The cold water of the shallow Autura swirled around my legs, reviving me somewhat. Looking up, I saw that the battle had been joined in the vineyard. Although the Romans still outnumbered us, our men were so angry that each fought like ten, and the century was suffering casualties.

The centurion had probably been told to find and destroy Gaulish vineyards and kill any stray resisters, but not to put his entire company at risk. After fighting long enough to satisfy honor, he barked a final order and the invaders wheeled about like a school of fish, setting off at double time toward the southeast. Our warriors raced along behind them, howling as they picked off the rear guard.

When I looked back to see how the women were, more men were still arriving to fight, most of them farmers and local small-holders who had grabbed up their tools to serve as weapons. They stood on the riverbank, brandishing forks and sickles and shouting imprecations at the departing Romans.

I caught my horse by the bridle and started leading him toward them. It felt as if I had been in the river for days, and I wanted to assure myself that Briga and the others were all right.

At first, thanks to the exhaustion that follows an excess of magic, I did not recognize the thing that lay before me in the shallow water. Then my horse arched his neck and snorted.

Tarvos drifted face downward on the sluggish current, with a spear through his neck.

CHAPTER TWENTY-SIX

IN THE the midriver collision between the retreating women and the advancing warriors, Tarvos must have lost his footing, I insisted to myself. He is not hurt, the breath is merely knocked out of him. There is no spear through his throat; it only looks that way.

"Tarvos," I heard myself say foolishly, "Tarvos, get up! Did you find Briga? Speak to me, Tarvos!"

Dropping my horse's reins, I gently turned him over and lifted his head and shoulders clear of the water. His head lolled. Instead of eyes I saw two white half-moons beneath partially closed lids. His face was the color of clay.

Now, now I ached for the strength to manipulate time again, to make it run backward! But my strength was spent. The arms that held Tarvos were trembling.

The people on the bank waded in to help me. "Can someone get that spear out of his neck?" I requested.

Hands touched us, guided us, helped carry him from the river and lay him on the bank. Sulis bent over us. I had not noticed her before; she must have been with the other women who had come to sing to the vines.

Giving me one sharp look, she then turned her attention to Tarvos. I watched helplessly as she listened for his heart, felt the bloodrivers in his neck, sniffed for his breathing. Then she shook her head. "The life has gone out of him, Ainvar." She made a signal to two of our men and between them they worked the spear out of my friend's neck as gently as if he could feel what they did.

Blood seeped sluggishly from the wound.

Someone pushed through the crowd around us and wrested Tarvos from my arms. Lakutu was making a weird moaning sound that rose and fell in awful ululation. Clutching Tarvos against her chest, she squatted on her heels and rocked back and forth, never ceasing that ghastly sound.

I had to turn away from them.

And there was Briga.

Without a word, she opened her arms to me and I stumbled into them.

"Tarvos is dead," I muttered into her hair.

"I know. He died saving us."

"But he isn't ready to be dead. He's too young. And he has Lakutu. So much life left to be lived . . . he isn't ready to be dead."

"I know," she repeated soothingly.

But she did not know. I knew. I knew that my friend still enjoyed warm sun and red wine and a good fight and a devoted woman. He was not ready to leave those things behind. Death was for the old, the ill, not for a man who was eagerly hurrying home because Lakutu was waiting for him.

Turning to the watching warriors, I said, "Take him to the grove."

One, a member of my own bodyguard so shaken by his captain's death that he dare argue with the chief druid, objected. "We should take him to the fort so the women can prepare him."

I whirled on the man. "Take him to the grove!" I commanded.

They cringed from me. They rolled their eyes and exchanged furtive glances. But they lifted Tarvos's body, extricating it from Lakutu's embrace with great difficulty, and we started on the way back. The long, long way back.

Tarvos was not our only casualty. Our warriors retrieved the body of the girl I had seen hit in the head, and found an older woman lying crumpled amid the vines, slain by a sword thrust. Several others were injured, a few seriously.

And the vineyard was destroyed.

I could not think of the vineyard yet; I could think only of Tarvos.

Sulis went back to the fort with the injured, but I insisted that the other dead be carried with Tarvos to the grove.

The time that I had locked and held now seemed to slow of its own accord, so that we spent years trudging toward the ridge, years of weariness and pain. I had been injured myself, as I discovered when a sharp stabbing sensation warned me of some damage to my side. A rib, perhaps. Nothing Sulis could not mend. Had spears been hurled at me there at the end? Had I stood in the deadly rain that killed Tarvos?

It did not matter. I walked on, watching my feet to avoid looking at Tarvos. Someone had relieved me of my poor horse and no doubt taken it, too, back to the fort for healing. The horse Tarvos had been riding still carried him, however, slung across its back, with Lakutu walking beside it, her arms around as much of the body as she could reach. She never stopped wailing.

With a sense of ineffable relief I saw the grove rising before me. The naked oaks stood with their arms upraised against oblivion.

I led the way to the central clearing where the stone of sacrifice waited. But I would not put Tarvos's body on the altar; he was not a sacrifice.

I ordered the three who had been killed to be laid in a row together, their heads to the sunrise. What was done for Tarvos must be done for all. By command of head and heart, the warriors arranged them tenderly. Then they stepped back and everyone watched me, waiting.

Even Lakutu finally fell silent—or perhaps the presence of the trees silenced her. She stood with her dark eyes fixed on me, and in them I read the same anguished, inarticulate pleading I had seen there once before—when she stood on the auction block.

How I wished I were not so tired! I had already strained my powers to the utmost and I was left drained, leaden with fatigue.

But, explaining to no one, I continued, preparing every step of the ritual meticulously. I arranged stones in an echo of the pattern of the stars in the winter sky; I asked Briga to bring water from the spring hidden in the grove; I kindled a fire. I made certain that the bodies were properly aligned, then I arranged the spectators in the exact positions the druids had taken on that long-ago day with Rosmerta.

Magic depends, in part, upon the replication of procedures and incantations that have worked before: fixed ritual to produce predictable result. The Goban Saor could strike iron with a hammer the same way every time and make it take a given shape; so it is with magic.

Most of the time.

But I was very tired, and the magic I would attempt was beyond the ability of any known druid.

If I let myself, I would be afraid.

Though I had not summoned them, the druids had come. Beyond the tight circle of my concentration I became aware of hooded figures silently filing into the glade. Grannus had been there from the beginning, limping up from the river with the rest of us. Now we were joined by Keryth, Narlos, Dian Cet . . . Aberth . . . the rest of the Order who lived near the great grove. I was thankful; their additional strength would be needed.

Speaking to no one, I continued my tasks, following the silent intuition of my spirit, for no one had ever designed this ritual before. At some stage Briga laid her hand on my arm.

No one else would have dared question me, but she did. "Ainvar, what are you going to attempt?"

Her choice of words was unfortunate. I must not think of myself as attempting, only as succeeding. Magic depends on the force of the mind and the druid's absolute confidence in that power. I shook my head at her and said nothing.

When all was ready, I closed my eyes and opened myself to the Source.

The ears of my spirit strained to catch the faintest whisper of guidance. They heard only the creaking of the branches and the subdued breathing of the circle of people around me.

Tell me! I pleaded with That Which Watched. Tell me what to do now. Shall I throw myself across the bodies and shout, "Live!" as I did before? Is that command sufficient? Is more needed?

I realized the extent of my presumption. Who was I to dare dream of striking the spark of life? For preempting the prerogative of the Creator, I risked reprisals beyond human imagining.

Yet Tarvos, whom I loved, was not ready to be dead. He deserved more of living. And Lakutu was watching me with those dark, tragic eyes, silently pleading. I felt no fear for myself, merely a consuming need to give.

Please, I implored in the caverns of my skull. Send me inspiration.

Standing beside the bodies as they lay on the earth, I bowed my head and waited.

Something entered the grove.

A tremor rippled through the earth. Wind soughed among the oaks. An intense, oppressive stillness like the eye of a storm settled around me. A great distance seemed to open up between myself and the circle of watchers, as if I were moving away from them at incredible speed. The druids had begun chanting, but the sound reached my ears as the humming of a thousand bees. The light in the glade dimmed, brightened, dimmed again.

When I looked down at the bodies, all light seemed to be concentrated on them.

I started to bend over Tarvos. Something drove me to my knees and a force sickening in its power slammed through me, leaving me writhing on the ground like an insect crushed beneath a giant heel.

The trees watched and the druids chanted and the earth was ancient and the Creator *was* . . .

. . . and the Creator *is* . . .

While a terrible power rent and tore me, I struggled to forge a link with the Source that transcends flesh and leaps in flame across the cosmos.

A voice screamed in agony.

In ecstasy.

And the Creator is!

My human body failed me, failed me utterly. I was lying on my face amid dead leaves, crying tears of weakness, my outflung arm touching the dead arm of my friend.

How long I lay there I do not know. No one dared disturb me. I lay as helpless as if newborn, hollowed out like a log canoe.

Then I knew the limitations of my gifts. Menua was wrong. The spirit housed in me was not powerful enough to raise the dead.

A far greater druid than I might someday achieve what I could not.

But lying shocked and battered in the glade, I realized that a different gift had been vouchsafed to me. Because of my love for my friend, I had, for one searing moment out of time, seen the ultimate face of the Source.

I pulled myself to my feet like a crippled old man. The others approached diffidently, their eyes wild and staring.

"Look," said Aberth, pointing.

On the far side of the glade a massive oak had been riven from crotch to root by lightning. Lightning in winter. The smell of burned wood thickened the air.

No one asked me to explain. I was chief druid.

"Carry the emptied bodies back to the fort so the women can prepare them to be given to the earth," I ordered. The procession moved through a blue twilight, myself at the head. Alone.

Lakutu walked beside the body of Tarvos as before, quietly sobbing.

Much later that night, when the fort was quiet and only the redoubled guard I had ordered kept vigil, I left my lodge and went out beneath the stars. Tarvos is there, I thought. Out of sight but not out of reach.

In the spring new buds will appear on the trees. They always do.

Meanwhile, we druids would have work to do. We are the eyes and ears of the earth. We think her thoughts. We feel her pain. As we would discover when we returned to our vineyard to inspect the damage, the Romans had not contented themselves with trampling the tender vines. The stench told us they had urinated on them as an expression of contempt. Even worse, they had scattered salt among the rows.

The polluted earth cried out to us, begging to be healed.

The horror we felt at the act was exceeded by the disgust we felt for the people who had committed it. What manner of beings poison the goddess who is mother to us all?

Standing in the desecrated vineyard, we wept. Then we commenced cleansing and healing rituals that would restore life to the earth. We had been well trained in the art, it was our obligation and our privilege.

My heart would always grieve that I was not permitted to do the same for Tarvos.

The experience in the grove left me a humbler and wiser man. I found I could not share it; the language of the spirit is alien to human tongues, there are no words to describe what I had seen and felt. Yet I was changed, in many ways.

From that day a broad streak of silver ran through my hair from just above my left temple; silver against dark bronze. My people remarked on it in awed whispers.

There was another change. The very next night, Briga appeared at the door of my lodge with her bedding rolled under her arm. "Don't just stand there, Ainvar. Let me in."

Trying to conceal my astonishment, I stepped aside so she could enter. "Why have you come?"

"Why do you think?" the hoarse little voice replied impudently. "I've come to be with you, you great gawking man."

"But why now . . . ?"

She dropped her bedding and, with a laugh, flung herself, the whole warm sweet weight of her, into my arms. Against my mouth she murmured, "Don't ask. I'm to be a druid and druids don't have to explain themselves."

Perhaps other men understand women.

That was a difficult winter. The weather was mild, but anxiety makes any season bleak. While we buried those the Romans had slain, I tensely awaited news from Cenabum, word from Rix, information about Caesar, and possible reprisals.

I began living more and more inside myself. Briga, with her abundant life, seemed to demand more of me than I had to spare. Even in our closest embraces I found myself distracted, with part of my mind listening. . . .

Menua's old raven screamed one morning from his perch on the rooftree.

I had been sitting by the fire, anointing my ash stick with oil to keep it from splitting. At the raven's cry I ran outside. There was nothing to be seen but the usual activity of the fort—yet I knew there was more. The raven had said so.

I went as far as the main gate and beyond, scanning the empty trackway. Nothing. Yet the day hummed with a peculiar tension, and the wind from the south was singing a low, sad song of death.

I ran for the grove, to listen to the trees.

When I returned to the fort and my lodge, I told Briga, "Tasgetius is dead."

She opened her eyes very wide. "What will happen now?"

I considered. There were undercurrents I did not like. "It depends on how he died," I told her.

The shouted news reached us shortly after midday. Tarvos was no longer there to come running to me with it, so I went down to the gates myself and waited, footshifting, watching the horizon to the south until I caught the first echoes. The sound came rolling toward us over the plain, from herder to hunter to woodsman.

The king had been killed in Cenabum during the night. That night was the longest of the year, which he had celebrated by ordering fires lighted everywhere in the town and spreading a great feast for his princes. The eating and drinking would last till sunrise, defying the night, and the crowd had overflowed the area of the king's lodge and had run through Cenabum with torches, laughing and singing.

Someone in the crowd had found an opportunity to run a sword through Tasgetius.

Cenabum was in turmoil; the chief druid was urgently needed.

I summoned Aberth. "Guard the grove in my absence. I must take the other senior members of the Order with me, a new king must be chosen. May I vote on your behalf?"

"Who are the candidates?"

I smiled with one side of my mouth only. "Men of my choosing."

Aberth showed me his teeth. "Then vote for the best in my name. Here." He took the fur arm ring, symbol of a sacrificer, from his upper arm and gave it to me. "Show them this as proof you speak for me."

"While I am gone, sleep standing. I shall send back more warriors from Cenabum to help guard the grove, but until they arrive, be doubly vigilant."

"You're certain the new king, whoever he may be, will let us have more warriors?"

"I'm certain," I replied. Aberth smiled.

I collected our oldest and wisest heads—Grannus, Dian Cet, Narlos, and a few others—and, together with my personal bodyguard, prepared to set off at the gallop.

Dian Cet objected strenuously. "I come from a line of craftsmen, Ainvar, I never learned to ride. Besides, druids *walk*."

"Not now, we don't have time. Life is change, remember? Just grit your teeth and hang on to the mane; there's a good healer at Cenabum who can put soothing ointment on your backside."

We arrived to find the stronghold still chaotic. The king's death was not the result of a unified uprising as I had hoped; it seemed that Cotuatus had nothing near the majority support he had claimed. One man alone had slain the king, for reasons as yet undetermined.

Tasgetius's relatives were wailing murder and demanding that the killer be found so they could receive the king's honor price to compensate for their loss. A number of warrior princes were clamoring to compete for the newly vacated royal lodge. The Roman traders, fearful for their own position, were planning to petition Caesar to "investigate the wanton slaughter of his friend."

The tribe was running and flapping like a headless chicken.

I sat beside Dian Cet in the assembly house as he listened to an endless parade of protests, lies, rumors, accusations, and occasionally shifted his weight to one side to rub his sore buttocks.

A familiar face appeared on the far side of the large room.

Crom Daral always looked surly; on this occasion he looked like a dog expecting a beating. I got up quietly, edged my way through the noisy crowd, and took him by the arm.

"Say nothing until we are outside," I warned him.

Raising my hood, I led him away from the assembly house until I found some privacy for us in the dark and stinking lean-to where some lodgeholder kept his pigs. "Now, Crom. What have you been doing?"

"Why do you think I've done anything?" he whined.

"I know you. You'd better tell me."

He turned his face from me and muttered something.

"Tell me!" commanded the chief druid of the Carnutes.

"I did it," he said reluctantly.

"You did what?"

"I killed the king."

CHAPTER TWENTY-SEVEN

"**W**HY DID you kill Tasgetius, Crom? Did Cotuatus order it?"

"No. He wouldn't even talk to me. I went out to his camp to tell him I hadn't betrayed him deliberately, I was just so angry when he went off without me . . . but he wouldn't even see me.

"So in the night, when no one was looking, I put my sword through Tasgetius. I had sworn that sword to Cotuatus, you see, and I thought with Tasgetius dead, he could come back into the town. I thought maybe then he would take me back." Crom's voice sank low in his chest. We stood together in the stink and darkness as I waited for him to speak again. "Will Cotuatus take me back, Ainvar?" he asked at last.

Crom Daral, our tangled knot. I sighed. "I don't know, Crom. I just wish you'd waited until Cotuatus had more followers. As it is . . . ah, one thing is certain. We have to get you away from here. Too many are howling for the killer's blood.

"I think the safest place for you would be back in the Fort of the Grove. You can take one of our horses, and I'll send an escort with you. Leave quietly; do nothing to attract attention."

He said gracelessly, "I don't want to be indebted to you for saving my life."

"No obligation is incurred. We druids are supposed to protect the tribe, and that includes you, Crom. Just do as I tell you."

As we left the shed, a thought struck me. "One other thing, Crom. You'd better know. Briga is living in my lodge now."

He gave me a terrible look. "You always get what you want, Ainvar, don't you?"

Later that day he left Cenabum as I had instructed, however, accompanied by two of my personal bodyguards. Crom Daral was not overly gifted with courage.

With the killer of Tasgetius undiscovered and out of the way, I set about repairing the damage while making the most of the opportunity. At least we were rid of Tasgetius. I would not, however, suggest Cotuatus too readily as his successor.

I did not want him to be accused of the killing. Also, the more I thought about his foolishness the more annoyed I became; the man had given in to the Celtic tendency to exaggerate when he assured me he had a large following. I had based my decisions on his word, which I now saw as untrustworthy to some extent. He would not necessarily be our best choice as king.

In fact, none of the men eligible by blood to contend for the kingship could claim majority support, either among the elders or the people. And the men who had been sworn to Tasgetius had coalesced into an angry group more devoted to the memory of the dead man than they had been to him while he lived, and determined to oppose anyone who took his place.

Death, my head observed, can put a bright shine on very tarnished metal.

My druids and I met with the council of elders to discuss the problem. After a long and argumentative day, nothing was resolved. We had not even agreed upon a list of men to be tested.

After the song for the sun next morning, I left Cenabum and went alone to the woodland beyond the town to think among the trees.

I could not solve the problem alone, but fortunately I was not really alone. None of us ever is. The Otherworld swirls in and around us, part of us always, giving the lie to the Roman priests who claim to be sole agents for the spirits. That Which Watched was with me in the woodland as it was with me in the sacred grove. I only needed to be by myself, to concentrate. . . .

My eye fell on a slim young birch, the tree symbolizing a new start. I paused. Then turned. And saw a beech, the tree of ancient knowledge, symbol of the aged and wise. I turned again. Directly in my path stood an elder, the wood of regeneration.

We must begin anew with the old, the trees told me, and trust the Source to supply the old with the needed strength.

I went back to Cenabum and asked that the council be reconvened. Addressing them in the assembly house, I held up my ash stick to put the weight of my authority behind my words as I said, "Among the eligible princes there is none right now who could command the support of all the tribe. We are in a dangerous situation, we must not be divided. But there is one among us whom everyone has always respected.

"I suggest we return the kingship to Nantorus for now," I said, ignoring their gasps of surprise. "At least until one strong new leader clearly emerges from the pack. An election now would just divide the tribe more, but they will stand behind Nantorus." Looking around at the seamed faces of the elders, I added, "The oldest heads contain the most."

Which was not necessarily true. But it was what they loved hearing.

"What of his physical abilities?" someone asked. "We do not deny his popularity, but he gave up the king's lodge before because he was not able to lead men into battle."

I told them, "If the Carnutes fight in the immediate future, our opponent will not be some other tribe. Like the rest of free Gaul we have one enemy now: the man Caesar. When the time comes to fight him, we will have a brilliant war leader, one both young and able enough to bring us victory. Nantorus will be our king, but when we need a true leader, I propose that Vercingetorix the Arvernian lead us in war!"

There was a stunned silence. Anticipating this moment, I had had a long discussion with Nantorus, who was standing quietly in the shadows at the rear of the assembly house. When I beckoned to him he came forward.

I stepped aside; the former king took my place. To arm him with the strength of anger, I had told him whose hand had hurled the spear into his back. But I had added, "Do not publicly accuse Tasgetius. Rocks thrown at the dead have a way of bouncing back. You can get a better revenge by helping us defeat his Roman friends."

Taut with held-in rage, Nantorus had never looked more kingly. There was the expected debate, but by the end of the day the council accepted Nantorus as the least divisive solution to our predicament. There need be no election; he had been elected once already. Even Tasgetius's men had once accepted him as king; they could hardly refuse to do so again.

More important, with Tasgetius dead no one opposed the concept of the Gaulish confederacy, and Nantorus gave it his whole-hearted support.

Cotuatus was a different matter. When I went out to his camp to tell him, he was furious. "I'll never return to Cenabum so long as another man occupies the king's lodge. It should have been mine!"

"It might have been," I told him, "if you'd had the support you claimed. But even among the elders there were only two who spoke for you. Learn from this experience, Cotuatus, and you may yet be king one day. Just not now."

"But—"

"Are you arguing with me?"

"No." He dropped his eyes.

I thought I could control him.

When we returned to the fort with the news of the kingship, my people were surprised but pleased. A different sort of surprise awaited me, however.

Briga, wreathed in smiles, met me at the gates. I received the welcome a man dreams of, but then she said, "Someone else is living in our lodge now, by the way."

My first, terrible thought was that Crom Daral had come dragging his bitterness under my rooftree, thrusting himself between me and Briga by demanding hospitality.

"You can't invite guests in my name!" I scolded her.

Briga merely smiled—mysteriously. "I only did what I knew you would have done," she said.

I had acquired a dislike for surprises.

When we entered the lodge was dark, for the fire had burned low and no lamps were lighted. Then a darker form stirred among the shadows.

Lakutu stepped forward, offering a shy smile.

Briga said, "With Tarvos dead she has no family. And she's pregnant. I knew you'd want to care for her for his sake."

"Did he know?"

"She only discovered it while you were away before. She was going to tell him when you returned, but . . . "

"So when you learned of it, you said she could live here?"

"Of course," Briga replied with the assurance of a prince's daughter.

The fort was amused. No one said anything to the chief druid outright, of course, but I saw the glances, the hidden smirks. Most of the time I pretended not to notice, but once in an unguarded moment I remarked to the Goban Saor, "I'm thinking of collecting women, starting a new tradition. I may take in a dozen or so."

"Druid humor," he observed correctly.

If I had had little time for Briga, I had none at all for two women. I found myself totally occupied with my responsibilities and with keeping abreast of Caesar's activities.

By early summer he had returned to Gaul to consolidate not only his conquest of the Veneti, but of all the tribes along the western seaboard. He had warships built and sailed them along the coast, keeping potential danger areas under constant surveillance. His winter camps in Gaul had made many tribes aware of what the Roman presence actually meant, and there were sporadic revolts throughout the land. But since the tribes revolted independently, Caesar met them one by one and cut them down, bloodily and savagely.

One by one.

In that terrible year we in central Gaul felt the Roman's fist tightening slowly but surely as he defeated the tribes around our perimeter. He also stationed a legion among the Nantuates southeast of the Aedui, to enable him to open a route through the Alps for more armies. He began negotiations with cowed kings in various areas to supply his forces with corn and other necessities.

He was sending considerable plunder back to Rome.

He also sent agents to Cenabum to investigate the death of Tasgetius.

Conco rode north to the grove to tell me what happened. "The Romans are enormously suspicious but they can't prove anything, Ainvar. No one can say who wielded the sword. The Romans have asked a lot of questions about Cotuatus and even a few about me, but gotten no satisfactory answers, I'm happy to say. And old Nantorus seems so harmless he has them puzzled. I don't think the problem is over; the traders will continue to complain because

Nantorus isn't cooperating with them as Tasgetius did. But Caesar's people have left Cenabum—for now."

It was that "for now" I did not like.

Obviously I had chosen wisely in urging Nantorus to be restored as king. Though Cotuatus would not like it, things must remain as they were until Rix was ready to make his move. He was not a boastful fool like Cotuatus; he would not claim support he did not have and act prematurely. The Gallic confederacy was growing; it was only a matter of time.

It was only a matter of time before Caesar closed his fist on free Gaul also.

I sent Conco back to Cotuatus to repeat the order to keep his head down and wait. Conco was not pleased to carry such a message; like his kinsman, he wanted action.

They did not understand that my desire for action was just as great as theirs.

Meanwhile, the killer of Tasgetius was, predictably, making trouble within the Fort of the Grove. He had returned as I ordered and taken up residence in his old lodge, but far from being grateful for the refuge afforded him, Crom complained constantly. He had found a kindred spirit in Baroc the porter, and the two could be found at any time of day or night, drinking together and condemning everyone but themselves.

The Goban Saor intercepted me one day as I returned from the vineyard, where we were still performing healing rituals on the ravaged earth in anticipation of planting new vines. "I'm afraid I passed along, quite in jest, your remark about collecting women, Ainvar," he told me. "Someone who heard me repeated it to someone else who repeated it to Crom Daral, and now . . . ah, you know how one word borrows another. He says you boast of having stolen his woman from him and plan to steal more."

"I'll talk to him," I said disgustedly.

But talking to Crom did no good. His head was stone, his opinions carved in. "I know what I know," was all he said.

I told Sulis, "I refused to give him the satisfaction of explaining in detail. I only told him Briga and I had always behaved with respect for his feelings, which is the truth. And as for Lakutu—I certainly didn't steal her!"

"What will become of her after the child is born?" the healer asked, giving me a sideways glance.

"I haven't thought that far ahead," was my honest answer.

"Beltaine is upon us; I assume you intend to marry Briga then?"

"I do."

"Hmmm," said Sulis.

Though I rejoiced with Lakutu that a part of Tarvos lived in her, her presence in the lodge was a disturbing influence. On the rare occasions when I had time to embrace Briga, I was always aware of Lakutu. Just knowing that she was under the same roof acted like a bucket of cold water thrown on my passion. I held myself in, I whispered instead of shouting with joy. I felt the disappointment in Briga.

But I could not enjoy her in privacy outside, somewhere among trees and grass, for whenever I emerged from my doorway someone appeared with a demand upon the time and effort of the chief druid.

My reputation for wisdom was growing. Every problem was brought to me—though I could not solve my own.

Once Lakutu's child is born, my head suggested, it might be wise to suggest her as a wife for Crom Daral.

I did not discuss this with Briga, who was fond of Lakutu. Briga was fond of anyone she helped.

There were many things I did not discuss with Briga, to my sorrow. I had once imagined that when we were together I would be able to open myself fully to her and share those aspects of Ainvar that only she would understand. Yet she did not open herself to me. She held something back, hidden in the shadows in her eyes. She was afraid to love because she was afraid to lose. So I, too, retreated, becoming critical, jealous, stung by a sense of incompletion I had not anticipated.

The magic was missing.

Yet sometimes in passing, Briga would reach up, very quickly, and just touch the streak of silver in my hair with her fingertips. At such moments there was a brief look of awe on her face. I longed to ask her what she had seen that day in the grove that made her come to me afterward, but I did not. I had her; that was enough.

Sometimes it was too much.

I began to suspect I wanted the dream of Briga more than the reality.

The reality was a woman who could distract me equally with her presence or her absence; a woman who could not be ignored, but could ignore me; who constantly gnawed her fingernails; who did not say the words I had imagined her saying to me; who sometimes looked at other men with speculation in her eyes; who made decisions on her own without asking my permission.

In short, a free person.

Trusting in the power of ritual, I expected marriage would change her. The ancient ceremonies at Beltaine had been designed not only to stimulate fertility, but also to enforce the pattern of female submission.

Ah, the beauty of Beltaine that year! Even with Rome's clouds in the sky, we rejoiced. The Great Fire burned hot above us, kindling an answering heat in me, and Briga threw back her flower-crowned head and laughed.

Dian Cet recited the laws of marrying, but I hardly heard him. My eyes kept straying to the plump little woman in the pleated skirt who blushed when I looked at her but then made sexually explicit gestures with her fingers where none but I could see them. Briga!

Her hair hung down her back in three heavy plaits, with a stem of grain from last year's harvest twisted through each. There was a golden glow in the air around her I thought everyone must surely see. Briga, my Briga.

The women who were being married stepped forward with great solemnity to reverence the Beltaine tree. We men watched, imagining those worshipful hands and mouths on our bodies. Then we all joined to dance the pattern that reenacted pursuit and capture and prepared the women to surrender.

We danced as Celts had done for countless centuries, stamping and singing, glorying in being alive. Through our linked hands I felt immortality running like a river from the past to the future. The ritual that was meant to influence Briga was speaking powerfully to me. As my feet danced the ancient pattern that was old when mankind was new, the meaning of existence was revealed to me, perfect and pure.

Life is.

We are.

The great and holy cosmological imperative is simply: *Be.*

When the dance ended, I stood behind Briga with no space between us. My thighs pressed against her buttocks, my hands slid up her rib cage to cup her breasts. I pulled her tightly against me, against every aching part of me, and shouted with the joy of being alive.

The flesh, more eloquent than words, took over.

We lay on the earth while the great thunder gathered in me. Briga buried her teeth in the muscle of my shoulder as I spun out of myself, whirled into a creative vortex where the Source was forever making and unmaking worlds, spinning with the ceaseless motion that maintains all in balance. Patterns formed behind my closed eyes in ever-increasing layers of complexity, then dissolved to build anew.

When at last I lay spent and throbbing, Briga whispered my name.

I raised my head. All around us people were murmuring and stirring as they slowly recovered themselves. Some always join the newly married pairs to reinforce their first wedded coupling, but this time participation had been total. Sulis lay with Dian Cet, and the Goban Saor with a pretty bondservant. Every man had a woman. Teyrnon the smith was embracing someone who was not his wife, while a little distance away, Damona was clinging happily to a young man who was certainly not her husband, but had made her feel young again, and filled with joy.

There was laughter around us, happy and unembarrassed, the sound of people delighted with themselves.

"Our strong young druid carried us all with him," I heard someone say.

Grannus came toward me, picking his way rather unsteadily among couples still lying locked on the earth. He had, I observed, a flushed face and his robe was hiked up on one side, with sticks and smears of dirt testifying to his recent activities.

Old Grannus, who had survived his seventieth winter.

"Take your wife to whatever private place you have prepared for her," he was saying formally to each married couple in turn, "and celebrate together until the honey moon wanes." When he came to us he added, "It's all right, Ainvar. Even the chief druid is not so indispensable we cannot spare him long enough to drink his cask of mead."

Following marriage, each new couple was traditionally given a cask of mead, which was honey wine, to drink, and for whatever remained of the Beltaine moon they were allowed to be alone together.

Briga and I made the most of the nights and days of the honey moon. I had made a nest for us in a secluded glade deep in the woods, with a leather tent against the rain and one of my body-guards on duty at all times, within shouting distance but out of sight. We were rarely in the tent, however.

Usually we slept beneath the trees and stars.

When our cask of honey wine was empty, we returned to the fort and my lodge, where I found a pile of gold ornaments just inside the door. "Where did these come from?" I asked Lakutu.

"They're mine," Briga interjected. "I sent for them."

"How? When?"

"After the Beltaine dance, while you were collecting our mead and supplies. I spoke to two of your men and asked them to go to my Sequani kinfolk and tell them that I was now married to the chief druid of the Carnutes, and must not be shamed before his tribe by my poverty. They sent this marriage portion," she added proudly.

"You sent my messengers on an errand of your own? After we were married?"

"But of course," she replied with a shrug.

Life resumed as before.

On a night of summer stars, Lakutu bore her child. When Briga told me she was in labor, I summoned help, for she was not a strong woman anymore. The lodge was soon crowded to overflowing. I wanted to leave, but Lakutu called out to me and I stayed, though some of the women frowned at me when I got in their way.

Sulis rubbed Lakutu's belly with imported oil of sandalwood, and Briga and Damona supported her in a squatting position to make birth easier. We chanted in rhythm with her efforts, all of us sweating together to produce life.

He came out roaring, a son of war and thunder.

"He will be a warrior like his father," I told Lakutu as I put him into her arms for the first time.

I had seen to it that all possible precautions were taken to give the infant the best chance at life. We had commandeered every lamp in the fort, arranging them so no shadow would fall on his emerging head. Sulis had then bathed him in sacred water from the spring in the grove, Keryth had read his first omens in the afterbirth, and Aberth had taken it to feed to the fire in due sacrifice. The women had woven tiny bands for the child's wrists from green twigs of rowan to protect him against malign spirits, and from holly to give strength to his arms. A miniature wreath of willow placed on his head ensured he would develop sharp night vision. Leaves of poplar scattered around him would ward off illness. Lastly, the massive gold arm ring of a warrior which had belonged to his father was laid at his tiny pink toes.

Lakutu gave me a wan smile. She was frighteningly thin and weak. "My people do not do these things."

"Tell me what your people do. I would be glad to learn of any helpful rituals."

She looked vaguely around, then back to my face as the eager baby sucked ferociously at her nipple. "In my land is so different. No man would be at birth."

"In my land," I told her, "we consider that a man is at least partially responsible."

Briga chuckled. Sulis laughed outright.

"Among my people would be much wailing now," Lakutu said, "for sorrows child will know in life."

"Here," I assured her, "we shall sing for joy."

She closed her eyes and sighed contentedly. "Let all be done your way. This my land now. These my people. Our clan," she added, snuggling the child.

Crom Daral shall not have her after all, I decided.

Menua had taught simplicity, but I had a large talent for complicating my life.

In the following seasons we Carnutes grew accustomed if not resigned to the sight of Roman patrols in our land, though a deed like the attack upon the vineyard was not repeated. Some of our more reckless princes clamored to attack the interlopers, but Nantorus and my druids urged caution and they reluctantly withheld their hands. "The whole pot must boil over at once and destroy Caesar," I told my people repeatedly. "A few scalding drops will only anger him and encourage him to crush the Carnutes as he has so many other tribes."

We found an unexpected ally. Caesar's attention was distracted from central Gaul by the Germanic tribes of the Usipetes and the Tencteri, who crossed the Rhine in large numbers near the seacoast. Once again, lesser tribes were fleeing the savage depredations of the Suebi.

Caesar joined his army very early in battle season, and entertained Germanic envoys who were supposedly suing for peace. There were the customary accusations and denials, then skirmishes, then an all-out war along the Rhine.

When his troops were finally victorious, Caesar turned his gaze in a new direction.

Rix himself brought me the news, riding that big black stallion of his up to the gates of the fort and bellowing my name so everyone in the fort heard him. He had a party of mixed warriors as escort, most of them Arvernian but a few from the other tribes who had given him their support.

Every time I met Rix he looked older, more weathered and drawn. Yet conversely he had more vitality than ever. Being in his presence was like warming oneself by a roaring fire.

As I was welcoming him to my lodge, I noticed him running appreciative eyes over Briga, who smiled back. Then he gave a start of surprise when he recognized Lakutu. "She's so changed, Ainvar! And what's she doing here? I thought she married our friend Tarvos."

I explained what had happened. He insisted on seeing Tarvos's son, who was lying asleep amid a pile of furs on Lakutu's bed. "No wonder this lodge smells of sour milk and urine," Rix laughed as he bent over the little warrior. "I never quite imagined you living like this, Ainvar."

"I'm as surprised as you are," I told him.

"The princes of a few tribes still take more than one wife, of course, but . . ."

"I haven't married Lakutu. I'm taking care of her and the boy for Tarvos's sake."

Rix raised a dubious eyebrow. Seeing Lakutu through his eyes —thin, graying, her breasts sagging from nursing—and knowing that she could understand what was said, I felt a perverse desire to clothe her in beauty. "I might marry her," I said defiantly. "Though you may not realize it, Rix, Lakutu is an extraordinary woman."

I heard a swiftly indrawn breath.

Briga, who was gouging hunks of cheese out of a pot, said sharply, "I know the law. You have to have permission from the first wife before you can take a second wife."

"When did you ever ask my permission about anything?" I countered.

Rix chuckled. "The two of you, bickering. Ah, Ainvar, this isn't what I imagined for you at all." He slapped his hands on his knees and let out a mighty peal of laughter.

When it subsided I tried to change the subject. "Surely you have women of your own, you understand how these things are."

"I have any number. But I've only married one of them: the one who caused me the least trouble." He was still grinning.

"You didn't come here to talk about women with me."

"Ah no." His manner sobered. "Have you heard? Caesar has undertaken an expedition to the land of the Britons before the onset of winter. He sailed on one of his warships from the territory of the Morini, nearest Briton-land."

"I hadn't heard—but I don't like it. How did you learn of this?"

"I've spent the summer quietly visiting the northern tribes, the ones Caesar has 'pacified.' I disguised myself and my men as traders"—he winked at me— "a ploy I learned from you, Ainvar. Though of course none of the tribes dare say so openly, I think most of them would stand with the confederacy in the event of an uprising. I'm certain of the Veneti, for one, and probably the Lexovii. It was they who told me about Caesar."

"Briton-land," I said gloomily, refusing the bread and cheese Lakutu was holding out to me. Suddenly I had no appetite. "Inhabited by Celtic tribes, Rix. Our people. Our druids even go there to study in the groves. Must Caesar crush every one of us beneath his heel?"

"I doubt if that's his purpose," Rix said, yawning. "He's probably after tin, and whatever else his traders now have to pay the Britons for."

"How large a force did he take with him?"

"Two legions, I was told. Over eighty ships."

I shuddered for the Britons. Until this year they had been free people. "At least," I said to Rix, "while Caesar is busy with the Britons he is not savaging us, and we have more time to prepare."

He nodded, but I did not think I had his entire attention. His eyes were following Briga's round little figure as she moved about the lodge.

And I saw her glance over her shoulder toward him.

CHAPTER TWENTY-EIGHT

WORKING TOGETHER in easy harmony, the two women prepared a fine meal for us and we ate gustily. I told Rix he must come back when I could offer him Gaulish wine.

"You're still working on that project in spite of everything else?"

"Of course. My obligation is to make the earth fruitful for my people. This very morning we held a ceremony propitiating the local gods of field and stream so the land would bear a good crop of grain."

Rix made an impatient gesture, scattering crumbs from the slab of black bread he held. "I spent my time this morning a great deal more effectively, scouting your defenses before we came in. On this plain you can see an enemy approaching from a long way off, but he can also see you. You're not making the most of the cover you have. You should have warriors in every clump of woodland, Ainvar, and a band of them on the ridge at all times, overlooking everything."

"The ridge is the sacred center of Gaul," I reminded him. "I will not station warriors in the grove."

"You will if you want to protect it."

"No."

He shrugged. "Please yourself. But if you refuse to take advantage of such a fine natural lookout, at least have more warriors on the plain around it."

I enjoyed a small smile. "There may be more fighting men there than you realize. With Roman patrols in the area I don't want to appear openly hostile, so I have clothed our warriors as plowmen and herders and woodsmen. You passed a number of them, you just didn't recognize them."

"I should have known that head of yours would put you a pace ahead of me," Rix said with a grin. He stretched out his long legs and sighed luxuriously. "It's pleasant here with your women to wait on me." He winked at Briga. "And I like not being on a horse for a change, not carrying that weight around." He nodded toward the doorway, where his great iron-bladed hacking sword stood propped against the wall.

"You still carry your father's sword, I see."

"Even when I'm in disguise, Ainvar. I always have it within reach."

"Be careful it doesn't give you away. Not many merchants wield two-handed swords with jewels in the hilt."

"Ah, I'm careful enough. But I never forget who I am."

"I should hope not," I replied. His remark reminded me of another of my concerns. My people were changing; were *being* changed, a crucial difference.

We were a people who sang. Yet we no longer surrendered to the spontaneous outbursts that used to occur for almost any reason, or just for the joy of living. My lyrical, generous, volatile, ebullient people were becoming cautious in company and suspicious of strangers; quiet, close-mouthed, wary. Since the Romans had dared destroy a vineyard in the heart of Gaul, my people were not the same.

Keryth, as chief of the vates, had offered one explanation. "We planted the vines in that place originally because it was inhabited by a benevolent spirit who would encourage them to grow and thrive. The invading Romans drove that spirit away; they frightened off many of our gentler nature gods. The people are reflecting the feelings of rape and impoverishment suffered by the land."

I said nothing of this to Rix, who would have scoffed. But I rejoiced that he at least was unchanged.

I did not, however, like the way he kept watching Briga.

"What are you going to be doing while Caesar is harassing the Britons?" I asked him.

"Making my endless rounds, trying to add to our allies," he said with a mock-weary shake of his head. "It doesn't seem to get easier."

"Of course not. You won the easiest ones first; the last will be the hardest." I understood the problem. The Celts had never had a sense of cohesion. To chieftains accustomed to autonomy the concept was absurd. Yet fortunately, some were finding the vital force of Vercingetorix irresistible.

I wondered if Briga would.

"When are you going back to Gergovia, Rix?" I asked abruptly.

"We're working our way in that direction now. I just thought we would rest here a few nights with you. My men are tired and we could use some fresh horses, if you have any to spare."

"Are you certain that's all you want here?"

"What do you mean?"

"Ah . . . I'm only saying we don't have much in the way of extra supplies. We can remount your men, but we have no horse that would be a suitable exchange for that black stallion of yours."

Rix laughed. "Don't worry about him, he isn't tired. And I wouldn't trade him anyway. What's mine I keep."

So do I, I vowed silently.

That night, with Rix sharing the hospitality of my lodge, I took Briga repeatedly, establishing my claim again and again so he could not help hearing.

He had no sooner ridden southward than I went to Sulis. I found her tending a man whose skin had begun to turn very yellow, a man who had lost his appetite. She had spread a layer of damp moss on his naked back as he lay on his belly, and was arranging heated stones in a pattern on the moss to stimulate the rivers of energy in his body to throw off the illness. We had used the same method to heal the ravaged earth of our vineyard. As the man lay drowsing, letting the cure do its work, I drew the healer aside.

"Sulis, is my wife barren?"

"Briga? Impossible. She is so full of the magic of life that it overflows. When we put one of her cloaks across a cow's back the animal invariably has a healthy calf."

"But she's never conceived."

"She's probably giving too much of the magic away."

"Help her then, Sulis. Redirect her gift to producing children for herself."

The woman gave me a wry and knowing look. "That magnificent Arvernian came riding in here, looking like a sun god, and immediately you want your wife to swell up with children so she'll be fat and clumsy. Men!"

Sulis always did have a nasty edge to her.

Caesar won a number of battles in the land of the Britons, we subsequently heard. For the most part, they were a backward people. They still did much of their fighting from chariots, a style we had abandoned as too awkward for anything but display. Being Celts they fought valiantly, however, and much Roman blood was shed. The Romans did not achieve a total conquest of the island. At the end of the fighting season, Caesar returned to northern Gaul and then went on to Latium, as was his custom, leaving fortified winter camps in Belgic territory to receive the expected influx of hostages he had demanded from the Britons he had defeated.

We were gratified to learn that only two of the British tribes complied.

The next spring Caesar led four legions and eight hundred cavalry from his Belgic bases to the lands of the Treveri, west of the Rhine. The Treveri were said to have good relations with some Germanic tribes. Caesar demanded they submit to him. Indutiomarus, a powerful Treveran prince, refused. At swords' point, Caesar's men took all his clan, including his sons, as hostages to ensure he would not join the Germans in an uprising. Then Caesar sailed back to the island of the Britons with more warships and an expanded fighting force.

The taking of hostages to ensure good behavior was an ancient custom, one we Celtic people practiced also. But in the hands of Gaius Caesar, it reached sinister proportions.

Still fearing a rebellion in some part of Gaul during his absence, Caesar decided to take with him to the land of the Britons the war leaders of the Gaulish tribes he had already "pacified."

One of these was Dumnorix of the Aedui, brother to Diviciacus. The Aedui now all professed loyalty to Caesar. Even the redoubtable Dumnorix moved his lips in the proper words. But Caesar was not convinced. He meant to keep Dumnorix where he could watch him.

The noble hostages were assembled on the north coast of Gaul, at the point of embarkation. As the warships were being loaded, Dumnorix took advantage of the confusion to escape with the aid of some Aeduan cavalrymen who were supposedly loyal to Caesar. Riding for his life, Dumnorix fled for home.

Caesar postponed the sailing and sent men in pursuit. After a wild chase, the Roman cavalry caught up with the fugitive. Dumnorix resisted and they killed him mercilessly, even as he was shouting that he was a free man and the inhabitant of a free land.

When news of this reached us, I ordered a herd of cattle to be sacrificed in the sacred grove in honor of a courageous man.

As I told Rix at our next meeting, "He was not of our tribe, but he was one of us. By offering such a tribute I show the people that all Gauls are in this together, linked by a common fate."

"Your druid symbolism may be wasted on Ollovico," Rix drawled. "He is more impressed by the sword that severed Dumnorix's neck."

Indeed we were meeting at Avaricum because Ollovico was wavering again. The killing of Dumnorix was causing him to doubt the wisdom of standing against Caesar. In response to a summons from Rix, I had come to help repersuade him.

I was just as happy meeting Rix away from the Fort of the Grove. Briga had asked at least twice if I had heard from him, and if he was well.

Prudence dictated another of my actions. Learning from Caesar's example, I impressed the spiteful Crom Daral into my bodyguard instead of leaving him behind to cause trouble in the fort.

"I don't ride well," Crom had whined. "I would just hold you back."

"That's foolishness, Crom. You could do more if you would just try."

"I cannot. My back . . . "

"Your back isn't as bad as you think it is."

"If you would just let Briga rub it for me the way she used to . . . "

"I'll send Sulis to you," I said briskly. "But I insist you go with me when I travel. In times of trouble we need to be surrounded by friends," I added rather deceitfully, for I no longer thought of Crom as a friend.

Neither was I willing to consider him an enemy.

In Avaricum, Rix and I met once more with Ollovico, ate with Ollovico, drank with Ollovico, argued with Ollovico. He was as stubborn as a stump in a grainfield. Several times Rix came close to losing his temper. If I had not put a restraining hand on his arm, he would have lost us the Bituriges in one violent explosion of anger. I understood; my imagination dwelled lovingly on images of us beating the man to a pulp.

But because of its location, we needed his tribe.

When we finally worked him around to joining with us again, Rix and I were both exhausted. We left Ollovico and went in search of some wine. Over a brimming cup, Rix asked me, "How's that plump little wife of yours, Ainvar? Briga, is that her name?"

"Plumper than ever," I assured him. "She's going to have my child."

He threw back his head and gave such a bellowing laugh that startled strangers nearby joined in. "You worked at it hard enough!" Rix cried, clapping me on the back.

I managed a smug smile.

"I'll bring your first son a gift for his name day," Rix promised me. "And a gift for your Briga, too. I'll select something for her myself, something that would suit her and no other woman. I think I know what she'd like."

He winked.

On the moon that marked the anniversary of his conception, we named the child of Tarvos and Lakutu Glas, a Celtic word for the color green.

Using a color as part of a child's name is not uncommon—if the child has black hair or red lips or a purple birthmark, for example. But when the vates read the portents and omens for Tarvos's son, every sign indicated verdure and lushness, grass and leaf, an emerald future.

So we called him Glas. And wondered where the name would lead him.

As Briga's pregnancy ripened, she grew calmer, quieter. Child-bearing women often subside into a milky serenity, I had observed. Many times I would find her and Lakutu with their heads together, murmuring away like conspirators about those aspects of creation from which the male is excluded.

I was jealous of their shared mysteries, but I was always jealous where Briga was concerned.

Encouraged by her prenatal tranquility, I decided it was safe to introduce her to an aspect of druidry that had been too long postponed. Though she had studied with Sulis and Grannus and Dian Cet and several others, I had never sent her to Aberth.

Her grief over her brother still lay in the deepest shadows behind her eyes.

Sacrifice is an integral part of the exchange between Man and Otherworld. If she was going to be a full member of the Order, Briga would have to learn to accept it.

I had been thinking a lot about sacrifice lately. The efficacy of Menua's offering of the Senonian prisoners of war had worn thin with time. The Carnutes had not yet felt the full force of Caesar as many other tribes had, but he was closing in on us. We would need fresh protections.

Everyone must be prepared.

On a morning when thick white mist rose from the river like the birth of clouds, I asked Briga to take a walk with me beyond the palisade.

"Are we going to the grove?"

"Not that far. We shall just . . . walk," I replied.

She looked toward Lakutu, who was sprinkling the floor with water in preparation for sweeping. Lakutu gave a very Gaulish shrug and Briga nodded, the eternal exchange of women acknowledging male vagaries.

I led my wife out into the mist.

Fog and mist are druid weather. When familiar landscape vanishes and there are no visible boundaries, one who knows the way may stumble into mystery. We are none of us solid. Nor are time and space immutable. It is claimed that the greatest of our druids, in ancient days, knew how to step from one reality into another, from one age into another. Sometimes, alone in the fog, wrapped in the hooded robe, I was tempted to try. . . .

But on this day my concern was the instruction of Briga. Taking her into the mist was merely a way of cutting her off from distractions and making her more vulnerable. She would resist what I was about to tell her; she must be isolated until she accepted.

I must be the chief druid.

As we passed out through the gate of the fort, the mist thickened until it swirled around us in clots and clouds. Briga put one hand on her swelling belly and pressed closer to me, but I did not put my arm around her. Instead, I began to speak. Quietly, calmly, gently; one strong and familiar voice amid white nothingness.

I wanted to hold her. But I wanted her to have nothing to hold on to but my words. "As you know," I began, "we consist of two parts: a spirit of fire and a fort of flesh. When the flesh dies the spirit does not cease to be. It merely alters the conditions of its existence."

"How can you be so sure?"

I explained it to her as Menua had once explained to me: "Imagine a lake in a hot, dry summer, with a cloudless blue sky burning above it. We have all seen this. Every day the level of the lake falls. Where is the water going?"

She walked in silence for a time before admitting, "I don't know."

I smiled to myself. The mist was making her uncertain. Good.

The mist grew even thicker.

"Remember what always happens," I told her. "Every day there is less water. Then at last clouds begin to form in that hot, bright sky. In time, they shed rain, and the rain replenishes the lake. Druids observed this for centuries before you were born, until they understood. The water had not ceased to be, Briga. Nothing ceases to be. It had merely altered the conditions of its existence. The lake water became a water spirit, was drawn up into the clouds, rested there for a time, then fell as rain to become part of the lake again.

"So it is with all spirits, including those housed in your flesh and mine. The body releases us—in our case, through death—and we move on through the cycles of existence."

"But why must there be death at all?" she asked resentfully.

"Look to nature again. Imagine a forest. If no tree ever died, the forest would become so crowded the trees would exist in a choking, lightless horror. There would be no light near the ground to encourage young seedlings, there would be only old trees growing older, drying, splitting, rotting, tormented by insects, with no way to let their spirits escape and start afresh.

"Instead, observe what happens when a tree dies. In old age its roots have already shrunk back so they do not grasp a great handful of earth as they did in their youthful vigor. This is one way in which the Source prepares the tree for its death. A wind comes and easily topples the ancient one and the forces of destruction cause it to decay, becoming part of the soil again. Where the old tree falls new trees grow, nourished by its discarded body as its spirit moves on.

"So the dual forces of construction and destruction keep the cycle of existence turning, freeing and re-housing spirits so each has a chance to grow and express itself in ways appropriate to its nature, while remaining part of the whole.

"We swim through spirits as we swim through air. Spirits caught between human lives and spirits that have never been and will never be human. Animal spirits, bird spirits, tree spirits, water spirits. Spirits of place. Spirits of being so different from ourselves we can no more understand them than wolves can understand rainbows. Yet all share the commonality of being and each commands respect.

"Sacrifice is one way of showing that respect."

At the mention of the word, I heard her swift intake of breath. Yet she had attended cattle sacrifices during her seasons of training for the Order. With her own small, calloused hands she had poured their blood upon the earth to beseech a good harvest.

She knew, however, that the sacrifice of a bullock was not the ultimate in offerings. She knew what I was about to tell her; she just did not want to hear it. Nor, remembering my own youthful ignorance, could I blame her.

"Sacrifice is an act of piety," I said in my gentlest voice as I guided her through a billowing mist that, wraithlike, extended tenuous, pleading arms to us. "The most potent form of sacrifice is human, Briga, because both sacrificer and victim can understand the nature of the act. Unlike animals, humans can go to their sacrifice willingly, as your brother did when he offered his life in a conscious effort to protect his people.

"Offering flesh and blood which has been sanctified through ritual is the utmost tribute, for it obligates the gods to give a gift of equal value in return. The most exalted intercourse between human and god takes place in the moment of sacrifice."

If I closed my eyes I could still see the golden sparks, flying upward. . . .

"You make it sound as if something wonderful happened to Bran," Briga said in a choked voice.

"It did."

"He was killed."

"No, Briga. His body was killed, only his body. The thing inside him that made him alive was his spirit, and that was not killed. Spirits cannot be unmade. Nothing ever ceases to be. Bran's flesh was transformed into ash, but his spirit was freed to intercede with the Otherworld on behalf of his people. He was successful, the plague was ended. Then the spirit of Bran, the essential, living Bran, moved on to other lives and other opportunities you and I cannot imagine."

We had stopped walking. Surrounded by a mist as thick as clotted cream, we stood facing one another. With my mind I held the mist around us like a palisade, keeping the distractions of the world at bay. Simultaneously I attempted to reach into Briga's head and instill her with belief.

The future might be terrible. The omens were increasingly dark. I wanted this woman who was more dear to me than any other to be able to meet whatever came without fear, secure in the wisdom of the druids. Knowing what druids know.

"Nothing ceases to be," I reiterated emphatically, forcing her to accept the law of nature. "Therefore we are, all of us, perfectly safe, even though the conditions of our existence change."

She was standing close to me, gazing up into my face with an expression so earnest, so hopeful yet so fearful that it made me ache. Concentrating every fiber of my being, I poured into her the full, unshielded force of my knowledge, all my experience, all my memories . . .

. . . until I saw the shadows fade from her eyes like the coming of dawn.

Filled with wonder, her dear little, hoarse little voice repeated at last, *"We are, all of us, perfectly safe."*

CHAPTER TWENTY-NINE

I OPENED my arms wide and she came into them. Lost in the mist, embracing my world, I was shaken by joy.

Between our tightly pressed bodies I felt the infant stir in her belly.

Briga laughed her gurgling laugh. "And the baby is safe too, yes?"

"Yes. That which causes it to move within you is its immortal spirit."

"I love you, Ainvar," Briga murmured.

In the silence of my head I murmured a prayer of profound gratitude to That Which Watched. Briga was entirely mine, she was no longer afraid to love me.

But I was afraid. Not of death. I was afraid that the child which was mine and Briga's would not have the chance to grow up as a free person among free people, a singer among people who sang. I was afraid that Tarvos's son, and the boy Briga had rescued from blindness, and all our other children would be denied their heritage.

Caesar's soldiers skewered Celtic children on their spears.

I had fought death for Tarvos's sake because it came to him too soon. For the sake of the children I would fight Caesar and all his armies. I would fight the world, I would sacrifice anything.

With redoubled fervor I devoted myself to studying the ancient rituals of protection and to searching for new ones. I exhaustively questioned every druid who visited the grove, seeking additional gestures, charms, and symbols to enlarge our druidical armory.

At the completion of a campaign in which he mercilessly slaughtered numerous unfortunate Britons and enslaved even more, Caesar sailed his warships back to the northern coast of Gaul. There he learned the region had just experienced a disastrous harvest. The warriors he had quartered in the lands of the Belgae would undergo serious shortages of grain and other supplies unless he took some action.

Calling a council of local kings to meet him at Samarobriva, on the river Somme, Caesar informed the council he was going to relocate the winter camps of his legions. They would now be distributed among many more tribes than before, to give them access to everyone's supplies.

I learned of this from druids of the Treveri and the Eburones, who had come to the great grove in preparation for the Samhain convocation. They pleaded with me to use the concentrated power of the grove to invoke the fertility of their lands, which had experienced crop failure that year. With the added burden of Roman warriors to feed, they, like many northern tribes, were facing famine before the wheel of the seasons had turned full circle again.

Listening to them, it became evident to me that the region was ripe for revolt. And a revolt in the north would distract Caesar a while longer from attacking central Gaul.

I conferred long and earnestly with the Treverans and the Eburones. Because they had already suffered under Roman control, I found them more amenable to my suggestions than many of our own free Gauls who had thus far been spared.

In return for my promise to work our most powerful magics on their behalf in the grove, visiting druids promised to use their influence with the leaders of their respective tribes. Then I reported to our local druids, with some satisfaction, "We are extending the network."

It did not take long for these efforts to bear fruit.

Uneasy over the situation, Caesar lingered in northern Gaul to supervise the fortifications of the new camps, rather than returning to Latium for the winter as usual. While he was there, a revolt broke out, led by Ambiorix, king of the Eburones, who claimed the support and encouragement of Indutiomarus of the large tribe of the Treveri. Sweeping battles followed throughout the land between the Rhine and the Meuse rivers. A substantial Roman force, including two high-ranking commanders, was annihilated.

Encouraged by the revolt's early successes, other northern tribes began joining in the uprising. Caesar soon found himself fighting on many fronts. Indutiomarus even sent envoys across the Rhine to invite the Germans to take part, promising them a share of the spoils and all the Roman iron they could carry home.

Avidly, I followed the accounts as the tides of battle turned one way, then another. Many bullocks were sacrificed in the grove on behalf of our northern allies. For a time it seemed as if they might win, but then the shrewd tactics of the Roman began to bite. Caesar's armies began to win more battles than they lost.

Then I learned I had been mistaken to assume the northern revolt would distract Caesar from central Gaul. The man had a layered mind; he could think of many things at once—which is the attribute that truly distinguishes humans from other animals. Even while conducting a campaign against tribes infuriated by his demands for their grain, he had remembered other angers—and the death of Tasgetius.

The news was shouted along the river valleys: Caesar had dispatched a legion from the lands of the Belgae to spend the winter among the Carnutians.

I was appalled.

I rode at once for Cenabum. The story was true; Caesar had ordered five thousand men under the command of one Lucius Plancus into the area to investigate the killing of Tasgetius and to, as the Romans put it, "keep the peace." The Romans claimed to suspect a combined revolt by the Carnutes and the Senones.

Caesar knew of the Gaulish confederacy; he had spies everywhere. It was obvious, however, that he did not know for certain just who was committed to the confederacy or what plans were being made. He must have assumed that an army sent into our territory—and another to the land of the Senones—would be sufficient to intimidate us both.

As I approached Cenabum, I saw the Roman encampment
spread across the level fields like an alien flood. My lips curled
with disgust. In order to avoid being spotted by the ubiquitous
Roman patrols in the vicinity of the camp, I led my companions
in a very large circle that eventually took us to a side gate of the
town.

The town gates were shut and barred. I had to shout up to the
sentry and identify myself with both hooded robe and triskele
before the gates were opened to us. While waiting, I thought about
the Roman style of intimidation.

Druids know something about intimidation.

Leaving my bodyguards to mingle with the warriors of Cenabum,
I headed for the king's lodge. The effect of the Roman presence
in the area was obvious. The Carnutes were subdued, going about
their daily affairs with downcast eyes and tight, nervous faces. They
spoke in brief phrases. No one was singing.

On the other hand, the Roman traders were more in evidence
than ever, strutting through Cenabum as jaunty as cockerels and
calling out cheery greetings as if they owned the place. I slipped
from shadow to shadow, avoiding them.

I found Nantorus in his lodge, submerged in gloom. His old wife
and his clanswomen made me welcome, but a soggy spirit looked
at me from the king's eyes. In the ruin of the man it was hard to
find the champion who had once been our most gifted warrior.
Whatever vitality he had regained was lost again, perhaps permanently this time.

"He treats me as if I were no more than a hound under the
table, Ainvar," Nantorus complained as soon as we had finished
the formalities.

"Who does?"

"The Roman commander, Lucius Plancus. He has some sort of
scroll from Caesar with symbols painted on it that he claims gives
him the right to govern here in the absence of a lawful king. *I* am
the lawful king, Ainvar!" he added querulously, his underlip quivering.

"I trust you told him his scroll carries no weight here. We are
not Caesar's to command, we are free people."

Nantorus would not meet my eyes. He sat on his bench, holding
a cup of wine he could not find the energy to drink, and said in a

rusty voice, "I tried. He wouldn't listen to me. I drove out to the camp and ordered him to leave, but his men laughed at my chariot, and almost before we knew what was happening, he had two cohorts at the main gates of Cenabum, threatening to kill anyone else who tried to come out. Plancus said we must stay within the walls and obey his orders or . . . or . . .

"I'm not afraid of him or any man, Ainvar, you know that. I'm not afraid of death." Nantorus lifted his head and found a vestige of his old pride to show me. "But I am terrified that I, the king of the Carnutes, will be unmanned before all my tribe. That's what Plancus promised to do to me, to have me gelded and beaten until I was lying helpless in a puddle of blood and urine, and then make my people spit on me.

"I thought I could fight him but . . . I could not find it in myself. Not anymore. So I stay here, and the Romans are out there. To-morrow they plan to begin questioning people about the death of Tasgetius. The people are frightened. I was . . . I represented their strength, their manhood. And I was able! Until the Roman . . . until his men laughed . . . until he said . . . "

I felt a great pity for him. It was because of me he was in this untenable position. An old man should be left his dignity; I should have foreseen his failing and had a stronger, younger man in place to face the Roman eagles. I thought briefly of Cotuatus, but to keep him away from what the Romans called justice I had left both him and Crom Daral at the Fort of the Grove.

"What princes are in Cenabum now, Nantorus?"

The king named them. Conconnetodumnus had gone off in search of a wife, taking his sworn warriors to attack the Turones, who bred handsome and fertile women. The other nobles currently penned within the walls of Cenabum were none of them impressive enough to intimidate a Roman commander. If only there were a Rix among them to meet Plancus. . . .

"Have your women bring me a prince's tunic," I ordered. "And all the gold jewelry they can gather, a torc, arm rings, finger rings, the bigger and showier the better. A wolf fur cloak, enameled brooches. Hurry!"

"But Ainvar, druids don't wear such things."

"When I meet the Roman commander, Nantorus, I won't be meeting him as a druid."

I dressed in the king's lodge. After the freedom of the hooded robe, the tight-fitting tunic and leggings were confining, and the weight of the jewelry threatened to drive me into the earth, as I told the giggling women.

When I thought myself ready, and perfectly disguised as a prince of horse rank, the king's old wife burst into laughter. "He'll know you are a druid as soon as he sees you," she said. "You wear the tonsure."

I had forgotten my tonsure. Since initiation into the Order I had, like all male druids, shaved the very front part of my head from ear to ear to allow the sun more access to my brain. The Fire of Creation nourishes the mind. The style gave, in my case, the impression of an unnaturally high forehead with a silver streak beginning above the temple, and was sufficient to identify me as a druid to anyone who had spent any time in Gaul.

"Do you have a tunic with a cowl? Or with some sort of hood that doesn't look like a druid's hood?" I asked, but a search of the lodge found nothing that would serve.

Then one of the king's sisters suggested, "Why not a wreath? If you are supposed to be a warrior, surely you take part in the endless contests and races with which they pass the time when not at war. We can make you a winner's wreath to wear and the Romans will never know the difference."

It was the wrong season for green leaves and the king's lodge lacked shrubbery, but the women contrived a dense circlet for me using kale and sorrel meant for the cooking pot, and twisted together with bindweed and thread from the loom. It might not have deceived one of our own, but it should suffice for the Romans, we all agreed.

When I was pronounced ready, we sent a messenger to the Roman camp to summon the commander to the king of the Carnutes.

We waited. Plancus did not come.

"You'll have to go to him," Nantorus said.

"Ah no. Send the messenger again, but this time let him say how distressed you are to learn that the Roman commander has been gravely incapacitated."

"But he hasn't . . . has he?"

"Not yet," I said, suppressing a smile. "But he won't want that sort of rumor going around Cenabum. He'll come to you to prove it isn't true. And just to be sure he does, I'll do a few spells for summoning while we wait."

We did not have to wait long before Lucius Plancus himself galloped through the gates of Cenabum at the head of a company of Roman cavalry. Hearing his approach, I stepped out in front of the lodge to read him before he could read me.

As I was predisposed to dislike the man for what he had done to Nantorus if for no other reason, I hated him on sight. Mounted on a snorting bay stallion with blood-flecked foam at the corners of its mouth, Plancus was short and swarthy and hard-eyed. A merciless man.

He had not shown compassion, so he would receive none from me; there must be a balance.

He slid from his horse, glanced around haughtily, and snapped his fingers. A man with the face of an Aeduan rode forward.

"We won't need an interpreter," I said hastily in Latin, half-turning so the Aeduan could not see my forehead too closely. I was grateful for the approaching twilight.

"And who are you?" Plancus demanded to know.

"Ainvar of the Carnutes. I speak your language, or we can use Greek if you prefer."

He was too experienced to let me see how that disconcerted him, but I could smell his surprise.

"Latin will do," he said, waving the Aeduan aside. "Take me to Nantorus."

I shifted weight and blocked his way. "The *king* Nantorus." I corrected him politely. "You must use his title."

"King, chieftain, call him what you like. He wanted to speak to me and I am here."

"I wanted to speak to you." I corrected him again. "You are here in response to my summons."

Plancus squinted at me as if seeing me for the first time. The Aeduan had also moved forward again and was looking at me curiously. I wondered if my wreath had slipped. We had better go into the lodge at once, before one of my own people happened by and revealed my true identity inadvertently.

"We can speak more comfortably inside," I told Plancus, pushing the oaken door open. "Unless you are afraid to come in and leave your army outside."

He shot me a barbed look, but he motioned his men to wait

and followed me into the lodge. I had to duck under the lintel. He did not.

Lucius Plancus did not greet or even acknowledge Nantorus, who arose from his bench as we entered. The Roman did not bother to give his face so much as a token splash from the basin of heated water the king's wife courteously offered to him. The interior of the big lodge gleamed with burnished metals and glowed with vividly dyed fabrics; lush furs were piled everywhere for comfort; the best food and drink were at hand. Yet the Roman flicked one glance of contempt around the walls and thereafter held himself aloof as if he were in a pen of animals.

"Now tell me what you want," he said to me in a voice long accustomed to command. "Speak fast, I have to get back to my men. You can begin by explaining just who you are, and what gives you the right to send for a Roman officer."

"I am of horse rank," I replied evenly, "like your Gaius Caesar. I have just returned to find Cenabum surrounded by armed foreigners who were not invited here. So of course I demand an explanation."

"*You* demand an explanation?" Plancus was perplexed. I was not acting in accordance with his expectations.

"I do. We have never marched an army into your land, why do you bring one into ours?"

"We have been sent to keep the peace," he said stiffly.

"There was peace here until you came. Now, with five thousand troops blundering across fields and meadowland and turning them into useless muck, the peace is destroyed. Men are angered by your intrusion, and even as we speak, they are polishing their weapons. Blood will flow and you will be to blame."

"Are you threatening a rebellion?"

"A rebellion is an uprising against the established authority," I told him with the confidence of one well educated by the Order. "We have no reason to resist our established authority, which is that of the king Nantorus, beloved of his people.

"We do have every reason to resist foreign invaders, however, and we are fully capable of doing so. You bring trouble with you. All I ask is that you take it away. Go. Take your legion elsewhere and leave us in peace."

Plancus glanced toward Nantorus. "I thought the old man was too smart for this, but obviously he is willing to let a fool speak for him. You are making a mistake, Ainvar. You do not understand the situation."

"It is you who does not understand the situation." I corrected him gently.

Like a clever war leader, Plancus tried to shift the area of conflict onto familiar ground. "We have been ordered to learn the name of the murderer of your king Tasgetius, and surrender him to justice."

"By whose authority?"

"That of Gaius Julius Caesar, on behalf of the citizens of Rome."

"A group that has no status in free Gaul," I replied. "You are here by no authority we recognize, Plancus, in the land of the Carnutes, who have six warriors to your every one." I paused to let him digest that fact. Romans, my head reminded me, believe death is permanent. Even a man as hard as Plancus must fear death as the ultimate threat.

"Whoever sent you here," I told him, "has ordered you to die for a matter of no consequence. Our princes can call in their sworn warriors from the surrounding countryside with a simple shout if Nantorus asks it of them. He has been lenient with you so far, because we are a people at peace, with a lawful king. You have come here in response to the unfounded accusations of a handful of disaffected traders, but are you willing to die for them, Plancus? Would any of them sacrifice himself for you? Are all of them together worth the destruction of a Roman legion?"

He snorted. "What makes you think your men could do any real damage to a legion of Rome?"

Without warning I seized his sword wrist. Locking his eyes with mine so I had access to his head, I began to squeeze.

Heavy. Stone. The weight of stone pressing inward on itself. The weight of the earth, the ultimate goddess, mother to us all, pressing in, pressing down, irresistible, grinding and crushing . . . and crushing . . .

Inside the man's head, in the place where each of us shapes our exterior form, consciously or not, I spoke to the bones of Plancus's wrist. Grind and crush, I ordered. Grind and crush each other.

The Roman's face went white beneath the layers of windburn.

Summoning memories of Vercingetorix, I spread his radiant, indomitable smile across my face and showed it to Lucius Plancus. Look upon the face of a free man! I commanded silently.

Fear him!

In the quiet lodge, the sudden crunching of bone being pulverized was shockingly loud.

Plancus sagged in my grip. He neither gasped nor cried out, however. Rome hammers her warriors hard. But I doubt if he ever thought his wrist could be crushed by a single squeeze.

When I released him, his hand flopped uselessly. He caught it with the other hand and tried to rotate the joint. There was a terrible grating noise and from the look of him, I thought Plancus would faint.

"You had better sit down," I said solicitously. "Here, on this bench. With a fur robe for your knees? And take some wine. Perhaps you would like one of our healers to attend you?"

Throughout the confrontation, Nantorus and his attendants had followed my instructions and kept quiet. Now the king's wife stepped forward to offer a cup of wine to the Roman. Taking the cup in his uninjured hand, he drained it in a gulp.

I thought of the earth, and darkness, and weight. Great weight, pressing down.

This time Plancus did gasp, but he fought back. "I do not want any of your barbarian healers to do me any more damage," he said through gritted teeth.

"As you wish," I agreed pleasantly. Still in conversational tones I remarked, "I am not the strongest of our tribe, you know. Far from it. Some of our warriors would consider me weak. You have never fought free Gauls, have you? There are those among us whom no sane man would dare to face in combat."

When he least expected it, I resurrected the radiant grin of Vercingetorix and showed it to him again.

Simultaneously I commanded the bones in his wrist to do my bidding one final time.

Plancus's eyes rolled up in his head. When he recovered he started to say something, but I forestalled him. "Shall I call your men to take you back to camp now? You do not seem to be enjoying yourself very much, which is a pity. We pride ourselves on our hospitality. I do not think you will want to tell your men what happened to you here, will you? It would do your reputation no good to admit you were so easily incapacitated by . . . a barbarian. Shall we just say you fell? It is so dark in these lodges."

Putting a hand under his good arm, I helped the Roman to his feet. He could not summon the strength to resist me. Pain was washing over him in waves, and his wrist hung at his side like a tube of skin filled with gravel. It would never wield a sword again, the joint was crushed. By the weight of the earth.

As we reached the door, all solicitude fell away from me in a blink, leaving a core of ice. In a low, intense voice, I hissed, "There is no reason for you to be here except to die, Lucius Plancus. To die horribly. You have already suffered. Leave while you can, before something much worse happens to you and to your men."

I walked him through the doorway. The sun was just setting in a blood-red sky. Turning my body precisely so the last, lurid rays were reflected in my eyes, I bent the full force of my gaze on the Roman.

"Leave," I commanded. "While you can."

CHAPTER THIRTY

MY PEOPLE were waiting for me at the gates of the Fort of the Grove, elbowing one another in their eagerness to hear what had happened at Cenabum. Even Crom Daral was there, not pressing forward with the others but standing beyond the crowd like a solitary raven on a branch.

Though I wanted to crawl into bed and sleep, I did my duty. I led the crowd to the assembly house, where I related my experience with the Romans. When telling of the confrontation with Plancus, I spun it out a bit, as Hanesa would have, enjoying the resultant gasps and murmurs. Perhaps in some other life I might be a good bard.

My druids asked the important questions. "Did the Romans leave?" Dian Cet insisted on knowing, several times, before I had quite finished the best part of the story.

"Plancus went back to his camp with much to think about," I replied. "I did not expect he would immediately pull out the legion; they continued to drill and march and countermarch as before. But no one appeared in Cenabum to investigate the death of Tasgetius.

"We waited.

"Plancus remained encamped near the town for a full seven nights, then on the eighth morning the sentries reported the legion was moving across the Liger, moving away from us in the general direction of the land of the Turones. Presumably Lucius Plancus had decided the peace could be better kept by watching the Turones instead of us."

The Goban Saor spoke up. "I don't understand why he didn't kill you. You had, after all, assaulted a commander of the Roman army."

I smiled. "I kept him too off-balance. Romans want everything to be clear, with sharp edges, and they train endlessly in preparation for predictable situations. But there was no way Plancus could have prepared himself for what befell him in the king's lodge. From the moment he arrived he was dealing with the unexpected.

"If he were a man who reacted rashly he would never have been put in charge of a Roman legion, so I was safe enough as long as I kept him confused, unable to sort out the situation in his head and decide on some sensible Roman response.

"By the time he returned to his own camp he must have felt something of a fool, but there was still the pain to be dealt with, and I relied on that pain. His injury was one no man could ignore. We all inadvertently tighten the tendons of our hands and fingers almost continually, and every time Plancus did so he must have been in agony. Agony prevents clear thought. Since he could not think clearly, he did what must have seemed the wisest thing— he made a strategic retreat. What reason he will give to Caesar I cannot say, but he will probably find a satisfactory justification."

"Will the legion return?"

"Not immediately. We have a little more time."

In truth, I felt as if I were conducting a complex trading negotiation with the unseen Caesar, using all of my cleverness to buy my people one day at a time, like one bead at a time to be strung on a string.

The two of us were engaged in a struggle whose true nature I understood far better than Caesar. For him, the campaigns in Gaul were merely stepping stones in his career.

For us, the issue was something more important than life itself.

Presumably he did not yet realize that the Order of the Wise was his true and implacable enemy.

The valiant Indutiomarus of the Treveri was captured by Caesar's men as he attempted to cross a river. We learned with great anger that his head had been carried on a pole to the Roman camp, where it was greeted with hoots and jeers.

In the great grove we offered a fitting sacrifice to the glory of the Treveran king; one of us, now and forever.

With the death of Indutiomarus northern resistance seemed to have abated, for the time being. Caesar called a council of the Gaulish leaders. He claimed afterward that most of them attended, which was a blatant lie.

An uneasy quiet that might have been mistaken for peace settled over Gaul, but underneath, the druid network was busy urging, persuading, arguing, suggesting.

I know. From the great grove at the heart of Gaul I guided them, playing my desperate, invisible game against the cruelty and cunning of Gaius Caesar.

One of the most frequent visitors to the grove had come to be Riommar, chief druid of the Senones. Like myself, he was young for his office; a man of talent and vigor, devoted to the protection of his tribe. His own diviners had seen portents that worried him, causing him to set aside any lingering resentment his people might have for mine over the matter of the long-ago sacrifice of the Senones prisoners of war. Such deeds were commonplace and understood by us both; the threat posed by Caesar was different, and Riommar was wise enough to realize that it superseded tribal rivalries.

If only kings were as wise!

It was at my urging that Riommar had warned Cavarinus, king of the Senones, not to attend Caesar's council. Cavarinus was beguiled by Rome's riches, but Riommar had managed to frighten him with dire portents.

"A temporary success," he told me in the grove. "Cavarinus is too much impressed by Caesar. It was with the Roman's support that he ousted our former king, Moritasgus, and took his place in the king's lodge at Vellaunodunum."

"That has come to be a familiar story in Gaul," I said. "But Moritasgus is still living, is he not?"

"He is."

"More fortunate than some," I murmured, thinking of Celtillus the Arvernian. "You would be better off if he became your king again, Riommar. He would not deliver you into the Roman's hands as I fear Cavarinus might."

Riommar nodded, his face shadowed with worry. "These are hard times."

"The addition of the Senones to the confederacy of free Gaul would greatly strengthen us," I suggested.

"Cavarinus would never . . ."

"No. But surely Moritasgus would. He must hate Caesar."

"If Cavarinus were assassinated the Romans would be suspicious. I do not want my tribe to be under their scrutiny as yours has been since the death of your Tasgetius."

"I was not thinking of overt murder," I assured Riommar. "That is the Roman way and to be avoided, as we have learned. There are other ways, older and better. Druid ways."

Our eyes met in understanding. "I defer to the wisdom of the Keeper of the Grove," said Riommar. "We seek your help because Cavarinus should not be king of our tribe; how you choose to help us is up to you."

"Nothing comes free. For every crop taken from the earth an offering must be given. If we use the power of the grove to help you, in return you must use your influence to persuade Moritasgus and the other princes of the Senones to join the Gaulish confederacy and follow Vercingetorix in battle against Caesar when the time comes."

"Agreed."

"What about those who are now most loyal to Cavarinus?"

We were walking in the forest, since Briga's time would soon be upon her and there were too many women in my lodge. On the bare branches of the trees tight new buds waited to spring into life.

Bending down, Riommar collected a handful of yellowish pebbles from the soft brown earth. He tossed them up, they fell into a pattern. Most fell together, but a few skipped and rolled apart from the others. "The majority will follow Moritasgus," Riommar said. "A few will go their own way. We are free people."

"We are. But if we are to remain free, how many can we afford to have go their own way? Caesar allows for no such individuality among those he controls."

Riommar could not answer my question.

When the chief druid of the Senones had departed for the tribe's stronghold at Vellaunodunum, I sent a message to Rix: Soon we will be able to add the Senones to the confederacy.

In the grove we began working powerful magic against Cavarinus. I never doubted it would be effective, so long as we were able to bring the full force of the sacred center to bear.

But it would take time, and we did not have much time left.

Reading the signs and portents, studying the entrails, communing with the spirits of water and wind, our vates foresaw the future. Keryth told me what they had learned. "Even on days of brightest sunshine, a shadow falls over the land of the Carnutes, Ainvar. It is the shadow of an eagle. Before the wheel of the seasons has turned full circle again the eagle will strike."

Riommar sent me a heartening message. Cavarinus, king of the Senones, was unaccountably suffering poor health. The princes Acco and Moritasgus were quietly taking over some of his responsibilities, with the agreement of most of the tribe, until such time as he might recover.

While I was rejoicing over this news, Briga gave birth to my daughter.

I had never imagined a daughter. Men think of sons. When I said this, Briga laughed at me. "I knew it was a girl before my belly began to swell, Ainvar. Sulis and Damona both told me so."

A girl. A girl so small I was afraid to touch her, with a long skull and damp, dark ringlets clustered around a red little face. A beautiful little face. At first glance I saw that she would be more lovely than any woman of the Carnutes had ever been.

Druids know these things.

How incredible that my thrusting maleness had been transmuted through Briga's magic into a fragile female with long eyelashes and tiny, crumpled ears. A spirit I would come to know and love was housed in this miniature being.

If Gaius Caesar had appeared at the door of my lodge just then, I would have strangled him with my bare hands, to make the world a safer place for my daughter.

He did not. I was free to stand and drink her with my eyes. We are not granted many such moments.

To my surprise, Crom Daral brought a gift for the child. "For Briga's daughter," he emphasized, as if I had played no part in the creation. He stood awkwardly in the doorway, holding something clenched in his fist and trying to peer past me into the lodge.

"Do you want to come in and see her, Crom?" I offered, feeling proud and magnanimous.

"Ah . . . no. I . . . just tell Briga this came from me." He thrust an object into my hands and fled.

When I looked I discovered he had given his gold arm ring, symbol of a warrior.

It was as if I had given away my hooded robe.

The gift was not suitable for a girl child, and certainly not for my daughter. I did not know how to respond.

"What is it, Ainvar?" Briga called from the bed, where she lay nursing the baby. Sulis had given her a concoction of cream and spices to stimulate her milk.

"Crom Daral brought the wrong gift by mistake," I said hastily.

"How like Crom," was her only reply. Lakutu came forward to see what I was holding. She recognized the warrior's ring at once; her son, Glas, had his father's ring.

"Good friend," she said. "He gives you gold."

"It was a mistake. I'll return it to him later." I put the ring out of sight in my chest of belongings, and other events soon captured my attention. Like the stone image the Goban Saor had once carved for Menua, Crom Daral's intended gift was forgotten in the press of daily concerns.

After the death of Indutiomarus his kinsmen continued to harass the Romans in the north. Ambiorix of the Eburones joined them. Caesar marched into the lands of the Treveri and built a bridge across the Rhine so he could threaten the Germanic tribes who had allied themselves with Indutiomarus. He did not dare advance too deeply into the dark German forests; the Germans did not engage in agriculture and there was no grain to feed his troops. He did take hostages, however, and laid waste to the land, as was his custom.

In the midst of this brutality he sent, to our total amazement, some German jewels as "gifts of friendship" to Vercingetorix of the Arverni! Rix was baffled and embarrassed. I saw it as an example of the Roman's calculating duplicity.

Having once more intimidated the Germans, Caesar recrossed the Rhine and attacked Ambiorix.

Meanwhile the Nervii, the Menapii, and the Aduatuci had also once more taken up arms against the Romans. Against them Caesar waged a relentless war of attrition. I received word from Riommar that prince Acco of the Senones was sending them support, and was also encouraging his tribesmen to join the confederation of free Gaul. "I am having great success among the leaders of the Senones," Riommar was pleased to inform me.

Then the Romans surrounded the forces of Ambiorix in the forest of the Ardennes, the largest in all Gaul. One prince of the Eburones poisoned himself with yew to avoid being taken prisoner, but Ambiorix escaped. Infuriated to be thwarted of his prey, Caesar declared that brave chieftain a criminal and put a price on his head to draw the jackals.

By now many of the small tribes in the north were scrambling frantically to protect themselves. They sent envoys to Caesar, disclaiming any connection with his enemies. In fact, various individuals from almost every tribe were making their way to Caesar, insisting they were his friends and eagerly denouncing others they wished him to punish instead.

Some of the borderland Carnutians went to him, I was saddened to learn. But recalling Riommar and his stones, I accepted. Each of us acts according to his nature, and even the bravest man may not be able to bear the thought of having his women and children slaughtered and his land laid waste.

By sheer weight of numbers, Caesar destroyed resistance in the Belgic lands. What his men did not eat or rape, they burned. Refugees were now flooding in upon the Senones, and upon the Parisii and the Carnutes as well, telling terrible tales.

A messenger from Vellaunodunum arrived on a lathered horse at the Fort of the Grove. "Riommar wishes you to know that Caesar has called another council of the kings of Gaul. Cavarinus of the Senones plans to attend, in spite of his illness."

I understood. My reply must be carefully worded, so Riommar would know what I meant but no one else could accuse us of conspiracy. There were too many spies abroad now; the most fresh-faced messenger was suspect. Caesar's coins clanked in too many Gaulish purses. "Return to Riommar at once and assure him that the power of the great grove is being concentrated upon the health of the king of the Senones," I said.

Even as the messenger was galloping away on a fresh horse, I was conferring with Aberth and Sulis.

In the grove we sacrificed a dozen white cattle with black manes, and mixed their blood with three kinds of poison. A fire was built using wood smeared with the blood. The druids chanted. Obeying our command, the wind veered toward Vellaunodunum, carrying the spirits of the poison to Cavarinus.

Someone warned him. Weak as he was, Cavarinus managed to drag himself onto a horse. Together with a small cavalry of his most devoted followers, he escaped to Caesar, but our efforts were rewarded with success. No sooner had he left Vellaunodunum than the Senones elected Moritasgus their king.

The new king of the Senonians did not attend Caesar's council.

Neither, of course, did Nantorus, nor any representative of the Treveri.

In a daring march to the very edge of Senonian territory some of Caesar's men captured the prince Acco and dragged him in chains to their leader. Caesar declared Acco to be an enemy of Rome and an instigator of conspiracies among Rome's enemies. He was slowly tortured to death. Some of the Senones who had gone willingly with Cavarinus were so appalled at this they fled, afraid they might be accused of secret involvement in Acco's plans.

In the harvest season Caesar made crushing demands upon the grain crop of the northern tribes. Then, satisfied they were now too cowed to resist, he set out for Latium, leaving two legions encamped for the winter on the Treveri borderlands, two more among the Lingones, and a full six legions just across the Sequana River from the heartland of the Senones.

Before leaving Gaul he took one more step, one I could not ignore. He sent Gaius Cita, a Roman official of horse rank, to Cenabum with instructions to secure the entire grain harvest of the Carnutes.

If Caesar was arranging supplies for his armies in the center of free Gaul, it meant only one thing. We were next. Our diviners' predictions were accurate.

I sent an urgent message to Vercingetorix, asking him to meet with me a safe distance from Roman eyes.

I told Briga, "In a way, I'm glad it's come. Waiting is harder than action. Now we not only know what to expect, but when."

"War," she said in the way women say that word. "You're meeting Vercingetorix to plan a huge war. When will I see you again?" She brightened. "I know! I'll go with you, Ainvar! We won't be separated."

"We'll be riding hard; it's best you stay here. Our daughter is still very small and she needs you," I reminded her.

She laughed. "But we are perfectly safe!"

I put on my most severe expression, a Menua frown I had used before with her—always to no effect. It had no effect this time, either. "I am going with you," she insisted.

When she was distracted by the child, I took Lakutu aside. "Briga is a willful woman," I told her. "She disobeys me, and I am worried. Where I am going is not a place for women."

Lakutu nodded. "Is bad thing, woman disobeys man."

"Can you convince her?"

The black eyes shone. "I do better. I keep her here."

"How?"

"She would not leave if she could not find child. When she sleeps, I hide baby, just until you are gone." She smiled broadly. "Play little joke on Briga, let you get away."

At the next Beltaine I must marry this woman, I thought. She has a clever head.

I no longer noticed her appearance; her thinness and gray hair went unremarked. I saw the real Lakutu shining out of her eyes in gentle, generous beauty. When you get to know and appreciate someone, the dwelling that contains them becomes unimportant; you go to see your friends, not the lodges they live in.

I would definitely marry my friend Lakutu. I would be the first chief druid of the Carnutes to have two wives.

Change was in the air. But some traditions in Gaul were being abandoned with unfortunate consequences.

At the instigation of Caesar, the Aedui had abolished kingship in favor of elected magistrates and were urging other tribes to follow their example. Caesar did not want the tribes to be led by kings. Those he could not immediately kill he was attempting to buy off with bribes and promises of friendship, but I knew he eventually meant to destroy them all. The Romans did not like kings.

We needed them, however. Over many generations we had evolved the pattern of living that best suited Celtic natures. Kings led noble warriors in battle that defined tribal territory and gave men a shape for their pride. Less aggressive common people farmed the land and did the labor of the tribe. Druids were responsible for the intangible essentials upon which all else depended. Man and Earth and Otherworld were thus held in balance—until the coming of Caesar, who wanted to destroy our warriors and our druids so he could make the rest of us his slaves.

My thoughts must be concentrated upon defeating him, so I agreed to Lakutu's plan. It was simple and required no mental effort from me. All I had to do was slip a potion in Briga's cup to make her fall asleep early, when we were almost ready to leave. Then I told Lakutu, "Hide the child well, so Briga will take a long time to find her when she wakes up. I need at least a half day's start."

Pleased to be part of a small conspiracy, Lakutu beamed like a child.

My bodyguard and I set off to meet Vercingetorix.

Along our way we met with the princes of Gaul in the dark woodlands I preferred, and I told them of the cruel death of Acco. Their eyes gleamed with anger; their lips curled.

"Any of you could meet a similar fate if Caesar's legions overrun free Gaul," I warned them. "Rome does not grant its enemies death with dignity. But if you rally behind the Arvernian king we can defeat Caesar. We can win a victory that will be commemorated for a thousand years!"

Inflamed by the prospect, they clenched their fists and beat their shields and shouted the name of Vercingetorix.

But Celts are easily aroused. Until we met Caesar on the field of battle, it was hard to say how many would actually stand with us.

The Roman had a talent for creating powerful partisans. Diviciacus of the Aedui, who as a druid should have been beyond his persuasions, was an example. Caesar could be generous or severe by turns with no thought of humanity or justice, only an implacable desire to win. He was unstinting of his resources in seducing allies and savage to those who resisted him. In this lay lessons for us, as I had pointed out to Rix.

Caesar had established a powerful personal influence almost independent of Rome. He was undoubtedly brilliant; in a different world I should have liked to learn from him and teach him.

Instead we were deadly enemies.

Rix and I met south of Avaricum, across the hills from the territory of the Boii. The mighty Boii had, through the urging of the Aedui, accepted Caesar's domination. Only a few princes were holding out and Rix had come in hopes of winning them for the Gaulish confederacy.

We met in a stand of trees that had grown up around a farmstead destroyed in some forgotten war. Little remained of it but a few weather-chewed rocks and rain-striped walls.

Accompanied by a well-armed cavalry, Rix came riding on that black horse of his. The animal was a fully mature stallion now, and the man who rode him was also fully mature, though young as men reckon age. The next winter would be the thirtieth for both of us if we lived to see it.

Memory is a dark tunnel with brightly lighted caves along its sides. In one of these I see Rix as he appeared that day. His body has thickened with muscle, his cheekbones thrust out like boulders above his flowing moustache. In his proud face the contradictory qualities of good humor and ferocity are balanced.

A man to match against Caesar.

Perhaps it is only memory that invests Rix with splendor. In reality he was human, muddy and tense and probably cold, for there was a fierce wind blowing. But he threw me the old, dazzling grin as he slid from his horse. He did not run to meet me like a boy, however. He strode forward like a king, with the wind lifting the wolf fur cloak that hung from his shoulders.

"Ainvar."

"Rix. Vercingetorix," I amended.

We did not hug and pound; time had taken that from us. Our eyes locked, then by unspoken agreement we walked a distance away from our followers and sat down together on the moss-crusted trunk of a fallen tree, beside a collapsed lodge.

Rix nodded toward Crom Daral, who was waiting with the rest of my bodyguard. "I see you brought the hunchback."

"He isn't a true hunchback. He exaggerates the crookedness of his spine to get sympathy."

"Pity," said Rix scornfully, calling Crom Daral's desire by its true name, "is the soggiest of emotions. I'm surprised you let such a person come anywhere near you."

"It seems wiser than leaving him behind. He's a proven troublemaker, I'm afraid, and I feel better when I have him where I can see what he's doing."

Rix directed a second and longer look at Crom Daral. "Do you think he's a spy?"

"Ah no, I don't believe he would willfully betray his tribe, for all his faults. But he sees things only in relation to himself, which

makes him unreliable. When we were ready to leave the Fort of
the Grove this time, he kept us waiting on our horses while he
went to take care of some personal matter he wouldn't explain. He
acted as if Crom Daral's problems were more important than the
defense of Gaul."

"Cut his throat," Rix advised. I could not be certain he was
joking. "I once warned you about Crom Daral, remember?"

"I remember. And I do watch him."

"And the Romans watch you," he reminded me.

"They do indeed." I told him then about Gaius Cita; I did not
try to keep the indignation from my voice as I said, "He's pressing
Nantorus to let him have our grain to feed to the Roman legions
next fighting season—in free Gaul!"

As I spoke, I was watching Rix. No muscle in his face twitched,
no eyelid flickered. Yet I was reminded of my earliest impression
of him, a feeling that he might explode at any moment.

With one square thumbnail he pried a section of vivid green
moss from the tree trunk on which we sat and turned it over and
over as if musing upon it. Then he tossed it away, a tiny piece of
spinning greenness. He looked at me. His eyes were clear and
cold. In the softest of voices, Rix said, "Instead of your grain we
shall give them spears to eat, Ainvar, and their own blood to drink.
The time has come."

"Yes." I could feel my heart beginning to race. "The time has
come."

The words were said. The trees heard them. The wind took
them from us and sang them across Gaul in a thin, bitter voice.

We were a people who enjoyed noise and display, but now we
must be secretive. Messengers were sent, soft-going as owls, to
summon the leaders of the allied tribes to meet with Rix at an
appointed time, deep in the forest.

They came. Senones, Parisii, Pictones, Helvii, Gabali, and more
. . . they came to the summons of Vercingetorix.

I stood just behind him as they lifted their standards to him.
Some we had not expected were there. Some we had expected
were not there. Some meant to fight their own way and were only
accepting Vercingetorix as leader in the heat of the moment, I
knew. But as long as he was standing in front of them, tall and
proud and brimming with energy, they were his.

So was I.

"My own Carnutes volunteer to strike the first blow," I announced. "We believe the war against Caesar should begin in the land of the great grove."

The princes of the other tribes cheered the courage of the Carnutes.

"Caesar is in Latium," Rix told them, "which gives us an advantage. We will take the Romans by surprise. They are not accustomed to undertaking a war when he is so far away from them. Attacking them in his absence will throw them into confusion."

So I hoped.

"Vercingetorix has an old head," I heard someone in the crowd say approvingly.

Rix had his father's sword. He held it up for them to see. "This belonged to Celtillus, who was a brave man. Every prince among you has warriors sworn to him on their swords. On this sword I swear myself to you; to all of you. I will fight for your freedom to the last breath in my body. Vercingetorix belongs to you now. Use him well."

The forest rang with their cheering voices. I can hear them still, through the long, dark tunnel of memory.

At the conclusion of the assembly, every man present took an oath, binding upon his tribe, not to desert the others once war began. They stood in a circle and one by one cut their arms with their daggers, then each one pressed his bleeding arm against another's.

The confederacy of Gaul was a reality, sworn in iron and blood.

I turned to share the moment of triumph with my bodyguard —and surprised a look on Crom Daral's face that made me distinctly uneasy. He looked guilty. But guilty of what? I tried to dismiss it from my mind. I wanted nothing to ruin the occasion.

That night I performed rituals of divination to determine the best time for the Carnutes to attack the might of Rome. Rix was skeptical. "The best time is whenever you're ready, Ainvar. There's no need for you to consult with stars and stones."

I did not reply, but I smiled to myself, remembering the way he had stared at a piece of moss as if it had a message for him. In time we will win you back, I thought. The conversation is not ended.

Chapter Thirty-one

THE WARLORDS of Gaul departed to make their preparations for war, and I took my leave of Rix. "The next time we meet we'll be fighting Caesar," I said.

"I want you beside me when we face him," Rix replied. His eyes glowed with eagerness to meet the Roman. He hungered to fight Caesar man to man, pitting himself against this most dangerous of opponents in a physical struggle. My duty was to outthink the Roman.

Once I had tried to keep them apart. Now I saw it was inevitable from the beginning that they come together like two stags in the forest, antler clashing on antler.

I was going north to Cenabum. Rix, having won pledges of support from at least some of the Boii, was returning to Gergovia somewhat reluctantly. "My uncle Gobannitio is back in Gergovia," he explained, "poisoning the air. Did I tell you that Caesar had found time to send me yet another 'gift of friendship'? Four excellent African mares, this time. Gobannitio at once began trumpeting how desirable it would be for the Arverni to accept a Roman alliance, and what a fool I was to attempt a Gaulish union. Alliance indeed," he snorted. "Domination, though Gobannitio refuses to see it that way."

"Did you send the horses back to Caesar? Four is a weak number."

"Are you mad? I kept them. Rather, I gave them to my black stallion there as a token of *my* friendship! But that didn't solve the problem of Gobannitio, of course."

"Cut his throat," I suggested.

Rix laughed.

When I was within sight of the walls of Cenabum, I had my men make camp for us in a secluded pocket of woodland. From there I sent the necessary messages. Then I waited, occupying myself with conducting rituals of power and protection and keeping an eye on Crom Daral.

There was something very wrong with Crom Daral, but I was too preoccupied with Caesar to be able to concentrate on reading him.

Those I had summoned converged upon Cenabum on the night appointed. Shortly before dawn we saw a lurid light in the sky above the fortified town and ran for our horses.

The gates of Cenabum were ajar, with no sentries manning them. The town was lit by flames. We were met by a cacophony of shrieks and yells and war cries, and the crashing of timbers as roofs collapsed from the fire. I reined my nervous horse to a dancing walk and rode between the lodges. People running in every direction repeated the same news: "They're killing the Romans! They're killing the Romans!"

Indeed they were.

At my command, the princes Cotuatus and Conconnetodumnus had led their followers in an assault against every Roman in Cenabum. Shortly before dawn the traders had been dragged from their beds and run through with swords, their bodies tossed in a bloody pile. The townspeople promptly began kicking and stoning the dead, settling old grudges. There was not a person in Cenabum who did not believe the traders had cheated him at some time. They were harvesting a brutal revenge; no grudge ever falls on barren soil.

A special punishment had been reserved for Gaius Cita, to balance the death of Acco. I, who had studied with Aberth the great sacrificer, was its designer.

The Roman official was stretched on the ground with his four limbs chained to four poles, his head making the fifth point of a star. A small platform of oak was placed upon his chest, and one by one the stones of Gaul were piled atop it until he screamed and blood ran from every aperture of his body. The hounds of Cenabum slunk forward on their bellies to lap it up.

When Cita was cold and staring, we put his head on a pole, as the Romans had done with Acco, and I sent a company of warriors to deliver the thing to the nearest Roman camp.

War was declared.

That night Nantorus and I feasted with the princes of the Carnutes, and many cheers were raised for Cotuatus and Conco. Meanwhile, the people of Cenabum plundered the ruined buildings of the traders and finished burning them to the ground.

When at last I sought a bed, I slept as soundly as a heap of stones. I did not dream. The Otherworld had no message for me, which puzzles me to this day.

By the time I was sleeping, the news of the devastating attack on the Romans at Cenabum had been shouted as far as the lands of the Arverni, and Rix knew of our success. While I was riding home to the Fort of the Grove, he was urging his own people to take up arms in the cause of freedom. His uncle argued; losing patience with Gobannitio, Rix drove him and the few who still agreed with him out of Gergovia. He then sent deputations to the tribes of free Gaul, reminding them of their oath to remain loyal when war broke out.

Rix demanded that each tribe send hostages to him to assure him of their obedience, and also warriors to serve as officers in the field under his command. Like Caesar, he was being simultaneously threatening and generous. He had prepared thoroughly, he knew exactly how many weapons he could demand of each tribe and what resources were available. In the matter of cavalry alone, he had a mighty force planned in his own head before the first horseman arrived from one of the allied tribes.

Preparing for war, Vercingetorix was like a flower blooming.

"I love battle," he had once said to me. "I love the feeling when I know I'm going to win and my enemy will die on my sword. There's a high, singing excitement to it, Ainvar, like drinking too much wine—only better. I love it."

Men are best at that which they love. I have never thought that

Vercingetorix loved killing; his spirit was not actually given over to bloodlust. He loved winning. The bloodlust only arose as an incidental.

Help me to help him win, I prayed to That Which Watched as I rode to the Fort of the Grove. Like Tarvos, I was more motivated by the fear of losing. Losing to Caesar would be catastrophic. The very thought made me ride harder, suddenly anxious to have Briga in my arms again and see our daughter's infant smile.

Then I realized one of our number was hanging back, falling behind almost deliberately.

"What's the matter with you, Crom Daral?" I snapped at him.

"I'm not a good rider, Ainvar, you know that. Let me go at my own pace."

"You can keep up with us if you want to; exert yourself for a change."

"I can't. Go on without me."

I scowled at him. He was becoming a constant unpleasantness. He made me feel like a man who has a giant wart on the end of his nose, spoiling his view in every direction. "As it is, then!" I shouted. "Ride slow or ride fast or sit right there and suck your thumb!" I urged my horse forward at the gallop and the rest of my bodyguard followed.

When I looked over my shoulder, Crom had halted and was sitting on his horse looking pathetic.

"You would think he didn't want to go in with us," remarked the man riding nearest to me.

We galloped on; soon enough the land rose to form the sacred ridge, and the oaks lifted their arms to the sky to welcome me.

Briga was waiting for me at the gate of the fort. Her eyes were red-rimmed. Lakutu was standing just behind her, wringing her hands. The rest of our women were crowded around them, wearing expressions that would give the mightiest warrior pause.

"Our daughter was stolen, Ainvar," was Briga's greeting to me. "Lakutu can tell you."

I slid from my horse. "Lakutu? Is this true?"

She flinched as if she expected me to strike her. "I do what we agree, Ainvar. Briga slept, I took baby to hide. For just little while. I met the one called Crom Daral going for his horse. He asked why I had your baby. He was your friend, he gave you gold. I thought it safe to tell him.

"He said to me, 'I hide baby for you.'

" 'No,' I say to him. But he insist. He say, 'We put baby in my lodge. No one look there.' It seemed good plan, Ainvar. He was your friend, I trusted!" Lakutu's voice rose in a wail of distress.

Briga's eyes were like chipped flint.

So while we were waiting for him, Crom Daral had been taking my daughter to his lodge and arranging for Baroc to look after the child. They had apparently agreed that once we had left, Baroc would sneak out of the fort with her and take her to some distant, prearranged place where Crom Daral would join them when we returned. Then he had come to us as if nothing had happened, and gone all the way to Rix to keep me from being suspicious.

While we were gone the fort and the entire area had been desperately searched, but neither Baroc nor the baby was found.

"How could you do this to me, Ainvar?" Briga asked in a tone that indicated I was like something to be scraped off her foot.

"I didn't steal her."

"You did. You stole her first—or arranged to have it done, you and Lakutu together. You drugged me and took her from me. The rest would never have happened otherwise."

"It was only to keep you safe, here in the fort. You are such a willful woman and you were determined to follow me."

"Why shouldn't I be with you? I'm your wife."

"You're the mother of a small child."

"I have no child now!" she cried, holding out her empty arms in an agonized gesture.

Lakutu moaned in sympathy. She took half a step, hesitated, then flung her arms around Briga and pressed my wife to her bosom. "Don't. Ah, don't," she soothed. "I . . . I give you my child," she offered. The watching women gasped. "He a *boy*," Lakutu added with shy pride.

Blinded by sudden, scalding tears, I turned toward the nearest of my bodyguards. "Give me your sword."

"What . . ."

I snatched it from him and vaulted back onto my horse. My men came pounding after me. By the time we reached the place we had last seen Crom Daral he was gone, of course, and an icy rain was washing away all trace of his tracks.

One of my men rode close beside me and said, "If you had killed him the moment you saw him, the way you wanted to, he could never have told us where to find Baroc and the child."

His words penetrated the red fog in my brain and it slowly lifted. I found myself sitting on a steaming horse in a deluge. Driven by the rain, a fox broke out of some underbrush nearby, peered sideways at me, then opened its mouth and laughed, pink tongue lolling, before it ran on.

One of my men started to hurl a spear at it, but I ordered him to let it go.

We turned our horses and rode back to the fort. All the way I kept seeing my daughter with the dark baby ringlets she had never lost, and her tiny, crumpled ears.

Nothing I had ever done was harder than returning to my lodge and facing the two women. Briga refused to speak to me, though her posture and the set of her head condemned me loudly.

She did not seem to blame Lakutu. Ainvar was the one who was supposed to be wise, she said with stamping feet and slamming pots. Ainvar should have known better than to follow poor Lakutu's foolish suggestion. She even put her arm around Lakutu as the two women built up the fire together.

Women, my head observed, cooperate. Men compete.

I went to Keryth. "Find my child."

"Bring me something of hers to hold."

"She's so new she has nothing yet, not even a name," I said despairingly.

Then I remembered the gold arm ring.

When I returned to the lodge and dug it out of the chest Briga's eyes widened. "Where did that come from?"

"It is the gift Crom Daral brought for the child."

She understood the implication at once. "He isn't her father, Ainvar," she said quickly.

"Perhaps he thinks he is." Those words had lain like poison at the back of my throat ever since Crom brought the ring. I should not have hurt her with them but I could not help it; I am human, and I need. I need.

She gave me a long, grave look. "It isn't possible, Ainvar. I've been with no one else since that first time with you."

"I know that."

"Do you?"

Crom's thinking was twisted, I told myself angrily. I must not become like him.

I took the warrior's arm ring and some blankets that had wrapped the baby to Keryth, then went with her to Crom Daral's lodge because that was the last place we knew the child had been.

Crom Daral, we were sickened to discover, had been living like an animal in its den. The floor was littered with gnawed bones. In places the filth was ankle-deep.

Keryth had brought a hare for sacrifice. She killed it and read its entrails on Crom's hearthstone. Then she circled the lodge three times sunwise, clutching the ring and blankets to her bosom. Her footsteps faltered, stopped. She stared into an unseeable distance. "There they are," she whispered. "Two men."

"Crom Daral and Baroc."

"Yes. They have met; they are fleeing together now, and they are carrying something. One man is afoot, the other on a horse. The horseman has the reins in one hand and a bundle in the crook of his other arm." She strained forward as if to see more clearly. "It stirs. It cries. . . ."

My daughter was crying! Crom Daral had my daughter and she was crying. I clenched impotent fists. "Where are they? We'll send men after them at once."

Keryth drew in a sharp breath. "Men are already after them. Men on horses . . . a patrol, a Roman patrol has spotted them and is overtaking them. . . ."

I stared at her in horror.

"The Romans have captured the two men," Keryth's relentless vision continued. "They are going toward the sunrise lands, they are moving beyond the limits of my vision. . . ." Her shoulders sagged. "I see nothing," she reported at last.

Crom's lodge contained only one broken bench. I eased her onto it and chafed her icy hands. "What have the Romans done with the child, Keryth?"

Her exhausted voice replied, "I cannot say. I saw them seize Baroc and Crom Daral, they bound them securely and then slung them over their horses. But whatever they did with the child was hidden from me. Now I can see nothing. I'm sorry, Ainvar."

So was I. She had seen too much.

"Don't tell Briga about the Romans, Keryth," I implored. "I'll find the child somehow, if she's still alive; I vow it by earth and fire and water!"

I was trying not to think of the stories refugees had told of Roman warriors tossing Celtic children on their spears.

Have them toss Crom Daral on their spears instead! I implored That Which Watched. I gladly offer him.

When Keryth had recovered sufficiently we searched her memory together for any detail that might tell us which of Caesar's tens of thousands of warriors had happened across our fugitives, or where they might have taken them. It was no use.

Trying to conceal my own despair, I reported to Briga, "The seer says they went east. I have already sent searchers after them, they'll find her."

She read the truth in my eyes. "All you had to do, Ainvar," she said bitterly, "was tell me I couldn't come with you. That's all you had to do. But that wasn't enough for you, you had to complicate matters. Are you happy now?"

Happy? I could not recall the taste of the word.

I sent a quarter of the fort's warriors eastward, seeking news of Crom Daral and my daughter. The rest remained at the fort, awaiting war.

Vercingetorix was moving swiftly. He had become a stricter disciplinarian than any warlord before him. Hanesa was traveling through free Gaul telling a tale of Rix cutting off the ears of attempted deserters—a tale with considerable power to discourage any others from trying to desert. Once I would not have judged deserters so harshly, but since Crom Daral's betrayal I was judging everyone harshly, myself most of all. I did not blame Vercingetorix for his deed.

Vercingetorix sent a prince called Lucteros south, to collect loyal warriors there, while he set out for the north to set up camp in the land of the Bituriges, a strategic location that would enable him to move in any direction.

Unfortunately, Ollovico had had another change of the unreliable organ he called his mind. When he learned that the Arvernian had almost reached the gates of Avaricum with an army, Ollovico decided his own sovereignty was threatened and sent a frantic message to the nearest Roman legate, who was encamped among the Aedui. Ollovico assured the Romans he had no part in the attempted uprising and asked that his lands be spared the retribution sure to come, and that his own position as leader of the Bituriges be protected.

The legate did not wait to consult with the distant Caesar, but ordered his loyal Aeduans to march to the aid of Ollovico.

The Aeduans advanced as far as the banks of the Liger, where they were met by a druidic deputation led by Nantua, chief druid of the Bituriges. Nantua assured them the whole thing was a trick meant to lure them into Ollovico's land, where they would be trapped between the Bituriges and the Arverni and destroyed.

The Aeduans turned around and went home.

Upon learning of this, so close on the heels of the massacre at Cenabum, Caesar abandoned whatever was keeping him in Latium and rushed to Gaul. But he was in a difficult position. He was physically in the south; the bulk of his legions was in the north. If he sent for them to come south and join him, they would have to fight their way down without the aid of his presence. If he attempted to go to them, he would have to pass through hostile territory. He was clever enough to realize that in Gaul, even tribes who professed loyalty to him might well change with the changing of the moon.

Meanwhile, Lucteros was leading the warriors of the Ruteni, the Nitiobriges, and the Gabali in a determined march toward the Province and its capital, Narbo.

Instead of going north Caesar hurried to Narbonese Gaul instead, killing several horses on the way, I understand. He swiftly fortified the local defenses and posted additional troops along the borders. Deciding the region was now too well defended, Lucteros withdrew to await further orders from Vercingetorix.

Caesar led his Provincial troops into the homelands of the Gabali and the Helvii and laid waste to their territories while their warriors were still farther west with Lucteros. The speed with which he accomplished this was unnerving.

The Arvernians in the south of their land were shocked to find Caesar suddenly within striking distance of their borders. Panicking, they sent messages to their kinsmen who were with Vercingetorix to plead with him not to leave his own tribeland defenseless against the Roman.

When I heard of this latest development, I hastily summoned my druids to the grove, where we concentrated our heads and spirits on the Otherworld, and received signs revealing Caesar's

intent. At once I sent an urgent message to Rix, to stay where he
was in central Gaul—which was an ideal location for preventing
Caesar from reaching his legions in the north.

But it was too late. Rix had already set out for Arvernian territory.
And as I knew, Caesar's action had been a ruse. Once Rix left the
land of the Bituriges, Caesar ceased menacing the Arvernians, sent
his Provincial forces back to guard Narbonese Gaul, and sped east
almost alone to the Rhone River, where a fresh contingent of cavalry
awaited him. Protected by these reinforcements, he made his way
safely through the mountainous Auvergne region to the land of the
Lingones, where he had two full legions in winter camps.

The unreliability of sending messages was obvious. I needed to
be with Rix. My daughter had not yet been found, but I did not
dare linger in the fort in vain hope. If she had been taken as far
as a Roman camp, then if I was with Rix the tides of war might
lead me to her.

I set out at once to join him, pausing at Cenabum only long
enough to collect Cotuatus and the Carnutian warriors. We left
Conco with old Nantorus to guard the tribal stronghold and headed
for the territory of the Bituriges, knowing Rix would return to his
camp there.

He and his army arrived soon after we did. He was angry.
"Caesar got us out of the way just long enough to allow him to
reach safety, and my men had a hard march for nothing."

"It won't happen again. We must outthink him."

"We can and will, now that you're here. I want you to help me
decide on the best plan for attacking his winter camps."

"Don't attack them."

"Why not?" he asked with sudden belligerence, the urge to strike
the enemy burning bright in his eyes.

"Because that's what Caesar wants you to do, Rix. He thinks the
wild and reckless Gauls will fling themselves into any danger for
the sake of battle."

"We always have."

"We have, but that must change. Caesar can't be defeated that
way. He has the strength of two legions in those camps, well
entrenched behind massive fortifications. We would exhaust ourselves in futile attack, then the Romans would come out and destroy
us. Instead, I suggest we attack Gorgobina."

He raised his eyebrows. "The stronghold of the Boii?"

"Exactly. Since the Boii have accepted Caesar's, ah, friendship, he's put them under the protection of his Aeduan allies. But as we know, and he must surely realize by now, the Aedui have lost heart. A successful attack on the Boii will show the other tribes that Caesar cannot protect his so-called friends, and he'll lose support throughout Gaul."

"Caesar will surely go to Gorgobina himself to prevent that happening."

"Ah, but in what manner? It is too early in the year for him to lead his legions out of the winter camps; it would be impossible for him to supply a large army along the route of march with the weather so bad. And it will stay bad. I, as a druid, assure you. Rain and wind and cold hamper the southerners.

"On the other hand, if he attempts to go to the aid of the Boii with a reduced force that he can supply, he will find himself facing our superior numbers."

Rix rewarded me with a huge grin. "We can't lose."

"I didn't say that, and you must not think it. Never underestimate the man. We shall have to be clever and careful if we are to defeat him. If you do decide to attack Gorgobina, at least whatever response he decides upon will present great difficulties for him and opportunities for us."

"We'll attack Gorgobina," Rix said unhesitatingly. "You are brilliant, Ainvar. Brilliant."

I warmed my hands in the heat of his praise. But alas, even the keenest head cannot foresee every possibility, or predict every accident and inspiration. I make a plan and I stand by it. But the burden of responsibility is cruel.

Vercingetorix led the Gaulish army east to attack Gorgobina, taking the Boii by surprise. As we had expected, no Aeduan came to their defense.

Caesar did. As soon as the news reached him, he left the main body of his two legions in winter camp, and set out with a picked force of men and cavalry. He did not, however, march directly south toward Gorgobina as we had anticipated.

In lashing rain and driving wind, he crossed the Liger and attacked Vellaunodunum.

In addition to being the stronghold of the Senones, Vellaunodunum, like all Gaulish towns, had what remained of the winter's grain supply in its storehouses.

Caesar's men encircled the fort. Those within lacked the ability for a sustained defense because the majority of the Senonian fighting men were, like my own Carnutes, with Vercingetorix. After a spirited but token resistance, the Senones sent out a deputation to discuss terms of surrender.

Caesar demanded their weapons, their grain and enough pack animals to carry it, and six hundred hostages who would inevitably be sold as slaves. Leaving a Roman legate behind to supervise arrangements concerning the latter, Caesar set out again.

In the direction of Cenabum.

Chapter Thirty-two

THE WARRIORS of the Boii were defending Gorgobina with considerable skill and we had settled in for a prolonged siege when we received somewhat garbled news of the surrender of Vellaunodunum to the Romans. The Senones among us were understandably upset and threatened to desert.

Rix rallied them with a stirring speech that raised the hair on the back of my neck. He shouted of victory until they were shouting too, clashing their fists against their shields and crying for vengeance against Caesar. When Vercingetorix stood tall and golden and unafraid, he was a light shining on us all.

That night a hundred campfires flickered in a vast circle around besieged Gorgobina. At the request of Vercingetorix, Hanesa went from one group to another, reciting tales of terrible punishments their Arvernian commander had been known to visit upon deserters. Over the keening of the wind, snatches of his rich, rolling voice came to us as we sat around the fire at the command camp, and from time to time I saw Rix smile to himself beneath his moustache.

Eventually Hanesa rejoined us to entertain us with less cautionary tales. Rix wanted to hear of Gaulish triumphs, and Hanesa happily complied. "Once," he declaimed, making extravagant gestures, "the men of Gaul were more ferocious in battle than even the Germans. Once, men of Gaul crossed the Rhine and occupied Germanic land!"

Rix remarked to no one in particular, "I wish we had some Germans fighting with us now."

Cotuatus commented, "By all accounts Ariovistus was very brave."

"How many brave men will it take to kill Caesar?" a prince of the Parisii wondered aloud.

The Otherworld moved through me. I heard my own voice say, "No brave man will kill him. The deed requires a coward."

Rix turned toward me. "What did you mean by that?"

"I cannot say," I replied honestly. "What you heard came from the spirits."

"Hunh," snorted Vercingetorix.

The assault on Gorgobina continued. It was a strongly fortified town and the Boii were defending it valiantly.

In the tent I shared with Hanesa the bard, I dreamed of my daughter, and awoke to feel tears on my cheeks.

"What's the matter, Ainvar?"

I opened my eyes. Above me loomed a fleshy face with a bulbous red nose and two very concerned eyes. In one hand Hanesa held a small bronze lamp, its flame guttering. "You were making a strange noise in your sleep," he told me. He held the lamp lower. "And you look dreadful."

"I'm all right." I sat up.

"Move over." Hanesa eased his increasingly ponderous bulk down on the ground beside me. We still slept rolled in our cloaks, but at least the leather tent overhead kept us dry during the cold, wet weather. "Tell me what's troubling you, Ainvar," Hanesa urged. His rich voice sank into me on waves of sympathy. I tried to resist but could not; the bard had a special magic. At last I told him about my child.

"Does Vercingetorix know of this?"

"I don't want him to. He has enough burdens to bear and this is a small problem by comparison."

"If we are one people, as you keep telling us, what happens to one child involves us all."

Our conversation was interrupted by the sudden shouts of sentries and then the clatter of galloping hooves. Hanesa and I scrambled to our feet and left the tent.

Rix was just emerging from the command tent nearby. In the light of the campfires his face looked as if he had not slept; as if he never needed sleep.

Two disheveled men whom I recognized at once as Carnutians came out of the night, accompanied by sentries. While Rix listened with thoughtfully lowered head, they related some excited message to him. He looked up, saw me, beckoned.

"These two men have ridden here at great risk to themselves all the way from Cenabum, Ainvar. They say Caesar halted his army outside its walls. It was twilight when he arrived; these two left as he was pitching camp. Nantorus sent them to tell me personally he fears a Roman attack."

The Carnutians were exhausted. They had ridden long and hard, stealing fresh horses on their way from farmsteads they passed, not daring to speak to anyone until they spoke to Vercingetorix.

Cenabum was a long distance from Gorgobina. Days had passed since Caesar arrived. Whatever happened had already happened. "We should have heard of this sooner!" I cried.

"We're in Boii territory," Rix reminded me. "They won't shout any messages for me." Lowering his voice, he said, "What do you advise me to do?"

Beyond the palisades of Gorgobina the dawn was gathering. The approaching sun had begun to stain the sky with a lurid light the color of blood. "There's no point in making decisions until we know exactly what happened, Rix. Caesar may have done no more than camp for the night near Cenabum, then move on."

"Is that what you think?"

I looked at the bloody sky. "No."

We resumed our assault on the sturdy walls of Gorgobina, from which spears and stones rained upon us. Soon the red sky filled with clouds and they rained upon us, too.

Late in the day another messenger arrived, one man alone, though he had started with four companions. All had been wounded; the others had died on the way. The survivor was sagging on his horse.

Caesar, he told us, had attacked Cenabum. In the night some of the inhabitants had tried to escape over the nearby bridge across the Liger, but they were captured. Setting fire to the gates of the fort, the Romans had penned the Carnutians inside and forced them to surrender. Only a few were killed. The majority were taken prisoner. My people. To become slaves.

Nantorus was slain in his own lodge. Conconnetodumnus, who had remained behind, was killed defending him.

The Romans had plundered Cenabum and left it in flames. Caesar was on the march again, but with a greatly expanded force. Having seized the supplies of two forts, he had called the legions to join him.

Rix was grim. We had no choice. We must lift the siege and march to meet Caesar or be caught between him and the Boii, who would gladly leave their stronghold to attack us from the rear while the Romans battered our faces.

As the army was breaking camp, I noticed that a strange silence had settled over the customarily voluble Gauls. We were used to winning or losing; the inconclusiveness of this incident made fighting men uncomfortable.

There would be battle soon enough, however.

I concentrated on wind and rain, hoping Caesar was thoroughly miserable.

Rix cast one farewell glance at the walls of Gorgobina. "I wish we had some of the siege machinery the Romans know how to build," he said wistfully.

"We can learn. As soon as we can I'll send to the Fort of the Grove for the Goban Saor; he can make anything if he has a model."

"We could have taken Gorgobina in another day, Ainvar."

"I know it. But Caesar isn't allowing us another day."

We set out to intercept Caesar, preferably in territory more friendly to us than Boii-land. For a time I rode with Rix. Then I dropped back and joined the silent, grim-faced Carnutians.

Cotuatus urged his horse beside mine. Warriors afoot and on horseback thronged around us, the vivid tribal colors of their clothing somehow inappropriate. The air smelled of anger and grief and steaming horse dung.

At last Cotuatus said, "My family was in Cenabum."

"I know."

"Yours is still at the Fort of the Grove?"

"Yes," I said simply.

"They're safe, then. Caesar didn't go that way."

I thought of my daughter and said nothing.

She must be given a name on her name day, even if we had not yet found her. For some reason, her lack of a name tormented me more than anything. Without one how could we invoke the Otherworld on her behalf? A stolen infant must leave an identity behind for her parents to weep over.

... my heart she was simply my little girl. Perhaps she would always be that and no more . . . my little girl.

"The days are growing longer," Cotuatus said abruptly, breaking into my reverie. "The farmers will be yoking their oxen for the plow."

I looked at the rolling, fertile land through which we were riding. "Gaulish farmers? Or Roman farmers?"

"Is that what Caesar really wants, Ainvar? Our land?"

"He wants it all."

"But we have been born here and buried here for generation after generation. He has no right."

"He has no right to yoke Gauls like those oxen you mentioned and march them off to sell into slavery, either, but he'll do it, and give the land they leave behind to his own followers."

My mouth had fallen into the old habit of running ahead of my mind. Too late I realized how painful those words must be to Cotuatus, who had left his family in Cenabum. But when I turned toward him, I saw that his jaw was set and his face was the face of a man.

He will make a good king after all, my head decided. The Carnutes need a king now, with Nantorus dead.

"I've been observing Vercingetorix," Cotuatus remarked, looking toward the forefront of the army where Rix rode at the head of his beloved Arvernian cavalry. The warriors of free Gaul followed him like a polychrome river snaking across the land, men on horseback or afoot, men who fought with sword or spear or bow or pike, men who divided themselves into tribes and watched the men of other tribes suspiciously, for all we were one army. The Carnutians were toward the front. At the rear, so far behind us we could not see them if we looked back, rumbled the supply wagons. As we marched through friendly territory, the allies of the Gaulish confederacy kept those supply wagons filled.

"I once thought your praise of the Arvernian was excessive," Cotuatus was saying, "but I don't think so anymore. He's skilled in the use of every weapon, he has frightening stamina, and he never takes a step backward. If anyone can defeat Caesar, he can."

"He can," I echoed. "And when he does, Cotuatus, we will find every man, woman, and child Caesar has captured as slaves and we will bring them home as free people. Including the inhabitants of Cenabum."

He nodded thoughtfully and said nothing more. We rode silently together, Cotuatus thinking of his family and I thinking of my daughter.

Following the river valley, we were approaching the fort of Noviodunum, easternmost settlement of the Bituriges. We heard a shout from the front of the army and drew rein, shading our eyes with our hands. We could see a small band of people running toward us across the fields.

I kicked my horse and galloped up the line to join Rix.

The men were brought to him at once. They were smallholders who had just begun plowing their land outside the walls of Noviodunum, a typical fortified Gaulish town on high ground above the river. They wore the coarse, simple clothing of the common class, rather than the vivid colors and brazen ornaments of warriors—and they were pale with fright.

I sat on my horse beside Rix as he listened to their tumbling, almost incoherent words.

Moving with his usual astonishing rapidity, Caesar had reached Noviodunum just before us and at once began setting up camp. While the farmers stood gaping, the inhabitants of the fort had sent out a deputation asking that they be spared. Caesar's response was to send two centurions and a company of men into Noviodunum to seize its weapons and horses, and take hostages.

While this was happening, some of the Bituriges on the palisade had seen Rix and the army in the distance. They had raised a loud cheer, telling their people within the fort that help was coming. The inhabitants took heart and began fighting the Romans, reclaiming their weapons. The centurions led their men out of the fort just in time to save their lives.

The watching farmers came running across the fields to us. "Defend us from the Roman!" they pleaded.

Rix moved swiftly. He had his trumpeters summon the horsemen from the various tribal groups, adding them to his own cavalry. Then he led the charge on the half-prepared Roman camp. My horse was so excited he leaped and plunged on the thin edge of control; I had all I could do to make him stay back. I wanted to join in the attack myself, and he knew it.

We topped a rise, and I saw the Roman camp. Caesar had indeed summoned his legions; thousands of men were assembled, blackening the earth. We had arrived before they were ready for us, and had the satisfaction of seeing them scramble as our cavalry thundered down upon them.

The Romans recovered quickly. Caesar sent his own cavalry forward to face ours, but we were superior in both numbers and anger and succeeded in breaking their line and scattering them.

It was a heady moment. I heard myself cheering; I looked around for Hanesa, trusting he was somewhere close enough to memorize every moment.

Then a fresh body of men on horseback came galloping toward us. Our horsemen checked in surprise. The newcomers were big blond men wearing raw leather and fur, and they rode thickset horses with bristling manes. Their guttural shouts identified them quickly enough.

Caesar had brought four hundred German horsemen with him!

Astonishment defeated us as much as anything else, though their attack was so savage that only the bravest could have withstood it. Our men were brave enough; their own fear of the Germans weakened them. It was our turn to be broken, and the horse warriors of Gaul went galloping back toward the main body of the army, many of them hacked and injured.

More lay dead on the ground, trampled by the German horses. Cotuatus, at least, was among the survivors.

Once we caught our breath and regrouped, Rix was furious. "Caesar supposedly invaded Gaul to fight the Germans. Now he uses them in his army! He has no true warrior style, he keeps changing the rules, Ainvar."

"Obviously that is his style, then. And a good one, because it is succeeding for him."

"I can get Germans, too, you know I can. I should have used them all along," he added, not bothering to conceal his anger with me in the matter.

However, that was in the past and could not be changed; I would

not react to it now. "You can't defeat Caesar by adopting his strategies, Rix. That way he shapes the war. You have to introduce a
pattern of your own, one he doesn't expect and will have to deal
with."

He raised an eyebrow. "I'm waiting for suggestions."

By twilight we had retired to make camp, some distance away
from the Romans. The two armies now had a river of water and a
sea of hostility between them, with commanders on both sides
considering the next step in the campaign. Ours must be one that
Caesar did not expect; one that would cripple him, if possible.

Leaving Rix, I walked alone to think. I did not throw pebbles
or read entrails. I opened the senses of my spirit, and waited to
know.

In time, inspiration came.

A large, sauntering circle took me past our grouped supply
wagons. They were already piled high, but even while the battle
was going on, local people had come from the surrounding farmsteads, gratefully bringing additional offerings of food for us and
fodder for our animals. We were in friendly territory now.

I stared long and hard at the supply wagons.

Think like Caesar, I commanded my head.

I returned to find Rix standing beside the campfire nearest his
command tent, listening with barely concealed irritation as the
princes of the tribes tried to outshout each other. Each one was
claiming his men had not been the first to run from the Germans,
but had been caught up in the panic of cavalry from some other
tribe.

I caught Rix's eye; he turned his back on the lot of them and
strode over to me.

"I have that suggestion you wanted," I told him, "but you may
not like it."

"I don't like losing. Tell me how to win."

"Caesar has several legions with him now, which means a huge
mass of men and horses to feed. Why did he pause to capture
Vellaunodunum and Cenabum and Noviodunum if he was in such
a hurry to fight the Gauls and defend the Boii? For their supplies,
of course. In hostile territory, the only way he can lay hands on
sufficient supplies for such a large army is by taking them from our
own storehouses in the forts and towns. His army can't live off the
land, it's too early in the year."

"So what are you suggesting? We haven't enough warriors to fight Caesar and defend every fort in Gaul at the same time."

"No," I agreed, "we don't. But we can offer a sacrifice."

He looked scornful. "Your druid magic won't . . ."

"It will. We'll sacrifice the forts."

Rix stared at me.

"We must set fire to any forts that are not made impregnable by their own fortifications or by their locations. We can disperse the inhabitants throughout the surrounding countryside. It will be hard on them to see their strongholds put to the torch, but not as hard as seeing themselves and their children enslaved.

"The Romans will be denied any centralized sources for supplies and plunder. They will have to send out foraging parties, and our own warriors can pick these off day by day."

"The unfortified villages and some of the larger farmsteads have large grain supplies in their storehouses, Ainvar."

"Then we must burn them, too. It will mean a hard year for Gaul—but we will be free. And the Roman armies won't stay here to starve. If our people are willing to make a large enough sacrifice, Rix, we can defeat Caesar now."

He never hesitated. Summoning the warlords of the tribes, he explained the proposal to them. Cotuatus was his first and most enthusiastic supporter. "If Cenabum had already been burned when Caesar got there, my family would have been safe in some friendly farmhouse far beyond the walls and he would not have had enough supplies to strengthen his men for today's battle. As it is, he has burned Cenabum anyway—after he finished looting it. And the people are led away to slavery."

Agreement was unanimous. Riders were dispersed in every direction, and by the following sundown there was not a village within a day's march where the Romans could find provisions. With their own hands the Bituriges denied twenty of their towns to Caesar.

Hanesa sang a great song of the valor of the Bituriges.

When Caesar sent out foraging parties from his camp near Noviodunum, our cavalry happily slaughtered them. The Romans swiftly broke camp, obviously preparing to move to some location with more to offer. The nearest was Avaricum.

The courage of the Bituriges did not extend to destroying the tribal stronghold that was their greatest pride. They went to Rix and begged him to spare the great fort.

"Avaricum is the most beautiful town in all of Gaul," they insisted, "and easily defended. It is surrounded by river and marsh, with only one narrow way through. Why should it be destroyed? Caesar can never take it."

Rix conferred privately with me; I conferred even more privately with the spirits. "The sacrifice must be total, Rix," I told him. "We can't afford to spare this one or that one because they are special. Every place is special to those who live there. Caesar's men are getting hungry and pressing him hard, the plan is working. Deny him Avaricum and he'll have to withdraw from free Gaul to some place where he can supply his army. Think of it! Imagine seeing his retreating back!"

Rix agreed, but unfortunately the others were persuaded by the arguments of the Bituriges. The princes began to accuse Rix of being too harsh to his supporters, of demanding sacrifice when none was necessary. Several kinsmen of Ollovico suggested the Arvernian simply wanted Avaricum destroyed to make it easier for him to establish Gergovia as the capital of free Gaul.

Vercingetorix acceded to the Bituriges's request; Avaricum was not to be destroyed before Caesar's army arrived. I told him he was making a mistake and I think he knew it also, but the word was shouted. The best warriors of the Bituriges sped off ahead of us to man the defenses of Avaricum. When Caesar himself got under way, our army moved with his, shadowing every step of his march.

Reaching the vicinity of Avaricum, Rix set up camp in a region protected by woodland and marsh. At my suggestion he sent out a network of patrols to relay information about Roman movements. Whenever enemy foraging parties set out, our cavalry attacked and destroyed them. Caesar began sending desperate messages to the Aedui and the Boii, asking them to aid him with grain supplies. But even if we had let his messengers get through, it would have been useless. The Aedui were no longer Caesar's unfailing allies. Having observed the size of the army of free Gaul, they were waiting to learn which way the wind blew. As for the Boii, they were a diminished tribe with no supplies to spare.

The Roman army was getting very lean and very hungry.

"I can taste victory the way other men taste wine," Rix boasted in an expansive moment. "Your plan has defeated Caesar."

"Not yet," I warned him. "You haven't followed my plan, not completely. Avaricum is still standing, stocked with everything the Romans need."

"The Romans can never capture it, it's as strong as any fort in Gaul. They're already beginning to be weakened by lack of adequate food. We'll let them exhaust themselves in a futile attack on Avaricum, then I'll order our armies in and we'll destroy them."

He said it with perfect confidence, as if he were actually seeing the future.

But Rix had not been given the gift of prophecy. He was a warrior.

The rains of early spring were as persistent as the winter storms had been, drumming tiresomely on our leather tent until both Hanesa and I suffered from headache.

I longed for Briga's touch; I wondered what effect so much rain would have on our vines. I wished I were home to help care for them.

In spite of the weather, Caesar apparently was planning to lay siege to Avaricum. "They won't go through with it," Rix said confidently. "They're too weakened by hunger."

Privately, I thought hunger might be the very goad to drive them to success.

By the time we were settled in our new camp, Caesar had moved siege towers up to the walls of Avaricum. At dawn Rix took most of the cavalry and set off in a wide sweep to attack Roman foraging parties. The day turned dark, with black clouds piling up like old regrets. The Romans appeared to abandon their efforts at the walls. When Rix was not back by dark, we knew he had encamped somewhere rather than risk the horses' legs by riding at night.

Under cover of night, Gaius Caesar approached our camp with an attack force.

Alerted by our patrols, we were not taken by surprise as he had hoped. We hid our wagons and supplies in a dense wood and then gathered our forces on high ground almost totally encircled by marsh. When Caesar met the warriors of Gaul in the dawn light, he saw brave, free men, standing tall in the open, defying him.

Hanesa would compose an epic about those warriors, later.

Our position served us well. It was my suggestion, softly murmured into the ears of various tribal princes, each of whom then thought it was his own idea. Trusting none of them totally, Rix had not named a commander to serve during his absence. Of course, none of us had anticipated a Roman attack on our camp; we thought Caesar preoccupied with his siege.

But we outsmarted him. If his soldiers attempted to charge through the marsh to reach us, we would attack them from the high ground as they floundered below us in cold water and sticky mud.

We could have done great damage to them. Realizing this, the Roman officers consulted among themselves, then ordered a withdrawal, knowing they were outmaneuvered.

How we cheered the sight of their backs!

When Rix returned we were eager to tell him of our victory. Some of the princes, denied the satisfaction of a battle, were suffering curdled dispositions, however. They found fault with the day's success. They even accused Rix of treachery for having left the army without putting one of them in supreme command. "As soon as you were gone the Romans moved in as if it were planned," the troublemakers said. "Was it? Did you think Caesar would give you the kingship of Gaul for betraying your people and leaving us undefended, with no cavalry?"

Rix was coldly furious. Answering the last charge first, he said, "What good is cavalry in a marsh? If every horseman we have had been there, they would not have been able to help you, whereas they were a great help to me and we destroyed every foraging party we found.

"I did not hand over command to anyone in my absence because there is not one among you who would not put his tribe's interests over the interests of Gaul. As for my seeking power from Caesar, there is no need. We will soon defeat Caesar and I will have, through my own achievement, all the power I want in Gaul, all I have ever sought . . . which is the kingship of the Arverni."

By revealing their pettiness and jealousy, he shamed them. The princes made no further accusations; they slipped away to their own campfires and began singing victory songs with their men.

But I who knew Rix best could not resist saying to him, "You want more than the kingship of the Arverni."

He did not deny it. He simply said, "I don't want anything from the hand of Caesar."

"What about those African mares he sent you? You kept those, I seem to remember."

"A horse is not the same as a kingship. And Caesar didn't buy me with them, Ainvar. You know that."

Yes. I knew that. But we had been boys together and sometimes I still had to tease him. Sometimes in private I even called him King of the World.

Watching him riding at the head of the army, however, it no longer seemed a ridiculous title.

CHAPTER THIRTY-THREE

Rix HAD taken several captives from the foraging parties. He had them tell our army of the hunger and privation in the Roman camp, the desperation that had driven them to seizing a stray cow or pillaging a solitary barn.

When their story was told Rix added, "Some of you accused me of treachery; yet thanks to me the invaders are wasting away without a drop of our blood being shed. When the Romans are sufficiently weakened we shall rout them and drive them from Gaul in disgrace!"

The warriors shouted and clashed their weapons, proclaiming Vercingetorix the greatest of all war leaders.

If Caesar was weakened, however, his intention was not. The siege of Avaricum continued.

The Bituriges within were staging an impressive defense, and their kinsmen with us began to claim their tribe was winning the war by itself and had no need of anyone else. Vercingetorix at once ordered a large force containing members of each tribe of the confederacy to go to the aid of the besieged fort.

"I have no intention of letting the Bituriges have all the glory," he explained to me. "Besides, we want to study Roman siege techniques more closely. We're going to have your Goban Saor help us imitate them."

"Shall I send riders to the Fort of the Grove?"

"Why not?"

I dispatched messengers at once, not only to bring back the Goban Saor, but also to inquire after the safety of my family.

And that of the grove.

The Romans threw up siege hooks to gain purchase on the timber walls of Avaricum; the defenders atop the walls caught hold of the hooks with nooses and hauled them inside by means of windlasses. The Romans built siege towers to allow their spearmen and archers to shoot over the walls, but the Gauls erected their own structures inside the fort, matching the Romans tower for tower so they could gain no advantage. Meanwhile, the attackers were constantly assaulted by spear and stone and boiling pitch—as well as by brutal weather.

Instead of singing the song for the sun, each morning I sang the song for the rain and sacrificed red cockerels.

At a great cost in lives, the Romans finally succeeded in constructing a huge siege terrace that almost touched the walls. Their plan was to send wave upon wave of warriors up this ramp, protected by a "turtle's back" device of interlocked shields held over their heads. But the Gauls included among their number miners from the iron mines in the region. They understood tunneling. They opened a tunnel beneath the siege terrace and then set fire to it, causing the whole thing to collapse. As the Romans were trying to extinguish the fire, the Bituriges poured from the gates of Avaricum to attack them, joined by the forces Vercingetorix had sent.

At first it seemed we must win. Caesar himself, as was his practice, had been supervising the work parties, and some of the tribal warriors set themselves the task of personally catching and killing him. But he managed to elude them—and to call up reserves from the Roman camp.

A terrible battle was waged around the walls of Avaricum.

The Romans moved a large siege tower up to the main gates of Avaricum, and used it to hurl down a deadly barrage that kept many of the defenders penned inside. One of our own men—a

Parisian, we later learned—placed himself in front of the gates and flung a torch at the base of the tower. Then he stood calmly throwing lumps of tallow and pitch to feed the flames. When an arrow from a Roman catapult killed him, another Gaul stepped over his body and took his place. When he died, another. And then another. They died free men. But they continued the doomed defense of their position until the Romans succeeded in putting out the fire on the siege terrace and pushed the Gauls back at every point.

The ashes of defeat were bitter and cold.

"Send a message to the defenders inside Avaricum to burn the stronghold and come to us," I urged Rix. "Deny Caesar their stores, at least."

"I'll deny him victory," Rix grated, refusing to listen to me.

In the night some of the Bituriges did try to escape, but there was a panic and they were captured. The next morning Caesar renewed his assault on the stronghold. Using every art and skill I possessed, I invoked a rainstorm of massive proportions. Even that was not enough to deter Caesar. The approaches to Avaricum were drowned in a sea of mud, but wherever there was a way through, he stationed troops to block our attack force from coming to the rescue. Then with one mighty, concerted, and very well-organized effort, he overcame the last defenses of the fort, entered, and massacred the inhabitants.

Women and children were indiscriminately slaughtered along with the men. To his credit, when Ollovico took a final stand it was on the side of the Gauls. He died a courageous death on the point of a Roman thrusting sword, but he died a free man.

Of the forty thousand Bituriges who had sought shelter within the walls of Avaricum, only eight hundred escaped to Vercingetorix.

"Those deaths were unnecessary," I told Rix bitterly. "We lost because the sacrifice that would have saved us was incomplete. You should have had Avaricum burned before Caesar arrived. Ollovico would have done it, you could have forced him."

The next day Rix called a council of war. "Do not be disheartened by this setback," he urged. "People who expect everything to go their way in a war are mistaken. The Romans did not win through valor, but because they have more skills in siegecraft than we do. If Avaricum had been burned as I originally urged, this never would have happened, but we will cast no blame now; we will go on to victory instead. Our greater success will wipe out this stain!"

They cheered him; they clashed their weapons.

The eight hundred refugees from Avaricum huddled together, eating our food and trying to forget nightmare.

Cotuatus told me, "Some of the princes thought Vercingetorix would be afraid to show his face after a defeat. His courage has impressed them. They think more of him than ever."

"It's generous of you to say so."

Cotuatus smiled without humor. "We're generous people."

Preparing for any eventuality, Vercingetorix ordered his troops to set about seriously fortifying their camp with walls, earthworks, log buildings—the strength and solidity the Romans brought to their own camps.

Unlike the Romans, however, our warriors were not laborers. They had not been trained to dig ditches and build walls, and the suggestion shocked them. But there was no one else to do it, so, driven by the sting of defeat, they undertook the work with more good humor than one would have expected.

Our scouts watched Caesar in his own camp and brought frequent reports to Rix. Winter was over; Caesar would not remain where he was for very long. But we had suffered sizable losses and Rix was reluctant to engage him in another battle until we were back up to strength. For that reason he was greatly heartened by the arrival of a large number of cavalry led by Teutomatus, king of the Nitiobriges, husband to a daughter of the late Ollovico.

Teutomatus had even recruited additional troops among the tribes of Aquitania, and was eager to avenge the death of his wife's father.

Another arrival cheered me. The Goban Saor rode into our camp as if trained to the horse, followed by a driver with a wagon covered in leather.

I ran to meet him. "I greet you as a free man. How are you?"

"How is everyone, you mean. They're all well at the Fort of the Grove, Ainvar, and the vines are growing again."

I hugged him.

"Briga and Lakutu send you special greetings," he went on.

"Is there any news of . . . ?"

"No, Ainvar, I'm sorry. We've learned nothing about your daughter, and no one's seen Crom Daral."

It is as it is, then, I thought. "Did you bring it as I asked?"

He followed my gaze to the wagon. "Ah yes, it's in there. Though what you mean to do with it I can't imagine. Briga was upset; she said she could have come in that wagon instead."

"She would. I trust you didn't let her." I peered hard at the leather covering, watching for moving bulges.

"I prevented it with the greatest difficulty. That's a stubborn woman you married."

"If she wanted to come with you, I take that to mean she's forgiven me," I said hopefully.

The Goban Saor considered. "I wouldn't say that."

Several warriors had sauntered past us to get a good look at the Goban Saor, whose size was impressive, and to cast curious glances at the covered wagon. I appointed one of the Carnutians to stand guard over it at all times and let no one see the contents. Then I took the craftsman to my tent.

That night we ate with Rix and discussed the techniques of siege. The Goban Saor made several ingenious suggestions. Rix told him, "If we'd had you with us at Gorgobina, we could have taken the fort quickly and intercepted Caesar before he did so much damage. Will you stay with us from now on?"

The Goban Saor's blue eyes met mine. "That is my intention," he said.

Enriched with the supplies and plunder of Avaricum, Caesar now had nine legions within half a day's march of our army. From their actions Rix deduced they would either attempt to lure us out of the marshes or blockade and attack us where we were. The Goban Saor built a number of clever traps for unwary invaders around the perimeter of our encampment, but it was increasingly obvious we were in a dangerous position.

Then, from a messenger we intercepted on his way to Caesar, we learned that dissension had once more erupted in the land of the Aedui. Following Diviciacus, a succession of men had been elected for annual terms as chief magistrate of the tribe. Current contenders for the office were two ambitious princes, each of whom had been educated by the druids, and each of whom had a large partisan following. The argument between the two sides was becoming violent. It was predicted that whoever lost would throw his entire support behind the Gaulish confederacy out of spite, thus dividing Caesar's Aeduan alliance. The elders of the tribe urgently requested Caesar's presence to resolve the issue and appoint one man as sole magistrate while appeasing the other.

Seeing an advantage in this for us, I advised Rix, "Let the messenger go on to Caesar with this news." The Roman reacted with alacrity. He prepared to go to the Aeduans by dividing his forces, sending four legions and part of his cavalry to the territories of the Senones and the Parisii in hopes of luring the warriors of those tribes away from Rix to defend their homelands. The rest of his legions he left in camp awaiting his return. Then he set off.

Rix refused to let the ruse divide the army of free Gaul. The Senones and Parisii argued vehemently, clamoring to go home, but he stood firm.

Through sheer force of personality, Vercingetorix held his army together. Deep in his spirit, however, the recent setbacks had shaken him more than he would let anyone know.

I read his eyes when he thought no one was looking.

He arranged for the refugees from Avaricum to be fed and clothed. Nantua the chief druid was among them; Hanesa and I took him into our own tent, which made it crowded but warmer, so a balance was struck.

After the losses suffered at Avaricum, Rix was anxious to bring his forces back to full strength and to expand them. I suggested, "Nantua and I between us have friends in the Order of the Wise in every tribe in Gaul. Let us use our persuasion to win those who have resisted you until now. After Avaricum it will become obvious where their self-interest lies. They just need gifted tongues to bring them to you, weapons in hand."

"How many men have your druids brought to me already, Ainvar?" Rix asked shrewdly.

I gave a modest answer. "We have done what we could."

His reply was typical of him: "Do more."

Being careful to attract no attention from Roman patrols, Nantua and I quietly left the Gaulish camp. He was going to visit fellow druids in the southern territory, while I rode north to use my druid network to enlist the last stragglers.

I rode north to see with my own eyes that the grove still stood, that Briga and Lakutu were still safe.

I took only six warriors with me as bodyguard, and I suspect Rix begrudged me even those.

We traveled through land brimming with incipient spring. I

wished there were time to dismount from my horse and walk so I could feel the earth hum. A cold high wind blew, but the sky at last was cloudless, the days crystalline. We were two moons from Beltaine.

My intention had been to marry Lakutu at Beltaine.

Where would the season find me?

In the swirl and stink of war, the earth is ravaged. She is scarred by galloping hooves and wagon wheels and tramping feet and leaping fires. Campaigning with Vercingetorix, I had for a time forgotten the beauty of a land at peace, but as I rode toward home I saw it and remembered. Skirting the swath cut by Caesar's army on its way from Cenabum to Avaricum, I rode through quiet meadows where the first brave blossoms of spring were beginning to peep through the awakening grass. I passed a hazel coppice, one seventh of its wood harvested every year for basketry and thatching and fish traps and bean poles, and saluted the trees as receptacles of knowledge. At a stand of alders, I paused to reverence the water spirits that protect alder trees. Everywhere I saw those things that tied me to the land, to Gaul.

To free Gaul. My land. Our land.

A painful lump rose in my throat.

Invaders have no right to this place. It is ours by love; they shall not take it by conquest.

That was my vow as I rode for home.

My head was filled with images. My land, my grove, my home, my hearth. Mine. My place.

I hated Caesar. Inside myself I discovered a cold and bitter hatred I had not known was there, a hatred intensified by my grudging admiration for the genius of the man. Caesar meant to enslave us, even to exterminate us, but worst of all was his desire to claim our land, the soil that nourished us and held the bones of our ancestors, the earth to which our bodies would be returned when our spirits were freed.

Earth, link between Man and Otherworld. Earth, whose every tree and bush and blade of grass and river and mountain and flower-starred meadow showed us another face of the Source. Our earth. Our Gaul. Beautiful Gaul.

I rode in a haze of love and pain. Something essential within us would be forever changed if the foreigners captured Gaul.

Then the sacred, grove-crowned ridge rose in the distance like a promise that nothing would ever change. I rode toward it with tears in my eyes.

Even before I went to the fort, I went to the trees. Leaving my bodyguard waiting, I walked alone among the oaks. Being.

We are, they reassured me. The Source is.

Relieved and comforted, I rode down to my people.

My two women met me at the gates of the fort, each with a child. For a moment my heart twisted before I realized the little one in Lakutu's arms was her own son, Glas, and the much older boy with Briga was the smallholder's son who had once been blind.

"I greet you as a free person," my wife said to me as I slid down from my horse. Then, more softly, "I am glad to see you, Ainvar."

"Glad!" echoed Lakutu happily.

Before we could say anything else to each other, my people crowded around me, begging for news of the war. Almost everyone had relatives at Cenabum, and demands for information came at me from every side: "How many did Caesar take as slaves?" "Where have they gone?" "Who was killed?" "Is Oncus the Beautiful still alive, do you know?" "Is Becuma?" "Is Nantosvelta?" "Or . . . ?"

I raised a hand for silence. "Cenabum is a ruin. I did not go all the way into the town, there was no point. It's nothing but burned timbers and tumbled stones, the people are gone. Most of them are still alive, we believe, and from all reports they have been sent across the Sequana River to the nearest permanent Roman camps. Caesar won't try to send them south until fighting season is over. So they are still within our reach and when we have defeated him we will get them back. We will," I said emphatically, meeting Briga's imploring eyes. "All of them."

Sulis pressed forward, wanting news of her brother, and I assured her the Goban Saor had reached Rix safely. She responded with a shaky laugh that revealed the depths of her concern. "He should have; he left here staggering under the weight of the charms and protections we heaped on him. We didn't want the Romans to get him."

I answered all the questions I could and then answered them again because the people could not stop asking. At last I was allowed to seek the sanctuary of my own lodge for a while, to eat and rest. There I had to observe all the little customs women hold dear. They must sit me on my bench, bathe my face and feet, exclaim to one another over the sad condition of my clothing. They worked in harmony; I wondered if they ever quarreled in my absence. If so, they hid it from me. In my presence Briga and Lakutu closed ranks and presented a unified front.

I looked curiously around the lodge. Each person who lives in a place leaves an imprint, rather in the way that the crisscrossing lines of power between Earth and stars leave tracks on human palms. Briga and Lakutu had succeeded in submerging almost every trace of me in their clutter, their busy, bright domesticity. A loom, piles of fabric, pottery, new blankets, unfamiliar household implements, stools, jars, infant smells, cages on the wall for hens, baskets of eggs and nets of onions, clothes drying on ropes strung from the rafters. Only the iron firedogs spoke of the past; those, and my carved wooden chest.

"Is there any news of our daughter?" I asked Briga as I took the first welcome bite of bread.

"Not yet. But on the anniversary of her conception the druids convened for her name day, Ainvar."

"Good. What name was discovered for her?"

"Maia. Daughter of the earth."

The rightness of the name sang in me. Maia, daughter of the earth. Daughter of Gaul.

"And that boy?" I inquired, nodding toward the formerly blind lad, who was now sitting comfortably cross-legged beside my hearthfire, eating my food as if he were accustomed to doing so.

Which he was, I learned from Briga. "His mother has a burning tumor in her belly, so while Sulis and I are working to heal we brought her children into the fort where they would be safer. We've divided them among the lodges. I took this one, of course."

Of course. "I'm surprised you didn't welcome the lot into my house," I said with a sarcasm Briga chose to ignore. "Were there dozens?"

She shook her head. "This is the oldest. His name is Cormiac Ru. The Red Wolf."

At the sound of his name Cormiac Ru looked up and met my eyes. I recalled holding him in my arms on a long-ago day and describing war for him. Now he was only a few seasons short of being of warrior age himself, had he been born into a noble clan. His hair was copper, his eyes were ice; his lean, intense face was not boyish.

"I defend these women," he told me flatly. Then he went back to his food.

His name suited him.

Under my breath, I said to Briga, "Are you going to send him back to his mother eventually?"

"If she regains her strength. But she's very ill, Ainvar. She didn't send for a healer when she should have and now it may be too late, even for the mistletoe. You've come at a most propitious time. Tomorrow is the sixth day of the moon."

I understood at once. Circumstance had denied me recent rituals in the grove, but I could conduct a major one tomorrow.

The ceremony of cutting the mistletoe was always held on the sixth day of the moon. The plant grew on a number of different trees, but was rarely found on oaks. When it was, it was called the Oak's Child and was an object of reverence, for it came with special gifts from the Otherworld. A decoction of the Oak's Child, prepared in a manner zealously guarded by the druids, was capable of destroying burning tumors. Indeed, it was the most powerful of all medicines.

Many oaks in the sacred grove were crowned with mistletoe.

We were not lavish in its use; we did not pillage and plunder the trees. Instead, we took the mistletoe only when we most needed it, and offered suitable sacrifices in return. The mistletoe would be cut from the oak with a special golden knife, and two fine young bulls would water the tree's roots with their blood while the druids chanted.

Administered in time, the medicine made from the Oak's Child might save the Red Wolf's mother. To my certain knowledge, it had saved many before her.

Also, after the ceremony I would have an excellent opportunity to speak to the druids and urge them to enlist more fighting men for Vercingetorix.

That night, sitting once more by my own fireside, I did not think of Vercingetorix. My eyes kept following Briga around the lodge, and the rising heat in me was not caused by the fire on the hearth. She seemed to have forgiven me for the loss of our daughter; her welcome had been warm and genuinely happy. When I lay down on my bed and opened my arms, she came into them willingly, and Lakutu and Cormiac Ru ignored us as people must when they share a lodge. Each person has their own hood of invisibility accorded to them by the courtesy of the others.

But Briga lay stiffly in my arms and I felt my heat cooling. "What is it?" I whispered to her.

"Nothing."

"Are you still angry with me?"

"Of course not. I'm glad you're alive, and here."

"Then what's the matter?"

"Nothing."

But something was, and its name was Maia. The lost child was like a shadow between us. "I'll give you another child," I said urgently, moving over her. I rammed my rigid self into Briga as if I would find Maia there, someplace inside her, and she cried out and clung to me as if we could create life from desperation.

Before dawn, as I was preparing to go out and sing the song for the sun, Cormiac Ru came to me. In a voice not meant for the women to hear, he said, "I'll go find your daughter. Give me a horse. I can do it. The women think I'm a child but I'm not."

I looked down at his earnest face in the weak light of the banked hearthfire. "No, you're not a child. I can see that. But you can't just go off and find her, it isn't that easy. You have no idea how large the world is beyond the palisade, Cormiac, or what waits for you out there."

"It doesn't matter," he said with the wonderful confidence of ignorance. "Briga cries for her at night; I want to go get her." He looked up at me with his ice-colored eyes, and I saw there was no fear in him, not in his body or his spirit. Briga had brought him out of the darkness and he owed her a debt. For Cormiac Ru it was simple. He was a Celt, a person of honor.

I felt a throb of triumph. These are my people, Caesar, I said in the silence of my head. Flawed and foolish and magnificent, these are my people and we will defeat you. We will survive when you and your ambitions are dust. The tribes will unite; our people will sing together.

I concentrated the full force of my will on those words as if, through them alone, I could shape the history to come.

The lodge seemed to fade away, leaving me standing in shadows that might have been the shadows of trees. A sound rang through me; one pure note from a song I had never heard before. I almost touched it, tasted it, saw it . . . then Cormiac tugged at my arm and the walls surrounded me again.

"Are you afraid of Caesar, Ainvar?" the boy was asking.

"Caesar?" I looked at the vibrant upturned face and smiled. "No, Cormiac. Caesar is nothing of consequence—a short wick in a small lamp."

He went out with me to sing the song for the sun.

That day we cut the mistletoe, and when the ceremony was concluded and the healers were hurrying away with the precious plant to prepare their decoction, I spoke with my druids. "Avoid Roman patrols, but visit every place known to you where there are strong men capable of fighting. They don't have to be nobles. Common men can fight, too; this is their land as well as ours. Perhaps more so, because they are the ones who work it. Urge them to take up whatever will serve as weapons and join in the resistance to the Romans. Use all your influence. Tell them the Otherworld requires it of them. When I return to Vercingetorix, I will guide those who are ready to go with me."

"How can we be certain this is what the Otherworld wants?" asked a jug-eared apprentice sacrificer who had accompanied Aberth.

With the full authority of the Keeper of the Grove, I thundered at him, "Because I tell you the spirit of Gaul demands it!"

There was no further argument. The druids dispersed to do my bidding, leaving me alone with the trees and my thoughts.

There was so little time. Soon Caesar must return to his legions. Soon I must rejoin Rix for what surely would be the decisive confrontation. Awareness of my prior errors of judgment weighed heavily on me. The advice I gave him from now on must be inspired. We could not afford any more mistakes. It was not enough that I had a good head; we needed the sort of assistance Vercingetorix scorned.

"Help me," I murmured to That Which Watched. "Let me see . . . let me *know* . . ." With all my strength I reached out, pleading, to the Otherworld.

The other world. Glowing just beyond the realm of earthly senses, yet so near I could almost touch it, could almost tear through the thin veil that separated us and feel its warm light on my face. There it was, just beyond the trees, over there . . . and in it the dead I had loved. When I thought of them, they could see me. I envied them their untrammeled spirits and their expanded knowledge. "Show me the future," I implored.

My stomach lurched. For the second time that day the world as I knew it dissolved around me. I found myself standing amid the shadows of trees that were not trees at all but pillars. My skin felt the cold echo of stone. A vertical immensity of stone.

I tilted my head back to follow the line of the pillars upward. There was no sky above me. Instead, incredibly, curving ceiling timbers arched upward to meet in a dim vastness higher than treetops. Or were they timbers? I had an impression of stone. And what was the source of the rainbowed light that dazzled my eyes? To one side a great circle shot through with vivid shades of blue and rose stopped my breath with its beauty.

Then the scene faded. I was in the grove again, amid the familiar oaks. But by the ringing in my ears and a sickening sense of dislocation I knew I had seen the future.

Chapter Thirty-four

Ttrue prophecy is the most elusive and the most ambiguous of druidic abilities. My own talent for it had always been negligible, my flare of prescience concerning the death of Caesar being the exception. Usually foretelling was a matter of recognizing patterns in nature, a form of divining rather than an inspiration from the Otherworld.

Nothing had prepared me for the shocking vision of the sacred grove of Gaul transformed into a structure of stone.

I told no one, not even the chief of the vates. Keryth would have been no more able to interpret the vision than I. Everything about it was alien, beyond comprehension. Yet the eerie beauty of the gigantic building in which I had so briefly stood, numb with awe, haunted me.

Was this the future Caesar brought? Somehow I did not think so. For all its size, the construction was too graceful to be Roman. It soared like the trees.

The trees it replaced.

I fought back terror.

When Briga and Sulis went to treat Cormiac Ru's mother with their mistletoe decoction, I went with them. The sight of her saddened me. She was no longer the creamy-skinned woman I remembered, but a sack of skin filled with knobby sticks. Her eyes stared blankly; I do not know if she recognized me or any of us. Her body was being eaten away from the inside, the tumor feeding on her as the mistletoe feeds on the oak.

The cure must be appropriate to the illness. The strength and life the mistletoe had taken from the oak, most powerful of trees, would now be given to the woman.

She stirred in pain on her bed of straw. "Where are my children? Someone . . . ?"

Briga bent tenderly over her. "They're housed and cherished, don't worry about them. Here, drink this."

"Where's your husband?" I interjected.

The woman tried feebly to push the cup away. "In the fields. Always in the fields. I should be with him, sowing the barley." To my dismay, she broke into a quavering, pitiful attempt to sing the song for sowing, while with one skeletal hand she broadcast invisible seeds from her bed.

She tore my heart. "Will she live?" I asked Sulis.

The healer looked doubtful. "She may have waited too long to admit she was ill. They only have a small holding here and in the spring everyone is needed to work. She said nothing until she collapsed. I don't know if there is enough of her left now for the mistletoe to restore, but we'll do our best, Ainvar."

I could not linger to learn the outcome. Daily, from every possible source, I was receiving news of Caesar. He would be leaving the Aeduans very soon indeed.

Meanwhile, my druids had collected as many recruits as they could for our army; they were a mixed group of woodsmen and craftsmen and half-grown boys. There were few farmers or herders, because of the season. The land claimed her own. She was pregnant with new life and would not wait upon the convenience of man.

In my lodge young Cormiac Ru announced, "I'm going to go with you and fight for Vercingetorix!" He planted himself resolutely in front of me, trying to stand taller than he was.

"You told me that you defend the women, remember? That is what I require of you now, stay here and be the man in this lodge while I am away."

His eyes sparkled at hearing himself called a man. "Just give me a sword and I'll cut anyone who tries to hurt them to bits!" He might have seemed ridiculous, standing there with his legs planted and his hairless chest inflated, but there was something in the child's eyes. . . .

From the very bottom of my carved chest, where it had lain untouched all these seasons, I took my father's sword. I was embarrassed to discover rust on the blade. "Can you wield this, Cormiac?"

He seized the sword with eager hands. At first the weight staggered him, but recovering quickly, he swung the weapon in a broad arc, making the air sing. Both my women jumped back.

"You'll have to practice using it," I said. "Rub that blade with vinegar and sand and borrow a whetstone for it."

He nodded, his eyes fixed on the sword with the expression most other farmers' sons wear when regarding a good team of oxen.

I spent the rest of the day in the grove. When I returned I felt restored, my brain burnished and sharpened. I had been too long away, my thoughts had grown rusty. But now I had an inspired plan. . . .

That night I held Briga very tightly, as if I would melt our flesh together. We mated with a desperate urgency and slept without ever separating our bodies.

In the gray light of morning I surveyed the inhabitants of the chief druid's lodge. Briga, Lakutu, the infant, Glas, the boy, Cormiac Ru. My acquired family. The bonds between us were invisible but very strong.

I beckoned to Briga to accompany me outside. "When Caesar is defeated and I return, we'll initiate you into the Order," I promised, adding on the same breath, "and at the next Beltaine I'll marry Lakutu."

Her eyebrows shot up alarmingly. "Just like that? Without asking me?"

"Are you and I supposed to ask one another's permission for things?" I could not resist inquiring in all innocence.

She opened her mouth, closed it, frowned; started again to speak, stopped. A laugh struggled to break through a mask of simulated anger. "While you're away, Ainvar, I'm going to learn how to outthink a chief druid!"

"Good. I like intelligent women."

I could tell she was not really displeased. If she and Lakutu had not become such good friends, I would never have considered the arrangement. But now Briga, prince's daughter, would have a woman to whom she was officially senior and whom she could order about if she chose.

But I knew her; she was too tenderhearted to order a friend about.

We had a more somber matter still to discuss. "While I'm away, I'm going to leave a heavy responsibility on your shoulders, Briga. If I don't return . . . if Caesar wins . . ." She started to protest, but I silenced her. "If Caesar wins, go to Aberth. Ask him to free your spirits before the Romans come to enslave you."

"Lakutu and the boys too?"

"And you. Yes. My family."

Here was the ultimate test of the faith I had tried to give her, the proof of my success as a druid. I watched her face anxiously.

Her chin came up. She met my eyes with a level, fearless gaze. "I shall do as you ask, Ainvar. Death is only a small thing. I know we are all perfectly safe."

Then she smiled. My Briga.

When I left the Fort of the Grove, people shouted, "Come back to us a free person!"

My bodyguards and I were forced to hold our horses to a trot so the recruits running with us could keep up. More promised to follow. We hardly paused for rest, since Caesar would speedily rejoin his legions. We made a brief visit to the sacred grove of the Bituriges so I could talk with Nantua, then hurried on to Vercingetorix at his camp beyond Avaricum. As our patrols subsequently informed me, I reached him on the same day Caesar returned to his army.

"I'm planning to attack immediately, before he has time to rest," Rix told me.

"I doubt if Caesar is tired, Rix. Or if he is, he won't let it hamper him, any more than you would. And his men are both rested and well fed, thanks to the stores of Avaricum. Our situation isn't as good as theirs. Before you fight Caesar we should be in a position of advantage. A stronghold."

"Avaricum and Cenabum are ruins, so what do you suggest?"

"Gergovia." I knew he would fight best on his own soil. And

the time it would take us to get there would allow my plan to mature.

Rix considered the suggestion, then nodded. "Gergovia."

Breaking camp, the army of Gaul marched southward. Along the way I met with various druids, and discussed with the Goban Saor methods of strengthening Gaulish strongholds.

We were following the river Allier, in flood at that season. Soon we learned that Caesar's army was coming after us down the opposite bank. At once Rix sent cavalry ahead to destroy all the bridges so Caesar could not cross the swollen river and attack us. The two armies then proceeded to march southward almost together, usually in sight of one another, separated only by a turbulent vein of swift brown water across which the men shouted challenges and occasional crude jokes.

Unnoticed by our patrols, Caesar detained a company of his men in a dense woodland opposite one of the broken bridges. When the two armies were out of sight, he emerged and proceeded to supervise the repair of the bridge. The Roman then recalled his legions, crossed the river, and at the next dawn our astonished patrols reported that the entire Roman army was coming up behind us.

The warriors of free Gaul cursed Caesar with every expletive known to the Celtic imagination.

Vercingetorix led us at utmost speed, hoping to reach the Arvernian stronghold before the Romans could force us to fight a pitched battle in the open. They outnumbered us; all the advantage would be theirs. Five days of hard marching brought us to Gergovia, which was perched atop a mountain with difficult approaches on every side, just as I remembered. Here was, indeed, a position of advantage for us.

Vercingetorix dispatched a company of cavalry to slow the Roman advance while his men set up camp on the heights around the stronghold, with a commanding view of the terrain below. Additional garrisons were established on nearby hillsides, to guard the fresh water sources that supplied Gergovia.

Rix assigned various tribes to stations around the outer walls of the fortified town. In plain view of the Romans below them, the warriors practiced their most intimidating battle feats and screamed their most terrifying war cries. Most of the tribes had archers who rained arrows down on the enemy troops whenever they came too close. We were less lavish with our spears, however, as they were more valuable.

Observing the preparations Rix made, I was impressed. Just as I had studied druidry, so he had studied war, and he was a champion.

Was it still a game for him on some level, a contest between honorable opponents even though he knew all the rules were changed? I did not know; we did not discuss it. Rix did not enjoy discussing the abstracts that fascinate druids.

He was warrior, I was druid. He commanded soldiers according to one pattern, I commanded the druid network according to another.

After meeting with me in the sacred grove of the Bituriges, Nantua had sent his druids east on fast horses to meet with Aeduan members of the Order. Together they then approached the new chief magistrate of the Aedui, whom Caesar had just confirmed in that office. The magistrate had been educated by the druids; he was susceptible to druidic persuasion.

The druids talked; the magistrate listened. With inspired tongues, the druids convinced him that the future of all Gaul lay in supporting the Gaulish confederacy against the invader. The magistrate then brought his influence to bear upon a young noble called Litaviccus, who had been commissioned by Caesar to lead ten thousand Aeduan warriors to join the Roman army.

Caesar already had a contingent of choice Aeduan cavalry with him, but demanded more fighting men.

Having been kept apprised of these developments, I had issued additional instructions during our march southward.

Under the command of Litaviccus and his brothers, the Aeduan reinforcements set out to rendezvous with Caesar at Gergovia. But when they entered Arvernian territory they encountered, thanks to Secumos, chief druid of the Arverni, a band of wild-eyed druids disguised as Gaulish deserters from the Roman army.

These druids told Litaviccus and his men a harrowing tale that had been concocted by me, with added flourishes by Hanesa the bard. The druids were very convincing. Afterward, Litaviccus addressed his followers with tears in his eyes, tears resulting from a potion slipped him by one of the druids.

"These men were witnesses to a monstrous deed!" he cried.

"They heard Caesar falsely accuse the leaders of his Aeduan cavalry of entering into a treacherous conspiracy with the Arverni. Then Caesar's followers massacred the Aeduan cavalry without proof or trial! Even the Aeduan princes were slain, men we knew and loved. This is the treatment we can expect of Caesar if we join him. We are warned to beware of Roman perfidy!"

Litaviccus's followers responded with a roar of rage. They fell upon the handful of Romans who were accompanying them with grain and provisions and slaughtered them to the last man. Then they turned back toward their homeland to spread the tale and avenge the slain cavalry by killing every Roman they found.

As I had taken into account when formulating this plan, Celts are impetuous and easily aroused.

Thus while Caesar was preparing to fight Vercingetorix, he received the distressing news of a potentially catastrophic revolt among the Aedui. If the revolt succeeded, it would undoubtedly spread to the other tribes still loyal to him around the perimeter of free Gaul, making his situation untenable.

I understood very well the handicap of a distracted mind, a handicap I had now inflicted on Caesar.

He would have to go after the Aeduans and persuade them of their error. There had been no treachery on the part of his Aeduan cavalry, and no massacre. The cavalry was alive and well, and astonished to hear of the defection of Litaviccus's ten thousand warriors. They pleaded with Caesar not to punish them for the deeds of their tribesmen.

However, simultaneously he was just solidifying his position before launching a siege on Gergovia. The Romans had overrun a small Arvernian garrison on a nearby hill, where they were building an entrenchment that would allow them to get closer to the town.

It was night. Rix and I stood together outside the gates of the fort, looking down on the lights of the sprawling Roman encampment: thousands and thousands of men.

"Caesar sits by one of those fires," Rix mused. "What do you suppose he's thinking tonight, Ainvar?"

I reached out, searching for the mind of the Roman. There was something magical about knowing he was so close, our thoughts mingling like smoke in the dark. "He's wondering what you're thinking," I hazarded.

"The Aeduan deception was brilliant, you know."

"Inspired," I said simply.

"Caesar will be forced to divide his army if he means to pursue the Aeduans."

"I know. I should think he'll leave at first light, with as many men remaining in camp as he can spare. He really has no other option."

"Then let's feast to our success!" cried Vercingetorix.

As long as the stars shone, the leaders of free Gaul ate and drank and sang in the king's lodge in Gergovia. Victory was like wine in the air and in the blood.

When men are certain of winning, they acquire a special arrogance. Listening to them as I sat beside Rix, I hoped the warlords realized this was a high point of their lives. I leaned over to say this to Hanesa, who was sitting across from me devouring a haunch of roast pig.

The bard wiped the grease from his mouth with the ends of his beard. "I once told you I would be able to compose an epic if I stayed with Vercingetorix," he reminded me.

"Have you begun it?"

"Begun it?" Hanesa bellowed with laughter and slapped his massive paunch. "I've nearly finished it. All I need is a triumphant climax. It's a pity Caesar won't meet Vercingetorix in single combat. In a battle of champions our leader would break that puny Roman in half!"

"Which is one reason why you never see Caesar anywhere near Vercingetorix on the battlefield," I pointed out. "The Roman is too clever to make that mistake. Besides, single combat is not part of his pattern."

He fights in other ways, my head silently remarked.

Caesar's brain, rather than his body, was the champion fighting for supremacy. And the brain matched against him was mine. We were a team, Rix and I. He the heart, I the head.

Two faces of Gaul.

Among the women serving the feast that night was Onuava, Rix's wife. I do not know what I had expected of the woman Rix had chosen to marry, but my first glimpse of her had been something of a surprise. She was a very fair, very tall, very sinewy woman with a lion's mane of hair and a catlike way of moving, a tawny creature who looked only half-tamed.

Under my breath, I said to Rix, "I thought you told me you married the woman who gave you the least trouble."

He slanted a sleepy-eyed look at Onuava. "I did. She gives me no trouble."

Feeling our eyes on her, Onuava threw the pair of us a bright, hot smile of blatantly sexual invitation. To both of us. At the same time.

"You're lying, King of the World," I told Rix.

He shrugged and laughed.

When the first light of dawn made tarnished silver of the eastern sky, Rix and I mounted the palisade of Gergovia to watch Caesar leave in pursuit of the Aeduans. He took four legions with him and all of his cavalry, which told me how serious he considered the Aeduan revolt to be. As the precise columns of men set off eastward, my eyes sought out one tiny figure at the very head of the foremost column, distinctive in a crimson cloak.

Though he was too far away to be certain, it seemed that Caesar paused, and looked back toward Gergovia.

On impulse, I raised my arm and waved.

Caesar was no sooner out of sight than Vercingetorix attacked his camp, where he had left something in excess of two legions. The Gauls sent wave after wave of men against the now-outnumbered Romans, forcing them to defend themselves without rest or respite. The fighting was savage, with heavy losses on both sides. The land around Gergovia was black with war and warriors.

Unfortunately, the worst of the fighting was taking place between the stronghold and the distant sacred grove of the Arverni. I could not get through to conduct rituals in the grove to help our warriors. I made the mistake of complaining about this to Rix when he was brimming with battle.

"Don't waste your effort on smoke and sacrifice, Ainvar," he said harshly. "We're winning through our own strength, not because of some dubious druid magic."

Winners, my head observed, believe they succeed on their own merit. It is only losers who require gods to blame.

The fighting continued. Clash and grunt and scream echoed from every ridge and valley. We had not given the Romans time to set up medical tents close to the battlefields, so at sundown, when our healers went out to collect the wounded, Rix ordered them to bring back the most gravely injured Romans as well for treatment.

I understood. It was a variation of the same impulse that had made me wave to Caesar.

We were Celts, men of honor.

The prince Litaviccus and his brothers arrived at a headlong gallop, requesting protection inside the walls of Gergovia. The sentries took them to the command tent at once, and Rix sent for me to hear their story.

When I arrived, Litaviccus was sitting with widespread knees on a stool outside the tent, enjoying the sun with the relish of a man who had feared he might never see it again. His was a typically Aeduan face, broad through the jaw, and he had the permanent squint of a mountain man.

"Caesar overtook us not far from the Allier," he was telling Rix when I joined them. "We had entered a strip of Boii territory and were looking for Romans. By then my men were wild with anger. I had sent messengers ahead to tell our tribesmen of the massacre and urge them to kill every Roman in Aeduan land.

"Then Caesar caught up with us. He is a clever man. He had brought with him the very leaders of the cavalry whom he had supposedly slain for treason. When my followers saw those men alive and unharmed, they threw down their weapons.

"It did not take Caesar long to convince them the whole thing had been a trick. They were afraid he would have them slain for desertion, but he made a disgustingly magnanimous speech about forgiveness and friendship that eventually had them fawning at his feet like hounds.

"But I was not such a fool as to think he would extend his mercy to myself and my brothers. So without waiting for the geese to cackle, we took advantage of the confusion and slipped away. We came straight here to you."

"You are welcome to both our protection and our gratitude," Rix replied. "You have been a great help to us. Being forced to split up his armies has cost Caesar almost half a legion already."

"And more Romans will die in the land of the Aedui," Litaviccus assured us. "My messengers will have gotten through. When my people hear the story of the massacre, they will not wait for confirmation, but will fall on every Roman trader and official they can find and tear them to bits and take their property. By the time they learn what really happened, there will be fewer Romans in my land."

"And here," said Rix, cocking his head toward the ongoing din of battle.

When Caesar returned from his pursuit of the ten thousand, he found the army he had left behind badly mauled. Men had become carrion; when he rode out to inspect the battlefield, he was greeted by lingering swarms of flies.

Meanwhile, our numbers were increasing. New recruits arrived daily, having been persuaded to take up arms by their tribal druids in places as far away as Aquitania. Caesar, on the other hand, had lost not only his battle casualties but the Aeduan ten thousand, because his trust in them had been destroyed and he dared not bring them back with him.

Caesar did send messengers to the land of the Aedui in an attempt to head off the burgeoning revolt there, but once you set fire to dry grass, it is not easily extinguished. It would not take long for the uprising to spread to nearby tribes, and soon they would all be killing Romans. Caesar would soon be flanked by hostile tribes where he had thought to have allies.

"He'll have to retreat," Rix said to me. "The most obvious thing for him to do now would be to withdraw to the Province and collect reinforcements."

"Caesar rarely does the obvious thing," I pointed out, "and I don't believe he's ready to withdraw." Caesar was not yet discouraged, I knew; I had observed the pattern of bird flight above his camp and tasted the soil of the battleground. In spite of his recent losses Caesar was relying on the valor and discipline of his men to overcome us; he still thought he had enough troops.

We must arrange for him to suffer losses he cannot ignore, I thought.

I suggested a plan to Vercingetorix.

A ragged stream of warriors claiming to be deserters from the army of free Gaul approached the Roman encampment. They allowed the Romans to coerce certain information from them concerning our terrain and vulnerability. Meanwhile, Rix withdrew his forces from the top of a strategic hill which gave access to a narrow, wooded ridge that led directly up the mountain on which Gergovia stood.

In the night, Caesar's legions converged on the deserted hill.

Dawn revealed them in control of the site. Our warriors swarmed to the attack, fighting to deny them the ridge. More Roman warriors emerged from hiding in the surrounding woodlands, and the battle was fierce.

Our men fell back gradually, letting the Romans win ground step by step but only with exhausting effort. The slope of the ground gave us the advantage. About halfway up the hill, the Goban Saor had erected a clever, complicated stone barrier the height of a Gaulish man, following the contour of the hill. Countless Romans fell to Gaulish spears as they tried to scramble over the barrier. But always we lured them on, taunting them, and eventually they succeeded and overran a few small camps of ours on the far side.

At about highsun the Romans surprised the king of the Nitiobriges in his tent. He barely managed to escape. As he told us later, "I had to ride for my life, half-naked and sitting astride a wounded horse!" He laughed; it was a good story because he was alive.

The Romans continued to advance. We fed them little victories to whet their appetites.

Had we not used the ruse of the undefended hill, Caesar would never have launched an assault on the stronghold itself, where all the advantage was ours. We had tricked him into coming too close to turn and go back. I had counted on his willingness to take a risk if he thought he saw the smallest opportunity was to be gained.

We kept the enemy fighting hard for the better part of a day. Caesar shifted troops from one place to another, hoping to confuse us, and eventually there were a number of men on the heights below the walls of Gergovia. But the Romans could advance no farther. Caesar even sent the Aeduan cavalry around the mountain to find a better means of approach, but there was none.

As the sun was setting, Caesar sounded recall. His men were exhausted, their senses dulled, their brains befogged. When the Aeduan cavalry rode toward them out of the twilight, they mistook their fellow warriors for men of free Gaul and attacked them savagely, killing many.

At the same time, another Roman contingent proved unwilling to fall back at all. They made a wild rush on the walls of the stronghold. It was exactly what we had planned.

Throughout the latter part of the day our warriors had been slipping back into the fortified town as they gave ground to the

Romans. Now there was not a space on the walls that was not crowded with them. They rained death down on the enemy directly below them. Spear and stone and boiling pitch did terrible damage. In their desperation to attack us, the Romans had thrown off discipline; they did not raise the roof of overlapped shields to protect themselves. Furthermore, those who had led the charge were now penned against the base of the walls by those who came up after them.

There was almost as much fighting taking place atop the walls. Everyone was struggling to find a spot to stand and watch. And to take part. I had secured an excellent position for myself near one of the watchtowers, with Cotuatus and many of our Carnutians, when I heard a great yell behind me and someone surged up, almost knocking me off the wall.

It was Onuava. "Where is my husband?" she shouted at me.

I peered into the confusion. "There, see him? On that black horse just in front of the gates."

We both strained forward, watching Rix run his sword through a crazed centurion who was shrieking at him like a madman. Suddenly Onuava leaned forward farther. I had to grasp her about the waist for fear she would topple off. Below us I saw one Roman balancing a second man on his shoulders. As this second man strained upward, Onuava bent toward him and tore open the bodice of her gown, baring her big white breasts.

CHAPTER THIRTY-FIVE

"COME UP here to me, you pretty little man," Onuava cooed down to the Roman as he gaped up at her from his precarious perch on his comrade's shoulders. "Come up here to me and claim your reward." She bounced her breasts at him, she tossed her glorious tawny mane.

Then she screamed and hurled a jagged stone straight into his upturned face.

The man tumbled backward and disappeared into the roiling mass below.

At once the other women on the walls began imitating Onuava, shouting invitations and offers of help to Romans trying to climb up, then mocking them, assaulting them with missiles, shrieking with laughter as they fell. Even tiny children clamored for something to throw at the enemy.

The Roman position was hopeless. At Rix's signal the warriors of free Gaul came pouring out all the side gates of Gergovia and circled around behind them, scything them down. Another centurion made one desperate, doomed attempt to storm the main gates, but Rix rode him down with his big black horse. Thereupon the centurion's men scattered, their nerve destroyed.

Our men smashed the enemy against the walls of Gergovia.

We could hear the Roman trumpets frantically shrilling recall now, and at last the legionaries were willing to hear it, too. Those who were still alive began running back down the mountain, and we stood on the ramparts and cheered them on their way in the twilight.

Seven hundred Romans died that day, including forty-six centurions, the backbone of Caesar's army. I saw Vercingetorix kill two of them himself.

I wondered what Caesar would say to the Romans who had lost control of themselves and disregarded his orders. "The sternest discipline can be overcome," I had told Rix when planning this strategy, "if you can hold our men longer than Caesar can control his."

"I can," he had said. And he had.

When they reached the level plain, the Romans had stopped and at last drawn themselves up into a ragged battle formation, but we had no intention of pursuing them. It was dark, and we knew as well as they who had won.

The next morning Rix fought a cavalry skirmish with them, and pride demanded that they try yet another the next day; but after that they struck camp and marched away.

Litaviccus came to us at once. "Let me take the survivors of the Aeduan cavalry," he pleaded with Rix. "They've deserted the Romans and are anxious to follow my standard. I can take them home and use them to consolidate the Aeduan revolt."

Some of the princes objected, saying we could use the Aeduans better as part of our own force. But Rix overrode them and let Litaviccus go. "It's more important to cost Caesar the Aedui," he said.

Our victory celebrations lasted for nights and days. Everyone had battle tales to tell; Hanesa exhausted himself trying to memorize them all. Onuava was much praised and her style greatly admired as the model of behavior for a warrior's wife.

She in turn seemed to be impressed by me. She personally undertook to keep my wine cup filled and rub the back of my neck when the night grew long. Her fingers snaked through my hair.

"Such a nice head," I heard her murmur behind me. "Full of

thoughts. All those twists and turns . . . there must be some very interesting pathways in your head, Ainvar. What would it be like to meander along them, I wonder."

"Tedious," I said, trying to keep my attention fixed on a conversation taking place between Rix and a prince of the Gabali about guarding the southern passes.

"Is it? Is it tedious, all that thinking?" Onuava slipped around and sat down on the bench beside me, pressing her round haunch against me.

I looked up to find Vercingetorix's heavy-lidded gaze upon us. I smiled back at him. I put my arm around Onuava.

Victory makes men more drunk than wine.

Rix held my eyes for a heartbeat longer, then deliberately looked away.

His wife leaned against me. "People wonder about you, you know," she said. "The druid who rides with the warriors. How much of your advice does my husband take, Ainvar?"

"I accompany him as his friend," I said sternly. "The king of the Arverni makes his own decisions, he is a brilliant warlord."

She was not misled. "Perhaps the final decision is his, but I know my husband. He is bold and straightforward; some of his most successful strategies are anything but straightforward. They must come from a devious mind, and I think that mind is yours. Am I right?"

What harm would there be in admitting it? The king's lodge was overheated and the fumes of the wine were swirling through my skull; it would be most pleasurable to boast to this magnificent woman with her knowing eyes and insinuating smile. I would be telling her nothing she did not already suspect. Surely everyone had guessed that I was Rix's principal, indeed his only, adviser.

But for once my brain ran faster than my tongue. Before I could open my mouth, my head warned: Leave the credit with Rix. Let the bards sing of his sagacity. Druids do not require praise for fulfilling the design of the Source.

I rewarded Onuava with my most opaque smile. "Perhaps your husband is simply more devious than you think—or should I say, clever? It is easy to underestimate the person you live with and overestimate the stranger."

Behind her eyes, something measured me. "I don't think I'm

overestimating you, Ainvar. I'll have to know you better to be sure."

"We won't have time to know one another better."

"Why not? Do you think the war is over?" Her fingers were rubbing the nape of my neck again.

"No," I told her honestly. "We shall have a respite for a little while, that's all. According to our patrols, Caesar has gone to the land of the Aedui to attempt to win the tribe back to him. But between our friend Litaviccus and the current chief magistrate, he's going to have a hard time of it. He will be occupied for a while. But he'll be back, Onuava; I assure you he hasn't abandoned his plans for Gaul."

"And what of your plans, Ainvar? Will you go home while Caesar is away?"

I had meant to, actually. But it was a long journey and I had already missed Beltaine. I would have to wait another year before I could dance around the Beltaine tree with Lakutu.

Next year for certain, I promised myself. When Caesar is finally defeated and driven out of Gaul. Next year.

In the meantime Onuava leaned her warm body against mine and refilled my cup.

The king of the Nitiobriges, who had escaped the Romans half-naked, riding a wounded horse, suddenly leaped onto the nearest table and gave a mighty shout. "I am free!" he cried in drunken exultation. "We are all free! And the earth is drinking Roman blood!" He bellowed with laughter and everyone joined in, yelling, stamping their feet, beating on the nearest surface with cup and fist and weapon.

Everyone but me. His reference to Roman blood had sobered me like cold water thrown in my face.

For the rest of the night, while the others celebrated, I sat quietly and thought druid thoughts. Onuava eventually moved away from me to lean on someone else but I hardly noticed her leaving. I was dismayed by a realization that I should have had much sooner—after our very first battle in free Gaul against Gaius Caesar.

I was a druid. I knew the power of blood.

At first light I left the king's lodge. Behind me, the drunken celebration continued unabated. As soon as I had joined Secumos in singing the song for the sun, I motioned to one of the sentries to open a gate and I left the fortress.

Below the massive walls of Gergovia the land fell away sharply. The whole area had seen savage fighting. Roman litter bearers had subsequently carried away their dead, but quantities of blood were still soaking into the earth.

Like a sacrifice.

Roman blood feeding and invigorating Gaulish soil.

Establishing a claim.

The earth is a goddess and not sentimental. As long as she receives her due, she does not ask the name of the sacrificer. Caesar had access to hundreds of thousands of men whose blood he could spend in the conquest of Gaul. Would his sacrifice ultimately outweigh ours? Would the claim of Roman blood be honored in the Otherworld?

I returned to Gergovia and sought out Secumos. For once I did not want to be with Rix.

The passage of the seasons was being kind to the Arvernian chief druid. His hair was as dark as ever, and his lean body and constantly moving hands were still agile. I could see the years in his eyes, though.

I wondered what he could see in mine.

I told him of my misgivings. "We need to discover a ritual to counteract the effect of all that Roman blood, Secumos."

He had survived more winters than I, but I was Keeper of the Grove. With disturbingly total faith he said, "You cost Caesar the Aeduans, Ainvar; you'll find the necessary ritual. The Otherworld will guide you to whatever needs to be done."

He was looking at me as the warriors looked at Rix after the victory of Gergovia.

The burden of another person's belief can be crushingly heavy.

Shortly after highsun that day, reports reached us of fierce fighting and much bloodshed in the land of the Parisii. The four legions that Caesar had sent north had gathered at a fishing village on the Sequana River, and were attacking a Parisian fort situated on an island in the river. After learning that Caesar had suffered a defeat at our hands and was having to deal with an Aeduan revolt, the neighboring tribes, including the ferocious Bellovaci, were all rising against the Romans.

Secumos and I went to the sacred grove of the Arverni. Amid

its trees, I opened the senses of my spirit and tried to reach the Otherworld, tried to find a new pattern of protection. But my bare feet were not touching earth I knew. The watching trees did not murmur my name. I needed to be in my own grove.

I could not admit failure to Secumos, however. Faith is magic too, and I must not destroy his, so I sent for his chief sacrificer and we offered cows and red cockerels and one of Rix's African mares . . . over his protests. We chanted, we danced, we invoked the Source.

Meanwhile, with the battle of Gergovia won, Rix's Parisian contingent was pleading more loudly than ever to be allowed to return home and defend its tribeland. Every tribe was being pulled in the direction of its self-interest. They all threatened to scatter like an explosion of stars.

Once more Rix held them. Summoning not only the princes but the warriors of all the tribes, he made a great speech, commending his army not only on its valor during the recent battle, but on something rarer to the Celtic nature, and more valuable in our current circumstances.

"You have accepted discipline," Vercingetorix said. "You kept calm and lured the Romans into a trap. Now they are trying to do the same thing to you, but we will outsmart them. It would do you no good to hurry home, men of the Parisii, because no matter how fast you travel, the outcome will have been decided by the time you get there. Do not be impetuous. Rein in your tempers as the cavalry reins in their horses.

"We shall fight Caesar again," he promised. "Not one of his commanders, but Caesar himself, and soon. But you must stay with me if you wish to take part in the battle that will win Gaul for us. It is not going to be determined by small victories in distant places, but by what happens when Gaius Caesar next confronts the King of the World!"

I was astonished to hear Rix apply that term in such an arrogant fashion, but it was exactly what the men needed to hear. They cheered him until some coughed blood.

Even upon learning that the Romans had won in the north, his men did not lose faith in Vercingetorix.

"Isn't he splendid?" Hanesa said enthusiastically. "He can do anything!"

We learned that following their victory in the north the four legions had marched to a permanent camp Caesar had established in the land of the Lingones. After a brief stay to collect additional supplies and weaponry, they set off on a three days' march to rejoin Caesar, who by this time was in the land of the Senones.

The Aeduans had risen against him almost totally. Upon his return to his homeland, Litaviccus had been welcomed as a hero in Bibracte, the Aeduan stronghold, and had been called brother by the chief magistrate of the tribe. Leaving his legions in camp, Caesar had made various diplomatic forays to try to reestablish alliances with the Aeduan princes, but he had been heartily rebuffed. The Aeduans had been plundering Roman settlements in the region and they liked the taste of the goods they had seized. Our victory at Gergovia convinced them ours was the winning side, and so they rejected Caesar.

Caesar had not given up all hope of reclaiming the Aeduans, however, so he refrained from a total attack. Besides, he needed supplies from them—supplies they were of course refusing to give him.

Caesar found he had two choices. He could withdraw into the Province, or he could go north.

He marched north into the land of the Senones, where the four legions joined him.

Now the Senones among us screamed to go home.

In his lodge at night, Rix watched the Senonian princes with brooding eyes. I caught his surreptitious signal and went to his side. "A messenger arrived just a little while ago from Bibracte," he said to me in a low voice not meant for anyone else to hear. "The Aeduans claim to be solidly in support of the Gaulish confederacy now. They want us to come to Bibracte to discuss a unified campaign to drive Caesar from Gaul."

"With the aid of Aeduan warriors? That's what you've been hoping for, Rix."

"I know. But . . . but I cannot totally trust the Aeduans."

"That is because your tribe and theirs are traditional enemies. You of all people know that tribalism must be set aside for the good of Gaul. You tell your princes that every day."

"It is easier to give advice than to take it," Rix said with a sigh. "We shall go to Bibracte, then."

I felt a faint tremor of intuition. "Let me take time first to visit the grove and read the signs and portents. . . ."

"No, Ainvar," he said, thrusting out his jaw. "Once my mind is decided, I act. We don't need all that magic. We march. We've defeated Caesar once; now is the time to close with him and inflict the final defeat. That's what he does to his enemies, isn't it? Once he has them on the run he follows them and slaughters them mercilessly!"

Yes, my head agreed. That is the Roman pattern. But it has never been ours. I felt an unease I could not set aside.

On the evening before our army left Gergovia, I was making a circuit of the walls, with the stars and my thoughts for company, when Onuava intercepted me. She strode up beside me and matched her pace to mine. Onuava was a big woman with long legs; I did not tower over her. "If you've come to ask me to invoke protections for your husband," I began, "I've already—"

"That isn't why I'm here," she interrupted. "No, don't stop, just keep walking. I need to talk to you . . . about myself."

Just then we saw the glow of a fire ahead of us. By its light several warriors were counting and stacking Roman weapons scavenged from the battlefield. They were removing iron javelin heads from broken wooden shafts and feeding the shafts to the flame, while arguing among themselves as to who would claim the best weapons.

Onuava approached them with a wide smile, clearly visible in the firelight. Her teeth gleamed. Stopping their work, the men gaped at the king's wife. She gathered them all up with her smile like fish in a net, then turned back toward me, triumphant. "You see how the men like me," she said.

I replied with a noncommittal murmur.

"Do you like me, Ainvar?"

Another murmur.

"You think I'm a simple woman, do you not? A big hearty female who enjoys men and food and probably snores."

This came so close to the truth that it made me uncomfortable.

Onuava laughed. "I do enjoy men, and food, but no one has ever complained about my snoring. And I'm not simple. I don't have a druid head, but I listen to everything said around me and I do my own thinking.

"I watch other people, too. I was watching you, the night after the battle. At first you were celebrating with the others, but then something gave you pause. Your expression changed and you seemed to gather a sort of darkness around you. You weren't paying attention to me anymore, but that isn't what bothered me. What bothered me was the expression on your face.

"You think Caesar is going to win, don't you? Or even worse, you know he is going to win."

"I don't know," I replied honestly, surprised to find she had thrown me so off balance that we were even having such a conversation. Onuava was right—she was not as simple as she seemed. I told her, "I've consulted for years with our best prophesiers and diviners and no one is able to give me a definite answer. There are just too many contradictory omens."

"What does that mean?"

"It means the situation could go either way."

"What will decide it, then?"

Once I would have given her some facile reply from an era when there were simpler answers and we of the Order thought we knew what there was to know. But life is change, and simplicity had been swept away on a Roman floodtide. Now, among the complex tangle of tribes and princes and personalities, ambitions and strategies and shifts of power, I could see no clear pattern. Even if there had been, Caesar and Vercingetorix, two men of inexhaustible energy and unyielding determination, would have pulled it apart between them and forced a new shape.

But if that were true, then living men, not the Otherworld, determined events.

Or was it possible that Caesar and Vercingetorix were but part of a still larger pattern, one I could not guess? Was the end to be determined not by them, or the Order, or even the world of the spirits as I understood it?

How much larger was reality than what I perceived?

What was really out there, beyond the firelight, in the night?

I came back from some lost and lonely pathway inside my head to find Onuava gripping my arm and peering intently into my face. "Ainvar? Speak to me, Ainvar!"

With an effort, I concentrated on her.

"For a moment I thought you were ill," she said.

I passed one hand across my forehead from the silver streak to the opposite temple, following the line of the druid tonsure. "I'm all right. I was just thinking. Why are you asking me these questions, Onuava?"

"I should think that would be perfectly obvious," she snapped. "Because I'm a woman."

"Your womanhood is perfectly obvious," I assured her, "but . . . "

"Women have to survive, Ainvar, don't you understand? I need to know what to expect so I can make preparations. My husband and his warriors will ride off to glory no matter which way the tree falls, but what about their women? We shall be left behind with the future on our hands and in our wombs. Women have to live in the future more than men do, so I want to know what's going to happen, if anyone can tell me. I hoped you could."

"If . . . if the unthinkable should happen and Vercingetorix dies, what will you do?" I wanted to know.

Her voluptuous lips narrowed to a thin line. "Find another strong man," she said mockingly.

There was iron in her eyes. Why had I thought women were soft?

The longer I lived the less I knew.

A ponderous presence came bustling up to us. "Ainvar, there you are, I've been looking everywhere for you!"

"What is it, Hanesa?"

"The army is leaving in the morning."

"I know."

"But the king just told me I'm not to go with them," the bard wailed. "He says I've gotten too fat, I couldn't keep up the pace."

"There is rather a lot of you," Onuava interjected.

I sensed an old and simmering antagonism between them as Hanesa replied huffily, "I'm very fast on my feet." He held out his hands to me. "Talk to him, Ainvar. Persuade him to change his mind. You can do it, no one else could."

Onuava was watching. "I don't have any exceptional influence with Vercingetorix, Hanesa. The command decisions are his; who am I to argue?"

The bard goggled at me. "This is me you're talking to, Ainvar. And I'm asking you for friendship's sake—tell the king he must bring me."

Onuava was smiling with one side of her mouth only. "Must, Ainvar? You can say 'must' to the king?"

Suddenly I wondered. "I'll talk to him, Hanesa, but I doubt if it will do any good."

I felt a weight leaning against me. Onuava said softly, "Speak to him on my behalf also, Ainvar. Tell him he must take me."

Hanesa and I both stared at her. "But you'll be safe here, in Gergovia," I argued. "We're going to *war*, Onuava!"

"Gaulish women fight beside their men."

"Sometimes, yes—in tribal battles, when the fighting is taking place close to their lodges and farms. But this is a different sort of war, we'll be marching for many days and facing soldiers who . . ."

"I know what Roman soldiers are like. I watched them from the walls."

"I thought you were concerned about the future. Going off to war is no way for a woman to guarantee herself a future."

"Ah, but it is, Ainvar. I have a bigger stake in this than you do. I don't mean to be left behind to worry and wonder. If I'm with you I shall know what happens as soon as it happens and can plan accordingly."

"And ride off with the victor," said Hanesa abruptly.

She whirled on him. "This is no business of yours!"

The bard said to me, "I've never mentioned the name of Onuava in my praise songs, and for good reason."

"You've never mentioned my name because I won't sit on the lap of a fat man."

"I wouldn't have you on my lap," he retorted. "Not a woman who would be willing to ride in a Roman chariot, which you will, if the Romans win."

"You don't know anything about me!" she shrieked.

"My wife wanted to go with me once but I refused," I interjected, hoping to distract them. But neither was listening.

"I know about you," said Hanesa. "Everyone knows about you."

She doubled her fists and sprang at him like a man.

With grave misgivings I stepped between them. Onuava hit me a jolting blow, then I caught her arm and twisted it back, holding her. She struggled violently; she was almost as strong as I was. I was aware we were gathering a crowd. People will always congregate to watch a fight, and a fight involving the king's wife and the chief druid of Gaul was not to be missed.

Hanesa, who was a prudent man, had stepped back into the night and left me struggling with the woman. I had no reason to fight his battle, but she was making a sincere effort to kill me and I did not dare turn her loose.

She hit me below the heart with her doubled fist, and the breath whooshed out of me. I twisted my body to protect my genitals from her knee, and she screamed at me as she had screamed at the Roman trying to scale the wall.

The watching crowd was laughing and making wagers as to the eventual winner.

The battle must be ended for the sake of the dignity of my office. I succeeded, briefly, in pinioning both her wrists with one hand, and simultaneously put my other hand on her head, concentrating on sending a stab of disabling pain through her skull without doing her any actual harm.

It had no effect at all.

When I had the time, I must contemplate the awful possibility that magic had no effect on women.

There was a clatter of hooves; Rix rode out of the night on his big black horse. He reined the animal in and sat staring down at us. I was too preoccupied to take time to read the expression on his face—and I was terribly embarrassed. Onuava took advantage of the distraction to break free from my grip and hit me as hard as she could on the side of the head with clubbed fists.

I staggered.

Somewhere above me, I heard Rix laugh. "That's enough, wife," he said mildly.

Enough for him perhaps, but not for me. I wanted to lift the woman over my head and hurl her from the walls of Gergovia. But it was too late. The battle was over. Onuava dropped her hands to her sides so I could not, in honor, hit her, and stepped back, tossing her hair out of her eyes. "I was just showing Ainvar how well I can fight," she said, breathing hard. "He had agreed to ask you to take me with you tomorrow, and I wanted to prove to him he had made the right decision."

How could I accuse the king's wife of being a liar in front of both the king and a large, very amused crowd? I looked around for Hanesa, but he had totally disappeared.

Rix shifted weight on his horse and the black stallion pranced sideways, making people scatter. "I did not know you wanted to go with us, Onuava," he called to her. "But if Ainvar approves I suppose it's all right." Then he laughed. "We need every fighter we can get!" He rode off.

Onuava and I looked at each other. I discovered that I did not want to hit her again.

I wanted to rape her.

It was the first time I had ever felt that specific desire. She was a woman made for conquest. Made for a conqueror. She aroused such contradictory emotions in me that I determined to avoid her in the future—which might not be easy, since she was obviously going with us.

CHAPTER THIRTY-SIX

RIX LEFT a sizable force to garrison Gergovia, but still we set out for the land of the Aedui with almost thirty-five thousand men, including his Arvernian warriors and the new recruits from the southern tribes. A great train of baggage wagons followed us, though they made no effort to keep up with the cavalry.

Onuava rode in one of those wagons. As I would learn later, she had even persuaded some of the other warriors' wives to accompany her.

Hanesa was also with us. Having lost the battle with Onuava, I had argued for him and won. If we had room in the wagons for the king's wife we surely had room for his personal praise singer.

No sooner did we enter Aeduan territory, than it became obvious how much the situation had changed. Signs of Romanization were stripped away. On every side we saw burned and looted houses with triumphant Gaulish standards fluttering above the ruins. Each face that greeted us was a Celtic face. If there were still any Roman traders or officials in the territory, they were in hiding.

When we camped at night I no longer shared a tent with Hanesa,

405

who was too far behind. I shared quarters instead with Cotuatus, who knew better than to question my frequent visits to the command tent.

Actually there was no advice I had to give Rix. He knew where he was going and exactly what he intended to accomplish. I simply sought him out as my soul friend—and because his was the force that drove us all.

Litaviccus himself met us before the gates of Bibracte. Leaving the warlords to discuss war, I withdrew to the sacred grove of the Aedui, site of the largest druidic school in all of Gaul. Its use had declined with the waxing influence of Rome, but young people were flocking there again to be taught and inspired, to establish links with the Source.

Whatever that might be.

The Aeduan druids were effusive in their welcome. With the coming of Caesar they had been facing the extinction of the Order, and now they wanted to credit me with having saved druidry. I urged them not to assume the battle for Gaulish freedom was won, however. "We are going to need every bit of wisdom and magic and force we can summon," I told them, "and even then it may not be enough. Caesar cannot afford to lose Gaul. His reputation back in the lands of Latium would be destroyed, to say nothing of his personal fortune. He will fight us as no enemy has fought before, and I want to be able to put the total strength of the Order at Vercingetorix's disposal."

Mindful of the magic of confidence, I did not reveal my secret fear—that a wisdom beyond my understanding had already decreed change for Gaul.

I told no one of the vision I had had in the grove of the Carnutes.

We must fight. We had to fight. What else could we do? We were a race of warriors.

We were too contentious, in fact. When I returned to the stronghold of Bibracte, a bitter quarrel had broken out. Vercingetorix had demanded to be put in charge of the combined tribal armies of Gaul, and the princes of the Aedui had balked, summoning the old arguments we had heard from Ollovico and so many others.

As I passed through the main gateway, I could hear the shouting coming from the assembly house, though it was almost in the center of the town. Soon Rix came striding toward me, white-lipped with anger.

"I've given Gaius Caesar his first major defeat," he snarled, "yet those woodenheads in there refuse to entrust me with command of the army. Of the army *I* inspired and created! They say I want to usurp their power in their own tribe!"

I fell into step beside him. "Other kings have had the same fear, but we convinced them, remember? And there is no believer as devout as the recently converted. Why not summon them here and let them persuade the Aeduans? They've given their warriors into your charge, yet they still control their own tribes; they would make the most persuasive argument on your behalf. Every one of them is no doubt very happy with you right now, after the triumph at Gergovia."

"Hmmm." Rix paced on beside me, but I could feel him cooling and relaxing. I was aware of this when he turned his head to glance at a handsome Aeduan woman, smiling at him from her doorway. He was ready to listen to reason; the deafness of anger had passed.

I repeated my suggestion and he nodded. "Yes, we can do that. And have them bring more warriors with them at the same time. That will make us even better prepared when the time comes to march against Caesar."

He sent out messengers recruited from the Arvernian cavalry, riding our swiftest horses. In response to his summons the most powerful men in Gaul came to us, except for the leaders of the Remi and the Lingones. The Remi were too thoroughly cowed by Caesar to want anything to do with the confederacy, and the Romans had too many men encamped in the land of the Lingones for that tribe to risk involving itself with us. Also absent were the Treveri, who were simply too far away—and the Nervii, upon whom Caesar had practiced almost total genocide.

When the tribal leaders had assembled at Bibracte, Rix gave them time to convince the Aeduans that he should be put in supreme command of the army—then requested that the issue be put to a vote.

In spite of pressure being brought to bear by their peers, the Aeduan princes continued to be stubborn. If Rix had been of any other tribe than the Arverni, they would have accepted him more easily, but the old animosity blinded them just as it had bothered him.

We had too much to lose; I did not mean to leave anything to chance. While they were preparing to take the vote, I was preparing to work magic.

Once a certain magic has proven itself it should be repeated with as little deviation in the ritual as possible. When Vercingetorix was elected king of the Arverni, I had been mating with Briga. I did not underestimate the power of sex magic. But Briga, unfortunately, was not available.

I saw the workings of the pattern in the fact that another woman with an intimate connection to Vercingetorix was available. But how could I ask Rix to let me use his wife in a druid ritual? I could not appeal to his self-interest, since he had no belief in magic.

I only hoped Onuava did not share his views.

Our wagons had long since reached Bibracte, adding their colorful confusion to the sprawling encampment around the base of the stronghold. It took me a while to find Onuava. Many claimed to have seen her but no one could remember just where.

I was beginning to grow desperate when one of the leather curtains screening the interior of a brightly painted wagon was pulled aside. Onuava looked out at me. "Ainvar! What brings you to this part of the camp?"

She sounded happy to see me, as if our recent battle were forgotten. She was in a strange land; every familiar face had become a cherished friend to her.

"I was looking for you, Onuava."

If she had been the sort of woman I originally thought she was, she might have smirked. Instead, she slitted her eyes at me, then drew the curtain farther aside and gestured at me to join her in the wagon. "If you want to talk to me, it's best to do it in here."

The interior of the wagon was a surprise. Designed for carrying baggage and supplies, the large four-wheeled cart had been converted into a home on wheels. Onuava had equipped herself with cushions and blankets and fur robes, with water jugs and wine amphorae, and even a little bronze brazier.

"If you light a fire in that," I remarked, "you'll burn down your wagon."

"I'm not going to light it in here, I'm no fool. I merely brought it in case the summer turns cold and wet, as it can in Gaul. And I brought my own supplies of dried meat and fruit and salt, in case you need any. I've thought of everything," she added smugly.

"I do have a need, but not for meat and fruit." Keeping my face impassive and my voice unemotional, I told her about sex magic.

Onuava gasped. "Are you saying that's how my husband was elected king?" I could see that she believed.

"I'm just telling you what happened. Now I want to repeat the ritual to assure he will be elected commander of the united armies of Gaul, because there is a chance the Aeduans may refuse to agree. I'm asking you to help me."

She made no reply. I could not even hear her breathing.

Perhaps, my head tardily suggested, Onuava does not want the Gauls to win. Perhaps she would prefer to ride in a Roman chariot, as Hanesa had suggested, and live in luxury in a Roman villa. You are no expert on women, my head reminded me, and this proud, sensual, savage female is like the Celtic women in the ancient legends, a law unto herself, as unsentimental as the earth.

"I'll help you," said Onuava abruptly.

She caught me off guard, while I was still thinking. "Ah . . . good. Good! That's good! But . . ."

"Yes?"

"We need not discuss this with your husband. He likes to believe he wins without any help from the Otherworld."

"Ah yes, Ainvar, I understand," she said, and I heard laughter hidden in her voice. "I understand very well."

I hoped I was not making another mistake.

The warlords of Gaul gathered in the assembly house of Bibracte; they were a band of tall and powerful warriors, each the symbol of manhood to his tribe. When all was in readiness, Cotuatus of the Carnutes demanded silence and announced that the matter of selecting a commander for their combined forces was now to be put to the vote.

While the vote was being taken, I was in the sacred grove of the Aedui with the wife of Vercingetorix.

No woman is like any other, though some share a blandness that makes them forgettable. Onuava was not forgettable. She threw herself into the ritual with such enthusiasm I had to restrain her; she was threatening to invade parts of my spirit reserved for Briga alone.

"Do you like this?" she kept asking. "Shall I put my hand here? Ah yes, rub me like that! Ah yes! And when I do this, how does it make you feel?"

Onuava was certainly not forgettable. Together we succeeded in making sex magic; when magic works, you know. We mated with a scorching joy. Joy is a force, an energy, a power. Joy soars.

At the peak of our soaring, Vercingetorix was elected commander in chief of the army of Gaul.

When the ritual in the grove was concluded, Onuava and I departed by separate paths. I hurried back to the fort to take part in the celebrations honoring Rix and the victory to come. Onuava slipped quietly back to her wagon, where she waited until when Rix sent a messenger to ask her to join us.

I sat on one side of him and she sat on the other as the Gauls cheered their chosen leader until the sky rang with the name "Vercingetorix!"

"Was the vote unanimous?" I asked Cotuatus later.

"Litaviccus was with us from the beginning, but those two princes who had been with the supposedly massacred cavalry held out almost until the end. Then they suddenly changed their minds and voted for Vercingetorix. And almost immediately afterward changed their minds again, but by then it was too late, fortunately, and he had been acclaimed as commander."

"Are they and their followers with us, though?"

"They are. Though I don't like the idea of fighting beside grudging men."

"You won't be," I assured him. "As always, the Aeduans will fight beside the Aeduans and the Carnutians beside the Carnutians. We may be one army now, but even Vercingetorix cannot make us one tribe." Which proves how wrong my prophecies could be.

His command confirmed, Rix acted with such speed I knew he had made his plans well in advance. He assembled a cavalry of fifteen thousand strong to be the principal attack force of the army. He personally examined the weaponry and supplies of the tens of thousands of foot warriors who would support them. He demanded noble hostages from several clans whose loyalty was still in question. He delivered a stirring speech in which he urged the army to be willing to burn its own towns rather than have them fall into Roman hands. I could not have spoken better myself on the importance of sacrifice.

Most of that speech was my own creation, actually.

Several times each day, messages from distant patrols reached the command tent, keeping Rix informed of Caesar's every move.

"Caesar has realized that we are superior in cavalry," Rix told me. "Our fifteen thousand horsemen are making him nervous. He has sent for German horsemen from across the Rhine, but because their animals are scrubby forest ponies, he is mounting them on quality animals taken away from his own officers so best horse and best rider will be together."

"I shouldn't think his officers like the plan," I remarked.

"If I tried that with the Gauls, they'd revolt. How *does* Caesar hold his men?"

"Fear. And respect."

"And love," said Vercingetorix, his hooded eyes brooding. "They must love him, too."

"Your men love you."

"Some of them, Ainvar. Only some of them. The ones who haven't been recent enemies."

At dawn the next day the war trumpets sounded and Rix addressed the army before the gates of Bibracte, a vast mass of men. In spite of Rix's deep voice and powerful lungs, only the foremost ranks could hear him, but they passed the word back quickly. "Caesar is on the march! He's taken his legions out of camp and is headed for the borderlands of the Lingones. He means to try to get back to the Province where he can get more reinforcements, but we won't allow him. We shall march at once to head him off and finally crush him!"

Making my way through the swirling frenzy of breaking camp, I got to Rix just as he was leaving the command tent. "Was there any news of what Caesar has done with the captives of Gaul?"

He stared past me; the captives were not uppermost in his thoughts. "Taken them with him, I suppose. You there!" he shouted abruptly, "Bring my black horse!"

Rix had the army under way very early in the day; Caesar could have done no better. There was no opportunity for me to visit the grove, commune with the Otherworld, examine the signs and portents at my leisure. Almost before I knew it, I was on a horse, galloping along in the dust raised by Vercingetorix, and all around me were the warriors of free Gaul, clashing their weapons against their shields and singing war songs to heat their blood.

When we topped the first rise I looked back. The earth that had hosted the army was scarred and trampled, blackened by campfires, disfigured by forests of jagged stumps where trees had been felled to feed those fires. Once green fields had rolled to meet the sky; now there were only quagmires of mud and manure and piles of rubbish.

The sight reminded me of the damage done by the migration of the Helvetians at the beginning of the Roman war in Gaul. No tribe had wanted the Helvetii to cross their land for fear of the same sort of destruction I was seeing; some had sent for Caesar to prevent it. Now the army of Gaul was ravaging the land it meant to save from Caesar.

The pattern of war, I mused.

I kicked my horse and galloped after Vercingetorix. Several times that first day I thought of turning back to see if Onuava was following with the baggage wagons, but my head chided me for such foolishness. She can take care of herself, and will, it reminded me.

But I could not quite forget her. We had worked magic together; she had become a presence in my mind.

We had not been many days on the march before our scouts reported the Romans were ahead. Rix ordered us to encamp near a river, then he walked among his warriors as they prepared their evening meal. In the twilight I caught glimpses of his golden hair gleaming amid a throng of his favorites, the cavalry, and heard them cheer him, heard them shout with laughter at some jest he made.

Wherever he went that night, Rix scattered confidence like seed broadcast. His men fell asleep anticipating victory.

According to the scouts, Caesar now had eleven legions with him. We had almost twice as many men. Later I would learn that Caesar had claimed still larger numbers for us, inflating the Gaulish army to impossible proportions to make any successes of his seem greater and any defeats more forgivable. Before the conflict was over, he would claim we had outnumbered him by more than four to one. Beware the Roman version of history.

That night in my tent I did not dream of victory, but of the Two-Faced One, with Caesar's face on one side and a Germanic visage on the other—glaring, terrifying. I awoke in a sweat, slipped from the tent without disturbing Cotuatus, and made my way through a felled forest of sleeping warriors to find Rix.

He was also awake, standing outside his tent and staring into the night. He did not even turn around as I approached. "Ainvar," he said, knowing it was.

"Have you told your men they will probably face Germanic horsemen tomorrow?"

"No, why should I? It doesn't matter who we face. We're going to win. That's all they need to know or think about. We're going to win."

"The southern and western tribes have never fought the Germans, Rix. They won't be prepared for their ferocity, they may panic."

"They'll be more likely to panic if we warn them in advance and give them time to frighten themselves with their own imaginings. No, Ainvar—the Germans may present a terrifying spectacle, but the odds are on our side now, and I have faith in our men."

Faith in men.

I returned to my tent and thought about my dream. The Goban Saor was back with the wagons, with one wagon in particular. I wished the baggage train had caught up with us, but unfortunately it was at least a half day behind.

While I was singing the song for the sun next morning, Rix was dividing our cavalry into three sections. Two sections were sent to attack the Roman flanks. The third rode ahead to block the Roman column's advance.

Sitting on my horse atop a nearby hill, I had a clear view of the action. The Roman column formed itself into a huge hollow square with baggage wagons in the center. I was not close enough to tell if any of the mass of people with the Romans were Gaulish prisoners, but they might be.

They might be.

There might be a tiny captive girl child in any of those covered wagons. If so, she had not been awakened by the song for the sun, but by the sonorous voice of the battle trumpet summoning men to slaughter.

I could almost feel her terror.

What price would my beautiful, perfect child bring on a Roman auction block?

Bile flooded my mouth.

Opposite the hill was a long, steep ridge. As I watched, a wave of horsemen crested the ridge and swept down into the valley below, behind our cavalry. Unearthly, savage screams carried clearly in the morning air as Caesar's German horsemen fell upon our men and began cutting them to pieces.

The Germans fought without style or grace, but with a deadly dedication to killing. The startled Gauls held their ground as long as they could, but then their nerve broke and they fled the savage horde. The Germans pursued them, roaring like wild beasts and killing every man they caught in the bloodiest possible way.

Meanwhile, Caesar's legionaries were peeling away from the outer edges of the hollow square in disturbingly precise order, making ready to follow up the attack.

Our horsemen, afraid of being surrounded, scattered in all directions.

The rout was complete. Vercingetorix on his black horse raced back and forth, trying to hold his men, trying to turn them, shouting defiance at the Germans and orders to his cavalry, making a desperate effort to rally them lest they keep riding all the way back to their tribelands. When it was obvious nothing would induce his men to turn and face the Germans, Rix surrendered to the inevitable and herded them back toward our former campsite on the river.

He was too far away for me to see his face, but anger was implicit in every line of his body.

We had lost perhaps a quarter of our cavalry, either to the Germans or to their own terror, and the rest were badly demoralized. They had seen the Germans hack the flesh off living men for the sheer pleasure of it and deliberately trample the wounded beneath their horses' hooves. They had seen a face of war that was neither stylized nor heroic, but merely brutal, an expression of the darkest recesses of the human spirit.

Vercingetorix ordered the tribal princes to assemble their warriors, and made a valiant speech praising them, attempting to soothe their fears, promising them a victory that would more than offset the loss. Yet all the time I saw the men glancing nervously first to one side and then to the other, as if they expected the Germans to come leaping out at them from the bushes.

Rix called the tribal leaders aside for a hurried conference. He did not beckon to me, but I walked over and stood quietly at the fringes, listening. "We have lost too many men," he said bitterly. "The cavalry are our principal attack force, or were, and they're all but shattered. We cannot afford to be caught in the open like that again until we've recovered ourselves.

"We are not very far from Alesia, the stronghold of the Mandubii." He turned to Litaviccus. "The Mandubians are old allies of the Aeduans, I believe?"

Litaviccus nodded.

"Then I ask you to ride ahead and tell them the army of Gaul is on its way to them. We shall use Alesia for a base the way we used Gergovia. With strong walls to rely on, our men will find their courage again and we shall hand Caesar a defeat to make the one he suffered at Gergovia look no worse than a skinned knee."

He spoke with all that vibrant confidence they had come to expect of him. As calmly as if nothing had gone wrong, Vercingetorix gathered his men, issued his orders, and soon had the army under way. To a casual observer it might have appeared we were an attack force. But I saw the fear and doubt carved deep in the faces of those who had survived the German onslaught.

And I saw in Rix's eyes the shadows he tried to keep hidden.

Men were dispatched to meet our wagons and provide them safe escort to Alesia, as well as to watch our rear for signs of Roman pursuit. There was no doubt Caesar would be after us all too soon.

As we set off, I moved up to ride beside Rix for a time. He knew I was there but said nothing to me. My presence reminded him that he had been wrong about our men's preparedness to face the Germans, and Rix did not like to be reminded of his mistakes.

But how else can we learn?

I edged my horse closer to the rangy brown horse he was riding. An aide was leading his black stallion, to keep it fresh for use in battle if needed. A hot summer sun was beaming down on us. The air was filled with dust and the smell of horse sweat. We rode to a music of jingling bits and creaking leather and rhythmic hooves. We were moving at a brisk pace, but Rix held it steady; he did not want the men to feel as if they were running away in panic.

"We weren't overcome by the enemy, but by our own fear," I told Rix in a conversational tone, keeping my eyes on the way ahead. "Caesar relied on the effect the Germans would have on us. They weren't any better than our men. Just more terrifying."

"My cavalry ran away. They *ran away*, Ainvar." Rix's voice sounded as if he were speaking from the bottom of a well. "I had made them my favorites; they had the best food, the best weapons, the choice horses taken from all the tribes. And they ran away. I could not hold them." His words were hollow with loathing and despair.

Vercingetorix had been as shocked as anyone else by what had happened, I realized. But because he was commander, he had to conceal it—except to his soul friend.

"They're only human, Rix," I said consolingly. "And it was the southerners and westerners who broke first. The Senones and the others of central Gaul faced up to the Germans."

"As long as they could, yes. But when hundreds of other horses started to run, they could not control their own indefinitely. The panic was like a brushfire, wasn't it? It has scorched everyone. I've watched the men; the foot warriors have caught fear from the cavalry. They're all afraid now. That's why I'm taking them to Alesia. We have to be in a position where we can win the next battle . . . or I'm afraid we'll lose the army of Gaul."

I had never heard him sound so bitter.

CHAPTER THIRTY-SEVEN

ALESIA OCCUPIED an extensive lozenge-shaped plateau protected by rivers on both sides, with steep hills to the north and south. Rix had chosen well. The actual stronghold was only of middle size, but stood on a height so imposing it was impregnable to every form of assault but blockade. As soon as we arrived, Rix ordered the army to set up camp on the slopes outside the walls and fortify its position with ditches and additional walls.

Litaviccus gave us a formal welcome at the gates of the town. I entered with Rix and the princes of Gaul; the Mandubian townspeople pressed forward from every side to offer us wine and food and victors' wreaths—"for saving us from the Romans," they said.

Rix refused the wreaths. "Offer them again when we have defeated Caesar," he said loudly.

He was given the hospitality of the king's lodge, but slept instead in his own tent with the army. And within another day, Caesar reached Alesia.

The Roman had wasted no time in following us. Expecting this,

Rix made every effort to present an unassailable face to Caesar when he arrived.

As Caesar, wearing his scarlet cloak, came galloping over the plain, the stronghold of Alesia must have looked daunting even to him.

To my relief, our wagons arrived shortly before the Romans. The Goban Saor came to my tent. I greeted him with a Celtic hug. "The wagons came up very fast. You must have thrown out everything you could spare for more speed."

"We did. Casks, boxes, anything heavy and dispensable."

"But not . . . ?"

The Goban Saor smiled at my anxiety. "Not that, no. It's still in my wagon. When I told people it belonged to the chief druid, no one touched it. If you'll help me unload it we can bring it into the tent now, if you like—but I still don't see how you can mean to use it."

"To work magic," I said simply.

The Goban Saor went off with Rix to examine the fortifications, and Cotuatus left to spend the day with the Carnutian warriors, who were repairing battle damage and making excuses to each other for the recent debacle. When they had gone I uncovered the object in the center of the tent.

I was alone with the Two-Faced One.

Once Celtic warriors had taken the heads of their most worthy adversaries to mount in places of honor as battle trophies, to impress their friends and intimidate their enemies. The custom had died out in recent generations, but members of the warrior nobility still observed the tradition symbolically by having trophy heads carved in wood or stone and mounted around their strongholds. In my travels through Gaul I had seen numerous examples of these.

The figure the Goban Saor had long ago carved for me as a gift for Menua was not a trophy head. The years had not diminished its impact. To look upon the Two-Faced One was to feel the cold breath of the Otherworld on my neck.

I sat down cross-legged on the ground to contemplate the image. Outside, the sounds of distant trumpets and shouting warned that our patrols had seen the Romans approaching; they were still far away but drawing nearer. Men began to run, dig in, prepare, watch, worry. But nothing would happen the first day, I knew.

Caesar would draw up his forces before Alesia and consider the
situation, set up a camp, make his preparations. The two great
armies would stare at each other with cold assessment for a time,
each looking for an advantage.

I stared at the image of the Two-Faced One.

The sun striking the leather walls of the tent imparted an ocher
glow to the surroundings. In that light the pale gray stone could
have been mistaken for flesh. It took little imagination to discover
awareness lurking in those blank eyes, to see those nostrils flare
with breath. So great was the artistry of the Goban Saor that he
had actually captured life, a disturbing, fearsome form of life, in
the stone. It crouched there, waiting.

Fearsome.

Fear is a tool of magic.

Once Menua believed I could strike the spark of life. Once I
had tried, for Tarvos's sake.

This was different. Life had not fled but was here, imprisoned
through the magic of the artisan. It only required another, greater
magic to bring it to the surface.

I closed my eyes and concentrated. With invisible fingers I
groped outward, seeking the limits of my power. I drew the Otherworld around me like a hooded robe until I could feel it, smell
it, taste it. I sank deeper, my lips forming the most potent words
I knew, the names of the gods of the abyss, the lords of night and
storm and the spaces between the stars, the darkest aspects of the
Source.

A cold tingling invaded my fingertips.

Without opening my eyes, I reached out and rested my fingers
on the surface of the carved image.

Sensation ran up my arms as if I had thrust my hands into a
raging fire.

It took all my willpower to keep from snatching my hands away
from the stone. Then I heard the voices. The deep and distant
voices of druids chanting, otherwhen, in the great grove of the
Carnutes.

"You will enter the light but never suffer the flame," they reminded me.

I opened my eyes.

* * *

By the time the Goban Saor returned to the tent, an oxhide painted with druidic symbols once more covered the Two-Faced One. The craftsman slanted a look at it, then led me outside to watch him draw various plans in the dirt with a spearhead, explaining the advantages of each and telling me which ones Rix had approved.

"If we erect a line of stakes just inside the perimeter walls of our encampment and then . . . you aren't listening, Ainvar."

"I am," I said hastily.

I pulled my thoughts away from the Two-Faced One and bent over to study the Goban Saor's latest design.

While we were making our arrangements, Caesar was making his. He deployed his legions in a huge irregular circuit around Alesia, erecting twenty-three small redoubts at various points from which observers could watch for activity among the Gauls. Under cover of night, he had his men start digging trenches and erecting palisades we did not discover until daylight.

Rix took the cavalry out on frequent sallies in an attempt to destroy these constructions, but each time he was repulsed. "My men aren't fighting as hard as they should," he told me grimly. "They advance on the enemy as if they expect something terrible to happen at any moment."

"They do," I said. "Caesar has clouded their minds with fear. Fear is a powerful magic, Rix. If you'll let me, I could undertake a ritual to counter . . ."

"My men don't need magic to make them fight! They need inspiration, and that is something *I* can give them!"

He gathered the warriors and made brave, exhortatory speeches that had them cheering and beating on their shields with spears. As long as they could hear his voice ringing in their ears, they were willing to face any danger. But he could not defeat Caesar with speeches alone. The time came when he must lead the men against the Romans, and when that happened and the Gauls heard Roman war trumpets and German battle cries, they seemed to shrink inside themselves.

When men who were once confident of winning have lost badly instead, something inside them is broken.

Using legionaries as ditchers and carpenters and engineers, Caesar continued inexorably to strengthen his position. Soon there were two lines of earthworks encircling Alesia, each composed of ditches and ramparts and banks and various traps of his devising. The inner earthwork was meant to keep us penned inside the town, while the outer one was obviously intended to deflect any reinforcements who might come to our aid.

Observing these constructions from the palisade of the stronghold, the Goban Saor was mightily impressed with their ingenuity. It seemed impossible that such a huge undertaking could have been done in so short a time by the Roman army, but it had.

Rix was furious. "Fifty thousand Romans cannot hold eighty thousand Gauls!"

But they could.

And in repeated engagements, we were learning at a great cost of blood that our warriors were no match for Caesar's men in the open. The Gauls attacked as they always had, wildly, haphazardly, heroically, each searching out an opponent who looked capable of testing his courage and giving him an honorable triumph, each fighting according to the dictates of his own inner nature.

The Romans, on the other hand, moved in precise formations according to one overriding design, and through a variety of long-practiced maneuvers trapped our warriors and cut them down.

In our tent at night after a particular disastrous battle, Cotuatus rolled his eyes at the covered image. "Are you going to work your magic now, Ainvar, and shrivel Caesar's army?"

"Even the Order of the Wise does not possess a magic strong enough to destroy so many men at once," I said. "It would be easier to roll the sea aside."

"But you must be planning to do something very powerful," interposed the Goban Saor, "or you would not have had me bring *that* so far." He nodded toward the covered image. "You have to tell us what you're going to do, Ainvar, we need to know."

I frowned. "Magic is weakened if you give it away beforehand."

"But—"

"Don't argue with him," Cotuatus interrupted. "Never, ever, argue with the Keeper of the Grove!"

The Goban Saor fell silent. I cast an approving nod at the new king of the Carnutes. Cotuatus had learned his lesson well.

Perhaps I should have sought to develop the same sort of control over Rix. But I doubt if I could have done so. Cotuatus believed in magic. Vercingetorix did not.

As Caesar's grip tightened, Rix made another attempt to

strengthen the cavalry, exhorting them to overcome once and for all the memory of their recent disgrace by crushing Caesar's horsemen in an engagement on the plain. I watched the battle from the walls of the stronghold.

It was a long and hard-fought fight. Sometimes it looked as if we might win. Rix led one brilliant, fearless charge after another and the Roman horsemen fell back. Then Caesar sent his Germans against us once more and once more the Gauls panicked and fled.

In despair, I turned away from the sight. I looked down to discover Onuava at the foot of the palisade, gazing up at me, shading her hand with her eyes. "What's happening, Ainvar?"

"We're losing. Our men are running away from Caesar's."

"They can't! They must not! Not the *Gauls!*" She stared at me fixedly for a heartbeat, then spun away and ran toward the king's lodge in the center of the stronghold. I lost sight of her in the milling crowd. Alesia was filled not only with the usual townspeople and members of the army, but also with the inhabitants of the surrounding countryside, driven by war to seek protection within its walls. The cleverest hound could not get from one side of Alesia to the other without being stepped upon.

I saw Onuava again soon enough. A side gate opened and a chariot emerged, the battered war cart of the king of the Mandubii. He was not in it, however. An Arvernian warrior held the reins, and beside him rode the wife of Vercingetorix.

Onuava was screaming and brandishing a sword. Her unbound hair streamed behind her like a tawny flag. Following her ran two-score women, warriors' wives, also screaming, also brandishing weapons. Like Onuava's, their faces were distorted with fury.

They were an awesome sight. When the women collided with the retreating warriors, many of the men stopped, turned, and went back with them to face the Germans once more. The battle resumed on a new level of savagery. I saw Gaulish women hurl themselves on the fiercest German horsemen and drag them from their animals to attack them with teeth and nails and fists and feet as well as knives. As an assault force, our women were more frightening than anything Caesar could send against us. It was a pity we did not have more of them. Led by the formidable Onuava, they displayed an awesome talent for survival against overwhelming odds.

Meanwhile, Caesar had drawn up his legions below our encampment to keep our foot warriors from going to the aid of Vercingetorix and the cavalry. Reassured by this, his own cavalry, including the Germans, redoubled their efforts and began relentlessly driving our people back toward Alesia.

We had too many untrained warriors. They got in each other's way as they attempted to retreat. The Germans pursued them all the way to the camp's fortifications, where many of our cavalry abandoned their horses so they could scramble over the walls to safety inside. The Germans caught many more; there was a terrible slaughter.

Caesar then ordered his legions to move forward. The sentries on the walls of Alesia interpreted this as a signal to storm the fort. They began shouting warnings, causing panic within the stronghold. I tried to reassure people by doing some yelling myself. "Caesar is no fool, he won't try to storm the fortress! He knows it would be futile! You are safe here, be calm, don't do anything foolish!"

But the frantic populace began opening the gates, begging our warriors outside to come in and protect them. A great crush took place in the gateways, injuring many.

Rix came riding toward the confusion on his black horse, yelling at the sentries to close and bar the gates of the fort so the warriors could not leave the camp deserted.

Once the stronghold was secured, Rix managed to rally his forces for a successful defense of their camp. Eventually the enemy withdrew, having killed a great number of our men and captured many of our horses.

I left the fort to join Rix in the camp. Onuava and a score of surviving female followers were already there. They had announced their intention of staying with the warriors, eating with them, sleeping with them, and no one had argued.

I think no one dared.

I met Onuava leaving the command tent as I was going in. Her face was filthy, she had a huge lump on her jaw and a purple swelling around a half-closed eye, and her arms were mottled with bruises. "I am going to ride back to Gergovia with the victor when he goes," she told me proudly. "With Vercingetorix!" Her head was high; her eyes were fierce.

I bowed my head in respect and went into the tent. Hanesa and I had both misjudged the woman.

Rix looked haggard. There was dried blood on a torn strip of cloth wrapped around his arm—not his sword arm, fortunately. He greeted me, saying, "We've lost too many warriors, Ainvar. Tonight I'm sending what's left of our cavalry to try to slip through the Roman lines and ride back to their own tribes to raise reinforcements.

"I want every person in free Gaul who is capable of wielding a pitchfork or throwing a stone to come to Alesia and stand with us, to fight with us for their freedom."

"There isn't enough food," I said sadly. "The grain supplies won't last thirty days as it is, never mind being stretched enough to feed more people. Caesar has us blockaded. And any additional mouth we attempt to feed will just lessen the length of time we can withstand a siege."

His eyes were sunk in sockets hollowed by fatigue. It was the first time I had ever seen Rix look exhausted. "Do you think I don't realize that, Ainvar? But what else can I do? This is the last chance we'll have to fight for Gaul. Do you know what will happen if Caesar wins? The Nervii could tell you. When he defeated them, only three of their elders were left alive, and out of all their warriors, tens of thousands, only five hundred lived. And they were sold for slaves.

"When the Eburones rose against him he invited all the neighboring tribes to come in and plunder and pillage them, and destroy 'their accursed race,' as he called it. And when his warriors captured Uxellodunum, they cut off the hands of all the defenders and sent them out into the countryside to be a warning to other Gauls not to resist the Romans.

"Can I let that happen to your tribe or mine, Ainvar? Or to any of those people out there who believe in me and in the idea of a confederacy of the Gauls? Caesar means to take all this land, settle it with his own people, and put those of us who survive into bondage forever.

"As for me," he added, staring down at his huge and battle-scarred hands, "I have no doubt he would thoroughly enjoy torturing me to death."

His voice was so calm, so uninflected, I had to ask, "Does that prospect frighten you?"

He met my eyes. "Nothing frightens me but losing," he said.

I recalled a conversation I had had long ago with Tarvos the

Bull. Men who are born to be warriors love to win, but they cannot bear to lose.

Gaius Julius Caesar could not bear to lose.

Vercingetorix took the grain supplies of Alesia under his personal control, measuring them out judiciously so they would last as long as possible. He also took charge of the Mandubian cattle to feed his own warriors. And as Caesar continued to build siegeworks nearer and nearer the stronghold, Rix began moving the army to safety within its walls.

If Alesia had been crowded before, it was impossible now.

Some of the princes came to him to complain about his sending for reinforcements. Like myself, they foresaw food shortages, and each was concerned about his own tribesmen. "You are too short-sighted," Vercingetorix told them. "Can you not withstand a little privation in order to have ultimate victory? It seems easier to get men to die willingly than to suffer discomfort willingly!

"But there is good news. We have just received a message that a great force of Gauls is gathering in the land of the Aedui in response to my summons, and will soon be coming to relieve us. So tell your people to hold out just a little longer. When the reinforcements arrive we shall trap Caesar and his army between us and them and it will all be over. We'll make a victory feast of the Roman supplies!"

Afterward, I asked Rix privately, "Is it true?"

"So I am told. I just hope they come quickly."

I longed to go to a grove and invoke the Otherworld. But at Alesia, as at Gergovia, the tribal grove was at some distance from the fort, and the Roman lines lay between. So I must content myself with finding links with nature's pattern within the walls of Alesia, amid throngs of anxious, frightened people, where the clamor of voices continued night and day and a druid could find no quiet place in which to listen for the Source.

I did my best. But I knew in my heart it was not enough. I began longing for silence as the others were longing for more food. There were too many people around me and my spirit cried out for the trees!

"Take care of the grove, Aberth," I sent out my whisper on the wind.

The day came when the relief force was to arrive, but there was no word of it. Caesar had closed his lines so tightly no message could get through. We could not even learn if the reinforcements had actually left the land of the Aedui.

Despair gripped the besieged Gauls. The grain in the storehouses was gone. Children were crying and rubbing their empty bellies. Women were white-faced and bitter-tongued, men were gaunt. Rix ordered the few remaining horses to be slaughtered and distributed for food, but this was not enough to feed even a portion of the eighty thousand people packed into Alesia.

Rix did not kill his black stallion. It was not to be a total sacrifice.

We were all hungry. Hunger can clarify the mind in strange ways. One morning I climbed onto the palisade to sing the song for the sun, and happened to notice a parade of geese beyond the walls, making its way to the river.

How the geese had survived being seized either by us or by Roman foraging parties I could not imagine. Yet there they were, as unconcerned as if there were no such thing as danger. The adults waddled along fat with self-importance, followed by a single file of half-grown goslings, which must have hatched unusually late in the season. The trip to the river was the major event of their day. Man and war meant nothing to them.

One word from me would have summoned a score of archers, and a fortunate few would have feasted on goose. But I did not shout. I stood silently watching, cherishing the sunlit vision of a reality isolated from what was happening at Alesia.

Yes. Reality was that line of geese. Adults leading their young into the future.

When they had passed from my sight, I heard my voice say dreamily, "Menua, when we are gone and forgotten, geese must continue to parade to the river on bright summer mornings."

A nearby sentry in his watchtower turned to stare at me as if I were mad. Perhaps I was. Perhaps we were all a little mad by then.

But I was thankful he had not noticed the geese.

When human excrement had become ankle-deep between the lodges and people were picking lice from each other's heads for food, the relief force at last arrived.

CHAPTER THIRTY-EIGHT

THE NIGHT before, a vote had been taken to send the old, the enfeebled, and the children away from Alesia. Some of the Mandubians had already slipped away, approaching the Roman lines and begging for food. But the Romans had turned them away. To save the remaining youngsters, it was resolved to find some stratagem to get them past Caesar's army, and various suggestions were put forth, but none seemed likely to succeed.

Several times I had opened my mouth to speak. Several times intuition had whispered to me, Wait. Wait.

When trumpets and shouts told us the relief force had arrived, I was thankful I had waited. The children of Alesia would see freedom won for all the children of Gaul.

For my daughter.

Everyone who could scrambled up onto the walls to watch the forthcoming battle. My hooded robe assured me of being ceded a good vantage point from which I could just make out the distant dark mass of the approaching Gauls coming up behind Caesar.

They occupied a hill beyond the Roman encampment and filled the plain with cavalry and foot warriors.

Inside the besieged fort, the people gave way to hysterical relief. I wanted to shout with joy also, but once again the voice whispered to me, Wait. Wait.

Mounted on his black horse, Vercingetorix led our warriors out of the stronghold and positioned them in front of the walls.

Caesar posted foot soldiers along both lines of his fortifications, one line facing inward toward us, the other facing outward toward the relief force.

The image of the Two-Faced One leaped into my head.

The Gauls attacked the Romans.

The newcomers had many archers, as well as a great number of foot warriors, so many that at first the Romans were overcome by the sheer size of the opposition. The battle was fought in full view of everyone on the walls of Alesia, which seemed to encourage men on both sides to show exceptional valor and determination. The fighting lasted from midday to almost sundeath, with neither side gaining a victory.

The inner line of Roman fortifications held, denying Rix the opportunity of joining the battle. I could see him just below me, riding back and forth in a frenzy of frustration, shouting encouragement to his allies.

The spectators on the wall were shouting, too, with such violence that in time the voices of Alesia were reduced to one great, hoarse whisper. Someone pounded me on the arm. I turned to find Hanesa beside me. "We're winning, we're winning," he rasped through a ravaged throat.

We were, for a time, and then the Romans were winning, and then our side seemed dominant again. The momentum shifted back and forth.

And then we saw a column of German cavalry sweep out from the Roman camp and hurl itself like a spear at our relief force.

Most of them were raw recruits. Many were farmers and herders who had abandoned their fields and their animals to answer the summons of Vercingetorix. They were not trained warriors, and they had never imagined facing men who appeared to be homicidal maniacs.

They broke and ran. A company of Germans surrounded many

of the archers and killed them very bloodily. The legions came up then and drove the confused and demoralized Gauls back to their most recent campsite on the horizon.

Looking down, I saw Rix slump on his horse. Then he gave the signal for the gates of Alesia to be opened, and he led our men back inside.

During the next day, the relief force in its camp quietly prepared wattles, ladders, and grappling hooks. In the darkest part of the night they crept forward and began throwing the wattles into the Roman trenches and storming the Roman line with ladders and hooks, at the same time shouting to Rix and his men to assault the Romans from the other side.

Chaos erupted within Alesia.

I cannot say how many warriors had been asleep. Perhaps most of them, like myself, had been lying, eyes open, too anxious and too exhausted to rest. But at Rix's call the men were soon on their feet and snatching up their weapons. There was great confusion at the gates as too many of them tried to get through at the same time.

I climbed onto the palisade once more, though it was impossible to see anything. The night was moonless and the stars hid behind shredded clouds. Once I had loved the darkness. Now I was peering into it with burning eyes, trying to see what was not to be seen.

The relief force was attacking courageously at a number of points around the Roman perimeter, as we learned later, but it was not able to break through anywhere. Having anticipated just such an attempt, Caesar had his forces so deployed that no vulnerable area could be found. We heard screams and yells and the thud of stones being hurled by the wooden machines the Romans called *ballistae*, but no Gaulish shouts of triumph.

As for Rix and his men, it took them too long to organize. They never got near to breaking through the inner circle of fortifications before the relief force had withdrawn from the outer one. Once more the warriors returned to the fort, defeated.

I had longed for silence, but the silence that now descended upon Alesia raked my nerves. Some people were too hoarse to speak, others were too dispirited. Only the children could be heard, crying with fear. Their thin, drawn faces were very pale, their eyes were full of questions no one could answer.

Later we heard music coming from the Roman encampment. Caesar's legions were celebrating their success with tympanum and cithara and horn.

My people were not singing.

I kept looking at the children.

At the council of war that night, the silence continued. No one accused Vercingetorix of having brought this upon us by pursuing Caesar and forcing battle with him. No one suggested we should have left well enough alone after Gergovia. Rix had done what Caesar would have done: pursued a beaten enemy to consolidate the defeat.

We should not have attempted to use the Roman's pattern, I thought, sitting cross-legged on the earth and staring into the fire. But I did not say anything.

No one said anything. At last we all withdrew to spend a sleepless night wrapped in our cloaks.

Back in our tent, the Goban Saor asked me, "Are the princes angry with Vercingetorix, Ainvar?"

"No. They know he will pay the price for his ambition and his dream."

"We shall all pay it."

"We all shared the dream," I reminded my companion. "We all thought we could remain free."

One more day and one more battle remained. This time the relief force sent its best warriors to attack a Roman camp on a large hill north of Alesia, one so vast Caesar had not been able to include it in his protective circle. Two legions were encamped there; their loss would have been a serious blow to the Romans.

Vercingetorix once more led his men outside the walls to try to break out while the Romans were occupied with defending the hill and protecting their own line. By daylight we could see that they were spread thin. It looked as if we had a chance. By now, our allies would have had time to brace themselves for any German attack and would not be so badly surprised. We did not dare hope, but we began to hope.

The fighting became more intense than ever. Some of the Gauls had adopted the Roman device of holding linked shields over their heads, and under this cover they advanced upon the enemy. The air sang with a deadly horizontal rain of spears and javelins. Rix and his men attacked the inner circle with grim determination, realizing this was their last chance, their third attempt.

Three is a number of great power. Three is the number of fate.

Watching from the walls of Alesia, I did not realize I was holding my breath until I began to feel dizzy.

There was a shout as if some of our men might have broken through the Roman line. At the same moment I caught sight of a lone figure in a vivid scarlet cloak riding through the rain of missiles as if impervious to them, encouraging his Romans to greater efforts by his presence.

I turned my eyes from Caesar to search for Rix. At first I did not see him anywhere. Then a black horse bounded up out of a ditch with a leap that would have unseated most riders, and Gaius Caesar found himself face to face with Vercingetorix.

Both men must have been taken by surprise. They halted their horses not a spear's throw from one another. I was so far away I could only identify them by scarlet cloak and black horse, yet even at that distance I felt, for the second time, the impact of their personalities colliding.

"A battle of champions?" Hanesa murmured hopefully beside me.

"No. Compared to our leader, the Roman is an old man. Vercingetorix would never fight him, it wouldn't be honorable."

"Does Caesar understand that, Ainvar? If he does, he must know what an advantage it gives him. He could attack Vercingetorix right now and win the war, because if the Gauls saw him killed, they would collapse."

Hanesa was right, I realized, my scalp prickling with panic.

Menua had taught that magic should be undertaken only after the most careful deliberation, and in full awareness of the possible consequences. "Read the signs and portents first," he had often told me. "Be certain of how you will affect the future before you act."

But when I saw Rix with Caesar, my discipline deserted me.

Without pausing for thought, I laced my fingers in the strongest pattern of protection and began chanting the name of Vercingetorix. All the strength of my spirit went into the chant, leaping out, crossing the space between us, seeking to wrap safety like a net around my soul friend. As soon as he realized what I was doing, Hanesa joined in, adding his voice to mine.

Chanting in unison, we watched and waited, hardly daring to hope. The two commanders held their positions, perhaps talking. Then, abruptly, Caesar wheeled his horse around and cantered away, arrogantly turning his back on Vercingetorix.

Had my magic caused the Roman to stay his hand? I shall never know. Standing on the wall of Alesia that day, Hanesa and I wanted to believe we had just saved the life of Vercingetorix.

But if I had to do it again today, I would pray a very different prayer and use all my force to urge Caesar's sword to cut my soul friend in half as he sat on his horse.

With the wisdom of bitter experience I acknowledge: How kind is the sacrificer's gift!

The fighting intensified. The majority of the Gauls penned at Alesia had failed to break through; only a trickle had gone with Rix. Those who remained behind were turning their full attention on Caesar's siege machinery, scaling the wooden towers from which missiles were being hurled into the fort and pulling the Romans off with their bare hands.

From the heights of Alesia we could clearly observe Caesar; his cloak was unmistakable. He had collected four fresh cohorts and a large body of cavalry and was circling around to attack our relief force from the rear.

We all screamed warnings, but at such a distance no one could have heard them. In fact, a great shout went up from both sides, echoing from the walls of Alesia and all down the line of the Roman reinforcements, adding to the pandemonium. It was as if everyone knew that the critical time had come.

We watched helplessly as the Romans fell upon the Gauls, who were exhausted from having hurled themselves in wave after futile wave against the outer Roman fortifications. The Romans now threw their spears aside and attacked our men with swords, hewing and hacking. The earth was soaked with blood. She was given too much to drink and could not absorb it, so it stood in puddles and men slipped and fell to be bathed in gore.

When the men of the relief force tried to fall back, they found Caesar's cavalry behind them, cutting off any hope of escape. The Gauls were rounded up and slaughtered like cattle, though to their credit they fought as cattle never fight, and it cost Caesar dear to kill them.

But the men had come a long way at great speed to try to save us, and they were tired, the majority of them unused to war. The Romans had done nothing more strenuous recently than build up their fortifications and yell derision over their ramparts at us. The long siege of Alesia had given them a chance to rest. They outfought the Gauls, and we who watched could not help.

"We have lost," said Hanesa beside me, in a voice as heavy and lusterless as lead. No rhetoric, no flourishes. Simply, "We have lost."

I turned to look at him. Hunger had carved away his jolly, affable excess, leaving the flesh sagging on his bones as if he were wearing the skin of a much larger person. His high color had faded, his eyes were dull.

I knew I looked no better. Caesar had leached the life out of all of us.

Our vantage point was no vantage now, yet we remained on the walls in horrified fascination, seeing what we did not want to see. Out of all that great army that had come so valiantly to rescue us and keep Gaul free, only a few survived. The Romans were relentlessly pursuing those few. Some might find safety if they made it to camp. Some others might even get back to their tribes to tell of this day. But most were dead. Our last chance lay dead on the battle-scarred earth, in plain view of Alesia.

As twilight fell, I saw a scarlet cloak in the center of the battlefield, drawing my eye like a flame. From all sides his officers were converging on Caesar, bringing him the torn and bloody standards of the fallen Gaulish leaders.

Incredibly, Vercingetorix had survived. I looked down from the walls in time to see him, still on his black horse, ride in through the gates of the stronghold, bringing the surviving warriors back inside for the night.

There was nothing else to be done.

In the aftermath of defeat, men avoid each other's eyes. Rix would need me as never before.

The access ladders were crammed with people going up and down, anxious to get to the top of the wall, then anxious to get back down again, people shouting, people cursing, people crying. Ignoring the ladders, I flexed my knees and jumped.

The impact of landing jolted me so hard it took my breath away.

As I waited for my legs to recover from the shock, I remembered the night I had gone over the wall at the Fort of the Grove to see the druids work great magic.

Everything circles, including time. Even the straight lines and precise columns of the Roman armies could not change that natural law.

I went to wait for Rix in his tent.

He came alone. Once he would have been surrounded by princes and followers praising him, seeking his ear. Now no one wanted to know him. Yet he was the same golden young giant who had been our champion.

Only his eyes looked a thousand years old.

I had wondered what I would say to him. "I jumped off the wall a little while ago," my voice spoke up conversationally. "I was surprised to find I was still young enough to do it without breaking my neck."

"Ainvar."

"Yes."

"Are we still young?"

"Yes."

"Ah." He sat down heavily and began massaging his aching arms. Swinging a sword is exhausting work. I noticed new wounds and fresh blood.

"Have you seen my wife, Ainvar?"

"She's with the other women."

"We have to get them out of here, the women and children. Caesar will be merciless. He'll enslave the Mandubians, but he'll probably kill anyone he thinks has a connection with me."

"Onuava isn't afraid of dying."

"I know. But she's carrying a child of mine, Ainvar."

"Oh."

We sat silently for a time.

"I can get them out, I think," I said at last. "I have a magic I've been saving."

His voice was bitter. "All your druid magic could not win this war."

"No, it could not. Nor did you want to win by magic, even if it were possible. But the gifts of the druids are meant to be used constructively wherever possible, Rix. Killing thousands of Romans would be . . ."

He waved his hand wearily. "Must we have this conversation? I don't want to discuss magic. I just want to know if you can get the women and children out."

"I'll do my best," I promised.

Vercingetorix sighed. "I did my best," he said.

I ached for him. "I'll need the Goban Saor and a couple of carpenters to build me a little framework on wheels tonight, Rix. And I'll need a couple of draft animals."

"We're a bit short on horses at the moment. And whatever happens to me, my black goes with me."

"It doesn't have to be your black stallion. Anything will do. A pair of asses, a pair of big dogs even."

"We've eaten all of them."

"Then we'll use human draft animals. All I really need is a wheeled platform and something to pull it with."

"Take the Goban Saor, then," said Rix. "I have no further use for him."

I could not leave him there, alone in the shadows, with his long legs stretched out and death in his face. "No one could have defeated Caesar, Rix," I said gently. "You came closer than anyone else could."

"Is that supposed to comfort me?"

"No. I know there is no comfort. It is just . . . the truth. What are you going to do now?"

"Call a last council. Tonight, after people have rested a little. Will you stand beside me one final time, Ainvar of the Carnutes? As my friend?"

I made a painful discovery. I was not only young enough to leap off a wall, I was still young enough to cry. I let him see the tears standing in my eyes.

I saw the tears in his.

While the Goban Saor built the device I had requested, I accompanied Rix to the final council of free Gaul.

Free Gaul. The words hung in the air like frost. Or perhaps they actually were frost; the siege of Alesia had seen the death of summer, and the first cold breath of autumn was blowing down upon us as we met in the Mandubian assembly house. The taste of a dead dream was flat on our tongues, the only food any of us had.

When Vercingetorix rose to address the surviving tribal leaders, the battered captains of his destroyed army, at first they did not respond. They stared at him as if he were a stranger. Then, as the meaning of his words sank into their dazed brains, their eyes began to glow with an agonized and despairing devotion.

For once we had not planned his speech in advance. The words were his own, spoken from his head and gut, and I listened to them with no more foreknowledge than anyone else.

Vercingetorix began by saying, "I did not undertake this war for my own personal advantage, but in hopes of maintaining the general freedom. If I had a selfish motive, it was that I wished to continue living as a free man among free men. But which man of you did not feel the same?

"When our freedom was threatened by invaders, I felt we had no choice but to fight. To that end I have spent my fortune, my followers, my strength, and would gladly have sacrificed my life.

"Yet though I was in the forefront of every charge and the midst of every battle, I find myself still alive. And Caesar has won." He sounded genuinely perplexed by both facts.

Drawing a deep breath, he went on. "Honor demands that I submit to the victor. But perhaps in so doing I can win some last concession for my people, some grain of mercy from that merciless man. I shall send a deputation to Caesar announcing my intention to surrender with no further struggle and no further loss of life on his side. Also, they will tell him, I am willing either to be slain here, by my own people, or to be handed over alive to him, whichever he prefers, if only he will grant safe conduct from Alesia for those who have served Gaul so long and so well."

I was deeply moved, and deeply ashamed. I had thought Rix indifferent to the concepts of druidry—yet he could teach us all about sacrifice. In his nobility he made the rest of us feel ennobled just by belonging to the same race of men.

Some of the men in the assembly house were openly weeping by now.

We were a people who cried.

"No!" a voice shouted.

Onuava ran forward, thrusting her way through the crowd until she stood in front of her husband. "No!" she cried again. "Don't leave it up to Caesar! Go to him alive! You are a resourceful man; as long as there is breath in your body you may find some way to escape him and come back to us."

He looked at her from under heavy lids. "You think I should grovel at his feet, then?"

She drew back in horror. "A king of the Arverni? Grovel at the feet of a Roman? I'd rather see you dead!"

In spite of himself, Rix laughed. Many of us did. Onuava reddened, a thing I would not have thought possible.

Rix said to his wife, "You see? It's an impossible choice. That's why I prefer to leave it to Caesar. It's the only bribe I have left to offer him, but the Romans understand bribes."

"It's too large a price to pay," said Cotuatus. "Your life for ours . . ."

"My life is forfeit in any case," Rix reminded him. "You know as well as I do that Caesar will kill me, one way or another. But there's no reason everyone here should die with me if it can be prevented."

"It is better to die than to live enslaved," I spoke up. "Death is only temporary."

Rix turned toward me. "You truly believe that, druid?" he asked as if the two of us were alone.

"I do. I know it."

He sighed. "If we had enough time, perhaps you could convince me. I wish you could. But we've run out of time. This will have to be just another of those unfinished conversations. . . ." He turned back toward the gathering. "Choose a deputation to send to Caesar," he told them. "Now."

Onuava put her hands over her face.

Rix patted her absentmindedly on the shoulder, then said to me, "If Caesar wants me killed now, Ainvar, I command you to do it."

I went cold. "I'm not a sacrificer!"

"You were taught to use the knife though, weren't you? And you're my friend. Who else could I ask?" Then he added, with ironic amusement, "Besides, if you don't believe in death you won't be doing anything so terrible to me."

He had a clever head! Vercingetorix would have made a great druid. He would have been superb at anything he did. His eyes locked with mine compellingly. I felt the final crushing weight of the final crushing responsibility press down on me.

When I was afraid to watch a sacrifice, all those long years ago, was I foreseeing and dreading this moment?

While we waited for the deputation to return from Caesar, Rix went to his tent. I wanted to be with him; Onuava wanted to be with him. The princes of Gaul wanted to be with him. But he insisted on being alone.

I understood. There are arrangements a man must make with his spirit that can only be made in privacy.

I had my own arrangements to make.

Sending for the Goban Saor, I asked him to search out the finest knife in the fort, and sharpen it to its utmost.

"Soul friend," I kept repeating to myself while I waited. "Soul friend."

The deputation returned from Caesar.

And Vercingetorix sent for me.

CHAPTER THIRTY-NINE

WITH THE sharpened knife thrust through my belt, I went to him. My mouth was dry. My emotions were hidden behind an impassive face.

The first light of dawn was staining the eastern sky, but I did not pause to sing the song for the sun. There was no singing left in me.

The inhabitants of Alesia and the surviving warriors, huddled in silent groups, watched as I passed. The warriors no longer divided themselves by tribe, my head observed. Aeduan, Arvernian, Parisian, Senonian, they stood together. They were now simply the Gauls.

Vercingetorix had made of them one tribe after all.

He was waiting for me inside his tent. "I greet you as a free person, Ainvar," he said as I entered.

"And I, you."

"I wanted to hear those words one more time. Caesar has sent for me to be brought to him alive."

A rush of contradictory emotions overwhelmed me so I could not speak.

Rix glanced at the knife in my belt. "You won't need that."

"Unfortunately," I managed to say.

"Yes, I think you are right. But . . . this is what the Roman wants. Myself, alive, in return for whatever mercy he may show my people."

"Do you really believe he will be merciful?"

"I'm gambling, Ainvar. Caesar has been known to make gestures of extraordinary generosity."

"To serve his own purposes."

"I know that. I'm gambling that this time it will serve his purpose to be generous to a defeated enemy in order to avoid stirring up further resistance."

"Caesar might not think that way," I warned.

"I know that too. If I am wrong, and he means to take revenge on our people even after I have given myself over to him . . . will you try to get the women and children out, Ainvar?"

"I will. I made plans for that eventuality some time ago."

"Ainvar the thinker. I should have known. How do you propose to rescue them?"

"Magic," I replied solemnly.

He laughed. It was the last time I ever heard Vercingetorix laugh.

I accompanied the deputation that escorted him to Caesar. He could not have kept me away and he knew it. The escorts had been promised safe conduct back to Alesia once Vercingetorix was delivered, but even if we knew Caesar meant to kill us all on the spot I would have gone with Rix.

He was my soul friend.

He dressed for the occasion in his best tunic, all his gold jewelry, his kingly cloak lined with wolf fur. The black stallion, last surviving horse in Alesia, was bony but burnished with loving hands, and when he sat on its back the animal snorted softly and curved its neck with pride in the old way.

Our silent group walked down the slope from Alesia toward the Roman camp. Caesar had set up his command tent on a little knoll, where the eagle standards could be seen stabbing the sky. Even at a distance the crimson dot that was the Roman's cloak was clearly visible as he waited for us.

Vercingetorix approached Caesar wearing the full regalia of a champion and carrying all his weapons of war. As we drew near the Roman line, I saw how the enemy eyes were assessing him. Even in defeat, without the braying of the trumpets and the screams of defiance and the clashing of shields, the Celt could arouse dread in his foes.

Vercingetorix had cast aside his battered and dented shield and carried a new one, patterned with spirals and set with bronze bosses. A gold-plated belt around his waist held a dagger, but at his right hip he wore his father's massive long sword, too heavy for a lesser man to wield. One hand held the reins of the black stallion. The other carried a casting spear with an iron head almost as long as a Roman sword.

Vercingetorix rode calmly at the walk, but he rode with his arm cocked back and the spear lifted, ready to be hurled.

The Romans watched him approach. Tension rippled along their lines. They raised their weapons. We heard Caesar bark a command, and his men froze.

Uttering one wild, free cry, Vercingetorix suddenly urged his horse forward in a full gallop. With a splendid feat of horsemanship he raced in a circle on the plain before the Roman command tent, letting the enemy see the full glory of who and what he was; who and what we were.

My heart ached in my breast. My eyes blurred with tears.

When the black horse had gone full circle, Vercingetorix reined him in so sharply the animal rose onto his hind legs and pawed the sky. At that moment, the King of the World threw his spear.

It sang a song of death through the air, and thudded into the earth, quivering, at the very feet of Julius Caesar.

Caesar was seated on a Roman campaign stool in front of the command tent. During Vercingetorix's display he had not moved. Even when the spear was thrown he reacted with no more than a flicker of his eyelids and an involuntary tensing of the muscles in his bare arms as they rested on the arms of the stool.

With the last brave flourish of his youth, Vercingetorix flung back his cloak and slid from his horse while the spear still quivered in the earth. He stood immobile beside it for a long moment, his head high. Then he knelt and laid his father's sword at Caesar's feet.

The conqueror only stared, stony and cold and silent.

"Do you speak the Roman tongue?" an aide beside Caesar asked.

"I can interpret," I said.

Caesar's gaze slanted toward me. I wore the hooded robe but the hood was thrown back; his eyes rested on my tonsure.

"Druid?" he inquired. His voice was high-pitched and rasping.

"I am of the Order of the Wise."

"Sorcerers," sneered the Roman. "We shall rid this land of your kind now. As for you," he addressed Vercingetorix, "what have you to say to me?"

I repeated his question to Rix, then carefully translated his reply.

"Once you sent me tokens of friendship, Caesar. If they were sincerely meant, I remind you of them now. I ask you in the name of friendship to spare the lives of the men who fought beside me. They fought nobly and sought no unfair advantage, and their cause was just, the cause of freedom, which you yourself must prize. Do what you like with me, I am your battle trophy. But spare my men as I would spare yours. It was never our way to humiliate a defeated enemy."

Caesar listened to this without shifting on his seat or taking his brooding gaze from Vercingetorix. When I finished speaking he said, in that waspish voice, "Barbarians have no concept of friendship or of honor. I have seen that proven time and again in Gaul. I have extended the hand of friendship on numerous occasions, only to be betrayed. I no longer make that mistake. The only enemy I do not fear is a dead enemy—or a man in chains."

He raised his chin and snapped his fingers. Men ran forward and seized Vercingetorix. It happened so fast he had no time to struggle, but he did not attempt to struggle. He let them bind him and pull him to his feet in front of Caesar.

As thin as he was, the Arvernian was impressive drawn up to his full height. His long Celtic bones made him a head taller than the tallest legionary. The ghost of a smile crossed Caesar's lips. "I shall take you back to Rome with me, to show the people just what sort of a creature I was able to conquer. You won't die, at least for a while. You will be my trophy, as you said."

I felt strong hands take hold of me from either side. The Romans grabbed and held each member of our deputation, forcing us to watch what happened next.

Caesar, looking amused, signaled to his watching centurions to come forward and examine the captured barbarian. It was a deliberate insult. We watched in helpless rage as they stepped forward to taunt Vercingetorix and spit on him.

But he did not notice. He stood immobile, gazing over the heads of the Romans into some distant, inner space they could not penetrate. He let them swarm over him like gnats, but paid them not the smallest attention. The Romans were less than nothing to him, his bearing said; they did not exist in any world he knew or understood. And so he was not touched by them, though they ran their hands brutally over his entire body, poking at the iron muscles in an admiration they could not quite conceal. Stroking up the great length of leg and arm bone, even hefting the genitals and exchanging meaningful glances, for who could fail to be impressed by the equipment he carried?

Yet none of this touched Vercingetorix. When they fumbled beneath his tunic, he did not even feel it. They had no power to make him feel it. At last they felt the stinging lash of ridicule turned back upon them in some silent, terrible way. They withdrew, smirking to preserve some sense of superiority, leaving Vercingetorix alone in a bright, hard place they could never reach.

I was glad, in that moment, that I had not killed him. His spirit had won a victory over them and everyone watching knew it.

Caesar knew it. His lips drew back in a snarl. "Go back to your fort," he said to me, "and tell your people to have all the gates thrown open to my men."

The Romans released us. They sent us back to Alesia at the run, shouting derision after us.

I risked one backward look. Vercingetorix was standing exactly as before, in front of Gaius Caesar, gazing beyond him.

I wondered what he saw.

The Gauls were waiting for us at the gates of Alesia. They crowded around, pulling at our clothes, imploring us to give them some sort of good news.

There was no good news.

"Is it to be slavery, then?" someone asked with a sob of despair.

I saw Onuava's white face staring toward me from the crowd.

I shook my head. "We can expect no mercy from Caesar. I think he'll take the most salable among us as slaves and have the rest of us killed. But we're going to try to save as many women and children as we can, especially the children. Now, listen to me . . ."

They listened. No druid ever had a more intense audience.

By the time the sentries on the wall warned us the legions were forming up and would soon advance on Alesia, we were ready. The children and the strongest of the mothers, the ones who stood the best chance of surviving, were gathered at a side gate. Just inside the gate stood the wheeled wooden platform the Goban Saor had made, carrying an object covered with leather painted with druidic symbols. The Goban Saor and Cotuatus would serve as draft horses for the strange vehicle. They stood in front of it, awaiting my signal.

I sent everyone else who was still strong enough to do so to climb the ladders to the tops of the walls. They had their instructions. "We are going to work magic together," I had told them. "Each of you is alive and life is magic, so there is magic inside each of you. Use it today."

There was little time for farewells, but I managed to find and embrace Hanesa. I had told him Vercingetorix's last words, committing them to his bardic memory, and he wanted to stay with the others to the end. "The climax of my epic," he said.

He was druid, and not afraid to die.

The conquering army started across the plain toward Alesia to claim its plunder. The Gauls on the palisade set up a great howling, meant to distract the Romans from what was happening at the side gate. The gate opened, and the king and the craftsman pulled the wheeled platform outside. I walked next to it, with one hand resting on the leather-covered object. The women and children clustered around it.

We struck off at an angle leading sharply away from Alesia. If we were fortunate, we could lose ourselves in the hills before the Romans saw us.

But we were not so fortunate. We heard the trumpets blow, and when I looked back, I saw that a detachment of German cavalry had been sent to head us off and bring us back. Some of the children screamed and several women stumbled in fear, but I shouted to them to be as brave as Vercingetorix. His name seemed to have a calming effect.

As the Germans bore down on us, I looked back toward the fort. Then I whipped the covering from the object on the wheeled platform and waved the leather in the air as a signal.

The watchers on the wall saw it. At once they began chanting as I had taught them, in one great and rhythmic voice.

I concentrated on pouring all the strength left in me into the uncovered image of the Two-Faced One.

When my fingers touched the surface of the stone, heat leaped along my arm. It pulsed in rhythm with the chanting coming from Alesia, the sound encircling and connecting us, amplifying my strength and the power in the stone.

The women and children screamed and shrank back. I knew what they were seeing, but I was not looking at the image. I was watching the German cavalry bearing down upon us.

They came at a headlong gallop, shrieking wildly, their faces distorted with smears of blood and dye meant to give them terrifying expressions. But when they saw the figure on the platform, their terror became real.

I watched panic seize them as it had once seized our warriors when the Germans attacked them. The foremost horsemen began desperately sawing at the reins, trying to turn their animals around. Those behind crashed into them. Horses and men screamed together. The air was filled with screaming.

And from the figure at my back pulsed a deadly, horrible heat.

I kept my face turned toward the Germans, my arm stretched back behind me so my fingers remained in contact with the image. I seemed to be held within a bubble of scalding light. The Germans tried to flee from that light, trampling each other in their manic fear, changing before my eyes from a military assault force into a pack of hysterical savages willing to kill each other just to escape the unknown.

They were broken completely. Faced with a magic beyond their comprehension, they fled in all directions—not a moment too soon. The last of my strength was devoured by the stone and I felt my knees give way.

Throwing off his harness, the Goban Saor caught me as I fell. Over his shoulder I had one glimpse of the thing the Germans had seen. On the wheeled platform crouched a two-faced monster burning with an unearthly fire, all four eyes rolling and glaring, two sets of nostrils snorting, two sets of lips writhing to reveal gnashing teeth.

Alive.

Blazingly, undeniably, alive.

As I collapsed, the fire faded.

Cotuatus threw the leather cover back over the figure. The Goban Saor propped me against the platform and rubbed life back into my limbs. Timidly, the women and children crept up to us. When they had all been collected, the two men took up the cart once more, and we set off at the trot, the women and children following like a parade of geese on their way to the river.

I do not know if any of the Germans recovered enough to report to Caesar. But no one else came after us.

At sundown we buried the stone image in the heart of a woodland. We burned the wooden platform in our campfire, and at dawn resumed our journey west and northward.

I was going home, to the great grove of the Carnutes.

Along the way I asked everyone we met if they had news of the army of Gaul. We were given conflicting reports. I began to hope Aberth had not learned of our defeat, though it was a foolish hope. I knew how fast word could travel.

As if to intensify our pain, the land was lovely that autumn. The earth wore amber and emerald, mornings were as sweet and crisp as the first bite of an apple, nights were soaked with starlight.

At first we hardly spoke to one another. We traveled numbly, each isolated in memories. Even the children were less fretful than I anticipated. They clung to their mothers and scuffed their toes in the earth as we walked. When people we met along the way gave us food, we fed the children first.

Some people gave us nothing. They cowered behind the walls of their dwellings, the Celtic tradition of hospitality forgotten, and their dogs snarled at us as we passed by. Rome was already an acknowledged presence in what had been free Gaul.

We saw Roman patrols several times. Each time I herded my little group into a woodland and hid until they passed by.

By our third-night camp, we were able to talk to one another, a little. I sat on a fallen tree beside Cotuatus and stretched my legs toward the fire.

"What do you suppose those Germans told Caesar?" he asked after a time.

"I doubt if they told him anything. I suspect they took the horses he'd given them and rode straight for the Rhine."

"Mmmmm." Cotuatus gazed into the flames. "I would have done the same thing myself. I wish you'd warned us first."

A child was crying somewhere, a thin, weak sound. A mother's gentle murmur quieted it. The night smelled of woodsmoke.

For some reason that most familiar of scents made me uneasy.

Onuava joined us. She never ceased to surprise me. I had expected that, of all the women, she would complain the most, longing for her abandoned comforts. Instead, she encouraged others when they were weary, and made light of our problems. If a weaker woman was too tired to carry her infant, Onuava took the child in her arms and strode on as if it weighed nothing.

Yet she must have been tired, too. And heartsick. And I knew she carried her own infant in her womb.

I moved over on the log to make room for her. Reaching down, Onuava picked up bits of bark and twig and began throwing them idly into the campfire. "What will happen to him, Ainvar?"

I knew who she meant. So did Cotuatus, who made a pained sound and stood up. Muttering something about needing to relieve himself, he left us.

Thinking about Vercingetorix was painful for all of us.

"Caesar said he would take him back to Rome. To exhibit. He's never had such a captive."

"He'll take care of him, then?" she asked hopefully.

"If you mean, will he feed him well and clothe him richly and give him the finest shelter as we do our noble hostages? the answer is no, Onuava. That isn't the Roman way."

"Then what will he do? Ainvar, you can see the future; look into it for me and tell me what will become of my husband."

"I cannot see the future. At least, not to order. I have random flashes sometimes, never when I want or expect them. It is not my gift. And even if it were, I don't want to see the future. I don't want to see any more pain."

"But haven't you tried to foresee what will happen to your own people? Your wife, your children . . ."

She felt me stiffen beside her.

"I have a daughter," I said, tight-lipped. "Had a daughter. She was stolen. We think she was taken to a Roman camp, but I don't know. I suspect I'll never know, now. She may have been one of the captives with Caesar. If we had won, I would have gone among them trying to find her. Now . . ."

"Oh, Ainvar." She put her hand on my arm and said nothing more, for which I was grateful.

That night when I spread my cloak on the ground to try to sleep, Onuava came to me. She lay down in my arms and pulled the cloak over the two of us. She was warm against my body, but I could not feel her warmth—nor, I suspect, could she feel mine. I clasped her more tightly, trying to restore the sense of touch, but I was numb. I put my hand on her full, soft breast, and it was just a hand on a breast. It might have been a hand on a lump of earth.

She touched my genitals, stroked their unresponsive flesh, then took her hand away and laid it instead on my chest, her palm over my heart.

I held her until the dawn, then we got up and went on.

We skirted the ruins of Cenabum. Neither Cotuatus nor I had any desire to go close enough to see the destruction. But as we continued northward and the soft brown earth welcomed my feet, I began extending my stride without realizing it.

"You're outrunning the women," the Goban Saor told me.

I checked myself, slowed, tried to wait for them. But there was a woman up ahead who was waiting for me. Briga was waiting for me.

And Lakutu, and Glas, and Cormiac Ru.

And the grove. My spirit was hungrier for the grove than my belly had been for food during the siege of Alesia. My feet broke into a trot without permission from my head, leaving the others behind.

Around highsun I circled a clump of alders and found a grizzled fisherman sitting on the bank of a tributary of the Autura. He was mending his net, patiently reknotting torn network. He looked up at me in surprise.

"Where did you come from?"

"Alesia."

His eyes opened wide. "I thought they were all dead in Alesia. The army of Gaul and everyone with them."

"When did you hear that?"

"Just this morning, about dawn. It was shouted up the river. We'd heard rumors for days, but this claimed to be truth."

I froze. "Would they have heard it at the Fort of the Grove?"

"I suppose so. I don't go that way much myself. It's half a day's walk, you know. This is my little patch and I stay with it." He looked back at his net, anxious to return to his task. His world was very narrow and self-contained; he really did not much care about Caesar, or Alesia.

Perhaps he was a fortunate man.

But his words had just destroyed my world.

By now Briga would have followed my instructions. The sacrificer's knife would have done its work.

I began to run.

It is better this way, my head tried to tell me. Better that they are dead, with their spirits set free, than alive to be sold into slavery.

But I am still alive, I argued. I wanted them to be alive with me!

I ran faster. Familiar landmarks blurred past. I ran until my lungs were tearing apart for want of breath and I found myself leaning against some smallholder's wattle-and-daub shed, gasping for air.

Cotuatus and the Goban Saor were far behind me. They would have to take care of the women and children and bring them on to the Fort of the Grove.

Where my family lay dead.

I knotted my fists and shook them at the sky and screamed.

Soft ash drifted onto my upturned face.

The smell of woodsmoke hung thick in the autumn air.

Too thick.

I stood very still, exploring with the senses of my spirit. Then I began to run again.

The great ridge rose from the surrounding plain as it had since before the Celts came to Gaul. Sacred heart of the land, place of awesome power.

Crowned in flame.

Even so far away, I could see that the grove was burning.

Transcending legs and lungs, I ran as I had never run before, keeping my eyes fixed on the terrible sight of leaping fire devouring the oaks. The wind blew the ash toward me, bringing me the dying whispers of the trees.

My trees.

I thought fleetingly of rain magic, but it was too late. The entire forested ridge was blazing furiously. By the time I could summon enough clouds to the clear sky, there would be nothing left to save.

I ran on.

How much pain can a spirit absorb? That is a question for druids to ponder. Kind death gives us a chance to forget those pains too cruel to remember. As I ran, my hand sought the knife I was still carrying in my belt, the one the Goban Saor had sharpened for Vercingetorix.

The Fort of the Grove loomed off to one side and I veered toward it, determined to die wherever my family was. By then I was sobbing a wild mixture of curses and invocations, calling upon the Source by every name I knew, with all the power of love and grief.

And Briga ran into my arms.

As simply as that, she ran out through the gateway of the fort and into my arms.

Joy can hurt more than pain and be harder to believe in. Crying and laughing, we clung to each other. Her fingers explored my face and I wrapped her in my arms and swung her around and around.

"You!" we cried to each other. "You, you, you!"

Then they were all there, gathering around us, shouting with surprise and relief: Lakutu, the children, Sulis, Keryth, Grannus, Teyrnon and Damona, Dian Cet . . .

I did not see Aberth.

"Where is the sacrificer, Briga?"

"Ah, Ainvar. Just this morning we heard that you . . ."

"I know. But you can see I'm still alive."

"Yes! But when I thought everything was lost I went to Aberth as you had asked me to do. While he was making . . . preparations for us, the sentry shouted that there was fire in the grove.

"A Roman patrol had set fire to the great grove! As soon as he heard that, Aberth forgot about us. He left like a wind blowing, running up there to fight the fire and the Romans. Narlos the exhorter went with him, and I had to hold back Cormiac Ru to keep him from joining them. We waited and hoped, but . . ."

"They never came back," I finished for her. "They are dead, then."

"Yes," she acknowledged in a whisper. "The Romans rode away; they never bothered to attack the fort. We didn't know what to do. We've just been waiting and watching."

We were waiting and watching now, gazing through gathering twilight toward the funeral pyre of the oaks.

Sacrificed, I thought. For what purpose?

The senses of my body and spirit flowed together to form a single awareness. I watched the blazing trees become pillars, soaring upward to meet spires of incomparable grace, crowning the ridge with a temple of flame.

I folded Briga into my arms and bowed my head over hers. We stood clasped together as the ash drifted softly down upon us.

CHAPTER FORTY

WE CEASED to be free people except in our hearts, and the wheel of the seasons turned.

After the fall of Alesia, Caesar had all who were unfit for slavery massacred, and gave the rest to his men as plunder. For himself he kept the Aeduan and Arvernian prisoners of war, hoping to use them to compel the loyalty of their tribes. He made a circuit of Gaul, claiming submission from each of the tribal leaders in turn. When Cotuatus appeared before him on behalf of the Carnutes and spat at his feet, the Roman ordered my friend beheaded.

Caesar's interdiction against the Order of the Wise forced me and my family to live a forest life, hiding among trees and shadows. But we lived. We survived to sing again, though in subdued voices, and to raise our children.

We never learned the fate of Maia—or of Crom Daral and Baroc. Perhaps it is better so.

After ten winters I did learn, through the hidden druid network, the fate of Vercingetorix. I never told Onuava, however, who was busy with the second son she had borne me. Briga had three, and the rivalry between them was intense.

Lakutu had a dimpled daughter, who was adored by Glas and Cormiac Ru and the son of Vercingetorix.

Vercingetorix . . . Caesar had indeed taken him to Rome, where he kept him imprisoned for years, starving him, trying to break his spirit. When it would not be broken, Caesar finally had him dragged in chains through the streets of Rome in what was called a "triumphal procession," and then executed.

I have met great men. Even Caesar must be given his due, in this life. But our lives do not evidence a progressive accumulation of rewards. As Menua once explained to me, a life of power is frequently followed by one of helplessness, a life of high rank by one of ignominy. There must be a balance. We command in one existence; we serve in another. What is left over is purged in the fire.

But life itself is immortal.

Vercingetorix no longer breathes the air I breathe, nor walks the earth I walk. Yet I go on talking to him, and he hears me. His awareness encircles me like a net wherever I go, whatever I do. Dead, Vercingetorix is more alive than ever. He is waiting somewhere in the future, like a promise.

Things he said and did come back to me. Not the splendid gestures, but the small ones: a grin, a wink. From the corner of my eye I glimpse the grace of his shadow. It is not the shadow itself, but the grace that endures. I move in and out of my soul friend, part of his pattern as he is part of mine.

He is.

We are.

The great unfinished conversation goes on and on.

HISTORICAL NOTE

Where the great grove of the Carnutes once crowned a ridge above the river Autura, the great Cathedral of Chartres now stands. Every year thousands of Gauls worship among its stone pillars as the magnificent rose window glows with the light of the Otherworld.

BIBLIOGRAPHY

Classical Sources:

Ammianus Marcellinus, Roman historian, died c. A.D. 391

Diodorus Siculus, Roman historian, died 21 B.C.

Livy, Roman historian, died A.D. 17

Pliny the Elder, Roman naturalist and procurator of Narbonese Gaul, died A.D. 79

Posidonius, Greek historian and philosopher, died 50 B.C.

Strabo, Greek geographer and historian, died c. A.D. 21

Tacitus, Roman historian, died A.D. 120

Contemporary Sources (a selected bibliography, as many other sources were also used for this book):

Caesar, Julius. *The Battle for Gaul*, Anne and Peter Wiseman, trans. Boston: Godine Press, 1980.

———. *The Conquest of Gaul*, S. A. Handford, trans. New York: Penguin Classics, 1951.

Chadwick, Nora. *The Celts*. New York: Penguin Books, 1977.

———. *The Druids*. Cardiff: University of Wales Press, 1966.

Cooperative Publication Society. *The Conquerors*. New York and London: 1910.

Cunliffe, Barry. *The Celtic World*. New York: McGraw-Hill, 1979.

Delaney, Frank. *The Celts*. London: Hodder and Stoughton, 1986.

Davis, Nigel. *Human Sacrifice*. New York: William Morrow, 1981.

Dottin, Georges. *The Celts*. New York: Minerva Books, Ltd., 1977.

———. *Civilization of the Celts*. New York: Crescent, n.d.

Elder, Isabel Hill. *Celt, Druid and Culdee*. London: Covenant Pub., Ltd., 1973.

Fraser, James G. *The Golden Bough*. New York: Avenel Books, 1981.

Grolier Society. *Lands and Peoples*, Vol. I. New York: 1948.

Guizot, M. *History of France from the Earliest Times*. Boston: Aldine Publishing Co., 1888.

Herm, Gerhard. *The Celts*. New York: St. Martin's Press, 1976.

James, E. C. *The Ancient Gods*. London: Weidenfeld and Nicholson, 1960.

Jukkian, Camille. *Vercingetorix*. Paris: Hachette, 1963.

Kendrick, T. D. *The Druids: A Study in Celtic Prehistory*. London: Methuen, 1927.

MacCulloch, J. A. *Celtic and Scandinavian Religions*. London: Hutchinson, 1911.

MacKendrick, Paul. *Roman France*. London: G. Bell and Sons, 1971.

Markale, Jean. *Celtic Civilization*. London: Gordon and Cremonesi, 1976.

Nock, A. D. *Essays on Religion in the Ancient World*. Oxford: Clarendon Press, 1972.

Norton-Taylor, Duncan. *The Celts*. New York: Time-Life Books, 1974.

Piggott, Stuart. *The Druids*. New York: Penguin Books, 1978; New York: Thames and Hudson, 1985.

Powell, T.G.E. *The Celts*. London: Thames and Hudson, 1980.

Raftery, Joseph, ed. *The Celts*. Cork, Ireland: Mercier Press, n.d.

Randers-Pherson, Justine. *Barbarians and Romans*. Enid: University of Oklahoma, 1983.

Ross, Ann, and Don Robins. *Life and Death of a Druid Prince*. London: Century Hutchinson, 1989.

Rutherford, Ward. *The Druids and Their Heritage.* London: Gordon and Cremonesi, 1978.

Sharkey, John. *Celtic Mysteries.* London: Thames and Hudson, 1975.

Tacitus, Cornelius. *Germania,* M. Hutton, trans. London: William Heinemann, Ltd., 1980.

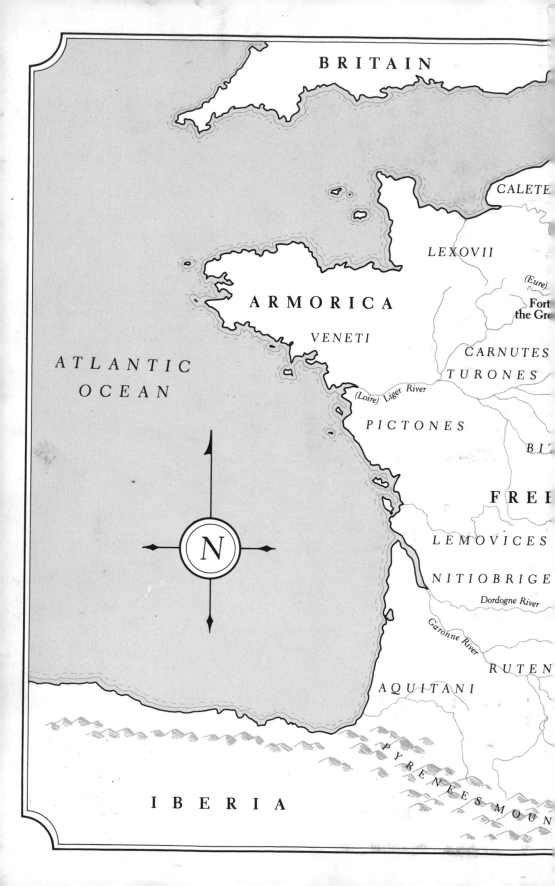